Praise for *Spots*

For people who haven't started reading this story there's a lot waiting under the surface for new readers. *Spots the Space Marine* provides a wide range of humanity through such small windows, fun and interesting characters, and a tradition of science fiction not often seen inked on the page. This story is worth attempting simply for the novelty of the subject matter and the way that Hogarth approaches the narrative.

—Kyt Dotson
DigitalScienceFiction.Com

It's the writing equivalent of a Chinese brush painting, where everything is powerfully conveyed in the minimal strokes. As such, it moves fast and the characters come across very vividly. A definite thumbs up for anyone who likes space opera and/or complex female characters.

—Cecilia Tan
Editor/Publisher, Circlet Press

Spots is gripping. Don't let the title fool you; this is no comedy. Prepare to be sucked in.

—Meilin Miranda
Author, *An Intimate History
of the Greater Kingdom*

Spots the Space Marine:
Defense of the Fiddler

Spots the Space Marine: Defense of the Fiddler

Copyright 2012 by M.C.A. Hogarth

ISBN-13: 978-1470131050
ISBN-10: 1470131056

Designed and typeset by Catspaw DTP Services
http://www.catspawdtp.com/

For Papo, from whom I inherited my love of explosions.

TABLE OF CONTENTS

Part 1 Contact 1

Part 2 In Deep 143

Part 3 Endgame 395

End Credits 496

INTRODUCTION

They came in
the year
2020

xi

...bearing news of invasion

and gifts,
such gifts:
ships, armor,
weapons....

Hope.

Spots the Space Marine: Defense of the Fiddler

Introduction ● *M. C. A. Hogarth*

Spots the Space Marine: Defense of the Fiddler

Among them,
two women:

A single reservist
to fill the hole
left by four men...

and a lieutenant,
to lead their
beheaded company.

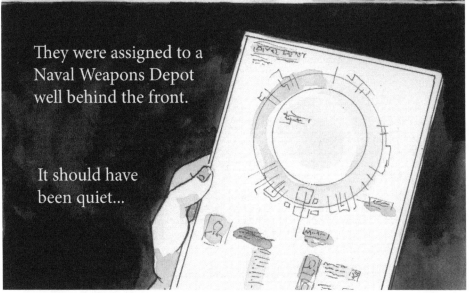

They were assigned to a
Naval Weapons Depot
well behind the front.

It should have
been quiet...

Introduction ● *M. C. A. Hogarth*

SPOTS THE SPACE MARINE: DEFENSE OF THE FIDDLER

M. C. A. HOGARTH

STUDIO
MCAH

PART 1:
CONTACT

01. Meeting Spots

Barracks. Claws enters the room to find a stranger in it: a woman in her early thirties, storing a duffel in the closet two bunks down. She's 5'5" and relatively fit, but has a rounded belly and soft edges. Her skin's a bisque color with a golden farmer's tan, and her hair is in a dark braid coiled and taped around her head.

Claws is a young man in his early twenties, built hard but narrow. What hair he has is very short and sandy; his eyes are hazel, his skin a faded tan.

Claws. "Well whoa, hey-lo. You must be new."

Stranger. "What gave me away?" *She smiles and extends a hand.* "Magda Guitart. Sergeant Holden told me I should bunk here."

Claws, shaking it. "Pleased to meetcha. I'm Walker, Travis. But call me Claws, everyone else does."

"Claws . . . no kidding?"

Claws. "Yeah, we all go by call-sign here. Sarge's Scythe if he ain't told you yet."

"How come? I mean, that's a little strange, isn't it?"

Claws. "Bit. You know about the Void Angels?"

Stranger. "You mean the air support, right?"

Claws. "Them's the ones. We had some of them layover here when we first deployed and picked up the habit from them. Pilots, you know."

She resumes unpacking. "Huh. I guess I need one, then, don't I."

Claws. "Sure do. If you're one of Scythe's you're part of Team Kitty. You can guess the theme."

Stranger, pausing in putting away her clothes. "Hmm. Is there a Spots yet?"

Claws. "Spots like a leopard or a cheetah? Huh, that'll work. We ain't got a Spots yet." *He nods at her face.* "For the freckles, eh?"

Spots, laughing. "All seven of them. You have more than I do."

Claws. "Can't see 'em as well, what with the skin bein' darker than yours. Where'd they send you from, space duty? You're pale as a china doll."

Spots. "Believe it or not, I just got plucked from my house and shipped out here." *She takes out a photo and carefully places it on the wall above her assigned bunk.*

Claws. "****, when was the last time you saw duty?"

Spots eyes him. "Do you always talk like that?"

Claws. "Talk like what?"

Spots, shaking her head. "Never mind. The war started after I retired from duty. I've been at a desk a few weekends a year for over a decade, but that's about the size of it. I've never been out of the solar system until now."

Claws stares at her. Then past her at the photo. "Your family?"

Spots. "Yes. Would you like to see?"

He looks: a solid man in his thirties with short blond hair is standing with his hand on the shoulder of a boy who looks to be 7 or 8 years old. The boy is holding a young girl, perhaps 3 years old. "Whoa. Those yours?"

"Both of them, yes. And the man too, I'm proud to say." *Spots grins.* "He's a miner, we spend half the year on an asteroid." *She sets her last item on the half-desk next to her bunk: a rosary.* "Sergeant Holden—Scythe, I guess—says I need to go check my suit. Do you know the way to the armory?"

Claws. "Sure, I'll show you." *Glances at her.* "Sure you're old enough to have two kids that size?"

Spots, laughing. "I can see I'm going to like you, Claws."

02. Spots is Dancing

Armory. Spots is checking the back of Claws's suit using a series of read-outs at the base of the back of the helmet. She's already in her own, so they're using suit-comm to communicate. The armor isn't overtly bulky and is a matte dark brown in color, almost black. Claws's suit has an additional series of marks down the back, mostly obscured by the power and ammo cells.

Spots. "All lights green. Seal checks. Check mine."

Claws. "All lights green. Seal checks. We're good to go. Control, this is Walkabout 1. You readin' me?"

Control. "Claws, this is Control. You're cleared for your walk. Remember to check in every fifteen, we could use the map updates. Otherwise, enjoy."

Claws. "Copy that, Control. Thanks. After you, Spots."

They enter the airlock leading to the planet's exterior and pause for the chunky door to shut behind them.

Spots. "Hey, Claws? Thank you for getting the okay for this from Scythe."

Claws. "No problem. It's been a couple of weeks since you've been in armor, what with them havin' to pack you onto the ship and send you way out to the middle of nowhere. I reckoned you'd appreciate some gettin'-to-know-you time before one of our ***es is on the line."

The exterior door opens and the two of them trudge out. The alien world is a series of murky sludge-like dunes scattered with brownish clouds in a heavy atmosphere flailed by constant winds.

Spots. "Just so. Ah, wow. It's such a beautiful planet, you know?"

Claws. "For somethin' with toxic soup for an atmosphere, sure."

Spots. "Come on, Claws. Just look at that sunset!"

Claws. "Guess it is kinda pretty. If you don't look at the rest of it. Let's head north, looks like last night's sandstorm blew holes in our latest map. How's the armor feel?"

Spots. "Good. Really good. God, it's good to be back."

Claws. "I can't imagine was much fun, shippin' out on such short notice. What were you up to when they plucked you up?"

Spots, chagrined. "Believe it or not . . . driving a desk. Not even a very important one."

Claws, glancing at her though he can't see her through the atmosphere. "Ah? You joshin' me?"

Spots. "Afraid not. I haven't seen active duty in this war yet."

Claws. "****, no kiddin'. Guess you're lucky you're out here, then . . . nothin' more strenuous than shootin' up your quota of crabs in the Warren and headin' back."

Spots. "Is it really that easy?"

Claws. "Honest. Most you gotta worry about is gettin' a sore trigger finger."

Spots laughs. "Guess that's not too bad, then."

Claws. "You'll see. Sit tight, I gotta check in. Control, this is Walkabout 1."

Control. "Walkabout 1, this is Control. Go ahead."

Claws. "I got terrain data, ready for the pulse?"

Control. "Standing by."

Claws. "All ri—"

Control. "Walkabout 1? Still waiting on that pulse?"

Claws. "I . . . uh . . . "

Control. "Walkabout 1, respond!"

Claws. "Spots is . . . well, just . . . look at the cam . . . "

Control. "What the hell is going—whoa!"

Out on the mire, beneath the thick clouds with the bright scarlet and magenta of the alien sunset reflecting off her helmet, Spots is dancing.

Claws. "Ain't that the damned finest thing I ever seen. Whoooo-eee! Go, Spots, go!"

In the Control room of the naval base, several of the staff crowd around to watch the cam footage. When Spots tires at last, Claws remembers the map data and sends the burst. They head back toward the base.

Claws. "So, uh . . . you do that a lot? Dance in armor?"

Spots with a grin. "Not as much as I'd want to."

Claws. "You serious?"

Spots. "Oh, Claws. Are you really wearing the same stuff I am? Have you noticed what it feels like? Like being alive, like being strong and alive. Who wouldn't dance?"

Claws. "Guess when you put it that way . . ."

She just smiles and follows him in.

03. FIRST KILL

The Warren. A series of maze-like corridors dug underground in the area around the naval base. Spots and Claws are currently patrolling their sector.

Claws, over the comm. "You doin' okay?"

Spots. "Yeah. Where are the aliens, though? I thought you said it was like . . . well, target practice."

Claws. "They're around here somewhere. Don't you fret, you'll get your chance."

Spots grimaces. "Tell me why we have to split up again?"

Claws. " 'Cause there's not enough of us to go around. You'll be fine."

Spots is about to respond when a hulking creature whips around the corner. It is fully ten feet tall, jet-black, armored like a tank and looks like a cross between a crab, a spider and a praying mantis. Without thinking, she shoots it and it collapses.

Spots. " . . ."

Spots. "Does one shot really kill these things?"

Claws. "Met your first crab, eh? Yep."

Spots. "How can it be this easy?"

Claws. "****, Spots, don't complain."

Spots starts to say something and shakes her head. She continues her patrol, dispatching several more crabs with equal ease. Her HUD reports her partner's position and ammo/power levels, which are fluctuating as he too fills his "quota."

A few hours later.

Claws, still a few corridors away. "Not too bad for your first go, eh?"

Spots. "Not at all . . . didn't really see much, actually."

Claws. "It's like this most of the time."

Spots. "Most of the--"

Fifteen crabs abruptly lurch from a side corridor. Thirteen of them are bulky tanks . . . but two are thin, tall, like elongated wasps on stilts. They rush her, a wall of black chitin and scything limbs.

Backing away, Spots, shouting. "CLAWS! CLAWS, GET YOUR TAIL OVER HERE NOW!"

Claws. "On my way, what's wrong!"

Spots. "Fifteen crabs, two Kings, HURRY!"

Claws. "****! Almost there, Spots, hang tight!"

The report of gunfire and the sound of scrabbling limbs . . .

. . . then silence . . .

. . . then the plangent noise of ichor, slowly dripping. Claws flies around the corridor behind Spots and comes to an abrupt halt at the sight of the bodies. Spots is standing very still, a death grip on her leveled weapon.

Claws, approaching cautiously. "****, Spots! Isn't almost *dyin'* a good enough reason to cuss? What's it take?"

Spots, prim and twitchy still. "Hush, Claws. You kiss your mother with that mouth."

Claws, frowning at the group. "I don't get it. They never bunch up like—whoa, Spots, what's wrong?"

Spots, who has abruptly listed to one side. "Adrenaline just gave out."

Claws, grasping her arm. "Control, this is Team Kitty."

Control. "Team Kitty, this is Control, go ahead."

Claws. "We're about up, time-wise. What's our sector lookin' like?"

Control. "Looking good."

Claws. "We got a weird bunchin' up here, you might want to give a heads-up to everyone. Fifteen buggers, two of 'em Kings, rushin' as a group. Spots handled it."

Control. "We'll review the cam footage. You're clear to come in."

Claws. "Understood, Kitty out." *To Spots,* "Come on, let's hoof it. Time to turn in."

Spots, with a shudder. "Thank God."

Claws, grinning. "Now, now, Spots . . . takin' the name of the lord in vain?"

Spots starts trudging after him. "That was a prayer, Claws, not an oath."

He nudges her. "Hey, not bad for your first outin'. How you feelin'?"

Spots the Space Marine: Defense of the Fiddler

Spots. "Like I want a shower. And a rack. And chocolate."

Claws. "Think you kinda got that backward there."

Spots, grim. "Trust me, if you've seen what passes for chocolate on-base, you'd know that the only way I'd be getting it is in my dreams."

04. FANG

Gym. There aren't many people in here. Probably because there aren't many people left. Spots and Claws have the equipment to themselves.

Claws. "Can you gimme another rep? Just another fifteen."

Spots. ". . . think so."

Claws. "All right, let's see it."

The bar clanks against the sockets with a rattle.

Claws. "Good job. You might be able to benchpress a bunny soon."

Spots. "C-claws!"

Claws. "Sorry, Spots. You're doin' good, seriously."

Spots. "Thanks. I'm trying."

———

Spots joins another member of Team Kitty in the showers, a younger woman with a lithe, hard body and dark skin. This woman's hair is shorn close to her scalp; she has tattoos on her arms and over her shoulder-blades: this is Fang. She glances once at Spots when she disrobes and then ignores her . . . until Spots peels her hair off the strip on her head.

Fang. "****ing A!"

Spots. "Pardon me?"

Fang. "What the hell is that, a rope? How'd they let you in with that much ****ing hair?"

Spots. "I guess they didn't care what I looked like, just that I showed up."

Fang. "You want to get us all killed with that?"

Spots. "It's usually under a helmet, Fang. The atmosphere is toxic, after all." *A pause. A sigh.* "Look, this is the first time you've noticed it, isn't it?"

Fang. "Well, since you keep it in that damned braid on your head, yeah."

Spots. "That braid is sealed on my head and I wear it that way all the time except once a week in this shower, when I wash it. Even when I sleep. I have less trouble getting my helmet on than Hairball does."

Spots the Space Marine: Defense of the Fiddler

Fang, disdainful. "Whatever you say."

Spots looks a little mournful as the younger woman steps out of the shower.

Later, in the Barracks.

Spots, sitting on the edge of her bunk as she unlaces her boots. "Hey, Claws?"

Claws, reading something on a tablet. "Yeah, what is it?"

Spots. "I don't think Fang likes me."

Claws. "Don't worry 'bout it. Fang don't like no one."

Spots. "Why is that?"

Claws. "She got assigned here when Dragon Team got destroyed. They were the best, they got the hardest assignment, and they died for it. Now she's here with us ****-ups."

Spots makes a face, though whether it's at his comment or the state of her foot once she peels her sock off is debatable. "We're not screw-ups, Claws."

Claws. "Can't say I disagree. But by her standards, we're a step down. Waaaaay down."

Spots. "But . . . hasn't she been with you a while? Surely she's gotten . . . well, used to it?"

Claws. "Hell, no." *A laugh.* "No one likes her attitude. That's why Fang-Two changed his name, just to **** her off. Now Scythe calls her Fang-One, it drives her ****ing insane."

Spots grimaces. "That wasn't very nice."

Claws. "No. But she had it comin'."

Spots. "Claws . . . we have to work together, you know. If we don't like one another—"

Claws. "We don't have to like each other. We just have to do our jobs."

Spots. "If you say so."

05. Trouble in the Team

Gym, again. Claws is sitting on a weight bench, watching the treadmill timer as Spots runs determinedly on it.

Claws. "Keep goin', almost done, and . . ."

He leans over and hits the timer, restarting the program.

"Go!"

Spots grimaces and keeps on. Fifteen minutes later . . .

Claws, grabbing her elbow. "Whoa! Hey, relax, I got ya. Gonna make a habit of fallin' off stuff?"

Spots, blowing hard. "N . . . n . . . no . . ."

Claws. "Did good. Here, sit. Get your breath back."

Quiet between them. Spots pants. Once she has her breath, he glances over at her.

Claws. "Hey. How come you didn't complain?"

Spots. "What?"

Claws. "You know. The suits practically run for us. 'S'no need for you to be hittin' the mat so hard."

Spots shakes her head. "Of course there is. If I rely on the suit, then I don't know if I can rely on myself. And if I can't do that . . . how can anyone else?"

Claws glances at her, then grips her shoulder. She smiles and stands to go shower.

Claws. "Hey, Spots? You got muscle definition in your back."

Spots pauses, looks over her shoulder with eyes wide. Then laughs.

A small common room. Fang is doing maintenance on a knife and its sheath, neither standard issue. Three men are playing cards. When Claws enters with a towel draped around his neck, Fang looks up.

"Still playing coach to Pollyanna?"

Claws, drawling even more than usual. "Why, Fang, I had no idea you knew how to read."

Spots the Space Marine: Defense of the Fiddler

Fang. "Why do you ****ing bother? She'll die first time something goes down."

The largest of the men speaks without looking up from his cards. "Hasn't yet."

Fang. "Newb's luck."

Claws. "It's not luck. And I ****in' bother because she actually works at it. You got a ****in' problem with that?"

Claws glares at Fang, who says nothing. Then at the others. One of them, a bald man with dark gold skin, holds up his hands.

"Hey, man, don't look at me. I'm all about the MILFs. Bring on the cookies."

Claws narrows his eyes and steps back. Fang waits until he's about to leave, then speaks to his back.

"Hey, Claws . . . **** you and your literary ***."

———————

A dark sleeping compartment. Spots is already asleep. Claws stops over her bunk to look at her. He goes to his own, sits down and rubs his face.

Claws, muttered. "Damn it."

Spots, sleepily. "Claws? You say something?"

Claws. "No. Go back to sleep." *A pause. Irritated:* "Where the hell did you get ears that fine? Steal 'em off a hare?"

". . . mmm. Try having a baby sometime, Claws . . . night . . ."

Claws, quietly, distracted. "Good night, Spots."

06. The Violinist

Armory. A narrow room of lockers, racked power and ammo cells, and suits in frames, terminating in an airlock.

Spots. "Are you sure we should be here this early?"

Claws. "Relax. Everyone checks their equipment before goin' out. Hairball and Whiskers were probably just here."

Spots. "If they were just here, doesn't that mean the equipment's already been checked?"

Claws. "We do our own—Spots, quick!"

Claws grabs Spots and pulls her behind an equipment locker as the door to the darkened armory opens. Two armed guards step through and take position beside the door. Then a thin, tall silhouette ducks to enter, and the smell of thyme and spice fills the air.

Spots, with a gasp. "Is that a . . . oh my gosh, Claws! That's a Violinist!"

"Spots, wait!"

Spots dashes out and almost into a nine-foot-tall alien resembling a streamlined praying mantis. It has a wedge-shaped head with large, multifaceted eyes and two backswept antenna. It has three pairs of arms: the topmost ending in long hand-like appendages, the middle sporting a set of scythe-like pincers with serrated edges, and a vestigial set near the joint of the thorax and abdomen. Its carapace is painted in fluorescent designs along its back, sides and up around six spiracles arranged in vertical rows on the thorax, three to a side.

It sees Spots, pauses, then "speaks" through these holes, a breathy, song-like sound. The vestigial arms glide together to add a counterpoint.

Alien. "Pardon, have we intruded?"

Spots. "Uh . . . no, no. We were just . . . just checking the armor."

Alien. "Ah! We also came for this purpose."

Claws hisses her name from the corner. She ignores him.

Spots. "Really?"

Alien. "Yes. We make a visual inspection and take data daily. This allows us to design better technology for your use."

Spots, wide-eyed. "Oh! You . . . you were one of the Violinists who gave us the technology?"

The alien approximates a bow. "We have that memory, yes."

Spots. "Wow. That's . . . that's amazing."

Alien. "We are glad you approve, Mother."

Spots. ". . . how . . . did you know I'm a mother?"

Alien. "Your body has the scent-memory of milk and blood. We have learned to associate this with mammalian mothers. You are here to inspect our work?"

Spots. "I . . . sort of. We're going out in a bit and—"

Alien. "Pardon us. Did you say you are going out? You mean in our work?"

Spots, hesitant. "Yes?"

"You, a mother?" *The lower arms make a somehow distressed trill.* "We did not know our work would be used for such important purposes."

Spots reaches to touch but thinks better of it. "It has served very well so far."

Alien. "We are glad to hear it." *A pause.* "You wished to know our lineage?"

15

Spots. "Know . . . your lineage?"

Alien, lifting an upper arm. "To smell the paint. It speaks of our lineage and its accomplishments."

Spots. "I . . . I don't know if my nose is that good, but . . . I'd be honored to try."

The alien extends its middle arm. Spots eyes the blade-like pincer and reaches over to sniff hesitantly at the fluorescent paint.

Spots. "I'm sorry. It smells . . . good, but I don't understand what it says."

Alien. "It is no surprise. Humans do not appear to have good talent in that way."

Spots. "Maybe you could explain it to me?" *Claws starts to say something.* "Uh . . . another day, when it's convenient."

Alien. "We would be honored, Mother-soldier. We have been named Samuel-Colt by the humans, if you wish to ask for us."

Spots. "Thank you, Samuel-Colt. I'll remember. Come on, Claws."

Claws inches around the locker, giving the alien a wide berth, and follows Spots out. In the corridor . . .

Claws. "Are you crazy? Talking to one of the fiddlers?"

Spots. "What's wrong with talking to them? They're our allies."

Claws. "Haven't you noticed they kind of look like the crabs we're fighting? They've admitted the crabs are from their planet."

Spots. "They also gave us the technology we use to kill them, Claws."

Claws. "You're way too trusting, Spots." *Claws squints at her, leans over and snaps fingers in front of her face*. "Hello! Earth to Spots, come in, Spots!"

Spots. "Sorry. I was just wondering why he kept saying 'we' all the time. Do you think he'd explain if I asked him later?"

Claws. "There ain't gonna be a later!"

Spots. "I guess you're right." *Wistful*. "I would have liked to have known."

16

07. The Corridor

[Base] Control : Team Kitty, you are go to clear the new corridor.

[Base] Scythe : Understood, Control. We're moving now.

[Base] Control : Good hunting, Kitty.

[Team Kitty] Scythe : All right, let's do this. I want to be back by dinner.

[Team Kitty] Fang2 : You actually look forward to that slop they serve us? You sure you're human?

[Team Kitty] Fang : Shut the **** up.

[Team Kitty] Scythe : Claws, Spots, you've got point-shield duty. Go.

[Team Kitty] Claws : On it.

[Team Kitty] Whiskers : Pretty damn quiet for a corridor.

[Private-to-Buddy] Claws : Hey, I don't like this. Stay close.

[Private-to-Buddy] Spots : Okay.

[Team Kitty] Fang2 : Where the hell are the bugs? Thought they built this out to make 'em pop up in a clump like they did for Spots.

[Team Kitty] Hairball : Halfway down now.

[Team Kitty] Fang2 : You hear something?

[Team Kitty] Fang : ****!!!

[Base] Control : Kitty, we've had no status from you for ten, what is your status?

[Team Kitty] Fang : NEW SHELLS! ONE O'CLOCK!

[Team Kitty] Scythe : SHIELDS! Cover the sniper!

[Team Kitty] Claws : Shields hot, go!

[Team Kitty] Fang : Got one—got 'em both!

[Team Kitty] Scythe : Close! Close up now! Finish off the rest, we need those bodies!

[Base] Control : Scythe, do you read!

[Base] Scythe : We have two new carapace designs, Control. Confirming . . . two body types not typical for this area. We're clearing to them now.

[Base] Control : ****. Good job. But ****.

[Base] Scythe : Copy that, Control.

[Private-to-Buddy] Claws : Did good on that.

[Private-to-Buddy] Spots : Just like practice. Just a little gorier.

[Private-to-Buddy] Claws : *laugh* You're all right, Spots.

08. Break for Rage

Warren, several days later. Claws and Spots are back on patrol. They're together now; after the discovery of the new shells, the pairs have been ordered not to split up.

Claws. "Quiet circuit. Makes me suspicious-like. You see anythin'?"

Spots. "Nothing."

Claws. "Let's hope it stays that way."

Spots. "From your mouth to God's ear."

Claws. " 'Nother hundred meters and we can go b—"

The wall between Spots and Claws erupts, smashing them apart on a wave of crabs. Twenty, thirty . . . it's hard to count them.

Claws, before he's lost to sight. "BREAKTHROUGH!"

Spots, desperate. "CLAWS!"

There is a stream of cursing from Claws and then silence.

Spots. "CLAWS!"

No answer.

oh God almighty, Claws claws hang on can't let them have you damn you all you won't have him you won't have any of them not my child not anyone's child NOT ANY MOTHER'S SON DAMN YOU ALL

NOT ANY MOTHER'S SON!

The corridor is carpeted with bodies. Claws has staggered to his feet and is staring at a very gory Spots.

"Jesus ****ing Christ!"

Spots turns and starts walking away. Claws lunges after her.

"Dammit, I'm sorry, I didn't mean to . . . to blaspheme, Spots . . . Spots . . . ! GUITART! Magda!"

At last Spots stops. Claws grabs her shoulders. "Are you okay? You're not supposed to wade into them like that! Remember the training? You get distance on these ****ers or they'll slice the ****in' hell outta your armor!"

Spots. "Sorry . . . I'm . . . sorry, Claws. I thought you were in trouble."

Claws. "I was, but . . . what the hell did you DO to them?"

Spots. "I . . . threw the shield forward of my arm and used the edge."

Claws stares at her. "Like the drill you screwed up and almost put a slice in the bulkhead."

Spots. "Well . . . yeah." *A lopsided, twisted sort of smile.* "They were in my face, it was kind of too late to get range on them."

A long pause. "Well, can't argue with results, I guess." *Still gripping her shoulder.* "Control, this is Claws. You read?"

"Control here. Go ahead, Claws."

Claws. "We've got two breakthrough tunnels in hall 7-Spoke-32, about a hundred meters from the end."

"Understood. We'll send a patch team. Can you guard?"

Claws. "Yeah. We're a bit shook up, but we can watch it."

"Patch team is on the way, ETA six minutes."

Claws. "Copy that." *Switching channels.* "Hey, Spots."

Spots. "Yes?"

Claws. "You with me?"

Spots. "Yes."

Claws. "Good."

———————

Armory, post-battle. Spots is crouching in her suit, helmet off. Claws is painting on its back with a red brush.

Spots. "How many was it?"

Claws. "That you went freaking ninja on? Musta been forty or fifty. I'm callin' it fifty, five ticks. We'll fill up your back soon enough."

Spots. "I never got to ask . . . why the different colors? Is that . . . by team or something?"

Claws. "No, that's keepin' count too. If you fill up the back panel and got no room left,

Spots the Space Marine: Defense of the Fiddler

you paint over it in the next color on the spectrum. Orange, yellow, 'cetera."

Spots glances at Fang's suit, which is already hung. "When do you get to white?"

Claws. "You don't get to white without dyin'." *Noting the direction of Spots's gaze.* "Unless you were part of Dragon Team."

Spots. "Right."

"Hey, Spots. Mind tellin' an ol' farm-boy where a cookie-bakin' mom comes by that much ***-kickin' wrath?"

Spots. "You don't know much about being a mom, do you, Claws."

Claws, working, lower lip rolled between his teeth. " 'Fraid I don't got the equipment."

Spots is quiet. Then she smiles. "It's all love."

Claws, cheerful. "Remind me not to date any moms."

"Claws!"

Claws. "Must sorta be like prayin' mantises. Snip, snip."

Spots is laughing. "Travis!"

21

Claws grins and keeps painting.

09. Shields

Small common room. There is a poster above the door that reads: "Varmint Gutter: Crawling Out of it So You Don't Have To." Scythe and two other squad leaders are playing cards at a round table: a tall, broad man, bald, with black skin and a green-eyed woman with light brown hair. There's a half-empty bottle (unmarked) and three glasses. The one nearest empty is next to the woman.

The black man speaks first.

"Need more, Dusty?"

Dusty, the woman. "Shut up."

Scythe. "Just deal the cards, Roach. She can pour a bottle same as you."

Roach. "Hey, just taking care of the lady. Varmint hospitality."

Dusty. "Is that what you're calling this **** we're drinking?"

Roach. "**** would taste better. At least mine would."

The door opens for another woman, Asian with bronze hair.

Roach. "Well hey-lo, Big Lion. What's the news?"

She sits. "We're ****ed. None of us special snowflakes are getting more warm bodies. Deal me in."

Dusty. "What! Have you seen what those new shells are doing to us? I've got three Dogs on biobeds tonight!"

Big Lion. "I know, Dusty."

Scythe is tense, but calmer than the other two. "We need more people. We can't send them out in pairs anymore. And if we start sending more we're going to run into serious fatigue issues."

Dusty. "**** it. I think Roach is the only left with a fire-team that knows any of its own by name."

Big Lion. "Doesn't change anything. We're a depot for the front, we're not supposed to need replacements. We'll talk more about it tomorrow, along with the really ****** parts."

Scythe. "There's worse?"

Spots the Space Marine: Defense of the Fiddler

Big Lion. "There's always worse. Pass the hooch."

Later. Scythe is coming back by way of Control.

Scythe, ducking in. "Any problems?"

"We were just about call. Your B-team had a breakthrough and they handled it. Alone."

Much later. Practice Room. Claws is leaning against a wall. Spots is in armor (without helmet) standing in front of a 3d target next to Scythe, a short, limber man with caramel-brown skin, black eyes, black brows and a Persian mouth. He speaks with a faint accent: Southern, maybe Cajun.

"So you cut them by shortening the shield's field. How did you keep them off your back while you were doing that?"

Claws. "By turning it back into a full shield, Sergeant."

Scythe looks over at Claws. "Didn't you have this talk with her?"

Claws. "Yep. Spots, didn't we have this talk?"

Spots. "About . . . oh, I'm not supposed to call Scythe 'sergeant'. Sorry, s—um, sorry."

Scythe shakes his head. "So you shortened the shield radius in the middle of a fight?"

Spots. "Yes. Claws showed me how to toggle on the interactive mode . . . he also said we never use it. 'Shields are for protecting snipers from enemy needles.' "

Scythe. "That's right. There's a reason for that. Do you remember?"

Spots. "Yes s . . . um, Scythe. We are to avoid closing with the enemy at all times. Because they can snip off a limb or cut through armor if you close."

Claws, dry. "Good t'know you were actually listenin' to my lectures, there."

Scythe. "Show me this shield modification."

Spots nods and faces off against the foam target. She lunges forward, swinging her arm in an arc in front of it, never actually hitting it. But as she redoubles, the top of the target slides off the bottom and bounces to the floor. Scythe picks it up.

"And you can reconfigure on the fly."

Spots. "I . . . guess I must ha—"

Scythe throws the target head at her. She brings up her arm and it bounces off with a splash of bright light.

Scythe. "Damn. Interesting."

Spots. "Is it? I . . . mean, I'm sure someone else has done it before. It's the same shield built into all the standard suits, right?"

Scythe. "Yes, but you might be the only one crazy enough to have rammed a forty-bug group with nothing but a shield. Why didn't you use your gun?"

Spots. "I . . . didn't think I could shoot them fast enough."

Claws coughs behind a fist.

Scythe eyes him as he addresses Spots. "Well, obviously you need to work on learning to shoot faster, yes?"

Spots. "Right."

Scythe. "Good. Somebody spent a lot of money shipping you all the way out here, Guitart, we don't need you dying yet."

Spots. "Yes. Um, right. I'll work on it."

Scythe shakes his head and leaves.

Spots sighs. "I guess I should go to the range."

Claws. "I guess we should. Come on, ninja. Lemme introduce you—again—to the wonders of automatic weapons."

10. INSOMNIA

The Real Window. A long window with four layers—an exterior surface for storm debris, two pressure panes and an interior panel—looking out on the dismal murk of an alien night. Spots is in a physical training uniform, loose shirt and pants; she is sitting on the broad sill, face turned toward the exterior. Her cheek is wet. She has a photo in one hand.

She is joined by a lean middle-aged man with stubble-short hair, a broken nose and a scar edging one cheekbone, in utility uniform.

He hands her a tissue. She wipes her face.

"Want to talk about it?"

Spots. "No."

"Fair enough." *A few moments later.* "Why the Real Window? There are plenty of others you can program to something nicer."

Spots. "Because it gets tiring, having to have everything be about you. It's good to face reality instead of trying to . . . to impose your personality on it all the time. I don't know if that makes sense . . ."

"Perfect. I like the Real Window better myself. Quite a storm out there."

Spots. "Yes."

"That your family?"

Spots. "Oh? Oh. Yes."

"May I see?"

She hands the picture over: a solid brick of a man with his hand on the shoulder of a young boy, who is holding a younger girl in his arms.

"Good-looking folks."

Spots. "I think so."

Quiet again. Then:

Spots. "Will I ever get any better at this? I mean . . . I enlisted over a decade ago, and not as Armor. I feel like . . ."

"Like you're too old to keep up?"

Spots sighs. "No. Like I'm too old to *catch* up. Maybe if I'd been doing this more than a few weekends a year . . ."

"You'll get there." *He nods at the photo.* "You've got a reason to go back."

Spots. "A lot of people have reasons to go back. They still die."

He's quiet a while.

"If you've been around long enough to understand that, then you're too old for my standard pep talk."

She looks up with a startled laugh. He grins.

"So your bones creak and maybe you were supposed to be riding a desk. You're not going to be benching what the eighteen-year-old kids are and you know that and I know that. You can't have that body back, or the years you could have spent working at it instead of, say, raising those beautiful kids. But you're here now, and you can get better at this: you can get as good at it as you, in particular, at this point in your life, have the potential to get. And that's a lot better than you think, and it's all in your hands. You wouldn't be sitting at the Real Window if you didn't know that. You'd be in front of some picture window, being reassured by things that aren't."

Spots inhales slowly, then blows out the breath and nods. He stands and clasps her shoulder.

"Besides, you know things those kids haven't learned yet. And they need that from you. You give it to them, they'll give you the strength of their best years."

Spots. "Do you really think those are the best years?"

He grins again. "No. But they don't know it."

She laughs, soft.

"Try to get some sleep, private."

"I will. And thank you."

11. TURMOIL

Kitty Common Room.

Scythe. "You've probably heard the news—"

Fang2. "Yeah, the crabs are getting more aggressive."

Scythe. "—yes. Which means from now on we patrol in teams of four. You're keeping your partners but we'll change out the pairs in the teams so that one pair can get extra rack-time between patrols."

Long pause. Then, Hairball.

"****, Boss."

Scythe. "I know. But Dusty's got three Dogs on their backs and it's only getting worse out there."

Claws. "Any plans for relief?"

Scythe, with teeth in his grin. "Yeah. Me. I'll be tagging along during my watch so one of you can sleep in."

Claws again. "Wow, that's mighty kind of you."

Scythe. "That's me. Sweet as your grandma. Any questions?" *No one speaks.* "Good. One final thing . . . word from up high is that we don't leave bodies anymore. Ever."

Fang2. "What the hell is that about?"

Whiskers. "We've always done retrieval."

Scythe. "When we could. But if we can't, we don't leave prisoners. And if you're taken, you don't either. You get my drift."

Hairball. "****."

Fang. "You planning on getting captured, Hairball?"

Hairball. "Way things are shaping, might be the only way I get any shut-eye."

———

Armory. Spots and Claws are climbing into their armor. They are listening to the comm channel while doing their checks.

[Base] Hairball : Control, maintenance 4B is clear. Heading home.

[Base] Control : Copy that, Hairball. Your relief is suiting up.

[Base] Hairball : Great, ETA ten minutes.

[Base] Fang : BREAKTHROUGH—

[Base] Fang2 : ****! Both walls!

Claws and Spots glance at one another, then start rushing through their final prep.

"Air supply, green. Ammo, topped. Reserve power, topped. All lights green. Seal checks—"

"Air supply, green ammo topped reserve power topped all lights green seal checks, airlock, go go go!"

They jump into the airlock. When the exterior door opens they burst through and sprint down the corridor. They turn a corner: the entire end of the hall is filled with flailing bodies. Hairball is running toward them with Whiskers over his back. Fang and Fang2 are laying down covering fire but aren't killing fast enough.

Claws and Spots add their guns. The bodies pile up so quickly the aliens have to stop to unplug the hall. The humans retreat.

[Team] Hairball : At the airlock.

[Team] Fang : Hold it open, we're almost there.

The ground beneath them shivers.

[Team] Fang2 : What the—

The ground falls from beneath the two Fangs. Claws grabs Fang2's arm, Spots Fang's belt. Pincers and legs everywhere.

[Team] Fang2 : **** DON'T LET GO

Claws hauls him back so hard he staggers backwards. Spots has an arm around Fang's waist, but the crabs are pulling her in.

[Team] Fang : LET GO!

[Team] Spots : No!

[Team] Fang : DAMMIT LET GO!

She shoves an elbow at Spots's faceplate. Spots is startled just enough to loosen her grip and Fang wrestles free. She vanishes into the pit.

[Team] Spots : FANG!

Fang pops back into view, jumping off the thorax of a heaving crab.

[Team] Fang : RUN RUN NOW

They start running. The pit explodes behind them, blowing them forward. They slam into the airlock and the exterior door closes behind them.

[Team] Fang2 : **** **** **** ****

[Team] Fang : Next time I tell you to do something, you do it. I know my job.

[Team] Claws : That was a damfool stunt and you know it.

[Team] Fang : I know what I'm doing.

[Team] Claws : You're not a super-special samurai, Fang, stop ****ing actin' like one.

[Team] Fang : I got news for you, newb. We're *all* supposed to be super-special samurai. If you think I'm acting like one it's because you can't ****ing cut it.

[Team] Fang2 : ****, Fang, tone it down. You got balls, we get it. You don't have to shove them in our face.

———————

Later. Barracks. Claws has just turned out the lights.

Spots. "Travis . . . does Fang want to die?"

Claws, tired. "Just go to sleep, Spots."

Spots. "Maybe I'll say a prayer for her. Do you think it would help?"

Claws, with a faint smirk as he turns over. "As long as she never finds out."

12. Conversations

Scythe and Fang, alone in one of the empty barracks.

"If you ever ****ing do that again, I will personally pack you up and ship you to the ****ing front. Without a ride. Do you understand me?"

Fang. "So the ****ing *mom* wades into a pack of crabs and she gets off, but I actually do my ****ing job and I get **** for it?"

Scythe. "Unlike the ****ing mom, Gordon, you should know the **** better. Am I going to have to tell you this again?"

Fang, surly. "No, Sergeant."

Scythe. "Good. Because like it or ****ing not, you're part of Team Kitty, and if you don't start acting like it I will use that ****ing kimono you brought back from Dragon Team to wipe my ***, understood?"

"Yes, Sergeant."

Scythe. "Get out of here and get some ****ing sleep."

———————

Sickbay. Whiskers is on one of the beds with his arm immobilized. Spots pulls up a stool next to him.

"I brought you your peanut butter bar."

Whiskers. "What?"

Spots. "Your peanut butter bar. Hairball was going to eat it but I told him that he can eat your food while you're on fluids but eating your candy is just rotten."

Whiskers. "I don't think the vampires want me eating on an IV."

Spots. "Oh, absolutely not." *She leans forward and whispers.* "When I was in the hospital my husband snuck in part of a breaded steak for me. It was cold and tough from the trip but it was the best thing I'd ever tasted. Totally worth it." *When he doesn't move to take it she sets it on the stand next to him.*

Whiskers. "Weren't you and Claws supposed to be out on patrol?"

Spots. "We were . . . there were so many crabs out there we had to change out rifles for grenade launchers and wait for engineering support. They started laying down grid flooring on the corridor so they couldn't break through that way again."

Spots the Space Marine: Defense of the Fiddler

Whiskers. "Grenade launchers, huh? Bet that was . . . exciting."

Spots makes a face. "That's not the word I would have chosen."

Whiskers grins. "Let me guess. 'Messy.' "

Spots starts laughing. "Good guess!"

He grins.

Spots. "You get better soon."

Whiskers. "Working on it."

Spots leaves. Whiskers drums his fingers on his blanketed chest. Then he snags the bar with his good arm and tears the wrapper with his teeth. Moments later he is chewing.

13. PEACHES

Two days later. Barracks. Spots is putting a rosary aside. Claws reaches for the compartment light.

"Done?"

Spots. "Yes, thank you."

"Righty. Good n—"

On the nightstand, Spots's earbug chirps. She places it against her ear. "Guitart." *Listens.* "On my way." *She rolls out of bed and starts dressing.*

"Spots?"

"Dunno . . . I'm supposed to report to the lieutenant at the Door." *She finishes dressing.* "Back . . . soon, I guess."

Once she's out the door Claws gets up and taps the screen beside his bunk. A disgruntled Scythe appears.

"This has better be good, I was just getting back to sleep."

Claws. "Dreamin' about ninety-two virgins?"

Scythe. "Oh, for God's sake. My ****ing grandmother would punch you in the ****ing mouth for that. What the **** is it?"

Claws. "Bonny Peaches just called for Spots. What gives?"

Scythe. "Dunno, had something to do with the Fiddler."

Claws. "With the *alien?*"

"Yep."

"****, Boss, this is our sack time. Sack time is sacred."

Scythe. "You don't argue with Peaches. Or do you want them to kick Rambo the First out of the grave, see if he can do better by us the second time around?"

Claws grimaces. "**** no, no. Dammit."

Scythe. "Go back to bed, Walker. She might be the noobiest of noobs, but she can handle a little quality time with the LT."

Claws. "You're not the **** who's going to have a sleepless buddy at your back tomorrow."

"Whine whine." *The circuit cuts. Claws grouses and throws himself on his bunk. The lights flick off.*

———————

Spots heads to the Door, which leads to high-security areas of the base. Three figures are waiting there: a short lanky man with stringy hair in civilian dress; and two Marines, a fit young woman and an older man with stubble for hair, the same who comforted Spots at the Real Window.

"Private Guitart reporting as ordered, ma'am."

"Come with us, Guitart."

"Yes, ma'am."

The civilian swipes an ID card through the door reader. After a few halls, they enter a room lined with computers and 3d imaging stations. Samuel-Colt is among them. In proper lighting, he is tan with brown markings. The fluorescing blue paint on his shell looks gray.

The civilian speaks first.

"Hey Sam, we brought her."

"Good, that is very good . . ." *The alien trails off. His vestigial arms squeak a sudden, disturbed note.* "Where is her escort?"

The civilian points at the two Marines. "They brought her."

"Those humans are strangers. They do not smell like her. Where is her escort? A mother should not be without her escort."

The civilian glares at Spots now. "Who were you with when he saw you?"

Spots, confused. "My squad-mate . . . ? Claws, he's in the barracks."

"Dammit."

Older man. "Is it important?"

Samuel-Colt. Sharp low sound. "A mother should never be without escort. Please retrieve him. Then we can speak."

Peaches. "Can you escort him through the Door, please, Gunny?"

Older man. "Sure thing, ma'am." *He steps outside.*

Civilian. "Might as well sit. We won't be able to start until he gets back."

Spots, bewildered. "Start . . . what?"

The civilian shrugs, offers his hand. "Will Kenyan. Senior Engineer, assistant to the Fiddler."

Spots. "Nice to meet you. I'm Magda."

The alien sits across from them: many arms, many legs, folded at strange angles. He studies Peaches, a young woman with blonde hair tied back in a very short ponytail. Her fresh girl-next-door face is responsible for her nickname. "We do not know this other human by name."

"I'm Lieutenant Savannah Bonnet. Nice to meet you, ah . . . Samuel-Colt, right?"

"That is my name. We know 'lieutenant' . . . that means you have authority in this situation, yes? Even over the mother?"

Peaches glances at Spots. "Ah, that's right. Yeah. Yes."

Samuel-Colt looks at Spots. Interrogatory glide (sounding almost skeptical). "This youth gives you orders?"

Firmly, Spots: "She's trained to deal with situations I'm not, Samuel-Colt. So yes, I follow her orders."

"Strange."

Spots. "Strange how?"

Kenyan, muttering. "****, don't ask him more questions."

Samuel-Colt. Single-note drone. "I will have been born, lived and died within a span that your young will live without fully maturing . . . and yet, despite having so many more years of experience than I would have, humans are still not considered adult. How can that be?"

Spots. "How old are you, Samuel-Colt?"

Falling pitch trill. "Fifteen years. We have already chosen my successor. Within five years, I will return to die and pass on our legacy. How old are you, Mother-soldier?"

Spots. "I'm thirty-two."

"Thirty-two years!" *A rising, startled glissando.* "And you, Lieutenant-Savannah-Bonnet?"

Spots the Space Marine: Defense of the Fiddler

Peaches glances at Spots again. "Twenty-two."

"A decade between you. It is not awkward?"

Spots laughs. "It probably wasn't until you asked."

Peaches flushes, then laughs too. The door slides open. "Here's Gunny and the . . . ah . . . mother's escort. At ease, Corporal."

Samuel-Colt, approvingly to Claws. "Very good. We apologize for separating you from your charge."

Claws, bewildered. "Ain't no trouble. Uh, what's this about now?"

Samuel-Colt, turning to Spots. Quick arpeggio, rising. "We have heard that you used our shields in a non-standard way. We were hoping to discuss this incident with you."

Spots, startled. "Really?"

"It was not our intent for the shields to be used in such a fashion, but you have made a proof of concept . . . we are not surprised. We did not design the shield protocol to allow for constant re-configuration, but if it is a viable weapon we would like to re-visit the technology."

Spots. "Oh! Of course. Anything I can do to help."

"Then perhaps we may repair to the testing facility?"

"Yes, of course!"

14. PARADIGMS

Testing Facility. There are multiple dummy targets in this room (crab-shaped) and a great deal of equipment. Samuel-Colt gives Spots a glove with a shield-generator, then picks up a clipboard.

Interrogative rising glide. "You were there also, mother's-escort?"

Claws. "Uh, yes, sir."

"The sir is not necessary . . . ours is a peer relationship. Since you were present, please speak freely when you have pertinent observations. Your views may be important." *Samuel-Colt glances at Peaches. Another glide, this one longer and more gradual.* "That is well with you Lieutenant-Savannah-Bonnet?"

"Yes, that's fine. Oblige him, Corporal, if you have anything relevant to add."

Claws. "Will do, ma'am."

Low drone. "Very good. Please proceed, Mother-soldier."

Spots demonstrates, slicing the targets. Samuel-Colt follows her with a clipboard, bent over her.

"So you are contracting the field's edge and using the bottom curve?"

Spots. "I . . . yes, I think so."

"By how great a margin?"

Spots. "I . . . don't know, I wasn't thinking about it. I guess short enough for my arm to handle?"

"Are you willing to demonstrate again?"

Spots. "Yes, of course."

"Then permit me a moment." *Samuel-Colt removes a clipper from the back of his clipboard and chops off two fingertips. He pops them into his mouth, crunches once and they're gone. Then he wiggles the new, shorter fingers, which have small visible holes at the ends.* "Continue."

Claws. "Jesus Christ! What the **** was that?"

Kenyan. "You get used to it."

Spots looks up at the alien, pained. "Doesn't that hurt?"

Spots the Space Marine: Defense of the Fiddler

Reassuring, alternating two notes. "No, Mother-soldier. And it allows me to better feel the shield resonances. I will be able to gauge their length myself from the sound. Please continue? More slowly. I will hold my hand near you."

Spots. "All right. Of course."

They run through the demonstration again.

Claws. "Uh, I have an observation. A more relevant one than my last one."

Peaches. "Go ahead."

Claws, with less of an accent. "This demo's not replicating the actual situation very well. You may be getting different data than you want."

Spots, frowning. "I think he's right, but sparring with this thing . . . it cuts through *armor*. I don't want to hurt anyone by accident!"

Samuel-Colt. Quick, excited notes. "That concern can be addressed if your partner is willing to wear a shield tuned off-key to yours. You will not be able to penetrate."

Claws is about to speak, but Gunny beats him to it. "I'll do it."

Ten minutes later after modification of the second generator, the two of them face off.

37

"Now don't feel weird about this, Guitart. Just cut loose. I can take it."

Spots. "Are you sure . . . ?"

"Positive."

Spots takes a deep breath . . . and goes for him. Samuel-Colt lunges after her, waving his hands in the periphery of their frenzied activity. She does not hold back or stop until the alien speaks.

"Good! Enough, thank you."

Peaches, frowning. "Strange to watch an armed fight with nothing to show you where the weapon is."

Gunny. "There's a rim of light when the cutting edge comes through, but it's quick."

Peaches. "So . . . this whole . . . novel use of the shield is because of the edge?"

Samuel-Colt. Tense, interested trill. "That is correct. Also, the rapid modulation of size. The mother's-escort was correct to change the parameters of the demonstration. The live-fight test was very different."

Peaches. "I'm not sure of the utility of using the shields this way. You'd need so much training to do it properly and then to coordinate it with your squadmates. What would be the advantage, weighed against that?"

Gunny, looking at Spots. "Why'd you do it this way, Guitart?"

Spots. "Um . . . instead of using the gun?"

"Yeah."

"I . . . I don't know." *She chews her lip, frowning.* "Maybe I didn't want to hit him? Rounds that pierce crab-armor do for ours as well."

Claws. "If I may?" *They look at him.* "I think she did it because the shield engages more of the enemy simultaneously. Look . . ." *He drags three of the foam targets together. They tower over him by several feet.* "If I'm standing here . . . right up in their faces . . . and I shoot one . . ." *He points his finger at the belly of one target.* "I don't have time to swing it far enough to engage the second target when they're this close. But the shield in weapon-shape—" *He lifts his arm, elbow out and forearm parallel to the ground.* "—that hits all three of them at the same time. And in shield-shape, it'll do a whole one-eighty bubble, nearly."

Peaches, musing. "It's a better weapon if you're in the middle of them."

Claws. "I surely wouldn't want to be shootin' crab-piercing rounds at point-blank myself, ma'am."

Spots, wide-eyed. "I . . . I don't think I was thinking all of that, Claws."

" 'Course not. You ain't doin' calculus when you catch a ball, but you'd need the math to describe the act. You don't have to know how to talk 'bout what you're doin' to do it." *He looks at Samuel-Colt.* "Look, so we get these shields and you tell us they're for sniper-shieldin' only, because the bullets passing through from the inside degrade the shield, right?"

Slow, thoughtful glide, falling. "That is correct. The interruptions are too abrupt, far more abrupt than humans brushing against them. That is why you can tap the inside with your finger but firing through it drains the power cell."

Claws. "I'll pretend I get the theory there. More important, though . . . two shields as shields work together, we do that already. Can two shields work together when one is being used as a weapon? Like, say . . . if Spots here's got the full half-bubble, can I slide my cutting edge through hers to hit what's coming?"

Samuel-Colt, studying Claws. He doesn't make any music at all. "Yesss . . . that should be possible. The shields are constructed to harmonize . . . that is why I had to re-tune the shield for the Mother-soldier's fighting partner."

Peaches. "I see where you're going with that, Corporal. But it would still take a lot of training."

Claws. "Maybe so, ma'am. Still, it's an alternative."

Peaches eyes him, speculatively. "So it is." *To Samuel-Colt.* "Is that enough, sir? These two need their down-time."

Samuel-Colt. Quick arpeggio, falling. "Yes, thank you. I have a great deal to consider."

Peaches. "Very good. Gunny, can you walk them to the Door?"

"Will do, ma'am."

Spots. "Goodbye, Samuel-Colt. And nice to meet you, Mr. Kenyan."

"Fare well, Mother-soldier." *A pause. A quick, almost laughing arpeggio, up first, then down.* "The fingers will grow back."

Spots laughs. "I'm glad to hear it!"

———

Back in the barracks.

Claws. "Can you sleep an hour?"

Spots. "Oh, yes."

Claws. "All right, I'll leave the light off then. No way I can put my head down that long and get anythin' out of it."

Spots. "Hey, Claws? The lieutenant was very impressed with you, I think."

Claws. "Aw shucks, Spots. She ain't my type. I like 'em older."

Spots. "Claws! That's not what I m—"

Claws. "Don't worry though, I'm not into brunettes. I prefer 'em red."

Spots. "You're terrible, Claws."

"Don't I know it. Night, Spots."

Claws turns the light off. In the dark, he puts a hand to his brow. Shortly after he whispers a curse. Spots opens her eyes a crack at the sound, but doesn't ask.

15. CHOW

Map room. Peaches is bent over a table, staring at a diagram of the base. The gunny is across from her.

Peaches. "I'm not seeing very many options."

Gunny. "That's because there aren't many, ma'am."

Peaches. "What about collapsing some of the tunnels?"

Gunny. "Could do that. It would give us less area to patrol."

Peaches, glancing at him. "I hear a 'but'."

Gunny. "But those tunnels were placed to route the crabs into areas of our choosing . . . and to keep them away from the donut. If we collapse too many of them, they might go for the collider."

Peaches grimaces. "Can't have that. Can we grid the existing tunnels? Make them harder to penetrate except where we choose?"

Gunny. "I'm not sure we have the materiel to cover the entire warren, but we can run the numbers."

Peaches. "Let's do that. It'll be my *** if we shut down the damn collider." *She presses a thumb against the bridge of her nose.* "I keep asking for replacements but none keep showing up."

Gunny. "We're not high on the priority list, ma'am."

Peaches. "We're not high on the priority list now, but stop making torpedoes and the entire Navy will be knocking on our door. With battering rams." *She smiles faintly.* "At least I did get the other thing I asked for."

"Ma'am?"

Peaches. "I read somewhere that you can compensate for fatigue a little with food, so I asked for extra rations. We should be getting those with the next supply ship."

Gunny. "No kidding. That'll go over well."

"Not as well as what's coming tonight." *At his arched brow, she continues.* "The Seabees offered to cook for us, since they've got a real kitchen."

Gunny, studying her. "They've got a real kitchen, ma'am, but I know for a fact they don't have extra food."

Spots the Space Marine: Defense of the Fiddler

"They don't, no. But the *contractors*, now . . ."

A pause. Then he laughs. "I like the way you think, ma'am. What's on the menu?"

"Pork chops, green beans and sweet potatos. And I hear there's a gigantic brownie somewhere with our name on it."

———————

Armory. Spots and Claws are stripping out of their armor; Hairball and Scythe are already suited up to replace them with the two Fangs, who are outside. Everyone is talking on comm, since some heads are out of suits.

Hairball. "You got good stuff waiting for you."

Claws. "What's this now?"

Scythe. "Real food. Hot food. In the mess."

Fang2. "Aww, ****, and I'm stuck out here for another round with ****ing Crab Delight?"

Scythe, grinning. "There'll be enough left over."

Claws. "Hot food. I've forgotten what that looks like."

Fang2. "Stop ****ing chatting and get out here so the rest of us can hurry up and get back!"

———————

Claws and Spots in the Mess Hall.

Claws. "****! He wasn't kiddin'!"

Spots. "This looks good! Oooh, chocolate."

Claws starts laughing. "Women."

Spots eyes him. "You don't like chocolate?"

Claws. "Nah, I'm more of a vanilla pers—aw, quit gigglin', you're ruinin' my image."

Spots, trying to compose herself. "Hey, you know, we should take some to Whiskers."

Claws. "Will they let him eat it? I thought he was on fluids."

Spots. "He's been there almost a week. That's long enough. Come on, let's do it. It won't take long, we won't miss much sleep."

Claws. "All right, sure."

———————

Sickbay.

Claws. "They gonna let you out of here anytime soon, Whiskers?"

Whiskers. "If they don't I'm gonna ****ing bust my way out. Hey, food!"

Claws and Spots pull up stools. The medical staff ignores them.

Spots, bringing a tray. "Here, need help?"

Whiskers. "Nah, I'm good. Pass that chop."

Claws, watching the medical staff. "How come they're not buggin' us? I woulda thought for sure they'd be all over us for messin' with your delicate health."

Whiskers. "They got other worries. One of them Wild Dogs isn't doing so well."

Spots glances over at the other side of sickbay. There is a man hooked up to more monitoring equipment than typical. "That looks bad. Coma?"

"Yeah, they think so."

Claws. "****."

Whiskers. "Yeah, serious ****. For the crabs. The Dogs are ****ing p***ed. What's this, dessert?"

Spots. "Aren't you going to eat it all?"

Whiskers. "Nah, not into chocolate, I'm all about the ice cre—why're you giggling?"

Claws. "Don't mind her. Brownies make her punchy."

Whiskers, shaking his head. "Women."

Claws. "Tell me about it."

16. JUST ANOTHER PATROL

Three days later, in the Warren. The Seabees are putting down grid flooring; they are not armored but carry rifles because so few Marines are available to escort their teams. Claws, Spots and the two Fangs stand guard.

Claws. "Wonder where our servin' is . . . everyone else's had one."

Spots. "Maybe we'll get lucky?"

Claws, making a face. "We're Marines, Spots. We never get lucky."

One Seabee looks up. "Hey, don't jinx it!"

Claws grins. The crew works steadily along the corridor's curve.

Fang2. "I think I feel som—BREAKTHROUGH!"

The corridor's walls erupt, separating Claws, Spots and one builder from the Fangs and the team. Grid flooring flies to the sides, crates of it spill. There are crabs everywhere.

"****!"

Claws. "GET THEM BACK TO BASE!"

Fang2. "Going!"

Claws pushes the unarmored builder in front of him. "RUN! First fox-run, go right!" *Claws and Spots cover the builder's retreat as the wave rushes for them.*

Claws. "TURN, TURN NOW!"

"****!! What the ****—"

Claws shoves him through the narrow tunnel. "Shield!"

Spots drops at the tunnel mouth, shield arm in front. Claws hovers over her shoulder, rifle pointed. The tunnel is small enough that the crabs have to come through one by one, hauling their dead out of the way. While Claws shoots—

Spots. "Fang! You good?"

Fang2, voice quick. "We got back, the team's fine. Most of the crabs ****ing chased off after you. You got them?"

The crabs stop trying to clamber through the hole. Spots squints. "I think we migh—"

Claws: "****! They're gonna come through! Go go go!"

They dash down the corridor, the builder streaming curses. Behind them, the fox-run explodes outward. The hall fills with a hail of thin alien needles. Spots puts her arm behind her head, shield still active. It flashes constantly as the projectiles bounce off it.

Claws. "****! Turn on three! One! Two! Thr—"

He and Spots fling themselves around and shoot. Beyond the oncoming rush of arms and pincers is the tall figure of a King. Claws aims—shoots—the King goes down and the other bugs begin flailing in confusion. Spots and Claws pick them off.

Then, silence.

"See, guns are handy."

Builder. "Nukes are handier. ****!"

Claws, grinning at builder. "You and I know that."

Spots. "I never said guns weren't useful, Claws." *Exasperation.* "Sometimes I think you people think I've never used one before I showed up here."

Claws. "Uh . . . guilty as charged."

Spots, wrinkling nose. "If I was the cursing kind . . ."

"You'd probably be saying '**** you' right now. I get it." *Pause.* "Sorry, Guitart."

Builder. "Uh . . . can we get back now?"

"In a minute, we have to call in the King. He's got a new shell."

"What's that mean?"

Spots. "It means we're in trouble."

Claws, grim. "**** yes. They've never worked around the ****ing fox-run before."

17. Righteous Anger

Gym. 3 AM. Spots, wearing gloves, sleepwear and an intent expression, is applying fists and feet to a punching bag. Scythe, in a physical training uniform and with a katana, enters and watches for a while. After a particularly violent kick:

"I think you put his lung out the back of his ribs."

Spots. "Oh! Um, Scythe. I didn't see you come in."

Scythe, wry. "I noticed. You're up during your sleep-shift."

Spots. "Just . . . a little bit. Couldn't sleep, thought I'd work it out."

Scythe. "Work what out?"

Spots eyes him. Sighs. "Guess if I said 'my aggression' you wouldn't believe me."

Scythe sits on a trunk used for safety equipment. "Actually, I would. What's eating you?"

"I'm getting a little tired of everyone treating me like a limp dishrag. I might have gone through boot camp over a decade before any of them, but I got through it." *She flexes her hands.* "And I qualified with a rifle while most of them were still in grade school. The gun jokes are getting old."

"You joined young."

She shrugs. "I wanted to go active, but I was engaged. It was that or get married and have kids." *She smiles.* "For an 18-year-old I was pretty clear about what I wanted."

Scythe. "You still with this guy you married as a teenager?"

"Huh? Yes, of course." *A smaller smile, private.* "Best decision I ever made."

Scythe. "You could try giving them as good as you get, you know."

Spots shakes her head. Strips off her gloves. "Not my style."

"What is your style, then?"

She thinks about it. Laughs, but not carefree. " 'Hang in there.' "

"I can see that. Hey, look, Guitart. At some point, you're going to have to lay down the law."

She grins at him. "Not going to fight my battles, are you."

"I could, but would you want me to?"

"Of course not. I've got a plan, I promise. But that doesn't mean I don't get angry when people dismiss me." *She puts the gloves away, glances at him.* "Aren't you on sleep-shift too?"

Scythe smiles, hands resting on the sword over his lap. "You're not the only one who has some aggression to work out."

"Want to talk about it?"

"No, I want to lop off some target heads. But thanks."

"No problem."

"Hey, Guitart."

She pauses at the door. "Yes?"

Scythe. "What *is* your plan?"

"Same as what worked with my kids. Wear 'em down. Night, Scythe."

———————

The Board Room: the lab where alien bodies are dissected. Next to the door is a photo of butterflies pinned to a board, supplying the room's nickname. Peaches is standing next to several people: Naval Intelligence, contractors, some specialists. On the board is the King Claws brought in.

Peaches. "So this isn't a new shell?"

"Not quite, Lieutenant. It's one of the new shells your sniper shot, but modified for a King body."

Peaches, frowning. "Are you sure about that?"

"Not completely, but the patterns and colors are the same, just . . . stretched out. We've never seen anything like it."

Peaches. "What about the inside?"

"That's . . . where it gets stranger. There's a nodule of nervous tissue at the base of the thorax. It's tempting to say it's a second brain, but we have no idea what it would be used for. Kings have bigger brains anyway, but . . . why the second node? I wish we could ask our resident alien."

Peaches glances at him. "Which you can't, because . . . ?"

Spots the Space Marine: Defense of the Fiddler

"Orders. We don't discuss these things with the friendlies. It's impolitic, makes them uncomfortable."

Peaches. "So we have a King with a shell we think might be quasi-new but we're not sure, and that we think might have a second brain, and we're not sure, and we don't know what any of it means or how it'll affect us."

"Basically."

Peaches. "****."

———————————

Twenty minutes later, Peaches is striding down the corridor. She picks up the gunny and keeps going, all the way to the secure area.

"Ma'am? What are we up to?"

Peaches. "Have you been through Sickbay lately, Gunny?"

"Yes, ma'am . . . ?"

"So have I." *Peaches swipes her security card, jaw hard.* "We're going to see Samuel-Colt."

47

18. Not Like Us

Design Lab. Peaches and Gunny enter without announcing themselves. Will Kenyan, the engineer, is working at one of the computers. He glances their way when they enter, stands.

Kenyan. "What are you doing here? No one sent for you."

Peaches. "We're looking for the alien."

"He's busy."

Peaches, impatient. "Who isn't? Where is he?"

Kenyan. "Seriously, you can't just walk in here and interrupt the research. Which we're doing for your benefit, I might add—"

Peaches, remembering herself. "This is important, Mister Kenyan. I assure you, I wouldn't have come for something trivial. Where is Samuel-Colt?"

Kenyan, throwing up his hands. "It's your ***. He's in the back room."

"Thank you, Mister Kenyan."

"Lieutenant? I wouldn't barge in there. Just an FYI."

Peaches eyes him, then heads for the back of the lab. There is a door there; Peaches hesitates, then keys the door intercom.

"Samuel-Colt? It's Lieutenant Savannah Bonnet and . . ." *Hesitates. Glances at the gunny.* "And my escort. May we come in?"

Pause. Then: "Please, enter."

Fiddler's "Restroom." This room is the size of a large closet, with a single pallet and a small sound system which is currently playing a Vivaldi flute concerto. The open door sheds enough light to reveal Samuel-Colt reclining.

Samuel-Colt. "Please close the door, Lieutenant-Savannah-Bonnet. The light is stressful."

She closes it, discomfited. In the dark, the Fiddler's eye glows like a faceted lamp.

Samuel-Colt, continuing. "How may we help you?"

Gathering herself. "We were hoping you could tell us about a situation we've encountered. We've run into a couple of new shells—which isn't unprecedented—but yesterday we picked up a King that seems to be wearing a modified version of one of them. He

Spots the Space Marine: Defense of the Fiddler

also has what appears to be a second brain in his thorax. Do you have any idea what that might be about?"

Samuel-Colt, strangely without fiddling. "I am sorry, Lieutenant-Savannah-Bonnet. I may not say."

"You *may* not?"

"That is correct."

Peaches, trying not to show her frustration. "But . . . why?"

"Because we were created for technology transfer and development. Others are designated for diplomacy and personal information-passage."

Peaches. "I have men and women out there getting hurt, Samuel-Colt. If you know something, it could help us."

"We regret the injuries of your people but we must not speak. Forgive us, but it is not done." *A pause.* "You should not stay any longer."

Peaches, trying to keep calm. "I'm sorry, I didn't mean to offend—"

"It is not a matter of offense. I must molt my arm and hand, and in our experience humans find this process wearisome and unsettling to witness."

"Molt your . . . okay." *Determinedly polite.* "Thank you for your time, Samuel-Colt."

"We regret we could not be more helpful, Lieutenant-Savannah-Bonnet." *A series of crackles sounds in the dark. The two leave quickly.*

Outside, Peaches frowns.

Kenyan, absently, still working. "Told you."

Peaches. "You could have mentioned the part that he was . . . indisposed."

Kenyan. "I said he was busy."

"There's 'busy' and then there's 'I'm about to shed my skin'!"

Kenyan. "It's not my fault you didn't ask. You can't make assumptions about these aliens. They're not like us. In the end, that's why we're going to lose."

Peaches, startled. "What?"

"We're going to lose. We can't think like them. 'If you know the enemy and know yourself, you need not fear the result of a hundred battles. If you know yourself but not the enemy, for every victory gained you will also suffer a defeat. If you know neither the enemy nor yourself, you will succumb in every battle.' "

Peaches. "We'll see about that."

Outside the Design Lab, walking back.

"What do you think, Gunny?"

"I think it's funny to hear Sun Tzu out of an engineer, ma'am."

"You know what I think? I think having the guy who makes guns saying he can't talk policy or state secrets isn't all that alien." *Sighs.* "We're running out of options. And information. I don't want to have to fight it out in the dark, but I'm not seeing much choice."

"They've got sixty percent of the grid laid, ma'am. That's something."

"Let's hope the last forty doesn't cost us as much as that sixty."

19. The First Mistake

Armory. Claws is already suited up in preparation for relieving Hairball and Scythe. Spots is working into hers.

Claws. "*****ing luck's gonna run out, I know it. Half of the Varmints are down, didya hear?"

Spots. "I heard."

Claws. "You'd think the damned things get high on blow-torches and metal shavin's, Jesus!"

"Claws—"

"****, Spots, sorry—"

"Not that." *She leans forward, touches his shoulder.* "Turn around again." *Pause.* "You're at half power."

"****!"

"It's the right power pack, it's empty." *Helping him strip it off.* "Didn't you see the indicator when you took it off the rack?"

"I looked . . ." *He glances at the rack where the swappable power modules are stored and pales. The last empty socket is yellow, not green.* "****! I almost went out half-empty. With the ****ing crabs eatin' us ****ing alive."

Spots. "Don't tear yourself up over it. We're all tired."

Claws, angry. "We can't afford to be tired. The game's awake or dead, there's no ****ing in-between."

She grasps his arm, meeting his eyes. "Well, then, good thing we do buddy-checks, isn't it."

"Yeah." *He breathes in.* "Yeah. Thanks."

"Let's get going."

———

Map Room. Peaches is pacing beside a table with a map of the Warren, marked up in red pencil. The gunny watches.

Peaches. "There's a pattern here, I know there is. And it's *changed*. But we're not going to get any more information out of our friendly."

Gunny. "Probably not, no, ma'am."

Peaches. "So we're going to have to get it directly from the source."

"Ma'am?"

Peaches points at the map with her red wax pencil. "There. From the new shells. I'm going out there."

Gunny, not quite alarmed but approaching it. "Ma'am, I'm not sure that's wise. You already know what the Warren's like, you went through it when you landed."

"That was before the crabs started getting so aggressive. Gunny, I have to look at them myself. I have to . . ." *Struggles.* "Just talking about it doesn't help. I want to face these new crabs, look them in the eye. Watch how they work. Second-hand reporting isn't doing it."

Gunny. "Lieutenant, you're the only officer on station. If you're incapacitated . . ."

Peaches. "Then they'll just drop-ship you another second lieutenant, hopefully a smarter one than me. Who's on patrol?"

Gunny, resigned. "We've got three teams out right now, ma'am."

"Pick one and tell them they've got company."

Team Kitty Common Room. The two Fangs, Spots and Claws are still out. Whiskers enters.

Whiskers. "Hairball! You look like ****."

Hairball, standing. "Yeah, well, some of us are ****ing working. Glad you finally decided to join the rest of us slobs."

Whiskers, clasping his hand. "Got tired of Spots rescuing my ****ing candy bars from you. Boss out with the team?"

Hairball. "Nah, he got called away. It's the Fangs and Claws and his newb out there."

Whiskers. "****. Wonder what's up."

Hairball. "Guess we'll find out. Game before rack-time?"

Whiskers, pulling out a chair. "You gonna wipe the mat with me?"

"Yep."

"****. Sure, deal."

Some time later, Scythe reappears, looking dour.

"What's up, boss?"

Scythe. "Whiskers! Glad you're out."

"Glad to be out, even if Hairball's ****ing cleaning my clock. Again."

Hairball, grinning. "I get all the ****ing luck, I know it."

Scythe. "Maybe I should send him to these meetings instead of me."

Hairball. "Bad news?"

Scythe. "Bonny Peaches is going out, and we're ****ing babysitting."

"Aww, ****, I'm going to miss it?"

Scythe. "Not funny, Hairball."

Hairball. "Sure it is. Fang-Bigger-Balls-Than-You-1, Fang-always-****ing-around-2, Mother-Hen-Claws and Pollyanna? Didn't they make that movie?"

Whiskers, snorting. "****ing Mr. Smith goes to Washington. The all-crab edition."

20. Confrontation

Warren. Claws and Spots are manning a machine-gun behind a stack of sandbags while the two Fangs stand guard beside the naval construction crew putting down the grid.

Fang2. "So, where do you want your scar?"

Claws. "What the *** are you talkin' about?"

Fang2. "Your scar. You know, the one we're all going to have before this **** is over. I want mine on my chest. So the girls I'm about to **** can get all hot about it.'"

Fang. "No girl is going to want to **** you."

Fang2. "Of course not. That's what the scar's for."

Claws. "Great. Your very own ****ing peacock tail."

Fang. "Un****ing believable."

Scythe, over com. "Scythe to Kitty, come in."

Claws. "Kitty here, go."

Scythe. "The LT's incoming."

Claws. "Say again?"

Scythe. "You heard me. She wants to look the new crabs in the eye."

Claws. "****!"

"Keep her alive, the gunny likes her. Scythe out."

Fang. "Great. Just ****ing great."

Fang2. "That must be her up there."

Peaches jogs in. Her suit is identical to the team's, though with fewer hash marks under her power packs. She exchanges terse greetings with the naval personnel and Team Kitty before crouching behind the sandbags. The silence grows tense.

Fang2. "I'm getting vibration, south."

Fang. "Finally."

Claws. "Through the grid?"

Spots the Space Marine: Defense of the Fiddler

Fang2. "Think so."

The crabs erupt several hundred feet in front of the sandbags.

Spots. "Contact north!"

Another group breaks through the corridor walls behind them.

Fang2. "**** here we go!"

They are cutting the enemy down when a third group crashes through the wall in the center of the team. Fang2's shot flies over Claws's head.

Claws. "**** you! Clear your area!"

Spots: "Contact north again! We're pinned!"

Claws. "****! Use the fox-run." *Grabbing Peaches as she starts toward the wrong hole.* "Other fox-run!"

They scramble through the tunnel as the three groups of crabs rip through the sandbags.

Claws. "Team B, meet us at Spoke 7!"

Fang. "Copy that!"

55

Claws, Spots and Peaches emerge from the fox-run. They run for the intersection when they are pinned by two new groups that erupt so quickly it's obvious they were waiting. One group includes the new King shell, with a guard composed entirely of the other two new shells.

There is a great pause.

Spots. "God Almighty."

And then they're rushed.

Claws. "Shields!" *Spots dives to a halt and puts up her arm. He crouches on the other side; between them they form a bubble around Peaches.* "Ma'am, shoot, ma'am!"

Peaches starts taking her shots as the crabs return fire.

Claws. "BACK-UP NOW."

Fangs in unison: "On our way."

The new shells take several shots to put down, so Peaches cuts the weaker force down first, leaving the new shells and the King between them and the intersection.

Spots. "Power at 20%."

Peaches. "Is it—it's staring at us."

The King is standing behind its legion, looking directly at her.

Peaches. ". . ."

Claws. "Fifteen percent—ma'am, stay back..!"

Claws's shield fails. One of the needles punches Peaches's shoulder. Claws pulls her down as the Fangs appear around the corner.

Fang, taking the shot. "STAY DOWN."

Spots's shield flickers and dies. The King goes down. Instead of pressing the attack, the crabs grab the King and retreat.

Fang. "What the ****? They've never done that before!"

Spots. "Lieutenant!"

Peaches, trying not to hold her arm. "I'm fine, Private. The Seabees okay?"

Fang. "Yes, ma'am."

Fang2. "A little shook up though."

Peaches, admirably upright. "Back to station, then." *She glances at Claws.* "One thing, though, Corporal."

Claws. "Ma'am?"

"Why the fox-run switch?"

Claws. "Ma'am, we're supposed to lead them away from the collider when we have the opportunity."

Peaches. "Ah, of course. Thank you."

Claws. "Ma'am, no problem. You should re-consider Sickbay, ma'am, you're listin'."

Peaches. "If I go back one of you will have to escort me. I don't want to leave the team undermanned. I can wait."

Claws. "Yes, ma'am. Back to station."

Spots, private channel to Claws. "Should you have been manhandling an officer like that?"

Spots the Space Marine: Defense of the Fiddler

Claws, annoyed, on private channel. "We're alive, ain't we?"

21. Mobilizing

Sickbay. Peaches is sitting on a bed while a corpsman checks her shoulder.

Peaches, hissing. "Dammit."

Corpsman. "Looks like you're going to be in a sling for a while, Lieutenant. Somehow you managed to break your collarbone."

Peaches. "Through my *armor*? The dent wasn't that big!"

Corpsman. "Don't ask me, ma'am, I don't know a thing about armor. Just telling you what I see, and what I see is that you need a sling and some painkillers."

Peaches. "Can't this be quick-fixed?"

Corpsman. "Sorry, ma'am. Medicine didn't get the upgrades other technologies did in the tech transfer . . . let's just say the Fiddlers aren't much like us when it comes to health care. Sit tight, I'll be right back with your prescription."

Peaches sighs. While he's gone, she is handed an electronic dispatch on a reader. She scans, curses. When the corpsman finishes fitting her with a sling, she thanks him and hurries back to the map room.

"Gunny!"

Gunny, concerned. "Ma'am, you're in a sling."

Peaches, impatient. "It's nothing. I need suitcam footage from the team that just got in ASAP. We have an opportunity."

Gunny. "An opportunity, ma'am?"

"Our sister depot just got nuked, Gunny. And their company's shot up, but right now they've got nothing to guard."

Gunny, lifting his brows. "You think you can get them re-assigned here?"

"Hell, I don't know, but I'm going to try! So get me that data!"

———

Fiddler's Restroom. Samuel-Colt is still reclining, listening to Mussorgsky's "Pictures at an Exhibition." The music ends. For a long moment, nothing.

Then Samuel-Colt rises and looks at his new arm, which is far more articulated and delicate than the one he just shed. He rotates it. In the dark, it is hard to see: the rest of his body fluo-

resces, thanks to his paint, but the new arm is naked.

He is still for some time, holding the new arm. Then he goes to a narrow cabinet alongside the sound system. From it he removes a jar and a slender reed. He studies these items, hesitates.
. . .

. . . then with great determination strides out of the Restroom, surprising Kenyan, his human assistant.

Kenyan. "Sam? You're done, finally—wait, where are you going?"

Samuel-Colt. "I am not done yet." *The door closes behind him.*

Kenyan. "Wa—dammit. Fine, whatever. ****ing aliens!"

59

22. LOOPHOLES

Barracks. Spots and Claws are preparing for bed.

Claws, yanking the sheets back. "What a cluster****. God al-****'in'-mighty."

Spots. "Everyone got back, Claws. It worked out. Let's just get some sleep, all right?"

"All ri—" *The door chimes.* "Hell, Spots, you expectin' a beau or somethin'?"

Spots looks at him funny, then answers the door . . . and steps back from the towering figure of Samuel-Colt.

"Samuel-Colt!"

The alien bows, makes a hesitant, interrogative sound with its vestigial limbs. "Mother-soldier. May I enter?"

"Of course!"

The alien is an overwhelming presence in such a small space. Both humans press against their bunks to give him enough room.

"Would it be more comfortable for you if we were to sit?"

Spots, glancing at wide-eyed Claws. "Uh . . . yes, please."

He folds himself down. Descending arpeggio. "Our apologies for disturbing you. We were hoping you might do us a service."

Spots. "Us? Help you?"

"I have recently made myself a new arm and hand to aid me in further refining the new shield technology. The arm is without decoration . . . " *Samuel-Colt trails off, then lifts the little jar and reed brush. Slow, rising note, somehow hopeful.*

"You want us to paint the designs on you?"

"Not you, Mother-soldier." *His head slowly turns to Claws. Single note drone.* "As a Mother's escort, this one is closest to us in rank and function. It is customary for peers who share a function to do this service for one another."

"Me?" *Claws starts.* "I'm your peer?"

Samuel-Colt inclines his head in assent. When Claws doesn't immediately respond, Spots nudges him.

"Um . . . of course, right." *He accepts the paint and brush with only the smallest tremor of hands.* "What . . . what do I do? Is there some specific design I need to copy?"

"Not for the arms. Lineage and honors are painted on the thorax; the extremities are reserved for personal statements. Since they are painted by others, they sometimes express the relationship between peers."

Claws squints. "So I'd put on you whatever I felt was . . . representative of our relationship."

Quick flourish. "Just so, Mother's escort."

Muttering. "Such as it is." *Louder.* "All right then. Hold out your arm."

The alien stretches out the arm and spreads the delicate hand on Claws's knee. Claws stares at it, then squares his shoulders and opens the jar. He studies the brush, frowns. "Hang tight, there, I have no idea how this thing writes." *He feels around his nightstand until he finds a towel and tries a few strokes on it.* "How the hell'd you get a reed to act like this?"

Samuel-Colt, amused trill. "It is naturally so. We toughen the barrel."

Claws, biting his lip, staring at the arm. "Damn. I have no idea where to start."

Spots. "Maybe if you could tell us more about . . . ah . . . being Claws's peer?"

"What do you wish to know?"

Claws. "Well . . . are all males peers?"

"No, Mother's escort. You and we both serve a mother. You are an escort; we perform a liaison function to the humans."

Spots. "What do you mean "we"?"

"We, myself and my lineage." *Samuel-Colt studies them, strangely intent.* "I have the memories of all the designers who have served the humans in generations past. When I speak of matters that concern their memories, I correctly include them."

Claws. "All the memories of . . . how do you do that?"

Samuel-Colt, without music. "It is not a matter we speak of."

Claws. "To humans?"

Samuel-Colt hesitates—no, waits.

Claws, catching the distinction. "What about to mothers?"

Spots, uneasy. "Claws. . . ."

"If the mother were to ask, we would answer." *No trill again.*

Claws glances at Spots, who shakes her head. "That feels like . . . like exploiting a loophole. It doesn't feel fair."

"You're a cookie-bakin' mom, Spots. Some things cross species. Right, Peer?"

"It is within your right, Mother-soldier." *There is a peculiar quality to Samuel-Colt's music: hope and resignation and tension.*

Spots glances at Claws. Then sighs too. "All right. Tell me how you pass memories, Samuel-Colt."

"We consume the bodies of our progenitors. While they are still alive."

Claws, standing abruptly. "****! Our people!"

23. BACKCHANNEL

Samuel-Colt lifts his upper arms, hands spread. His lower limbs trill a tense, high note.

Claws. "They're eating them alive . . . to get their memories??"

Samuel-Colt, urgent falling trill. "I cannot answer you."

Claws, leaning toward him. "DAMN YOU! TELL ME!"

Spots, putting herself between them. "Claws! Stop! He can't talk to you!"

"So ask him dammit!!"

Spots, swallowing. "Samuel-Colt? Is it true? Do the crabs eat our dead to steal their memories?"

Samuel-Colt, with a shivery falling arpeggio. "You are too different from us, Mother-soldier. They try, but their attempts have not succeeded. Thus far."

Spots. "Thus . . . far."

Samuel-Colt. "Lieutenant-Savannah-Bonnet asked about an evolution in the tactics of our enemies. Something has changed."

Spots. "You mean they've figured out how to do it?"

Samuel-Colt, shaking his head in a learned human mannerism. Quick arpeggio, up, down. "No. If they had, you would not be here alive. The passage of memories is very complete; they would know everything you know, including security codes and procedures, your command chain, weaknesses of the base . . . even where everyone sleeps."

Claws, backing down, thinking. "Can they have picked up partial memories?"

Samuel-Colt, slow, long sawing. "It is remotely possible. Remotely."

Claws, glancing at the paint, then at Spots. "So . . . this was an elaborate pretense so you could tell us somethin' you couldn't tell the LT . . . because she ain't had a baby."

Samuel-Colt. "I would be honored if you fulfilled our request."

Claws, eyeing him. "That's not exactly denying it."

Spots. "Enough, Claws. We all get the picture. So now what?"

Claws. "So now, we go have a chat with Bonny Peaches."

Spots, firm. "And the arm, Claws."

Claws. "I gotta think about the arm." *At Samuel-Colts falling trill,* "Look, it's complicated."

Spots. "He just went out on a limb for us, Claws.

Claws. "Yeah, well, I haven't said I won't do it."

Samuel-Colt rises. He leans over and places the ink and brush back in Claws's palm, then closes the human's fingers over it. "Keep them until you decide." *And then he exits.*

Spots. "Claws? You want to tell me what's wrong?"

Claws stares at the jar and puts it and the brush down. "Come on, we've got a report to make."

24. Skip-leveling

"Claws? Claws, where are you going? Scythe is that way."

"Yes, and if we wake up Scythe, he'll just have to turn around and wake up a bunch of people who will eventually wake up the Gunny . . . who'll wake up the LT . . . who'll drag us right back in front of her. Let's just say we're skippin' to the chase."

"But that's not the way things are done—" *Spots grabs Claws's arm, stopping him.* "Travis! What is the matter with you? This isn't like you at all."

"They're ****in' eatin' our people. While they're *alive. On purpose.*"

"Yes . . . and there's nothing we can do about it right this minute, so can't it go up the normal chain, the way it's supposed to?"

He eyes her. "This from the woman who kept callin' Scythe 'sergeant'?"

"Call it exaggerated respect for authority."

Claws looks up the corridor, eyes distant. Then looks at Spots again. "You comin' or not?"

Spots sighs. "Yes."

———————

Office, Depot's Senior Marine Officer. Has an unused air, metal desk and mostly empty shelving; Peaches obviously doesn't spend much time here. She's here now, working on the computer.

Peaches, leaning over her sling and cursing. ". . . one hand, ****, how does anyone use a computer with *one* hand?"

Door chime. Peaches looks up. Glances at computer clock. Frowns. "Come in."

Claws steps through first, followed by Spots. They come to attention and wait to be recognized by Peaches, who looks puzzled. "At ease. Corporal, Private, why aren't you asleep?"

"Ma'am, we had information we thought you needed. Immediately."

Peaches. "There's a procedure for this sort of thing, Corporal."

"Yes, ma'am."

Peaches glances at Spots, back at Claws. "All right. Tell me what's so damned important that you decided to come straight here."

"Ma'am, the crabs eat the dead to absorb their memories."

Peaches. "Excuse me?"

Spots, speaking for the first time. "Samuel-Colt told us. He said it doesn't work cross-species, as far as he knows."

Peaches, tense. "As far as he knows."

Claws. "You saw, ma'am . . . they dragged off their King. Maybe they planned to absorb his observations. Maybe that's why they're changing their tactics."

Peaches, frowning. "Or why he has an extra brain. Maybe he's storing something there for them to access. Damn, using their own kind as recon drones . . . that's low." *She rubs her mouth then looks up.* "You said 'as far as he knows'. Does he think they're *trying* to do the same with us?"

Spots glances at Claws, then says, "He said so, ma'am."

Peaches's eyes narrow. "And he talked to you because . . ."

Claws. "Because she's a mom, ma'am."

Spots, embarrassed. "He wanted you to know, though."

"But he had to go through you to do it . . ." *Peaches frowns.* "It's not fathers, is it? Just mothers?"

Claws. "As far as we know, ma'am."

"Well, then, since I think you might be the only mother on station . . . you get to be my liaison to the alien, Private Guitart."

Spots, wide-eyed. "Of course, ma'am." *Adds,* "I can't talk to him without Claws."

"You can't . . . ah, right. He wouldn't talk to you without an escort." *She glances at Claws.* "All right. Then you get to go with her whenever I need information. Think of it as your reward for showing so much 'initiative' in coming to me directly."

Claws. "Glad to be of service, ma'am."

"No doubt. Next time, do it the right way, Corporal. You don't want me to write a letter for your personnel file."

"Ma'am, no ma'am. I'll remember."

Peaches, thinking. "Their memories. All of them?"

Claws. "So completely it's like they live on in the recipient's head."

Peaches. "****." She looks up. "Dismissed. Go get some God-damned sleep."

Spots. "Yes, ma'am." *Outside in the corridor, she eyes Claws.*

Claws. "Bonny Peaches got the info and we didn't have to stay up half the night gettin' passed up the chain explainin' and explainin' how we got it to five different people. Everyone's gonna get more sleep. That's a net good, right?"

Spots, studying him. "Let's not do that again."

"We won't have to. You're the Liaison to the Alien, remember?"

Spots sighs.

67

25. Taking Care of Business

Captain—

~~I am very sorry to hear about the destruction of Naval Depot A~~ The destruction of Naval Depot A leaves Depot B as the ~~single point of failure~~ sole supplier of the Navy's heavy weapons in this sector. As such, I am requesting the re-assignment of ~~the Marine company from Depot A~~ Depot A's Marine company here. The tactical situation is ~~desperate~~ growing more complex: according to local sources, the crabs are able to absorb the memories of their dead, and they appear to be using this ability to grow their data on our deployments.

Attached find footage of a skirmish in which the crabs demonstrate ~~more intelligence~~ new tactics. ~~We believe they're learning.~~ They are growing more effective.

Again, I urgently request reinforcement.

———————

Following day. Scythe is coming off duty as Spots and Claws are going on.

Claws. "Hey, can I talk to you?"

Scythe. "Sure."

Outside, leaning against the wall.

Claws. "I sorta got Spots more work."

Scythe, folding arms. "This should be good."

"The Fiddler came in last night to have a talk with us, told us some stuff I thought Bonny Peaches should know . . . so I hauled Guitart up to her office. Peaches decided to appoint her as our liaison to the alien."

Scythe, studying him. "What was this stuff?"

"The crabs. They eat each other to absorb one another's memories. All of them. And their victims are alive when they do it."

Scythe's hands tighten on his arms. Then he turns away. "****! Are they doing that to us?"

Claws. "They can't get anything out of us . . . but . . . yeah, the Fiddler thinks so."

Scythe. "****!"

Spots the Space Marine: Defense of the Fiddler

"Yeah."

Scythe. "****! They told us not to leave anyone behind, but not because they'd get ****ing eaten *alive*."

"I don't think they knew, boss."

Scythe. "I'm surprised Peaches didn't throw a ****ing fit!"

"Yeah, well, I didn't emphasize that part. She's gotta worry about the big picture, eh? The rest of us . . . *we* take care of the important stuff. Don't we."

Scythe turns to look at him, eyes hard. "**** yes."

Claws nods. "Thought you'd wanna know. And by the way, you're welcome."

"What for?"

"For not wakin' you up last night to parade us all the way to officer country."

"**** you, Walker."

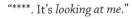

Office. Peaches is sitting in front of her computer still. Hitting Play, backing up and hitting Play. Over and over again.

"****. It's *looking at me*."

26. Picking the Wrong Fight

Claws walks back into the Armory after his discussion in the corridor with Scythe, finishes suiting up and goes out with Spots to join the two Fangs.

The Warren. The engineers continue laying grid. Claws goes to talk to the engineering team lead.

Fang. "Will you stop hanging so ****ing close to me?"

Spots. "I thought it would be a good idea, since the last couple of times we were attacked we got separated."

Fang. "And that worked out fine. I already got one ****ing growth, I don't need another."

Fang2. "Harsh, man. Harsh. I'd like to at least think I'd merit being called a *cancerous* growth. Maybe even a tumor."

Spots. "I really think it would be better not to get too far apart. They're changing tactics, they might not let one pair of us go next time."

Fang. "And I really think you should ****ing get off my back. I don't take orders from a ****ing reservist."

Fang2. "Well, technically she's got seniority." *Sly.* "Actually, she might have had seniority before we were even born."

Fang. "****ing office work doesn't count. What did you do for fifty years, Spots? Shine your boots and type up memos on a ****ing manual typewriter?"

Fang2. "Ouch."

Unruffled, Spots doesn't move.

Fang. "I said—"

Spots. "I heard what you said. I'm not moving."

Fang. "The hell you're not!"

Claws, returning from talk with engineer. "What the **** is goin' on?"

Fang2. "Pissing match."

Fang. "She won't get off my back."

Claws. "What the hell is she talkin' about, Spots?"

Spots the Space Marine: Defense of the Fiddler

Spots. "I'm just worried about getting separated if we're attacked again."

Fang2. "I'm thinking you should be more worried about her getting too un-separated. If you know what I mean." *He mimes a punch.*

Claws. "Oh for ****'s sake. Get off it, Fang. She wants to watch your back, that's what we're ****in' supposed to do. Remember?"

Fang2. "Actually, that might be kinda hot. Wrestling in armor . . ."

Claws. "You're not ****in' HELPIN', Chao."

Fang2. "I'd say I was sorry, but damn, I'm not."

Claws. "We'll stick the **** together."

Fang. "I knew you'd come down on her side."

Claws. "Of course you did, because she's ****in' RIGHT. When she's ****in' wrong, I'll tell her that too. Got a ****in' problem with that?"

Fang. "Yeah. Who died and made you Scythe?"

Claws steps toward her. Spots grabs his arm. He stops moving. Finally, he says, "You got an issue, Fang, you take it out on someone else. Not the team shielding your ****in' rifle while you shoot the bad guys."

Fang. "You calling me a glory hound?"

Absolute silence.

Fang2. "Uh, guys . . . the engineers are staring. Can we keep it in the family? Like, later?"

Fang. "This isn't over."

Claws. "The hell it's not."

Fang2, relieved. "Crabs!"

They spend a tense patrol handling minor crab incursions. Shift change approaches.

Claws. "Claws to Relief, you up?"

[Team Kitty] [Hairball] : Yeah, we're up.

Fang2. "****, what's wrong, you sound like your mom died."

[Team Kitty] [Hairball] : One of Dusty's dogs just bit it.

Claws. "****, say again?"

[Team Kitty] [Hairball] : One of the guys in the coma. They just lost him.

Fang, whispering. "****."

27. SOLIDARITY

Front Hall. There is a casket here draped in a flag. All the Marines on base except those currently on patrol are present in their dress uniforms. Peaches is standing to the side of the chaplain.

The ceremony is short—it is a memorial service, not a funeral. After Taps, the casket is wheeled to cold-storage until the next transport can take it home. The Marines process out after it, subdued, and from there to the mess hall where the food has been augmented by a punch bowl provided by the company still.

Almost everyone takes one drink. No one takes a second. They are mourning but all too aware of having to be alert for their own patrols.

———————

Office. Peaches is sitting at the desk, leaning forward, brow against her good hand. A cup is set by her elbow. She looks up.

Gunny. "You didn't have any at the wake."

Peaches. "I thought it would look bad."

Gunny. "Probably. Drink it."

She looks at it from under the shadow of her hand, glum. Then does it in one swallow. She pushes the cup away from her; Gunny picks it up.

Then: "Someone died. On my watch."

"He won't be the last."

Peaches looks up, startled. He squeezes her shoulder and leaves. Outside in the corridor, his face shows a trace of regret as he walks away.

———————

Gym. Dusty is slamming her fist into a target dummy while fellow squad leaders Scythe, Roach and platoon leader Big Lion watch.

"****ing crabs! ****ing doctors! **** **** ****! I can't even get properly ****ing wasted because we don't have enough ****ing people to keep the ****ing crabs from ****ing the damned donut when our backs are turned! **** the donut anyway!"

Roach. "Want me to take your shift?"

Dusty, rubbing her wrist. "****. No, Roach. No, you're tired too. **** it." *She sits on a bench.*

"****. Dying on your back in a bed. Saved from the crabs just to ****ing die anyway."

Scythe, tense. "It's a good death."

Roach. "Aw, ****, Scythe. How the hell is that a good death?"

Scythe, fierce and quiet. "The crabs eat us alive if they catch us. So, yeah. Dying in bed surrounded by your brothers is a ****ing good death."

All three of the others stare at him.

Dusty. "W-what?"

Scythe. "You know that retiree they gave me? Seems like the bug on base likes to talk to her. Told her the crabs ****ing eat people alive, hoping to suck their memories out of their brains. Doesn't work, but they keep trying."

Big Lion, low. "**** all."

Roach. "Damn, Scythe. We get new folks and they're regular joes. You get saddled with G.I. Jane and the alien whisperer. Your god have it out for you?"

Scythe. "**** you, Roach."

Dusty. "So . . . we can put questions to the bug."

Scythe. "You can bring questions to me and I'll have her relay, yeah. If you've got a *useful* question. **** if I know what a useful question is right now. 'What flavors are you allergic to?' "

Roach. "****. Eating us alive!" *He eyes Big Lion.* "You didn't know?"

Big Lion. "**** no. They just told me 'never leave anyone behind.' "

Scythe, hard. "Peaches didn't even know. Guess they thought it would make us *angry*."

Silence. Then Dusty gets up. "I got patrol." *Eyes Scythe.* "I'll think of something."

Roach. "I'll walk you home."

Dusty. "Bastard. I can ****ing walk myself home, I'm not some paper doll."

Roach, grinning. "I know. That's why I like you." *More serious.* "Come on."

The two of them leave.

Big Lion. "You running interference for your alien whisperer?"

Scythe. "Of course I am. Dusty's ****ing pissed. I don't need her waking up my people and giving them **** before she's got her head together."

Big Lion, sounding tense. "Good."

Scythe glances up at her.

"I don't think her other two are going to make it either."

Scythe. "****."

28. Half the Story

Gym, late night after the wake. Scythe is moving through iaido forms with sword. Spots enters and watches in silence until he's done.

Scythe, without facing her. "Up late again."

"I don't sleep well after funerals."

Scythe, turning now. "You been to a lot of them?"

Spots, faint smile. "My husband's a miner. I live half the year on an asteroid. It's dangerous work."

Scythe. "Ah." *He slides his sword back into its sheath, formal.* "You're not here because of that, though."

Spots. "Not entirely. I was looking for you."

". . . because?"

"What's going on with Claws?"

Scythe glances at her. "I don't like to talk about other people's business."

Spots. ". . . but?"

"But you work with him. You need to know."

"Know what?"

Scythe sits on a bench, sword on lap. "You'll have noticed we're understrength."

"Yes."

He nods. "And you know Peaches is new?"

Spots. "Yes. I came in on her transport."

"She was replacing the LT who died flinging us at the crabs. He was convinced we had to take the offensive."

Spots, cocking her head. "Isn't that sound tactics?"

"Maybe against humans. Against crabs? You need to know the location of the lab and the nest. Otherwise you might as well never have gone."

Spots the Space Marine: Defense of the Fiddler

Spots. "And you didn't know."

"No. And we died for it. I lost one man, Fang2's partner Scratch. But Claws was my assistant squad leader and he lost his entire team. Rosey, Snarl and Hack . . . all of them gone. We almost lost him too when he tried to go back for them."

Spots, paling. "God."

"He's still assistant squad leader, but you're it, Guitart. Fang rotated in for Scratch but we never got enough to fill out his half of the squad."

Spots, thinking. "He still acts like the assistant squad leader sometimes."

Scythe nods. "He's good at it. I don't want to lose him because I pushed him too fast after it went bad on his watch. He needs to come around on his own." *As Spots turns away, pacing,* "You were a piece of luck. You're nothing like the men he lost. And you're easy to manage."

"So I don't remind him of them."

Scythe, smiling a little. "You don't remind anyone of anything, Guitart."

Spots, making a face. "Gee, thanks."

"You already know that or you wouldn't be having problems. You are having problems, aren't you?"

Spots. "Nothing serious."

"This business with the Fiddler . . . you're not careful, it'll make things worse for you."

Spots. "I know what they say about people who like the aliens too much, Scythe."

"It goes a little beyond name-calling in the Marines."

Spots, eyeing him. "Are you saying someone's going to beat the tar out of me because I'm talking to the Violinist, Scythe?"

Scythe. "No, just warning you. Tension's running high."

"I noticed. I'll handle it."

He nods, getting up. "Gym's all yours."

"Thanks. Hey, Scythe?"

He pauses.

"Thanks for not saying 'don't tell him I told you.' "

Scythe smiles. "You're not the type."

Spots the Space Marine: Defense of the Fiddler

29. GIRLS

The Warren. Spots and Claws are advancing to replace Whiskers and Hairball on the patrol, when—

"AAAaaaahhHHHH!"

Spots. "Is that . . ."

Claws. "Fang2!"

Spots and Claws sprint down the corridor and turn the corner to find Fang calmly firing into a mob of crabs. One of them has Fang2 in its largest pincers. Cursing, Claws skids to a stop on the new grid. His is the shot that inspires Fang2's opponent to drop him. Claws darts forth and drags him back.

Claws. "****!"

Fang2. "Don't . . . feel so good."

Claws pulls him up. "I gotta get him back, there's a ****ing hole in his side."

Spots. "Go, we've got it handled."

The crabs are mostly scattered or dead. After a glance around, Claws nods and starts back. Once he's down the corridor . . .

Fang, cold. "So, you going to say it?"

Spots. "Say what?"

Fang. "Something about the cold-hearted ***** that wasn't trying hard enough to save a buddy?"

Spots. "Actually, I want to know what you were shooting at."

Fang turns to stare at her.

Spots, checking her ammunition levels. "You were shooting at something, weren't you?"

Fang, slowly. "Yessss."

"So what was it?"

Fang. "I saw a new shell behind them."

Spots, looking up. "Did you get it?"

Fang shakes her head. "I think it ran."

Spots nods. "So, we going hunting?"

Fang hesitates. "Think you can take it, old woman?"

Spots rolls her eyes. "Right, you've got to get the breast-beating out of the way. 'Yes, yes, I can take it, let's go.' Is that good? Are we done?"

Fang pauses, then laughs a little unwillingly.

Spots. "Which way did it go?"

Fang. "That way."

Spots. "You lead. I'll cover you."

Fang, pausing. "You really believe me?"

Spots, smiling a little. "I believe you're a pain in the rear, Fang. But that you'd lie about something like this, no. So let's go, they're opening the lead."

Fang. "All right."

30. Ambush

Fang and Claws are running, armored boots clanking against the new grid.

[**Base**] **Spots** : Control, this is Team Kitty.

[**Base**] **Control** : Team Kitty, this is Control. Go ahead.

[**Base**] **Spots** : We're chasing a possible new shell. Permission to leave patrol area if necessary?

[**Base**] **Control** : Which cam, Kitty?

[**Base**] **Spots** : Fang's, just now.

[**Base**] **Control** : Copy that, will check.

Fang. "****. I don't see them. They run fast."

Spots. "They must be off the grid, then."

Fang. "Yeah, they went inward."

Spots. "Uhn. Not toward the donut!"

Fang. "This way."

[**Base**] **Control** : Team Kitty, this is Control.

[**Base**] **Spots** : This is Kitty.

[**Base**] **Control** : Your footage is ambiguous. Stay in your patrol zone.

Fang. "Dammit! Come on, we're still in the area—"

They run, turn a corner. The corridor is empty.

Fang. "****, ****, ****! I saw it, I know I did!"

Spots, frowning. "Come on, we have to turn back."

Still cursing, Fang leads the way back around the corner . . .

. . . into a wall of crabs, so close they almost step into them.

Spots throws her arm up over her head, shield on. "Holy Mother!"

"****!"

"Shoot them, Fang! God!"

"They're too close—"

Spots. "Mmph, wish me luck!"

Fang. "What are you—****!"

Spots turns her shield to maximum breadth and power, walling in the corridor. She's using this to slowly push the crabs back. They are plastered against the shield, banging on it.

[**Team Kitty**] **Spots** : Claws, now would be a good time . . . !

[**Team Kitty**] **Claws** : ****, Spots, I'm ****in' half the Warren away!

Fang, shooting now. "Keep going, keep ****ing going!"

Spots. "My power's half out—"

Fang. "—the shield?"

Spots. "—the *suit*. There's a fox-run in two meters, get ready to take it."

Fang, grim, shooting still. "I'm there. Keep pushing, Mama."

"Almost . . . there. . . . NOW!"

Fang bolts into the fox-run. Spots gives the crabs a good shove and then scrambles after her. Instantly the crabs are digging at the wall.

Fang. "Out! Out! Come on!" *She hauls Spots out by the arm.* "Run! There's a trap up-corridor, we can take them there!"

[**Team Kitty**] **Claws** : I'm on my way! ****in' don't DIE!

31. Evolving Tactics

Spots. "Breakthrough!"

Fang. "****, run faster!"

[Team Kitty] Claws : ****, ****, ****, I'm almost there!

Fang. "****ing tell me something useful, Claws!"

[Team Kitty] Claws : I'll set the trap, give me three minutes!

Fang, running. "**** you, we don't have three minutes!"

Spots. "I can hold them for one."

Fang. "One! Then what!"

Spots. "Then you hold them and I shoot. Ready? NOW." *She flings herself around and makes the shield wall again . . . when the crabs hit it, the impact shoves her back half a meter. She hisses.* "SHOOT, FANG!"

Fang starts picking them off. Her movements are quick, competent and steady . . . but she's cursing continuously.

Suddenly, from the com:

[Team Kitty] Claws : ****!!!!

Spots. "Claws . . . ?"

[Team Kitty] Claws : The ****in' grid is OVER THE TRAP!

Fang. "You have got to be kidding me!"

Spots. "I'm almost to quarter power, I've got to stop or I won't have anything to run with."

Fang lunges toward her, activates shield, stares at settings. "****! How do I do this??"

Spots grabs her arm with her free hand, resets the shield and springs back as it opens to fill the corridor. She starts shooting, stops—"Keep your head down, for God's sake! Kneel!"

Fang, dropping. "****! I am not a kneeler!"

Spots ignores her. "Claws? Where are you?"

[*Team Kitty*] Claws : Comin'. . . .

Spots. "Come faster, please."

Fang, muttering, sweating. "Fang-two would have run with that."

Spots. "He's going to be fine. And so are we."

Fang, staring at shield settings. "****, I'm down a third already!"

[*Team Kitty*] Claws : What's the shield strength at?

Fang. "Still 100%, but my suit power's draining fast."

[*Team Kitty*] Claws : Spots, get behind her. DO IT NOW!

Spots dives behind Fang . . . as a grenade bounces off the shield wall.

Detonation—

32. Rapport

Crab parts and ichor everywhere. A piece of a crab claw flexes, then collapses. Silence/stillness.

. . . then the thud of boots as Claws runs over.

Claws. "Spots! Fang!"

Fang, sitting up slowly. The explosion pushed both of them back two meters. "**** . . ."

Claws. "Spots!!" *Bending over her.* "Spots?"

Spots. "—ine, I'm fine."

Claws. "****, you're limp!"

Spots. "I'm fine, the suit is just down."

Claws. "What??"

Spots. "I linked shields with Fang when you tossed that grenade. Figured we'd need it."

Fang. "****, she's right, I'm almost completely down too. What the **** do we put in our grenades?"

Claws. "It worked."

Fang. "Yeah, I guess it did." *Eyes him.* "Thanks."

Claws. "****. Control, this is Team Kitty.

[*Base*] **Control :** Team Kitty, this is Control, go ahead.

Claws. "We got two spent suits and one man in Sickbay. We need relief."

[*Base*] **Control :** Copy that, Kitty. We'll see who we can send.

Claws. "Can the two of you walk?"

Fang. "I've got power for it."

Spots tries to rise and grimaces. "I need a charge."

Claws. "All right, hold still." *After messing with the inter-suit hook-ups:* "Try now. You good?"

Spots flexes her hand. "Yeah."

Claws. "Right, we'll just sit tight until they get here."

Fang. "They who? We're stretched too ****ing thin as it is."

Claws. "Dunno. Their problem."

Fang, staring at the gruesome corridor. "****ing mess."

Claws. "Beautiful, ain't it?"

Fang, grinning. "Most beautiful thing I've ever seen."

Claws. "You're welcome."

Fang snorts, but she's still smiling.

Spots. "Claws . . . ?"

"Yeah?"

Spots. "Tell me . . . that's not what I think it is."

Claws twists around to face the opposite end of the corridor, then leaps to his feet, gun out. "****! ****!"

Fang. "CONTROL THIS IS KITTY GET US THAT RELIEF NOW!"

33. Close Calls

A new wall of crabs is advancing on them from behind. The three start shooting.

Claws. "Get behind us, Spots."

Fang. "****, she can still shoot!"

Claws. "Not for long. And neither can you."

Spots. "You can put up your shield."

Claws. "And end up like the two of you? *Hell-no*."

[Base] Control : Team Kitty, this is Control. Relief inbound from Sector C. Coyote requests direct.

Claws. "SECTOR ****IN' C! You want them to collect our BODIES?" *Switching to command circuit.* "Control-this-is-Team-Kitty-put-them-through."

[Company] Coyote : Kitty, this is Coyote. Location?

Claws. "Patching HUD, no time to talk."

[Company] Coyote : . . . right, I see you, we'll flank them in . . . 7 minutes."

Fang. "****! We don't have 7 minutes!"

Spots. "We have to run."

Claws. "Can you?"

Spots. "We're going to find out."

Claws. "Right. On three—"

One.

Two.

Three—

They flee, the crabs rushing after. Spots's suit runs out of power; it's too heavy to be operated without it. She hits the grid, skidding.

Claws. "SPOTS!" *Turns and lunges for her.*

Fang turns and starts shooting. "****! I can't keep this up!"

Claws. "Fang, help!"

Fang. "I can't shoot them *and* carry her with you!"

Spots. "SHOOT THEM, CLAWS."

Claws. "I won't leave you!"

Spots. "I have a plan, damn it, *shoot them!*"

Claws. "What the **** plan can you possibly have?" *But he joins Fang in shooting the on-rushing crabs.*

Spots. "Always wondered about this emergency eject—"

Claws. "What?? NO!"

Spots, wearing only her skinsuit, flees up the corridor.

Fang. "****, follow her!"

Claws keys his shield, scoops Spots up under his arm. They run.

Claws. "Coyote, now would be ****in' good . . . !"

[**Company**] **Coyote** : Two minutes!

Fang. "Grenade!"

Claws. "We'd have to block them or they'll run past it!"

Fang, sliding to a stop. "**** **** ****!"

Claws. "****!!!!"

The corridor is blocked with new dirt.

Claws. "****! This isn't supposed to be here!"

They turn. Spots points at the crabs and shouts something.

Claws. "You must be ****in' kidding!"

Spots hits his faceplate and points again.

Fang grabs Claws's arm and pulls him after her. "She's got a point, GO!"

Spots the Space Marine: Defense of the Fiddler

Claws. "****!" *And then they run straight at the oncoming crabs . . .*

       . . . into them . . .

    . . . through them.

Fang. "I'm almost out of juice!"

Claws throws the grenade, pushes Fang in front of him. As they flee, the grenade goes off. A few moments later, Coyote's team flashes past and starts shooting the survivors. There aren't that many left.

Fang. "And . . . out!" *Her suit goes dark. Claws stops, sets Spots down. He slumps against the wall, hands to his faceplate.*

When all the crabs are dead, Coyote comes over. "That was some quick thinking there, breaking through and then blowing them. Risky, but quick."

Claws, low. "****."

89

34. SLOW REPAIRS

Sickbay, after action. Spots is standing over Fang2's bed when the corpsman appears behind her.

Spots. "How is he?"

Corpsman. "He'll be fine. You're supposed to be in bed 12, Private."

Spots. "Sorry about that." *She lets him guide her back.*

"You're limping, did you know?"

"I can feel it, yes."

"Hold still." *The corpsman starts running a diagnostic.* "You came out of there lucky. Usually suit failures break a bone or sprain something. How do you feel?"

"Like I've seen better days."

He nods. "You're going to be a solid bruise in a couple of days." *He pauses at something on the monitor.* "Uh . . . did you yank yourself out of that suit?"

"Sort of. Emergency eject."

"Emergency . . . Jesus! Lie down. We're going to need someone to have a look at the plumbing."

Spots sighs and lies down. As they're waiting for the doctor: "The repair shouldn't take long. You came away pretty clean, given the circumstances." *A pause.* "Doesn't it hurt?"

"I've had worse."

———

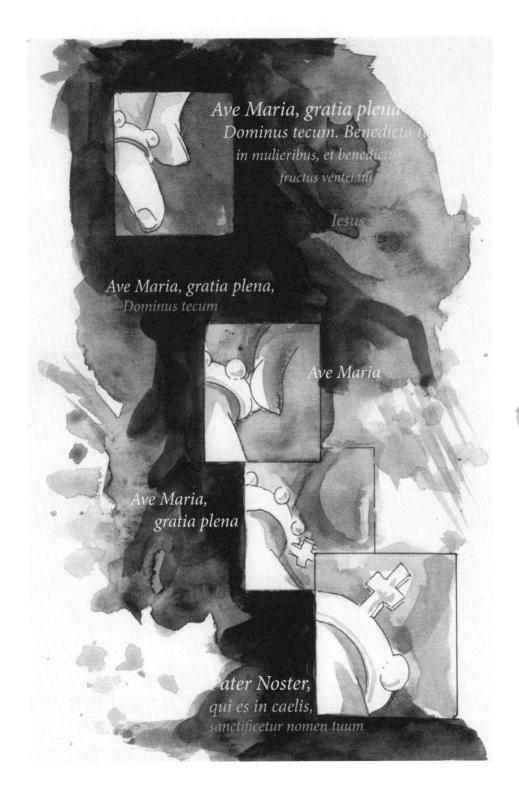

Part 1: Contact   ●   M. C. A. Hogarth

Spots exits the common shower in her PT shirt and a pair of loose sweatpants, pocketing her ring rosary, and finds Claws leaning on the wall outside.

"Claws? Shouldn't you be in bed?"

"Just got done checkin' in your suit, reckoned I'd wait up for you. How you feelin'?"

Spots smiles. "Worn thin."

Claws. "I figured. You good for a little air?"

"A little air?"

"Got a message while you were showerin'. Seems the Fiddler wants to talk to you, and Peaches wants us to make nice."

Spots sighs. "I was hoping to sleep."

Claws eyes her. "Wow, a complaint outta the cookie-bakin' mom. Maybe I should take you back to sickbay, this might be serious-like."

Spots laughs. "No, it's okay. Lead the way." *They start down the corridor.* "Travis?"

"Yeah?"

"Thanks. I wouldn't have gotten out of there except under your arm."

"Ain't nothin'."

She stops, grasps his shoulder. "It was something to me. And to Fang. And Fang2—I saw him in Sickbay, that was a serious injury. He could have bled out."

He meets her eyes, suddenly angry. "You did your part too. You all did."

"Yes. But you pulled it together and made it work. So thanks." *She shakes him a little.* "Say 'you're welcome.' Or did that mother you profess to write to all the time teach you no manners?"

Claws coughs a laugh. "All right, all right. Don't be puttin' down my momma."

Spots waits, brow lifted. Claws covers her hand on his shoulder. "You're welcome." *He pulls away, uncomfortable.* "The Fiddler now, okay? 'Mother's Escort' insists."

"Yessir." *She sways away from his elbow jab.* "You missed."

"Fu—aw, hell, I can't say it."

Spots laughs.

Spots the Space Marine: Defense of the Fiddler

35. After-Action with Aliens

Claws and Spots are passed through security and directed to the Testing Facility. Their arrival causes Samuel-Colt to rise.

Samuel-Colt, trilling an agitated rising-and-falling arpeggio. "Mother-soldier? You smell wrong. Are you injured?"

Spots, smiling. "Only slightly. I'll be fine, Samuel-Colt. You wanted to see me?"

Slower trill, soothed. "If the time is not inconvenient. We would like to discuss some footage we were given from your suit."

"Footage?"

Samuel-Colt brings it up on a wall-screen. "If you permit. We would like to ask your reasoning for some of your actions. We wish to refine the shield further."

Spots. "Oh! Sure. Of course."

Interrogative rising trill. "Here. What are you doing?"

Spots squints. "Oh, right, with Fang right in front of the fox-run. I'm shoving them back."

"You appear to be . . ." *The Fiddler pauses, then mimes a jerk of the arm with another interrogative trill.* "Flicking? What behavior did you expect?"

Spots. "I . . . don't know. I just wanted to push them away."

"Was there any significance to the violence of the motion?"

"I . . . guess I was just in a rush."

Claws. "Hey, go back a moment? Play it again." *The Fiddler obliges.* "You know . . . I think you wanted to throw it, Spots."

Spots and Samuel-Colt, the latter with rising arpeggio. "Throw it?"

"Not far." *Claws looks around, heads for a target.* "Shoving's like this." *He pushes into the target, which wobbles.* "You see me leanin' into it? You weren't there, look at the cam angle. You were leanin' back. But if you toss it and the shield slides out, just a fraction, then you get more of a snap going. Surprises them, springs 'em back more. All without you having to lean into it, which brings you closer to 'em."

Samuel-Colt, sharp note jumping. "Intriguing! Of course, the shield could not be thrown in a literal sense. But it could slide outward."

Spots. "What if you don't want it to?"

Samuel-Colt, slow sawing notes. "There would have to be a control to activate the movement. Perhaps gestural."

Claws, musing. "Just to make it loose. It could decide the angle of motion just from the motion of your arm, yeah?"

Samuel-Colt. "It could. Would this be sufficiently useful? It is a minor modification, but it would require significant training to use. We would have to retool the entire interface to allow fine control of the breadth, size, permeability and "looseness" of the shield."

Claws glances at Spots. "What do you think?"

Spots frowns. "Come at me?"

Claws. "Come at—oh, right." *He steps toward her, deliberate. She twists, arm facing him and stops.*

Spots. "I seem to act like it would work. That probably means if it was there, I'd use it. Does that mean we get the cutting edge flicking out? That could be nasty. Like being punched with a razor."

Claws. "I like that idea."

Spots. "Of course, none of it matters if we run out of power. Did they tell you about today, Samuel-Colt?"

"No, Mother-soldier?"

Spots turns to the interface. "Let me find the footage." *She brings up the segment where she's using the shield as a wall.*

Samuel-Colt, rising trill. "Mother-soldier! Brilliant!"

Claws, droll. "Brilliant until it used up her suit and left her runnin' round in her skivvies."

Samuel-Colt. "Yes, we imagine so. But it can be re-engineered, if we know you are planning to use it so. We were told not to expect you to use it often so we did not allocate much time to its design."

Claws, frowning. "Really?"

Samuel-Colt. "Yes. A . . . last resort, we were told. Soldiers are gun-users, so we designed appropriately. The shield technology is not old. A year, perhaps."

Spots, curious. "So why did you add it?"

Spots the Space Marine: Defense of the Fiddler

Samuel-Colt. "Because it offers a defensive option."

Claws, chuckling. "Which we're turnin' into an offensive one."

Samuel-Colt, long rising trill. "Truly you are generalists in violence."

Claws. "What now?"

Samuel-Colt spreads his six arms. "All of you are exquisitely adaptable to the protection of yourselves and others. It is admirable, this trait."

Claws. "And you, not so much, is that it? That why we're doin' your fightin' for you?"

Spots. "Claws!"

Claws. "What, no answer for that?"

Samuel-Colt, one sharp note. "I would discuss such things with a peer. But you have not accepted that role."

"I haven't done what?"

Spots, quiet. "The arm, Claws."

Claws. "Oh. Right." *Pause.* "Well, that's fair. There oughtta be consequences, right?"

Samuel-Colt. "And privileges, yes."

Claws. "But if Spots asked . . ."

Spots. "That would be cheating." *Claws eyes her; her arms are folded.* "It is. He's not just a source of information to be milked, Claws. He's the representative of an allied power. An alien one."

Claws glances at Samuel-Colt. "Guess that's so."

Samuel-Colt indicates the the screen with a low drone. "Shall we continue our technology review?"

Claws. "Hell yeah!" *Cracks his knuckles.* "Designin' my own weapons tech? Hell yeah!"

36. Desperate Quarters

Testing Center. Spots, Claws and Samuel-Colt continue their discussion. This involves frequent demonstrations of unarmed techniques, gesticulation on Claws's part and note-taking by the Fiddler. Samuel-Colt brings out a test shield-generator. More discussion.

Spots goes from demonstration . . .

to talking . . .

to sitting. . . .

Claws notices her asleep on a bench. "Aw, ****. What time is it?"

Samuel-Colt, quick back-and-forth notes. "We have been here three hours."

Claws. "****, we have to get back or we won't get any sleep." *He crouches beside Spots.* "Hey. Hey, lady."

Spots opens her eyes.

Claws. "You didn't tell us we were borin' you."

Spots laughs muzzily and gets up.

Claws to Samuel-Colt. "So, more later?"

Samuel-Colt, single long note. "I should have a prototype for you within two days."

Claws. "If we live that long . . . sounds good."

Samuel-Colt, rising agitated arpeggio. "Is it so serious?"

Claws. "Hell yeah, it's so serious. See ya, Sam."

Outside, in the corridor. Spots. "You don't have to scare him."

Claws. "In case you ain't noticed, Spots, things *are* pretty scary." *More bitterly.* "If he can't take the heat, he shouldn't be in this kitchen with the rest of us."

Spots. "But he is. I wonder why?"

Claws glances at her and frowns.

"They did WHAT?"

Spots the Space Marine: Defense of the Fiddler

Gunny. "They gridded over the traps, ma'am."

Peaches. "What . . . the . . . ****."

"A mistake."

Peaches. "A mistake that almost killed four people!"

"Three. One of them was already in Sickbay."

"Even better!" *Peaches scrubs a hand over her face.* "How close to finishing are they?"

"Fifteen percent now."

"We can't have them gridding over the traps."

"They say they can't guarantee the integrity of the floor if we leave holes in it, ma'am. It's either we have a floor they can't tunnel through, or we have the traps. Otherwise . . ."

"Otherwise, we have points of failure." *Peaches frowns.* "Or choke points."

Gunny, fighting a grin. "Or choke points."

"Think they'll take the bait?"

"I don't know, ma'am. They're not acting predictably anymore."

Peaches sighs. "All right. Let me think about this."

"I'd think fast, ma'am."

"Right. I'll get right on it."

―――――――

Sickbay. The door opens for Peaches. She wanders through, greeting the medical personnel and talking with the injured who are awake. Fang2 manages a weak pass at her, which she pretends to misinterpret; she leaves him smiling. She moves on to the two coma patients, sits next to each and tells them both stories before patting them on their arms and telling them to feel better.

Then she walks out of Sickbay and back to her office. She stares at the casualty reports, eyes unfocused. Some time later, she calls the Gunny.

"Let's leave the choke points. We're almost out of options . . . and people. If we can't get them to take the bait, we're going to have to shut down the outer perimeter of the Warren."

Part 1: Contact ● *M. C. A. Hogarth*

"You sure about that, ma'am?"

"Do you have better advice, Gunny?" *She looks up at him.* "Any advice? I'll take anything."

He hesitates, then shakes his head. "No, ma'am. I wish I did."

Peaches, grim. "Then we go with what we've got. And pray to God it's enough."

Spots the Space Marine: Defense of the Fiddler

37. Spit and Bailing Wire

Senior Enlisted Meeting Room. Dusty and Roach, Scythe's peers, are sitting around a table along with Big Lion, the platoon leader.

Dusty. "We can't keep going like this."

Scythe, to himself. " 'The center will not hold.' "

Roach. "She's right, Lion. This is ****, no mistake."

Big Lion. "Tell me something I don't know. Can we get less complaining and more suggestions?"

Roach. "I think we're gonna have to fill in the gaps in the teams with each other's people."

Dusty. "We can't do that without enlarging the patrol zones. The shifts will be longer."

Roach. "Yeah, but at least the teams will be full-strength. Right now we're covering smaller areas with teams that are down, sometimes by half."

Scythe. "He's right. Plus, unit cohesion is failing. Our squads haven't worked together in ages. Hell, even inside the squad it's been too long since we've worked in anything but pairs or fire-teams."

Dusty. "What're you going to do? We sure haven't got time for training."

Roach, wry. "Sure we do. On-the-job training, best kind." *He glances at Big Lion.* "You're quiet."

"Just thinking you're right." *She doesn't look pleased.* "But we've got too many injured. There aren't many ways to solve manpower problems. And we can't do less sleep, performance is already degrading."

"How long is this going to keep on?" *Dusty.* "Any word *at all* on possible relief?"

Big Lion shakes her head.

Roach. "The men are saying we're gonna die on this rock, just like the company guarding the other donut."

Big Lion, scowling. "How'd they find out about that?"

Roach. "People hear things, you know that."

Big Lion. "****. We don't need a morale problem on top of this."

Scythe. "I think it's a little late to worry about a morale problem."

Roach. "Unless Peaches has more brownies somewhere."

Dusty. "**** the brownies, we need moonshine."

Roach. "We can breathe on the crabs, they'll drop dead from the vapors."

Big Lion. "All right. Let's get to work scheduling the new teams and re-zoning the patrol areas."

Outside the room as the meeting disbands. Scythe pauses alongside Big Lion.

"This isn't going to work for long. You know that."

"Yeah, I know that. Everyone does."

———

Barracks. Spots enters; Claws looks up from his terminal.

"Hey, where've ya been?"

Spots, subdued. "Sickbay. Have you been there lately?"

"No . . . ?" *When she doesn't answer, Claws gets up and sits on the bunk across from her.* "You okay?"

She nods.

Claws. "You sure?"

She rouses herself, shoulders straightening. "Yes. I just haven't seen an infirmary that full since the last accident on the asteroid."

Claws watches her. Then says, "You're really tired. Sure you want to go see the Fiddler?"

"He's asked for us again?"

"He's got that prototype ready."

Spots, rubbing her eyes. "That was fast."

"Guess he was motivated."

"Guess so. Yes, let's go."

As they're leaving, Claws asks. "Fang-two?"

"He's doing better."

"Good. I didn't want his job."

"What exactly is his job, Claws?"

"Tweakin' Fang-one. Professional-like. The rest of us do it by accident."

Spots laughs, quiet. "Right. By accident. So what's my job?"

"Bakin' cookies, of course."

"And your job?"

"Findin' you an oven."

Spots laughs in earnest. "You find me an oven, Claws and I'll bake the whole company cookies."

"Deal."

38. PROTOTYPE

Testing Facility. Samuel-Colt is fitting Claws and Spots with gloves with prototype shield-generators.

Samuel-Colt, leaning back, single note marcato. "There. To turn it on, use this gesture."

Claws. "Hey, is that a visible gradient?" *He tilts his arm.* "There, toward the edges. It is, isn't it."

Samuel-Colt, rising arpeggio, staccato. "A slight one, yes. It is not obtrusive?"

Spots. "I didn't even see it at first. But . . . now I can see the edge, that's nice. Why don't the existing shields have something like this?"

Samuel-Colt, quick melody. "It was not necessary: the shield was always the same size and shape, so with little training a soldier could memorize its boundaries. These changes make the shield too malleable; it is imperative that its boundaries be delineated in some manner. We judged a visual aid would be best, since your species is visually-oriented."

Spots, curious. "Instead of . . . some other sense? What would you have used for yourself?"

"Sound, most probably. Scent can become too diffuse or confused in long engagements."

Claws, brows lifted. "And sound doesn't?"

"It is our observation that we hear sounds more accurately than you do." *The Fiddler taps his abdomen as his vestigial arms bow a melody, detache.* "We hear with our entire bodies. Shell thickness, density of the matter behind it and breadth of the part reverberating, all give us a broad spectrum of surfaces with which to hear a single sound." *He pauses, tilts his head, ending the melody abruptly.* "Even now, I must use visual words to describe it accurately in your language. A 'spectrum.' "

"Wow." *Spots, soft.* "You must have amazing music."

Samuel-Colt. "Our passage through life creates it."

Spots. "That sounds almost like a proverb."

Samuel-Colt. "You have a good . . ." *Pause, single note, sharp.* "Ear. I suppose. We would say 'good body,' but I suspect that has a different meaning to you."

Claws, chuckling. "You've been payin' attention to notice that."

Samuel-Colt, rising and falling arpeggios, spiccato. "We have had many lives here to pay attention, mother's-escort. If we did not observe accurately, we would be very poor at designing proper weapons for such a different species."

Claws. "Which brings us back to this." *Pats shield-generator.* "Please, go on."

Samuel-Colt. "Yes. To toggle the slide . . ."

After instruction, Spots and Claws experiment against target dummies and (lightly) against Samuel-Colt himself.

Claws. "This is complicated."

Spots. "This feels good." *Sweetly.* "It's not complicated, unless all you're used to is pulling a trigger."

Claws. "Hey! Ow! She's got teeth!"

Spots, grinning. To Samuel-Colt. "How much testing have you done? Enough to put it in the suit?"

Long note, held. "We can do no more testing without it being in a suit."

Spots nods. "Put it in mine, then." *She glances at the clock, makes a face.* "Uh, after the next shift."

Samuel-Colt, rising arpeggio with flourish. "It will be done, mother-soldier."

Claws. "Y' know, if you're gonna call her something, it should be 'mother-Marine'."

Samuel-Colt, three quick notes, spiccato, rising. "Because she is an underwater mother?"

Claws and Spots pause.

Slowly, Claws: "You . . . just made a joke?"

Samuel-Colt, arpeggio softening, legato. "I am aware of your designations, yes. It is amusing to us because we have special feeling for water."

Spots. "Really? How come?"

Samuel-Colt, legato. "We live in water." *Another long pause from the humans. This time the Fiddler correctly interprets it.* "We—I and my lineage—were designed to live in human environments."

Spots. "But . . . what do you do when you go home?"

Samuel-Colt, single soft note. "We can never go home, mother-soldier."

Claws. "Never?"

Samuel-Colt, silence, then slow melody. "Every designer of my lineage has given up water to fulfill our mother's request. We design weapons for the humans. That is the price we pay for the privilege of serving her, and you." *A curious tremolo note, rising.* "Do you not give up something to be here, both of you? Do you think it is a worthy cause, for the price?"

Spots. "We do, yes. Thank you, Samuel-Colt. Your sacrifice honors us."

The Fiddler bows. Spots bows back.

In the corridor, on the way back to the barracks.

Claws. "So, you around royalty much or do you just like fantasy flicks?"

Spots. "It just seemed like the right thing to do. You could say thank you, you know."

Claws. "For bowin' for me? I'm not the bowin' type . . ."

Spots. ". . . for covering up the fact that you couldn't immediately answer that there was a good reason for being out here."

Claws. "Caught that, did you."

Spots. "Red-handed."

Claws. "Hey, Spots—"

Spots. "You don't have to explain anything to me, Claws. Why you're out here is your business. But if you don't know the answer to that one, maybe you have some explaining to do, to yourself."

Claws. "****, you really are a mom, aren't you."

Spots. "Twice over. And—"

Claws. "—mind my manners, sorry, sorry, I'll wash my mouth out with what passes for soap when we get back, Scout's honor."

Spots's mouth quirks.

39. UNDER TENSION

Barracks. Spots is just settling in after the trip to the Testing Facility. Claws is staring at the ceiling. Long after Spots has stopped moving, he's still staring.

Montage. Engineers laying down grid. One squad guarding. Then another. Shot of the flooring being put down around the trap. Marines shooting crabs.

Control Center. Peaches is leaning over the console, watching the video from several different suit-cams. Gunny's standing behind her, arms folded.

[**Base**] **Coyote** : Control, this is Team Doggy.

Controller. "Team Doggy, this is Control. Go ahead."

[**Base**] **Coyote** : The grid is finished. Repeat: Grid is finished. We are escorting the engineers back now.

Controller. "Great news, Team Doggy. We'll pass it on."

Peaches straightens. "That's my cue. What squad's up next?"

Controller, consulting different screen. "Team Kitty, ma'am."

"Tell them I'm on my way."

Armory. Team Kitty is suiting up, along with a couple of Varmints.

Over the intercom. "Team Kitty, the grid is complete. Advise you have the LT on her way down."

Whiskers. "Babysitting again?"

Hairball. "Maybe she just wants to have a look at the thing now that it's done."

Claws. "I know I do."

Scythe, holding down the button on the intercom. "Team Kitty copies, Control. Thanks for the heads-up."

Spots is sitting on a corner, studying the new shield generator.

Claws, under his breath. "Son of a gun!"

Spots. "Claws?"

Claws laughs and shows her his arm. "He gave me one too. I was thinkin' of askin' him for it but didn't want to climb through all the security hoops between us an' his hide-out."

Spots grins. "He really has been around humans long."

Claws. "Either that, or guys are the same everywhere."

Spots. "How's that?"

Claws. "Don't want the girls havin' all the best toys. An' particularly not *first.*"

Fang, eyeing them. "What've you got there?"

Spots. "New shield prototype. We're testing for Samuel-Colt."

Scythe, calling. "You could have remembered to say something about that to me."

Claws. "Sorry, boss, slipped m'mind. Lack of sleep an' all."

Scythe. "No joke, Walker. This is serious." *He comes over to have a look.* "Was this thing tested?"

Spots. "In the lab, extensively. It's got to be field-tested at some point, Scythe. I volunteered."

Scythe, resigned. "Of course you did. All right, fall in before Bonny Peaches surprises us *en deshabille.*"

Claws. "Fancy, boss. Real fancy."

Scythe. "Yeah, but you got it, didn't you."

Spots. "He pleads the fifth."

Claws shoots her a glare as Peaches enters the compartment, already suited.

Scythe. "Attention!"

The squad stands at attention. Peaches sweeps them with her gaze, then nods.

Peaches. "Looking good. Finish suiting up and let's go have a look at our new flooring."

"Yes, ma'am!"

40. Entrapment

Warren. Peaches is crouching next to one of the two traps left open by the Seabees.

Peaches. "Little more complicated than I expected. What's this?"

Scythe. "Looks like they gave it a retractable floor, ma'am."

Peaches. "Why? Do they think . . . uhm, mm. What, to trap some of them in it so they can't get out?"

Claws, peering into it. "They did give it metal walls." *Adds, distracted.* "Ma'am."

Peaches. "That's—" *Stops herself.* "Did they give this cage wheels so we could get it safely into the base for dissection? Because that's the only way we're going to get a crab out of these tunnels without killing it."

Scythe. "Maybe they're expecting us to neutralize it some other way."

Peaches. "Like a tranq gun?" *She glances up.* "Guitart? Want to ask the Fiddler about that?"

Spots. "I can do that, ma'am." *Quieter.* "I'd rather not."

Peaches, frowning. "Why?"

Spots, heart-beat pause. "He's a weapons-designer, not a biologist or doctor, ma'am. Designing something more complicated than "puts holes in it" might be beyond him."

Peaches. "Good point. Ask him anyway."

Spots. "Yes, ma'am."

Peaches. "Sergeant, give me a hand here. I'd like to see how this thing works."

Scythe. "Yes, ma'am."

While he and Peaches puzzle out the mechanism, the rest of the squad takes points along the corridor.

[**Squad**] **Flea :** So it's true you're in bed with the Fiddler, Spots? I hear you spend enough nights there.

[**Squad**] **Claws :** I'm thinkin' Team Kitty guests oughta be more polite.

[**Squad**] **Flea :** What's wrong, can't take the truth? How about it, Spots? How come you don't wanna ****ing talk to the Fiddler about helping us out?

[*Squad*] **Spots** : I'll be glad to talk to him about helping us out, on things he can actually help us with.

[*Squad*] **Silverfish** : Ohhh, right. It's too complicated for us stupid varmints to get. A kitty thing, getting friendly with the ****ing enemy.

[*Squad*] **Hairball** : Thought the enemy was in front of us, not back at base.

[*Squad*] **Claws** : I'm thinkin' Team Kitty Guests oughta be a lot more ****ing polite. You guys got a problem?

[*Squad*] **Flea** : Wow, you her nanny or her lover?

Claws looks down the corridor in Flea's direction, almost taking a step—

[*Squad*] **Spots** : ENOUGH.

Silence on the squad channel.

[*Squad*] **Spots** : I'm doing my job to win this fight, just like the rest of us. You have a problem with that? You go down there and give up your rack time to play diplomat to aliens. I'll be interested to see how far you get.

No comment. Then:

[*Squad*] **Scythe** : I could use a hand over here.

Claws, closest to him, troops over to help out. While he's holding the grid ceiling steady:

[*Buddy-to-Buddy*] **Claws** : Hey, Spots? What gives?

[*Buddy-to-Buddy*] **Spots** : What do you mean?

[*Buddy-to-Buddy*] **Claws** : I've got your back, but it would help knowin' why. How come you don't want to ask Sam Colt 'bout the tranq gun?

[*Buddy-to-Buddy*] **Spots** : *sigh* It's one thing to kill a brother, Claws. It's another thing to arrange for him to become someone's science experiment.

[*Buddy-to-Buddy*] **Claws** : We have to play this one to win, Spots. Or else there ain't gonna be any other games, ever.

[*Buddy-to-Buddy*] **Spots** : I know that, Claws. I'll ask.

Peaches finishes inspecting the trap to her satisfaction and leads the patrol further up the corridor, toward the next. On their way:

[*NCO*] **Claws** : I know that walk. You're pissed. Think I didn't handle it?

Spots the Space Marine: Defense of the Fiddler

[*NCO*] **Scythe** : It's fine.

[*NCO*] **Claws** : So?

[*NCO*] **Scythe** : That damned trap. Is way too clever.

[*NCO*] **Claws** : Think it'll break?

[*NCO*] **Scythe** : I don't know. But the way things are going, I won't be ****ing surprised.

41. Conversations

Peaches and the squad investigate the other trap, which works the same way as the first, then resume their patrol duty. They find isolated bands of crabs; no major incursions. They dispatch them and return to base for shift-change.

The armory is unusually silent as the squad and its Varmint guests un-suit and the incoming Wild Dogs start hooking up. Some of the Dogs glance at the Kitties but no one asks.

Team Kitty Common Room.

Fang. "What the **** was that?"

Scythe. "Just go to bed, Fang."

Fang. "No, really. I want to know. Why the **** were they giving us grief?"

Spots. "Don't look at me. I'm just doing the job the lieutenant asked me to do."

Fang. "I'm not talking about that. I want to know why they're giving us **** about it. What did we ever do to the ****ing Varmints?"

There is a surprised pause, since this is the first time Fang's talked about "us." As if she's a part of the team.

Claws. "Uh . . . "

Spots. "They're just tense and tired, like the rest of us. I'm sure it was just blowing off steam."

Scythe. "Good answer. And now, sack time."

Hairball, nonplussed. "Cards first."

Whiskers. "I'm in."

Fang. "Huh, me too."

Scythe, hesitates. "****. Fine, I'll play."

Hairball, without looking up from shuffling. "**** the crabs, anyway."

Whiskers. "You two in?"

Spots. "I'm going to go see Fang2 . . . then talk to Samuel-Colt, as commanded."

Claws. "Guess I'm with her, then."

Whiskers. "Your loss." *Eyes Hairball.* "Or maybe you're just being smart, I don't know yet."

Hairball, serene. "Not my fault the rest of you suck at this game."

Fang. "****! We'll see about that."

Scythe chuckles.

Officer's Armory. Peaches is stripping off her gloves when Gunny enters.

Peaches. "You were watching the footage?"

Gunny. "Yes, ma'am. Those are interesting additions the engineers made."

Peaches. "Maybe too interesting. I guess we'll have to see how they work, though I'm all fresh out of ideas what to do with a trapped crab, besides kill it."

Gunny. "Actually, that sounds like a fine plan, ma'am."

Peaches snorts. "More importantly, were you listening?"

113

Gunny. "To what, ma'am?"

Peaches. "You know what I mean, Gunny. The squad."

Gunny. "Ma'am, officers aren't supposed to be listening to—"

Peaches. "But every single one I've ever talked to does. Or the ones worth their salt, anyway. So yeah, I was listening . . . were you?"

Gunny nods once, mouth tight.

Peaches. "You think they took care of it?"

Gunny. "As well as they could, anyway. You know how Marines feel about aliens."

Peaches. "Yeah. But we kind of have to be able to make the distinction between "alien giving us technology that we'd be dead without" and "alien trying to kill us" before we point our weapons." *She sighs.* "Do you think I need to step in?"

Gunny. "Not yet. Let the non-coms handle it for now, ma'am. If it gets bad, they'll bring it to you."

Peaches. "You hope they'll bring it to me."

Gunny, wry. "Yes, ma'am. I hope."

Peaches rises to strip out of the rest of the suit. "Just enough crabs out there so the men could say 'goody, the LT got some target practice, now she can go home.' A lot fewer than I was expecting. Do you think they're waiting for something?"

Gunny, with emphasis. "Ma'am, I hope not."

42. OBJECTIFYING

Spots and Claws stop at Sickbay and find Fang2 sleeping. Spots leaves him a protein bar (coconut flavor). They head to the Testing Facility and find it empty. Likewise the Lab.

Claws, to nearest guard. "Hey, where's the Fiddler?"

Guard. "Personal quarters."

Claws. "Which way is—"

Spots, interrupting. "Is he on sleep-shift?"

Guard. "I don't know, Private."

Spots sighs. "Can you tell us the way?"

The guard leads them down the hall, around a corner. A little further. Leaves them at a door. Claws watches Spots as she hits the door-announce. After a moment:

Samuel-Colt, through intercom. "Yes?"

Spots. "Samuel-Colt? Are you accepting guests?"

A pause. Then: "Enter."

Fiddler's Room. The size of this room is hard to gauge, because it is painted in shades of blue and green and there are blue and green lights rippling over it in simulated water patterns. There are translucent scarves (some threaded with clear beads) hanging from the ceilings and in the corners, like strands of gossamer kelp. There's an audio system somewhere; Holst's Venus is playing.

Samuel-Colt is rising from a flat low platform bed, which is suspended from the ceiling by nearly invisible cables.

"Mother-soldier? And escort. How may we assist you?"

Spots, agape. "Oh, Samuel-Colt! It's beautiful!"

Even Claws is silent.

Samuel-Colt, legato melody. "We thank you, Mother. We find it soothing."

Spots, softer. "Like home." *Touching her mouth.* "I'm sorry, I don't mean to remind you of painful things."

Samuel-Colt, still legato, rising melody lines. "It is like home. It was my intention, and so you do not hurt me by noticing."

Spots. "I'm glad. I'm . . . sorry but I came on business. My lieutenant had a question."

Samuel-Colt cuts off the melody with a bounced note, spreading upper hands. "Continue."

Spots. "She wondered if you know of some way to . . . tranquilize a crab, instead of killing it."

Samuel-Colt, rising arpeggio. "Why would she wish that?"

Spots, squaring shoulders. "She was thinking of scientific experimentation."

Samuel-Colt. "That is well done of her. The enemy has been dissected before but they continually evolve. It would be wise to inspect one of the current iterations."

Claws. "What? Seriously?"

Samuel-Colt, spiccato up an arpeggio. "Knowledge of the enemy is never wasted, Mother's-escort. You agree?"

Claws. "Yeah, but . . . I kinda thought you'd be more against, uh . . . you know. Crab cruelty?"

Samuel-Colt, slower, but still staccato. "The enemy does not understand cruelty, Mother's-escort. Or have you not noticed?"

Claws. "It's sorta expected for us to be objectifyin' the enemy, Sam, but not because the things we think are true. They're usually not, we just think 'em so we can become killers without completely rippin' apart."

Spots is staring at him now.

Samuel-Colt, softer bowing. "You are not fighting a human enemy. The creatures you fight are designed not to have your higher instincts. Not only would they interfere with their function, but it would make them too costly to create."

Spots. "So . . . you'll help us?"

Samuel-Colt, staccato, rising melody. "We will try, yes. But we cannot guarantee success, and the danger to the soldier administering the tranquilizer would be great. The enemy does not have convenient flesh over its entire surface. The places one can aim to be effective are very small and very few."

Claws. "Lucky for you, you got the best snipers in the whole ****ing armed forces, right here."

Spots. "Thank you, Samuel-Colt. I thought . . . maybe it would bother you, to fulfill this request. I guess I was thinking like a human."

Samuel-Colt, spiccato. "As you are a human, Mother-soldier, that is perhaps a good thing."

Claws. "Wow, another joke. You're enjoyin' this, eh?"

Samuel-Colt, one long note, sustained. "Having an audience is gratifying."

Claws, grinning. "You sayin' that assistant of yours ain't got ears?"

Samuel-Colt, silence. "Perhaps it would be more accurate to say he hasn't the Mother's. Or yours." *At Claws's look, staccato:* "He does not expect humor from an alien, so he does not hear it."

Claws snorts. "His loss."

Spots, curious. "Do you make a lot of jokes at home? I guess it's harder here."

Samuel-Colt, rising and falling arpeggio. "You understand clearly, Mother. It is hard to guess what humans will find funny from us, even after several generations of living among them. Something said by a human may fall flat said by us."

Spots. "I bet your humor at home is musical."

117

Samuel-Colt, marcato. "Yes!"

Claws. "****. I'd love to hear some musical humor! Like dueling banjos, or those tricks where people make violins sound like arguin' folks."

Spots. "Ooh, yes!"

Samuel-Colt, legato, falling arpeggio. "Ah, I wish you could hear one of our humorists, both of you. I can tell a joke, but I am no expert."

Spots. "What's it like?"

Samuel-Colt, slow melody. "Like . . . one of your concerts. Everyone floats in a circle around the humorist, a great sphere of an audience. There is a . . . a rope? A star? A knot? Of braided seaweed—synthetic or natural depending on the performer's taste—and the humorist stands in the center. The strands extend so the audience can anchor themselves if they wish. And then they drift through the ocean, and listen to the anecdotes and jokes, and . . . they laugh!" *Single note, marcato: vring!*

Spots. Soft. "Wow."

Claws, quiet but intense. "That must be ****ing awesome."

Spots. "I guess human humor is one-dimensional, compared to that. . . ."

Samuel-Colt, legato. "Oh, no . . . merely different, Mother. Merely different. And there is music running through your voices, also. You don't often notice it the same way we would."

Claws, to himself. "Huh."

Samuel-Colt, rising arpeggio. "Is there anything more? You are in the middle of your rest periods, we think. We are also."

Spots. "No, that's . . . that's all we came for. But thank you, Samuel-Colt."

This time after she bows, Claws hesitates, then nods to the alien. They are quiet all the way to the Barracks. While they are turning back their beds:

Claws. "So, you going to tease me yet?"

Spots. "What about?"

Claws. "Ouch. So many choices you don't even know which one I'm talkin' about."

Spots smiles without comment.

Claws. "He's still an alien."

Spots, lying down. "Yes. But now he's an alien who likes stand-up comics."

Claws. "*Underwater* stand-up comics."

Spots. "Yes."

Claws. "That's fu—freakin' awesome."

Spots, smiling to herself. "Good night, Claws."

"Night, Spots."

43. GUESTING

Corridor. Spots, Claws and Fang are heading to the Armory.

Fang. "How come we're the lucky ones who have to pull an extra half-shift?"

Claws. "It's the sleep thing. Moms don't need it and ex-Dragons are too hardcore for it."

Fang, snorting. "And you?"

Claws. "I'm the poor chump who has to keep up with you two."

Spots grins as they enter the Armory. Team Doggie's suiting up.

Dusty. "Hey, Kitties. You have Guest Channel 4. Squad channel's inclusive."

Claws. "We copy that, Sergeant. Channel 4, all kitties, all the time."

One of the Wild Dogs: "Meow."

Another: "Woof."

Fang. "Oh, shut it."

Claws. "Ex-Dragon. Ya know how they are." *He ducks Fang's swing.*

Dusty. "Enough horsing around, we got crabs to kill. Into your armor, dogs. And guests."

After suiting up, the Wild Dog squad, augmented by the three Kitties, heads into the Warren.

[*Guest*] Fang : Seriously, Claws. I know everyone's supposed to filling out the squads . . . but do you know why Scythe sent us? Us in particular?

[*Guest*] Claws: Cross mah heart, Fang. I got no idea. We'll probably rotate through, next time it'll be Whiskers, Hairball and Fang2 if he's outta sickbay.

[*Guest*] Fang : At least it's the Doggies and not the ****ing Varmints. *Caressing the barrel of her rifle.*

[*Guest*] Spots : For now, anyway.

Fang shoots her a look.

[*Guest*] Claws : Let's just concentrate on givin' good support, eh?

[*Guest*] Fang : Right. The band of brothers ****. I can do that. As long as they do it back.

The squad begins patrol duty. After weeks of escorting engineers, equipment and materiel, the Warren is very quiet.

[*Squad*] **Coyote** : So, I hear we got the Alien-Whisperer with us.

[*Squad*] **Claws** : You have got to be ****in' kiddin' me.

[*Squad*] **Spots** : You mean me?

[*Squad*] **Coyote** : Yeah, so . . . can you tell us when they're gonna attack? That would be handy.

[*Guest*] **Spots** : *Anticipating.* Don't, Claws. It's an honest question. *Switching channels.* I don't know, I wish I did.

[*Squad*] **Fang** : Yeah, for that we'd need my tumor, Fang-****ing-two. He can feel them coming through his boots. I swear. You hear Fang2 saying 'I feel something' and next thing you know there's a crab in your ****ing face.

[*Squad*] **Coyote** : ****! When's he guesting?

[*Squad*] **Fang** : When he gets out of sickbay. Two of us got caught between two breakthroughs. Rough ****.

[*Squad*] **Coyote** : We'll kill a ****ing crab for him.

All the Wild Dogs chant on the channel: We'll kill a ****ing crab for him!

[*Squad*] **Claws** : Whoa.

[*Squad*] **Coyote** : We kill a ****ing crab for every Dog who's down. We'll do one for you kitties, since we're rubbing elbows.

[*Squad*] **Spots** : Hey, thank you.

[*Squad*] **Dusty** : Now if there were only some crabs to *kill* . . . where *are* they?

In the Command Center, Peaches is scowling at the live-cam footage.

"She's right. Where the hell *are* they?"

44. REHASH

Team Doggie and guests continue their patrol with some grumbling, much banter and no incident. Halfway through the shift finds them back near base.

[**Squad**] **Dusty** : Time for your drop-off, Kitties. Thanks for filling us out.

[**Squad**] **Claws** : No problem.

[**Squad**] **Coyote** : And next time bring your canary with you!

[**Squad**] **Spots** : We'll tell him you asked for him.

[**Squad**] **Fang** : He'll love that . . . 'My legend grows.'

[**Squad**] **Claws** : Hell, you sound just like him!

[**Squad**] **Fang** : Shu—SHIELDS!

A knot of crabs with one King, so sudden. Spots's shield flares with a golden ripple, Claws's comes up in blue; they flicker green where they intersect in front of Fang. Her shot brings down the King; the Wild Dog sniper is fast but not as fast as this ex-Dragon. The rest of the team mows through the enemy.

[**Squad**] **Fang** : ****! ****! ****! What the hell? *She wades through the bodies to kick the King in the abdomen.* What is this ****? They insulting us?

[**Squad**] **Claws** : ****!

The entire squad is looking at the downed crabs. The King, the soldiers . . . all the earliest models, from before the new carapaces Fang brought down.

[**Squad**] **Dusty** : ****, this is *not* good.

[**Squad**] **Fang** : ****ing target practice, what this is.

[**Squad**] **Claws** : They're cookin' somethin, and I reckon we ain't gonna like it when they're done.

[**Squad**] **Dusty** : You Kitties get back, and send us your replacements pronto. I don't know where this is heading, but I'm not happy.

[**Squad**] **Claws** : You got it.

The Varmints replacing Claws, Spots and Fang are already entering the Warren. The Kitties nod in passing and get inside.

Fang, sitting, helmet off. "*****. What does it mean?"

Claws. "Like I said. No good."

Spots is looking at the markers next to the first locker. "Fang?"

"Yeah?"

Spots picks out the black one. "Turn around, let's get your newest King painted on."

"What? Oh, right. I stopped keeping count." *She hesitates.*

Claws. "Scared we'll catch up to ya?"

Fang snorts. "Hell no. Come put that star on, and let's see if I can remember the rest."

Spots winks at Claws when Fang turns her back and crouches to do the honors.

———————

Later, preparing for bed:

"That was good thinkin' back there."

Spots. "I noticed her kill count wasn't incrementing. I thought it was because no one wanted to paint them for her."

Claws. "You were right."

Spots. "You know, Fang might have been a pain when she first came on, but you didn't exactly make it easy for her to integrate either."

Claws. "Hell, we're Marines, Spots. We don't do easy."

Spots, turning in her bunk to look at him. "That's an excuse and you know it."

Claws, uncomfortable. "She was a *****, Spots. A real *****, and there's no other word for it, sorry."

Spots. "Yeah, and? When she joined Team Kitty, she became ours. Attitude and all."

Silence.

Then Claws nods. "Yeah. Guess we shoulda tried harder."

Spots nods and turns out the light.

In the dark: "*****, Spots, you are one hard mother."

Spots the Space Marine: Defense of the Fiddler

"Claws!"

"I know, I know. I'll soap up in the mornin'."

Spots. "Actually, I'm just glad you didn't finish that."

Claws. "Finish . . . ?"

Spots. "Mother- . . . you know. I mean, what would that make me?"

"One very dangerous lesbian."

"Claws!"

"Or bisexual, I guess, what with the kids and the husband and all. . . ."

"Claws!"

"I guess I'd better stop now or I'll have to eat that bar in the mornin', won't I."

"Yes!"

"Night, Spots."

123

45. LIVE OR DEAD

The Board Room, again, where the aliens are dissected. Peaches is standing next to a lab technician and an ONI specialist. They are looking at a crab corpse.

Lab Tech. "This is their standard soldier carapace, Lieutenant. First revision."

Peaches. "First? Aren't we on third revision?"

Lab Tech nods. "This is the design that was typical when we first dug in."

Peaches. "But that makes no sense. I've been looking through the records, and the crabs have never sent old carapaces back at us. Have they?"

The other two exchange a look. The specialist says, "They've never done it here, no."

"But elsewhere?"

Specialist shakes her head. "I can't say." *At Peaches's look:* "I mean that literally, Lieutenant. I just don't know. If there's more information on it, I can't read it."

Peaches. "****. No clue what it might mean, then."

"None."

Peaches rubs her forehead. "All right. Then I need you working on something new."

Lab Tech. "Ma'am?"

Peaches. "Find some way for us to destroy the utility of these things once they're dead. I don't want the crabs making use of them."

Specialist. "We don't have any evidence that they can use these carapaces that way."

Peaches. "We don't have any evidence that they can't, either." *Looks at Lab Tech.* "I need fast, complete and safe. No compromise, I want all three."

Lab Tech. "I can experiment with compounds, but what you're talking about is really more of a weapons matter."

Peaches. "Not if what we want is to disintegrate whatever they're using for brains."

Lab Tech. "That's the problem, ma'am. How do we *know* what they're using for brains? For all I know they could be storing memories on the insides of their chitin with scent markers."

Peaches frowns. Then strides to the wall and toggles the intercom. "Lieutenant here. I'm in the Board Room. Get Private Guitart for me, please, and tell her to bring Samuel-Colt here. We have questions."

When she turns away from the intercom . . .

Specialist. "The alien's talking to you?"

Peaches. "The alien's talking to one of my people. She's talking to me."

Lab Tech. "Nice!"

Specialist. "****, I've known Samuel-Colt for a year and he's never said a word to me."

A little bit later, Spots arrives with Claws escorting and Samuel-Colt behind her. The alien watches the military courtesies between Spots, Claws and the lieutenant but does not interrupt.

Peaches. "Thank you for coming, Samuel-Colt."

Samuel-Colt. "You are welcome, Lieutenant-Savannah-Bonnet. There is an issue?"

Peaches nods toward the table with the dead crab. "We were looking for a way to make the bodies unusable to the enemy for their . . . memory-eating."

Samuel-Colt. "Lieutenant-Savannah-Bonnet, they are already useless if they are dead. Memories can only be consumed from the living."

Peaches. "Always?"

Samuel-Colt. "Always." *A hesitation.*

Spots, watching his bowing. "Is there something else you wanted to say, Samuel-Colt?"

Samuel-Colt. "Mother-soldier; if they plan to cannibalize their base soldier models for memories, they will probably design them to fall insensate in advance of a true killing blow. It's what we would do."

Claws. "Oh, that's just great. So we'll have to go through piles of maybe-dead crabs to make sure they're really dead?"

Peaches. "Well, that just brings us back to the beginning. We have to make sure they can't be used for reconnaissance, so we'll just have to kill them dead-dead." *She glances at Samuel-Colt.* "I'm right?"

Samuel-Colt. "Essentially, yes."

Spots. "Essentially?"

Samuel-Colt spreads his middle, claw-bearing arms (causing the specialist and lab tech to edge away). "We are assuming they are working the way we understand, Mother-Marine. But they no less than we advance, and their biotechnology is their weapons technology. What if they have evolved some new method? We will not know until we see its effects."

Peaches, low. "****." *Then clearer.* "Well, that's war. We signed up for it. Is there anything else?"

Spots glances at Samuel-Colt. He shakes his head in a very human gesture, which looks strange on his stalk of a neck.

Peaches. "All right. Thank you all."

Once they've left:

Specialist. "****."

Lab Tech. "Get me some more specimens, Lieutenant, if they send new ones. I'll see what I can do."

Peaches. "Right. Specimens of new killer crabs. You want them dead or alive?"

Lab Tech. ". . . is that a joke?"

Peaches, fell smile. "We're the ****ing Marines. If you need a live crab, we'll get you one."

Silence.

Lab Tech. "Dead will do. For a start."

Peaches. "You got it."

———————

In the hall, Spots bows to Samuel-Colt. "Thank you."

Samuel-Colt. "You make my duty easy, Mother-soldier. Thank you. Do you go back to your rest now?"

Claws. "Think by now we should be gettin' to the Armory, actually."

Samuel-Colt. "May I accompany you? It has been some time since I checked the statistics on your gear. The shield modifications were distracting."

Spots. "We'd be delighted."

46. Bars of Soap

Armory as Spots, Claws and Samuel-Colt enter.

Spots. "We're the first ones here!"

Samuel-Colt. "We will check the data on your suits first, if that is acceptable. The new shield data should be valuable."

Spots. "Go ahead."

Claws, taking down one of the power cells. "Hey, Sam . . . how *do* you make sure a crab is dead, anyway?"

Spots. "I assume you shoot it with the guns you keep telling me I need practice with."

Claws. "Man, you are never gonna let me forget that, are you."

Spots. "Nope."

Samuel-Colt. "Your escort asks a valid question, Mother. The answer is not a simple one."

Spots. "It's not? But we shoot them and they go down. Or explode, depending on the round."

Samuel-Colt. "The soldier class, perhaps. Different classes have different nervous systems. For example, Kings commonly have two neural nodes, a brain and a nexus at the base of the thorax. This second node handles music and scent, so it retains memories related to those senses. In order to neutralize the King you must destroy both nodes."

Claws. "****! You mean all this time we've been leavin' them mostly not-dead?"

Samuel-Colt. "The Kings do die if you damage them, Mother's Escort. But it isn't immediate. If you are asking how to keep their memories from being used by the enemy, then these are nuances you need to understand."

Claws. "****! And the normal bugs?"

Samuel-Colt. "As far as we know, a head shot should be sufficient."

Claws. "But not the body shots we usually use to mow 'em down."

Samuel-Colt bows a regretful note.

Claws. "****.****! Do you know how much harder that's gonna make our jobs?" *Sockets the power cells into his suit.* "****! Also, I've probably earned six bars of soap cussin' about this. **—crap!"

Spots makes no comment, but her mouth is quirking. The door opens for Scythe, who halts at the scene.

Spots, pulling her suit on. "Hi, Sergeant. Have you met Samuel-Colt?"

Scythe. "I . . . haven't had the pleasure."

Spots. "Samuel-Colt, this is Scythe, our sergeant. Scythe, Samuel-Colt, the designer. He's downloading suit data for evaluation."

Samuel-Colt, melody with flourish. "We are glad to make your acquaintance."

Scythe, a little off-balance, but taking it in stride. "Likewise." *He takes down his suit.* "You two are early."

Claws. "Bonny Peaches called us down to have a look at a crab corpse, tryin' to figure out how come they're sendin' us their dregs."

Scythe. "And?"

Claws. "Sam thinks it's cuz they're preparin' to sic some super-crabs on us. All at once."

Scythe. "****ing wonderful."

Samuel-Colt to Spots, with rising arpeggio. "Do you make the Scythe eat bars of soap also?"

Scythe. "Make me what?"

Spots, laughing. "No, no, if every Marine on this base had to wash out their mouths every time they cursed in front of me, we'd be out of soap in a day."

Claws, muttering. "In an hour."

Scythe. "A few minutes, I think."

They're all laughing, Samuel-Colt's a springing melody, when the rest of the team enters with the Varmint guests.

Silence.

Claws. "So, you got your data, Sam?"

Samuel-Colt, no music. "Yes. Thank you." *He inclines his body to Spots.* "Mother."

Spots. "Samuel-Colt. Rest well."

The alien exits. Another silence. Then the team resumes suiting up.

Spots the Space Marine: Defense of the Fiddler

[***Buddy-to-Buddy***] [**Claws**] : If they give us trouble . . .

[***Buddy-to-Buddy***] [**Spots**] : They won't. Turn around so I can do your check.

47. Veteran's Day, with Crabs

The Warren. Team Kitty and Guests are patrolling, casually killing the first revision crabs.

Fang. "****ing insult, I tell you."

Claws. "Think of it as an opportunity to practice."

Fang, gunning down another three crabs. "How the **** is this practice? I could do it in my ****ing sleep."

Claws. "Well, I hear tell the only way to really be sure a crab is dead is to shoot it in the head."

Fang shoots the next group of three in the head, *bam* *bam* *bam*.

Claws, drawling. "And the Kings, you gotta shoot 'em at the base of the thorax too."

Fang. "I'll keep that in mind when we actually see one."

Scythe. "What's this now?"

Spots. "The lieutenant wants to make sure we deny the enemy the chance to use their own for reconnaissance. If you don't get the head on the commoners and the head and second brain on the Kings, they might live long enough to be useful."

Scythe. "****. I'm guessing she'll be wanting us to do that then."

Whiskers. "Even when we're looking at a ****ing wall of them?"

Flea, the Varmint Guest. "You saying you can't make that many headshots?"

Fang. "Get real, you ****ing ***. Even I can't take down every head on an advancing wall, and if you think you can do better we've got a date on a ****ing range where you can prove it."

Flea. "Oooh, a date. She likes me."

Fang. "Don't make me rip your ***** up through your ***, you ****er."

Flea. "Mmm, I like spicy—"

The wall beside them falls in: writhing bodies, arms, a solid wall of the new carapaces Fang found, not the older ones they've been shooting.

Spots. "Breakthrough!" *Her new shield slices through four of them with a corner-of-the-eye flash of gold.*

Spots the Space Marine: Defense of the Fiddler

Scythe: "NORTH!"

The squad breaks that way, with Spots and Claws in the rear with shields up, intercepting a hail of alien needles.

Fang. "Finally! Something worth the ammo!"

Claws. "**** that, I didn't want more excitement!"

Scythe. "****!"

The old revision crabs have poured out of the intersection in front of them.

Scythe. "Mow them down."

Fang. "Here's your ****ing chance to make your wall of headshots, moron, let's see it."

Flea. "Are you always this much of a ****?"

Spots. "Hey! Don't call her that!"

They are in the middle of shooting a way clear through the second group.

Flea. "What? A ****? She sure acts like one."

Spots. "That's uncalled for. Don't do it again."

Flea. "Or what? ****, can't take a little—"

Spots, still shielding the rear. "SHUT UP. And tell her you're sorry."

Flea. "For ****'s sake, isn't anyone gonna say 'we're a little *busy* right now for this kind of ****?'"

Claws, covering the rear with Spots. "Nope."

Hairball, shooting. "Uh-uh."

Scythe, shooting. "I'm with them."

Flea. "**** you. At least I'm not getting cozy with the en—"

Spots. "Don't you *dare* finish that."

They kill off the second group, leaving the crabs behind them to clamber over the dead.

Scythe. "Next fox-run, take it. Let's head them off and set up on the corner."

Whiskers is the first one in the fox-run, then Hairball, then Fang. Flea is just going in after her when:

Whiskers: "****! ****! Go back!"

Hairball: "Uh, there's no going back—"

Whiskers: "****!"

The wall starts shaking. Scythe looks up at it. "Oh, ****."

48. Surrounded

Control Room. Several stacked screens of cam footage from Team Kitty: all show flailing crabs, or nothing at all, just a shimmering, writhing dark.

[*Base*] Control 1: Team Kitty, this is Control. Come in, Team Kitty.

[*Base*] Control 2 : Scythe, this is Control. Report.

[*Base*] Control 1 : Team Kitty, sitrep please. We can't see a thing here.

Control 1. "**** . . . ! Oh God! Where are they in that mess?"

[*Base*] Control 2 : Team Kitty, report please.

The Warren. The first revision crabs have caught up with the new attackers. Nothing can be seen in the corridor except the remains of the wall and the mound of crabs.

. . . closer . . .

. . . closer, squeezing between two crabs . . .

Spots. "Crap."

The entire team is packed under Spots's and Claws's second-generation shield, forming a tight hemispherical bubble around them. The crabs are plastered to the edges, trying to get to them.

Whiskers. "Wow. Now I know we're in trouble."

Hairball and Fang chuckle. Scythe grins. Even Fang snorts with a smile.

Spots, squinting as a crab claw scrapes against the shield wall a few inches above her head. "I think we can hold like this for at least ten minutes."

Scythe. "Great, we can shoot our way clear, then."

Fang. "If we can ****ing get a clear shot . . ."

Scythe. "Well, let's get our backs to one another."

Some writhing ensues.

"****, that was my kidney!"

"Didn't need it anyway."

"Get outta my lap, Hairball."

"Thought you liked me."

"Not that much."

Scythe. "****, Control's been hammering on my circuit and I didn't see it." *Changes channels.* "Control, this is Team Kitty. Sitrep is ****ed up, but we're alive. We could use back-up."

"Hey, keep your elbow out of my face!"

[*Base*] Control 1 : Team Kitty, this is Control. All we're seeing is bug parts."

Scythe. "That's because we're under them."

Pause.

Claws, sotto voce. "Bet they're going dot-dot-dot."

Flea, disgusted. "This is so ****ed up."

49. CRUSHED

Control Room.

Control 1. "**** . . . !"

[*Base*] **Control 2** : Team Kitty, can you get out from under them?

[*Base*] **Control 1** : How are you even keeping them off? *Off mic.* "****! Where are we going to find reinforcements?"

In the Warren.

Scythe, on the base channel. "We're under a shield bubble."

Claws, low. "Told you. You can just hear them gibberin'."

Flea. "I don't exactly ****ing BLAME them."

[*Base*] **Control 2** : Repeating, can you get out?

Scythe. "We'll get back to you." *Switching channels again.* "All right, everyone got a target? One, two, three, now!"

Everyone under the shield shoots several times. Crabs explode. Ichor and parts fly. Silence.

Claws. "Well, ****. Now we've just got dead crabs piled on us insteada live ones."

Spots, squinting. "Do you think the living ones will move them out of the way?"

Scythe. "I don't know. Let's see."

Two minutes later . . . nothing.

Scythe. "****."

Hairball. "Maybe we could try grenades?"

Whiskers. "How are we gonna get those ****ers through the dead bugs? Wedge them out?"

Claws. "We'll just end up blowin' up more crabs to lie dead on top of us."

Flea. "****! This is NOT how I was planning to go! Buried alive under a hundred dead crabs??"

Scythe. "More like fifty."

Flea. "****! Can't we move out from under them? Kind of scoot the shield along with us?"

Everyone looks at Spots. She shakes her head.

Spots. "It might be a force-field but it's attached to my arm, and Claws's. We've got a lot of weight on top of us. I don't know if we can move it without breaking something."

Scythe. "Even supported by your suits."

Spots. "Call it a feeling."

Claws. "She might be right. Right now we got the weight in a straight line, arm-spine-ground. We start shiftin' too much we might get shear."

Hairball. "Well, we can't go down. We got this grid under us now."

Whiskers. "And we can't go side to side."

Spots, musing. "I guess that leaves . . ."

Fang, with teeth. "Up."

[*Base*] **Control 1** : Team Kitty, this is Control. Sitrep.

Scythe. "Now we're under a shield bubble with a layer of dead crabs on top. ETA on back-up?"

[*Base*] **Control 2** : Seven to ten minutes.

Scythe. "You have anything on exterior cameras?"

[*Base*] **Control 2** : Negative, Team Kitty.

Scythe. "****. Anything could be out there, waiting for us."

Hairball. "We can't stay here, though. Ten minutes is what we had on the shield a few minutes ago."

Spots nods. "Unless we contract it. We could probably squeeze in tighter."

Flea. "****, I'm close enough to all you ****ers as it is!"

Fang. "So the choice is wait or fight."

Claws. "That's the size of it."

Fang. "The answer's obvious, then, isn't it?"

Everyone looks at Scythe, who grins. "**** yeah. We fight!"

50. Platform Games

Claws. "So how exactly are we gonna do this?"

Spots squints at one of the bodies above them. "Flea, can you hold this crab in place?"

Flea. "****, that would mean poking my ****ing hand outside this thing."

Scythe. "Shut up and do it."

Spots, to Claws. "Just keep the shield up when I take mine down. It should last as long as we need even without me helping." *She sets a timer on a grenade. When she looks up, Flea is grumbling but holding the body in place.*

Spots. "All right, here goes nothing." *She stands up, head above the shield, grabs the crab body and scrabbles on top of it, pushing through a narrow space between corpses.*

Claws. "****! Spots—"

Spots. "I'm okay. It's all dead stuff up here."

Whiskers. "****, I had no idea you could do that."

Spots wedges herself between bodies until she can stand straight—more or less. She squeezes a hand up to place the grenade in between the corpses, then wiggles back down, steps off the crab she was using as platform and drops back into the bubble.

Spots. "Okay. Twenty seconds."

Hairball, eyeing her. "How'd you think of that?"

Flea. "**** that, how'd you shimmy like that in *armor*? Jesus!"

Claws starts laughing. "You ain't seen the ****in' half of it."

Fang, ignoring them. ". . . four . . . three . . . two . . . one!"

The shield flickers and dies as crab parts go flying. Through the broken mosaic of the explosion, Team Kitty can see the rest of the living crabs.

Whiskers. "Here they come!"

138

51. Rescue

Flea. "****. We're gonna die."

Scythe. "Can that **** and do your job."

The crabs are streaming from both corridors and over the fallen wall. The team has its backs to one another, facing out. They expend their first-generation shields against the hail of alien needles.

The crabs keep coming.

Spots. "Claws! Shield power?"

Claws. "Zip."

Spots. "Rewire from something else!"

Claws. "There's nothing ****in' nonessential LEFT."

The crabs keep coming until they're climbing over their dead and into Team Kitty's faces.

Scythe. "****! Back up!"

Hairball. "Got a wall here, boss!"

Spots punches a final combination on her glove and shoves her way in front, slicing through the first three crabs with the edge of her shield.

Claws. "****! Spots!"

Spots. "Help. Me. NOW."

Claws fumbles through the power shunt and jumps after her, clearing the crabs in front. Fang recovers first and shoots past the falling pieces.

Claws. "****. ****. ****. ****." *He nearly gets punctured by a crab pincer.* "****!"

Fang. "****, stay alive, you ****er, you're the only thing keeping us up!"

Claws. "**** you!"

Scythe. "KING!"

Fang. "MINE!" *She aims past Spots and Claws.* "****, stop weaving!"

Hairball grabs the back of her suit and pulls her. "Up!"

Part 1: Contact ● M. C. A. Hogarth

Fang glances back, then jumps onto his knee and aims past the crabs Spots and Claws are killing. First shot: head explodes. Second shot: thorax explodes before the head has time to fall past it.

Scythe, catching green marks on his HUD. "Watch your shots, we've got friendlies!"

[**Company**] [**Peaches**] : Good plan, Sergeant.

[**Company**] [**Flea**] : ****, if we're not happy to see you!

Peaches and the relief cut away from the crabs from behind, Team Kitty from in front. They meet in the gore-soaked middle surrounded by mounds of crab parts.

[**Company**] [**Scythe**] : It's good to see you, ma'am.

[**Company**] [**Peaches**] : You all in one piece?

[**Company**] [**Scythe**] : Yes, though we burned through our power cells.

[**Company**] [**Peaches**] : Head on back, then. We'll mop up and take the rest of your shift.

[**Company**] [**Scythe**] : Yes, ma'am. *Switching to squad channel.* "You heard her. Let's go."

Fang. "Nothing left to do here anyway. Hey, Flea."

Flea. "What?"

Fang, grinning. "I'm waiting for your tally of headshots."

Flea. Long pause. Then: "**** you!"

———————

Armory, six hours later. Peaches is unlocking her helmet when Gunny shows up. She is exhausted, sweat streaking her hair to her temples.

"Ma'am?"

She looks over. "What's up, Gunny?"

"Priority message."

She nods and steps outside the door, leaving the rest of the relief team to unsuit. Once there: "Let's have it, then."

He hands her a tablet, which she scans . . . and then closes her eyes.

Spots the Space Marine: Defense of the Fiddler

"They're coming. . . ." *She looks at him.* "My God, Gunny, we *got them*. We got the company from Depot A! We're going to be reinforced! We might live through this assignment after all!"

Gunny. "From your lips to God's ear, ma'am."

PART 2:

IN DEEP

52. Seniority

Lieutenant's office. Peaches is sitting at the desk, the Gunny's across from her.

Peaches. "I have a bad feeling about this."

Gunny. "Ma'am?"

Peaches. "Every naval depot has a company assigned to it to keep a permanent staff here, I get that. But we've never had a full company here that I know of. I got here to two platoons, pretty battered."

Gunny. "That's correct, ma'am."

Peaches. "Have a look at this. Am I reading it wrong? Naval Depot A did have a full company."

Gunny, scanning the list. "*Had* a full company."

Peaches, wincing. "Yeah, they're down almost their entire complement. Including . . ."

Gunny. "****. Their captain."

Peaches. "How are we going to do this? They've got what looks 22 people, plus 6 casualties they're shipping in. We've got 54, not counting our casualties and the staff. Should we fill out the holes in our squads or keep the groups separate?"

Gunny. "That might be up to the new lieutenant, ma'am . . ." *He hands her back the message board.* "He's got seniority."

Peaches. ". . ."

Peaches. "****."

Long pause.

Peaches. "Think they'll ship us a new captain?"

Gunny. "Maybe. Or they might give one of you a field promotion."

Peaches. "And I'm betting it's not going to be me."

Gunny says nothing.

Peaches. "****. Well, they're arriving in a week. Let's put together a couple of plans, one for integration and one for keeping the groups separate. Who knows, maybe the new guy will be easy to work with."

Spots the Space Marine: Defense of the Fiddler

—

Barracks. Spots is just getting back from visiting Fang2 in Sickbay when Scythe stops her.

Scythe. "Going to get some sleep?"

Spots. "Hoping to soon."

Scythe. "That new shield . . ."

Spots pauses, lifts a brow.

Scythe. "Can you do a demo for me?"

53. DISTANCE-NO DISTANCE

Practice Room. Spots and Scythe are in physical training uniforms; the former has a test glove on with the second-generation shield generator. Spots is showing Scythe the variable sizing, the types of cuts and the sliding function against some foam dummies.

Scythe. "And this is all based on gesture?"

Spots. "Yes. It takes some practice."

Scythe. "I'm a little concerned about power usage. It seemed to give out pretty quickly out there."

Spots. "I'm not sure holding a ceiling between us and that many dead crabs was how it was intended to be used . . . ! But it's a prototype, I'm guessing this is the kind of thing Samuel-Colt needs data on. The next revision should be better."

Scythe is silent, studying the foam targets. Then: "It makes a clean cut. I wonder how sharp it is."

Spots, sitting down. "The edge of the shield? As sharp as a molecule? An atom? Who knows. It's magic as far as I'm concerned."

He glances at her sharply. "You sound pretty attached to it."

Spots. "I love it." *At his raised brow:* "I do. Guns are . . . kind of impersonal."

Scythe. "Are you sure you're a Marine, Guitart?"

Spots. "I know, I know. I'm supposed to love my rifle next to God. But you shoot some-one so they don't get close. It's about keeping a distance. This is . . . less about distance and more about being able to punch something in the eyes."

Scythe laughs. "I never would have figured you for so violent."

Spots, uncomfortable. "Not violent. Just . . . if I'm going to kill something—someone—I want to have made that connection."

Scythe. "We don't kill someones, Guitart. The crabs aren't people."

Spots. "Are you sure you're a Marine, Scythe? We haven't always been alien-killers."

Scythe. "Point." *He looks at the targets again.*

Spots. "I can get Samuel-Colt to issue you one."

Scythe. "Yeah . . . yeah." *He straightens.* "If two of you are going to be getting into trouble

Spots the Space Marine: Defense of the Fiddler

with it, I should at least know my way around the thing."

Spots. "You'll be slicing the heads off practice dummies in no time. Faster than I learned, I bet."

Scythe. "You think?"

Spots. "You do a pretty good job with your sword." *She smiles a little.* "No distance, right?"

He glances at her. Chuckles. "No distance."

"So if you like swords, why did you choose 'Scythe' for a call-sign?"

He grins, wry. "There's a section in the Book of Five Rings about weapons on the battlefield. It discusses spears and scythes, and notes that the scythe is good only for the battlefield, being not suitable for taking prisoners. But that it is inferior to the spear because it is a defensive weapon only."

A long pause. Then Spots leans back and laughs.

Spots. "So all this time I've been preaching to the choir."

Scythe grins. But: "There's a time and place for everything, Guitart. Distance and no distance. That's part of being effective in combat, not just here—" *Taps his fist.* "—but here." *Taps his heart and then his forehead.*

Spots. "I'll think about that. And I'll get Samuel-Colt to make you a new glove."

Scythe. "Thanks. And for the demo. Go get some sleep."

Spots. "You too, boss."

Scythe, smiling. "Yes, mom."

Spots, on her way out. "Oh boy. No, you're not allowed to say that . . . if I'm old enough to be your mom I'll cry myself to sleep!"

54. The New Guys

"The Birdcage," officially the Landing Bay, a large hangar. Men and women are marching out of a shuttle; behind them come an additional line of six stretchers. More people are unloading what remains of the ordnance from Depot A from the back of the shuttle.

Peaches is standing rigidly erect. She doesn't wait long: a young man approaches her, wearing a lieutenant's service uniform. Ordinarily he'd be handsome, with blue eyes, a fading tan and a Gallic nose. However, impeccable grooming does nothing for the circles under his eyes and the hard and distant look his gaze defaults to. She salutes him; he returns it.

"Lieutenant Savannah Bonnet."

"Paul Avril." *He offers her his hand. She shakes it.* "Good to meet you, Lieutenant Bonnet."

"Savannah, please."

"Then call me Paul." *He smiles.* "Nice of you to offer your hospitality. I hear you have a pest problem."

"Like a bad motel, I'm afraid."

He grasps her shoulder, a gesture both natural and genuine. "I read all about it on the way here. Tell me how we can help."

Peaches, surprised. "Well, we could use some warm bodies to spread out the patrol schedule. . . ."

"You have some suggestions?"

Peaches. "Ah . . . yeah, I drew up a few tables based on your ready reports."

He grins. "Another go-getter! Great, we'll take care of that the moment you show me my office. Get your people some rest."

Peaches, surprised. "That would be great. This way, I'll introduce you to the staff."

———

Barracks. Focus on a clock: it's 0730. Spots slowly opens her eyes, sees the numbers and sits up, throwing off her blankets.

Claws. "Whoa, lady. Slow down there."

Spots jumps; he's sitting on the edge of her bunk. "Claws! We're two hours late!"

Claws. "Not anymore, we ain't." *He grins.* "Some relief shipped in last night. Poor bastards barely touched down and they're already hoofin' it through the Warren. While *we* get to sleep in. We're gonna be clockin' an extra four hours, all to ourselves, *every* God-blessed day."

Spots slowly lies back. "Wow. Four hours."

"Sounds like Heaven, don't it?"

Spots. "Yes! Who are the new people?"

Claws. "Members of Alpha Company. They were on asteroid duty."

"An entire company!"

Claws. "Well . . . sorta."

She eyes him.

"They came with a lieutenant. All twenty-ish of 'em." *At Spots's look, he nods.* "Yeah. Scuttlebutt says they lost a good sixty people in their last engagement."

Spots, whispering. "Mother of God." *Then, frowning again.* "If they came with a lieutenant . . . who's in charge?"

Claws. "Damned if I know."

149

———

Sickbay. Fang2, who is just ambulatory, stops at one of the newly occupied beds which now holds a man in his early thirties with a recruitment-poster look, complete with lantern jaw.

Fang2. "Wow, someone I haven't fleeced yet! Who the hell are you?"

Man, eyeing him. "Hawk Abrams, Sergeant, Alpha Company. Who the hell are you?"

"I'm Low-*** Private Fang2 Chao, Team Kitty." *He grins.* "Is that Abrams like the tank?"

"Is that Fang2 like you're missing something? That why you're here?"

Fang2 laughs. "You got me. Fang-Prime stole my balls, she wanted some extras. Want to play some cards? I'm ****ing bored."

Hawk. "Sure."

Fang2 hobbles back to his bed and comes back with a pack of cards. He shuffles. "So, Alpha Company . . . when you'd get in?"

Hawk. "Last night. We're your relief."

Fang2, eyeing the cast on his leg. "Some ****ing relief. Where were you before?"

"Naval Depot A, the asteroid."

Fang2, dealing. "No kidding! Zero-g, huh? What's that like?"

Hawk. "Interesting the first few times. After that, same ****, different life support."

Fang2. "Ain't that always the way."

Hawk. "Yep. So what's your officer like?"

Fang2. "Bonny Peaches? ****ing hot for a white girl."

Hawk eyes him over his cards. "Other than her shagability."

Fang2. "Oh, she's cool. Works the hell out of us, but she got the Seabees to cook for us. Man, pork chops." *He licks his lips.* "Was like Thanksgiving. *In space.*"

Hawk. "Hot food sounds great."

Fang2 grins. "Yeah, it was all that and more. There was even a brownie for the ladies. What about your LT?"

Hawk, suddenly intense. "I'd follow him into Hell."

Fang2, uneasy. "Uh . . . huh. So . . . um, how come 'Hawk'? I thought winged call-signs were reserved for the aviation units."

Hawk. "Zero-g's sort of like flying."

Fang2, a little wistful. "I bet. Your whole team's birds, then?"

Hawk. "Yep. Team PYEO."

Fang2. "Pee-yoh? What the hell is that?"

Hawk. "PYEO. Stands for "Peck Your Eyes Out." "

Fang2. "Man, that's some ****-up ****."

Hawk. "It was better than the alternative."

Fang2. "What was that?

Hawk. "PYFEO. "Peck Your ****ing Eyes Out." Try saying that. Pee-fyoh? PIE-fee-oh?"

As Fang2 laughs, a nurse shows up behind him, shakes his head. "Private Chao—"

Spots the Space Marine: Defense of the Fiddler

Fang2 with a theatrical sigh. "I know, I'm supposed to be in bed—"

Nurse. "Actually, no. You're reaching the point where you really need to be doing regular exercise again. How do you feel about the gym?"

Fang2. "Aww, ****, I just sat down."

55. 'Cause Moms Are Always Planning Ahead

Claws. "So what are we up to again?"

Spots. "You're playing Mother's Escort."

"Right, the bug."

"The Violinist, yes."

Claws. "So what we liaisonin' about?"

Spots, eyeing him. "Is that even a word?"

Claws. "Is now."

Spots shakes her head. The security guards at the Door recognize the two of them and wave them through.

Claws. "Hey . . . wait a minute."

Spots glances at him.

Claws scowls. "You know liaison ain't a verb. You did that to get out of answering the question, didn't you."

Spots grins at him and chimes for admittance to the lab. The door opens for Will Kenyan, who peers at them. "What are you back for? Did something break? We're busy."

Spots, politely obstinate. "We'd like to speak to Samuel-Colt, please."

"Fine, go on. I'm not his secretary."

Samuel-Colt is standing at one of the 3-D imaging stations, frowning at what looks like a circuit diagram. He looks up at the arrival of the two Marines and plays a sprightly welcome. "The Mother-Soldier, and her escort! What brings you here?"

Claws eyes her.

Spots. "A couple of things. First, could you please fit Scythe's armor with a new shield? He's asked."

Samuel-Colt, ripple of sound, rising. "Of course. We would welcome additional test data. And the second of the couple?"

Spots. "Could you make us some test versions of the shields?" *She lifts her hands.* "Not

Spots the Space Marine: Defense of the Fiddler

test-like-prototype, test-like-blunt-edges. Something we could practice with without slicing one another in half."

Samuel-Colt, quick note, spiccato. "Ah . . . as when you sparred with Scythe. Yes, an excellent idea."

Spots. "And . . . could you tint them permanently? I think that would help, practicing with them visible."

Samuel-Colt, a slow sustained note, contemplative. "We forget you cannot hear as well as we do. Yes, of course."

Claws, curious despite himself. "You can hear the shields?"

Samuel-Colt. "I am not sure I'd call it hearing as much as feeling. But yes. We can tell where they end and where they begin without sight."

Claws. "**--er, crap, that sounds handy."

Samuel-Colt, spreading his upper hands. "May we do anything else for you? Elsewise we will return to our work." *He indicates the station with a lower claw-hand and bows an agitated sound.* "We are not happy with the power consumption curves."

Claws. "Yeah, neither are we. I've already done more power-sharin' to keep those things active than I've done since Basic."

153

Samuel-Colt suddenly looks at him, intent, vestigial arms silent. "Excuse us? Say again?"

Claws mimes plugging a cord in. "You know . . . jackin' in? Because someone," *eyeing Spots,* "keeps drainin' herself dry usin' the new-fangled shields?"

Samuel-Colt stares at him.

Claws. "Uh . . . Sam . . . you're kinda creepin' me out there. Why are you givin' me the gimlet glare?"

Samuel-Colt, drawing out a long note, rising. "If in a squad there are nine individuals, each using power at different rates . . . why can't the power levels be equalized between them all? Draw more from someone who is not using it as much?"

Claws, frowning. "You want to make it easier to power-share? Lasers, maybe?"

Samuel-Colt. "It is a possibility."

Claws. "That's only a stopgap, though. The real issue is that the damn shield eats too much juice. If you fix that, you won't need the power-share. Or, I guess, power-load balancing is what you're really talkin' about."

Spots. "That's kind of a nice idea." *They both glance at her.* "You know, the team hangs together or the team falls apart."

Claws. "Dunno . . . it would mean that if someone's down on power, everyone is. So instead of just one person being down, everyone's down. At the same time."

Spots. "But everyone would be up much longer."

Claws. "Hell. That's a hard equation. I kinda don't like the idea and I can't tell if it's because I'm being an untrustin' sort or not."

Samuel-Colt, rising arpeggio, questioning. "Perhaps you might take the matter to your lieutenant."

Claws. "Yeah, suppose we should."

Samuel-Colt, a variation of the sprightly welcoming melody. "We will have Scythe's shield ready for him tomorrow, and your test-as-blunt-edges shields as soon as possible."

Spots bows. Claws watches her, a touch uncomfortable. But the alien bows back, hands clasped in front of his chest. Soon they are out the door again.

Claws. "So, you got some trainin' program planned for us I don't know about?"

Spots. "No . . . you've got some training program planned for us that I don't know about. I'm just requisitioning our hardware for you."

Claws. "Wait, what?"

Spots. "Come on, Claws. You talked me through all my work-outs. Well, now we have this new tech and we hardly know what to do with it. Shouldn't we be working out some ideas in the gym before we improvise them in the Warren?"

Claws. "Yeeeahhhhh . . . guess I can't argue with that."

Noting the sudden distant look, Spots says nothing. But she smiles all the way back to the barracks.

56. FAVORITES

The Warren. Team Kitty is patrolling, mostly without incident.

Hairball. "Favorite home-cooking, go."

Whiskers. "Damn, I can only pick one thing?"

Fang. "Stick with the pattern."

Whiskers. "Mph. Shrimp. Deep-fried."

Fang. "Your mom deep-fried ****?"

Whiskers. "Hell yeah."

Fang. "****, my mom wouldn't touch anything fried with a ten-foot pole."

Scythe. "So what did she make you?"

Fang. "Toast. Burnt."

Claws. "****, no wonder you grew up mean."

Everyone laughs, including Fang.

Hairball. "Mine's potato pancakes with applesauce."

Claws. "Never had that but it sounds deadly."

Hairball. "It's like the best kind of white **** you're not supposed to eat in vegetables combined with the best kind of white **** you're not supposed to eat in grains, covered in sugar. Or sour cream. It's ****ing awesome. What about you?"

Claws. "I'm a breakfast man. Hash browns, eggs and ham steak all the way. Scythe? Spots?"

Scythe. "Macaroni and cheese."

Whiskers. "You're ****ing us."

Scythe. "Nope. My grandmother's the only Iraqi in the family. Rest of us are crackers. She makes it with bacon."

Hairball. "****, everything's better with bacon. Macaroni and bacon!"

Fang. "Hey, aren't Muslims supposed to not eat pigs?"

Scythe. "I didn't say she ate it. Just that she made it, for the rest of us."

Whiskers. "That's love, right there."

Scythe. "Yep. Spots?"

Whiskers. "Heh, you don't count, right? You're a mom."

Scythe. "That just means she gets two answers, what she likes and what she cooks for her kids."

Spots. "French toast. And guava pastries."

Hairball. "What's a guava?"

Spots laughs. "It's a tropical fruit and it's delicious. All right, my turn. Awesome teachers you had growing up, go."

"Good one!"

Several hours later Team Kitty finishes their shift, gets back to the Armory and strips down, still talking. They disperse to their showers. Spots watches Fang enter before her, then follows. Once inside under the water:

"Hey, Fang?"

"Yeah?"

"Did your mom make you anything you liked? You didn't really get a chance to answer."

Fang pauses in scrubbing her head, then resumes. "She didn't like to cook."

Spots nods. "Ah."

After a moment: "Dad made most of our meals. He was much better at it anyway. Kind of fancy. Other people had peanut butter sandwiches at school and I'd have . . . chicken and almond with mango avocado salsa."

Spots. "Wow!" *And then rueful.* "I can't imagine my kids eating that."

Fang. "You got used to it." *She sluices off and reaches for a towel. As she's leaving:* "But Mom used to let me drink her coffee. Sometimes."

Spots. "Really? How'd she take it?"

Fang. "Really bitter. And sweet. And dark. I'd sit on her lap and it was like the strongest candy you ever had. My eyes used to water."

Spots the Space Marine: Defense of the Fiddler

Spots says, quiet, "I bet that's one of her favorite memories too."

Fang glances at her, then looks away quickly and leaves.

57. Boss

"You have a Fiddler on station?"

Peaches and the new lieutenant, Avril, are in the base office.

"Yeah. That a problem?"

Avril glances at her. "No, I'm just . . . surprised, I guess. What's he doing here?"

Peaches. "Observing. He's one of the original weapons designers from the first meet, apparently he gets shipped around from place to place to see how the tech's working for us."

Avril. "So . . . what, he goes out with the squads?"

Peaches. "No, mostly he does what we're doing, looking at cam footage and checking suit statistics and forensic data from dead crabs. Then he tweaks stuff based on that."

Avril. "You mean we're prototyping new weapons designs? In the field?"

Peaches. "Sort of."

Avril. "****."

Peaches. "It's mostly tweaks though."

Avril. "Mostly?"

Peaches. "Well, yeah. He's done some more experimental modification by request."

Avril, frowning at her. "You let your people mod their suits so they're different from one another?"

Peaches. "I let our Violinist consultant develop new weapons tech with my company's cooperation."

Avril is silent. Then: "I should meet him."

"I'll make arrangements."

———

Barracks. Claws is looking at the new test shield, which is sitting on his night-stand next to the reed and ink well Samuel-Colt left with him. When Spots enters in her PT uniform: "Ah, you're ready?"

Spots the Space Marine: Defense of the Fiddler

Spots. "Sure, let's head out."

Claws. "Actually, I was thinkin' we'd stay here."

Spots. "Here? In the barracks?" *She looks around.* "There's not exactly much room here to practice anything."

Claws. "Bingo." *At her glance:* "The Warren ain't too big and the fox-runs are even littler. We need to make moves that work in confined spaces."

Spots. "Huh. There are some open chambers, though."

Claws. "And we'll do some practicin' in bigger rooms later. But let's start here in friendly territory."

Spots eyes him. "Is that the other part of it? Friendly territory?"

Claws. "Hell yeah. I don't want to stop to explain what we're doin' to every Tom, Dick and Harry who's never seen our new fancy Mcfancypants shields. I'd prefer to use our trainin' time to train, not chat with the rubberneckers."

Spots. "All right, then . . . you're the boss. Lead on."

58. NO ONE EXPECTS

Two days later. Base Office. Peaches and Gunny are both at desks, going through paperwork.

"I know I shouldn't be asking . . . but what do you think of him, Gunny?"

"The new lieutenant?"

"Yeah."

"That would be talking, ma'am."

Peaches narrows her eyes, taps a finger on her desk. Then: "Gunny?"

"Yes, ma'am?"

"How would you characterize the condition and morale of our relief forces?"

Unseen by Peaches, Gunny grins. His voice shows no sign of it, though. "Despite their recent defeat, they're holding together well. Their training sessions and patrols show consistency and discipline."

"So even though they should be slacking off or coming apart, they're not."

"Yes, ma'am."

"That's . . . a little weird, isn't it? Have the medical personnel said anything? The chaplain? Anyone using the counseling service?"

"I haven't seen any reports of them utilizing any of those services, ma'am."

Peaches frowns, thinking. "Any advice?"

"Ma'am?"

Peaches. "They just got decimated, Gunny, and I think I'm only off by a few people when I use that word to describe what happened to them. Their previous base didn't have any staffers offering support services like this. At least one or two of them should be seeking counseling. Right?"

"We're talking about only twenty people or so, ma'am. That's a pretty small sample size. Maybe they're all emotional hardcases."

Peaches. "Maybe. You sure you don't want to tell me anything about the new LT?"

Gunny. "That would be talking. If I may, ma'am . . . why are you asking?"

Peaches. "Because I'm about to take him to see the Fiddler and I want to know if I'm about to walk into an emotional IED."

Gunny hesitates. Then says: "I haven't heard anything, ma'am."

Peaches sighs. "Yeah, I didn't think so. No one expects the land mine. It's like the Spanish Inquisition that way." *She sleeps her computer and rises.* "Wish me luck."

He waits until she's gone to laugh.

59. I See What You Did There

Avril and Peaches are walking down the corridor to the Door.

Avril. "So why can't he just come to our office?"

Peaches, glancing at him askance. "I can't exactly order him over like an errant private. He's not in our chain of command."

Avril. "No, but we are fighting his war for him."

Peaches. "..."

Avril. "Oh come on, Savannah. You can't tell me you haven't thought it."

Their arrival at the Door saves Peaches from having to respond as the guards check their credentials. Shortly afterwards they arrive at the lab, where they are admitted by a taciturn Will Kenyan.

Peaches. "Lieutenant, this is Will Kenyan, Samuel-Colt's assistant engineer. Mister Kenyan, this is Lieutenant Paul Avril."

Kenyan nods to them. "He's in the back."

Peaches leads Avril further into the lab, where they find Samuel-Colt standing at a full-size hologram of what looks like circuitry. The alien steps away from it and bows to her. "Apologies, Lieutenant-Savannah-Bonnet. Time slipped away from us while we were working. We did not realize it was time for your meeting."

Peaches. "It's not necessary to apologize. I just wanted to introduce you to Lieutenant Paul Avril."

Avril. "Samuel . . . Colt? Is it?"

Samuel-Colt, with a slow sustained note: "That is correct. Lieutenant-Savannah-Bonnet, this is your new escort?"

Avril. "Her new what?"

Peaches, embarrassed. "Um, no, no. Actually, Paul is technically my senior."

Samuel-Colt, a staccato arpeggio, falling. "Ah. You came without your escort, we presumed it was because this one was filling that role now."

Avril. "Uh . . . Savannah?"

Samuel-Colt, studying him. "You are replacing Lieutenant-Savannah-Bonnet?"

Spots the Space Marine: Defense of the Fiddler

Avril. " 'Replacing' is a strong word."

Samuel-Colt, no bowing. "We would tend to agree."

Avril. "It's more like . . . my seniority gives me command of the existing company here."

Samuel-Colt. "We see."

Avril. "So, I just wanted to . . . ah . . . introduce myself." *He offers his hand.* "In case you have any . . . requests. Or . . . needs. I understand you're working with some of Bravo Company on weapons development?"

Samuel-Colt, politely ignoring the hand. "That is correct."

Avril, folding his arms behind his back again. "I hope you'll feel comfortable keeping me apprised of your plans?"

Samuel-Colt. "We share that hope, Lieutenant-Paul-Avril."

Avril. "Good, great. I'm glad to hear that."

Samuel-Colt, with a suspiciously amused-sounding trill. "We are the first Violinist you have met, Lieutenant-Paul-Avril?"

Avril. "What gave me away? The attempted handshake?"

Samuel-Colt. "Ah, no, we understand the custom. You are staring everywhere but my face."

Avril. "You have . . . interesting eyes."

Samuel-Colt. "So we have been told."

Avril. "I haven't offended, I hope?"

Samuel-Colt. "Not at all. But if you will pardon us? This—" *indicating the display,* "— needs our attention."

Avril. "Of course, please. Carry on. Nice to meet you, Samuel."

"Likewise, Lieutenant-Paul-Avril." *To Peaches,* "Lieutenant-Savannah-Bonnet."

She nods to him and leads Avril back out of the lab; Kenyan doesn't lift his head when they pass. Outside, Avril blows out a breath. "****. Did I botch that?"

Peaches. "I have no idea."

Avril. "I hope not. What was that all about, the escort business?"

Peaches. "Um . . . well, the Fiddlers, they have female leadership, and women are expected to be surrounded by male guards. It's considered a breach of courtesy to deal with a woman who isn't escorted, it's like . . . I don't know. Noticing someone's pants are down."

Avril. "Strange, never heard anything like that about them. I mean, I knew they had kings and queens, but not that there was . . . protocol, I guess, that we had to navigate when dealing with them."

Peaches. "Like I said, it's not like they're in our chain of command. We aren't supposed to make problems for the diplomats. Fortunately Samuel-Colt seems pretty easy-going."

"For an alien."

Peaches. "For an alien."

Avril. "Anyway, thanks for doing that, Savannah. And . . . for being so professional about the seniority issue. I know a lot of people who would have taken it personally."

Peaches. "Our people've got enough of a morale problem without their officers sniping at one another."

Avril. "Still. I wanted you to know I appreciate it."

Peaches smiles. "No problem."

60. Getting to Know You

Several days later, Barracks. Spots and Claws are sitting on their bunks, wearing physical training uniforms and their practice gloves.

Spots. "So, I'm not prepared to say this isn't working . . ."

Claws. "But it's sure as hell limitin', yeah, I know, I know."

Spots. "Can I make a suggestion, O sensei?"

Claws, eyeing her. "Yeah, mom, spit it out."

Spots. "If you don't want to use the gym still, there is another place."

Claws. "And that would be . . . what, outside the compound?"

Spots. "The test facility."

Claws. ". . ."

Spots. "It's big. It's empty all the time. And we'd have ready access to Samuel-Colt if something strange happens." *Claws is staring at nothing while listening to this.* "If you want, I could ask him if we could use it for practice?"

Claws, rousing himself. "No. No, I'll ask him. Peer to peer. Sorta."

Spots glances at the unused bottle on his table. Then looks at him and nods. "All right. Tell me if he says yes."

"Will do."

———

Claws heads through the Door, looking for the alien, and is directed to his room. He hesitates, then hits the door-announce.

"Samuel-Colt? It's me. Uh, the Mother's Escort."

"Enter."

Claws steps inside, finding Samuel-Colt sitting on the low-platform bed, upper hands resting on his knees and lower claw-hands spread.

"****, am I interruptin' your . . . uh, meditation or somethin'?"

Samuel-Colt, low, amused note. "No, it's fine. Where is the mother?"

Claws. "I left her home when she suggested she do something for me to make things easier on me."

Samuel-Colt, another amused ripple. "The maternal tendency to over-nurture is cross-species, then."

Claws. "Say that again."

Samuel-Colt. "So then. What was she attempting to make easier for you?"

Claws. "We're lookin' for a place to practice with these test gloves you made us, and she suggested your facility. So I came to ask if we could use it."

Samuel-Colt. "Of course. Make free."

Claws. "That's it? Just like that?"

Samuel-Colt, long quizzical tone. "Should I make it more difficult?"

Claws. "Well, I haven't exactly been the nicest to you. You know, what with the not paintin' your arm thing."

Samuel-Colt. "And why have you not done this thing, Claws-Mother's-Escort?"

Claws, uncomfortable. "The arm-paintin'? ****, I don't even know what I'd put on you. We don't have a ****in' relationship yet for me to be makin' ink on your arm. Maybe if I was some pro tattoo artist or somethin', but this isn't about you payin' for a service, it's supposed to be personal, yeah?"

Samuel-Colt, studying him. "Yes."

Claws. "Well . . . there you go. I'm admittin' it. I don't feel it."

Samuel-Colt. "And that is precisely why I am content."

Claws. "Come again?"

Samuel-Colt. "I would not want a thoughtless souvenir. If you paint my arm, it will have meaning to us both, worth the chitin." *His expression remains fixed, but he suddenly bows a leaping, sprightly arpeggio.* "To use a better metaphor, we will just say I am not into casual sex."

Claws. "****!" *And then he starts laughing, embarrassed.* "Um, ****, don't say stuff like that around Spots, she'll fluster somethin' awful."

Samuel-Colt, satisfied. "I thought you would understand."

Claws. "I ain't gonna have sex with you, Sam. Just so you know. Ever."

Spots the Space Marine: Defense of the Fiddler

Samuel-Colt. "I had no doubt, Claws. The testing facility is yours."

Claws bows. "Thanks."

Samuel-Colt, amused note. "Don't mention it."

61. ALIEN PORN, ALIEN HUMOR

*Claws stops a few steps away in the hall . . . then mutters ****! under his breath and heads straight back into the Fiddler's Room. As Samuel-Colt looks up, surprised:*

Claws. "What the **** do you know about sex?"

Samuel-Colt. "I presume you mean the human kind?"

Claws. "**** yes, the human kind!" *He points.* "I think you've creeped me the hell out with that comment about casual sex."

Samuel-Colt's vestigial limbs tremble, but he suppresses their bowing. "It is hard not to be exposed to human sex, Mother's-Escort. It permeates every part of your society. Even your invective."

Claws pauses. Then bulls ahead. "Yeah, but seeing it don't necessarily mean gettin' it. You're an alien. Hell, do you even *have* sex?"

Samuel-Colt. "You do observe that there are more Violinists from generation to generation?"

Claws pauses again, eyes the shaking vestigial limbs. Then exclaims, "****! You're laughin' at me."

Samuel-Colt. "Now, now. You were not supposed to notice, since I was trying to be polite about not doing it out loud."

Claws smirks. "Yeah, yeah, okay. Sorry. But still. Do you even know what casual sex is?"

Samuel-Colt rises and goes to a small refrigerator next to a desk. He returns and hands Claws a bottle. "We have some understanding of the notion. Intellectual, admittedly."

Claws. "Is this *booze*?"

Samuel-Colt. "You seem to need it."

Claws. "Hell, I don't want to drink alone. Do you drink?"

Samuel-Colt. "I can, but my blood volume is much lower for my size than it would be in a human. Drinking is more toxic than pleasurable. We can however have a blackvein incense? That would be the Violinist equivalent of . . . ah . . . getting buzzed."

Claws, eyeing him. "You know a lot of slang."

Samuel-Colt. "We have been living among and designing weapons for human soldiers for generations."

Spots the Space Marine: Defense of the Fiddler

"How come you don't use it around anyone else?"

Samuel-Colt. "We do. But not the Mother, nor Lieutenant-Savannah-Bonnet. Females, yes? It's uncomfortable for us to be informal around females."

Claws. "****. We're more alike than I thought. Yeah, light your incense."

Samuel-Colt brings out a small cone and sets it on a clean burner. The resulting smoke is thin and clear and smells piquant; he waves it toward his face with one upper hand, then sits back down across from Claws. "The comment was literal. If I am lucky, I won't have sex at all before I die."

Claws stares at him. "You'll forgive me if I say that sounds bass-ackwards. *Never*? Have sex?"

Samuel-Colt. "No. Reproduction is . . . complicated."

Claws. "Tell me about it."

Samuel-Colt. "Do you have a woman of your own?"

Claws. "Uh . . . no. Not right now." *He pauses to drink.* "Didn't seem like a good idea, what with me deployin' out to the middle of ****in' nowhere for five years. You? Do you get married? Find some Mother or somethin' to settle down with? And then . . . I guess, never have sex with? ****, that's messed up."

Samuel-Colt. "It doesn't work that way, no. Fertilization of a Mother's eggs requires the death of the male in question."

Claws. "****! So you only get to have sex once?"

Samuel-Colt. "If we do, yes. And then the Mother eats your body."

Claws. "****, there's a lot of eatin' each other's brains and guts and bodies goin' on in your society, Sam."

Samuel-Colt, with a somewhat grimly-amused minor arpeggio: "Am I creeping you out properly now?"

Claws. "Keep goin'."

Samuel-Colt. "The problem being, when a Mother consumes a male, she gives his personality and memories to the eggs. Which would raise up a generation of clones. It stifles evolution, both individually and as a species. So we have developed a special set of males—blanks—without personalities or higher-functioning minds. They fertilize the eggs, the Mothers consume them and the babies are therefore born with unprinted minds."

Claws, staring. "That is . . . spectacularly messed up. Wow." *Then, shaking himself.* "But wait, didn't you say at some point . . . you're going to get eaten by someone? To pass on your memories?"

Samuel-Colt. "That is correct. When I am old, I will return to the homeworld where I will retire to a maturation chamber with an egg. In the two weeks it takes for it to grow to its adult form, it will consume my body and finally my brain, completing its adolescence."

Claws. ". . ."

Claws. "So for two weeks you lie there while a ravenous mindless kid eats your body from the limbs in?"

Samuel-Colt. "And then I will die, and become a father thereby. And be reborn, of sorts."

Claws, drawing the word out: "**********." *Gathering himself.* "****, that's hardcore. ****! I don't think I could sit still for that."

Samuel-Colt. "I don't know if I will be able to either. My memories indicate that some of us have taken it better than others." *Another of those minor arpeggios, falling.* "They keep the doors locked, just in case."

Claws, over his bottle. "So lemme get this straight. If you have sex, even once, you'll die when your sex partner eats you. And if you don't have sex, eventually you'll get eaten by someone else's kid."

Samuel-Colt. "If I am deemed worthy of being preserved."

Claws. "****! Do you people ever have sex for fun? There's got to be some insect version of non-procreative sex. Or hell, alien condoms!"

Samuel-Colt. "We admit, Claws, it is not something that would occur to us to do for fun. The adrenaline rush one feels when narrowly avoiding death is very nice, but one would hardly build a culture around throwing oneself off buildings or into weapons' fire just to reproduce the feeling."

Claws. "So what do you do for fun? Besides go to concerts."

Samuel-Colt's laugh is a ripple of music. "That topic we could fill a year with. But at least one thing we have in common . . ."

Claws. "Oh?"

Samuel-Colt. "I will send you a few pictures to your terminal. You can tell your friends you are looking at alien porn."

Claws. "This oughtta be good." *He gets up.* "Thanks for the bottle."

Spots the Space Marine: Defense of the Fiddler

Samuel-Colt. "Keep it."

Claws caps it and tosses it back to him. "Naw. Scythe catches me with this stuff he'll tan my hide. You keep it. I'll be back for it. We'll discuss what I think of your email."

Samuel-Colt. "It's a deal." *As Claws turns away:* "Mother's-Escort?"

"Yeah?"

"Just to make clear: We make our reports on our weapons research to the Mother."

Claws looks over his shoulder and frowns. "Eh?"

Samuel-Colt, fiddling silent. "To the Mother. What she chooses to do with those reports is her business."

Claws. "That's awful exactin' of you, Sam. Somethin' goin' on I should know about?"

Samuel-Colt. "Just making the chain of command clear. Lest we inadvertently give offense to someone."

Claws, eyes narrowing. "This 'bout the new LT?" *When the alien doesn't respond.* "What's wrong with him?"

Samuel-Colt. "He won't meet my eyes."

Claws. "Well, you've got damn-strange ones, Sam, what with the color-changin' and the size and the facets and whatnot."

Samuel-Colt. "Yet you look at them. Even on the first day in the Armory, you looked at them."

Claws. "Well, yeah . . . where else am I gonna look?"

Samuel-Colt, spreading his hands. "Exactly."

Claws. "All right, all right. I can't say I don't understand. But you are an alien, you know? It's kinda natural for humans not to be comfortable around aliens."

Samuel-Colt. "Maybe so. But that's a long discussion, perhaps for another day." *At Claws's look:* "You humans and the Other."

Claws. "****. Yes, that's definitely for another day. But . . . yeah. Your reports go to Spots. And Spots's opinions go through me to officer country. 'Cause I love Spots but hell if she's not a little too by-the-book sometimes. She'd tell them everythin', and then how would they get anythin' done?"

Samuel-Colt's bounced note sounds like a snort. "Truly some things are the same."

"Just enough to make the things that ain't feel like they come outta left field. Anyway. Night, Sam. We'll be back to use your test facility tomorrow."

"Good night, Claws."

Back at the Barracks, Claws finds Spots napping. He glances at her, then sits at his terminal. Hesitates . . . then checks it for mail and opens the files he finds from the Violinist. And then he starts laughing.

"Well, I'll be damned. The ****in' bugs *surf . . . !*"

62. NEW DIGS

The Warren. Team Kitty is on patrol.

Fang. "This has been like a ****ing vacation lately."

Claws. "Complain, complain."

Whiskers. "You got to practice your headshots a couple times last corridor over."

Fang. "I don't need practice making shots that ****ing easy."

Hairball. "It is weird. The new guys get here and the crabs hole up."

Whiskers. "Or maybe we killed them all?"

Fang. "You never finish killing the ****ing crabs."

Whiskers. "Still wish there was more for the newbies to do. Makes us look like ****ing ****ies, having them get here to relieve us from ****ing nothing."

Spots. "Does it really bother you that much?"

Whiskers, glancing her way. "**** yes. You seen them in the gym? They're ****ing hardcore."

Fang. "I like them. They're serious about ****."

Whiskers. "You would like them. But like you said before, we're no Dragon Team."

Claws. "Maybe. But this ain't no summer blockbuster either. They think they can go Rambo on **—crap here, they're gonna learn different real quick."

Scythe. "I'm sure there'll be enough work for all of us eventually." *At the sudden silence on the com line:* "Like Fang says. You never finish killing the ****ing crabs."

A few moments later:

Whiskers. ". . ."

Whiskers. "Did you say . . . crap just then? Crap? Seriously?"

Claws. "I'm man enough to use the word "crap," I promise. You're not sure, we can duke it out after class."

They patrol in silence until the next bend, then:

173

Whiskers. "Seriously?"

Claws shakes an armored fist at him. Hairball snickers. Spots says nothing, but she's grinning.

They complete their patrol with minimal action, return to the Armory and peel down. In the corridor, Spots says to Claws, "Back to the barracks?"

He puts his hand on her shoulder. "Nope. New digs, remember?"

Spots. "You talked to him? He said yes?"

Claws. "I think I can handle *one* alien, Spots."

Spots laughs. "All right. Let's go!"

They retrieve their practice gear and head up-country to the Door, are waved through and make their way to the testing facility. Claws palms open the door and they step inside: a huge open space, high-tech target dummies, projector fields, recording equipment . . .

Claws. "Aww, yeah. Now we're talkin'. We just leveled up, you and me. Let's get crackin'!"

174

63. SICKBAY

Sickbay. Spots enters with a handful of granola bars. She checks Fang2's bed and finds it empty; a nurse tells her he's with a doctor, so she heads over to the Wild Dogs who are still in a coma. She sits next to them and reads from one of the stack of battered books on their night-stands, donations from everyone in the company: science fiction, history, westerns, sports magazines, a romance novel or two.

Then she checks on a couple of the new people, who are unconscious.

From a nearby bed, Hawk Abrams speaks. "Who are you?"

Spots. "Oh, I didn't see you were awake. I'm Spots Guitart, Team Kitty."

Hawk. "What are you doing here?"

Spots holds up the granola bars. "Distributing carbohydrate cheer. Want one?"

Hawk, uncertain. "You serious?"

Spots. "Sure. I bring one for Fang2, the extras go to anyone else who looks like they need it. I've got peanut butter, cherry-walnut and . . . um . . . I don't know what this flavor is. They say it's chocolate, but it tastes like mud."

Hawk. "I'll take the cherry."

Spots hands it over. He continues looking at her funny. "You come here often?"

Spots. "Yeah?"

Hawk. "You Team Kitty's ASL?"

Spots. "What? Oh, no. I just do it because . . ." *She trails off, then shrugs.* "No one likes to be stuck in bed."

Hawk. "No." *He unwraps the bar slowly.* "I see your LT in here pretty often. She does the same thing, reading to them."

Spots. "She might have started it, actually."

Hawk. "Our LT does it too. Comes by. Does the pep talk. No food, though."

Spots. "One out of two's still good." *She glances at the read-out next to his bed.* "You did a real number on your hip and leg there."

Hawk. "You read that gibberish?"

Spots. "Oh? Yeah, you get used to it. What happened?"

Hawk. "Took a bad fall."

Spots. "In *armor?* That must have hurt something awful."

Hawk, looking at her funny. "Yeah."

Spots. "Oh, there's Fang2. Do you mind . . . ?"

Hawk. "No. Nice to meet you, Guitart."

Spots. "Sure thing . . . um, I didn't catch your name?"

"Hawk."

"Good to meet you too, Hawk." *She waves, leaving him with a perplexed expression, and goes to perch on the stool next to Fang2's bed as the latter limps in.* "Hey, I got fake-chocolate or peanut butter here."

Fang2. "Sweet! Thanks, Mom." *He snitches the peanut butter.*

Spots. "So you leaving here soon?"

Fang2. "Yeah." *He makes a face.* "They got me working out in the gym and it's driving me . . . uh, nuts."

Spots. "How come?"

Fang2. "The place is always crammed full of the new people, and they're . . . eh."

Spots glances back at Hawk, who is chewing slowly on his granola bar. "Pretty serious, huh."

Fang2. "Yeah. It's ****ing embarrassing."

Spots. "Hmm. You think they'd let Claws take over? He's good at planning exercise programs and we've got a place no one would see you."

Fang2. "For serious? That would be great!"

Spots. "Yeah, I'll go talk to the doctor, see if he'll clear it. But you know Claws won't be soft on you."

Fang2. "****, if I'd wanted soft I would have stayed in the states and let Mom cook for me while I played games in the basement. Besides, better a teammate chewing my *** off than some white-coat with an attitude."

Spots shakes her head. "Fang2 . . ."

Spots the Space Marine: Defense of the Fiddler

Fang2. "Okay, okay, I didn't mean it. Sort of. I know they're the good guys."

Spots slides off the stool. "I'll go make arrangements."

64. Taking Care of Your Own

Following day, after patrol.

"Hey, Spots? Door's this way."

Spots. "I know. But we have to pick up Fang2 first."

Claws. "Do what now?"

Spots, heading toward Sickbay. "Fang2 is at the point where he needs physical therapy. I volunteered you to walk him through that."

Claws. "Whoa, what now? Isn't that, like, complicated work? That requires a license?"

Spots. "He's not that far gone. He just needs someone to walk him through a list of exercises."

Claws. "And you volunteered me for this . . . why?"

Spots. "He wasn't comfortable doing it in the gym with everyone else watching. He's one of the squad, Claws. We take care of our own, right?"

Claws falls silent. He follows her to Sickbay where she says, "Go get Fang2? I'll pick up his exercise list."

Claws. "All right."

Spots. "Thanks."

Claws finds Fang2 sitting up on his bed, waiting.

Claws. "So . . . I hear I'm in charge of floggin' your *** now."

Fang2, smacking his hip. "**** yeah, I know you've always wanted a piece of this."

Claws, rolling his eyes. "Get off the ****in' bed and lets get goin'."

Fang2. "Thought you'd never ask, sweetie." *He slides off the bed. Spots meets them at the door and they head out. Claws sets a normal pace, notices that Fang2 isn't keeping up and slows down. He frowns a little. At the Door, the guards examine Fang2 and make a call before allowing him in.*

Fang2. "Wow, fancy. I feel all super-spytastic doing this."

Claws. "You have no idea." *He palms open the door to the Testing Facility.*

Fang2. "Sweet! Where'd you get clearance for this?"

Claws points a thumb at Spots. "Her idea." *To Spots:* "Start with the warm-ups. I'll see what we're supposed to be doin' to Fang2 here."

While Claws reads, Fang2 watches Spots start solo practice with the test-glove. "****, can I do what she's doing?"

Claws. "Later, when you're not limpin' like a horse in need of a mercy killin'."

Fang2. "Promise?"

Claws is about to retort but Fang2 doesn't notice; he's watching Spots, intent.

Claws, quiet. "Promise. Hit the mat, mister, you've got an excitin' regimen of . . . lessee. Sixty stretches to do."

Fang2. "****. They've got me doing yoga like some kind of soccer mom."

Spots. "I heard that!"

Fang2. "You're no soccer mom, woman. You're a gun-toting, ***-kicking, eats-rations-and-crabs-for-breakfast-and-then-makes-cookies mom."

Spots. "Hey, there were days before I was a gun-toting, backside-kicking mom that I wished my life was as easy as 'point guns at things and shoot them'." *She pauses, looking wistful.* "Actually, it would have been nice to be able to solve most of my problems that way back then. There were a lot of times . . ."

Claws. "Now look what you've done. You've given her ideas."

Fang2 cackles.

Claws. "Get to work. Both of you."

65. Hunches

"God, Gunny, I feel stupid."

"Ma'am?"

"Look at this." *Peaches points at all the footage running concurrently on her monitor.* "All these patrols and . . . nothing. Just those Mark 1 bugs we were killing when I first got here. The guys are tearing them up like cake after all the trouble I went through bleating for relief."

"I'm sure no one blames you for that, ma'am."

"No, but it sure is embarrassing." *Peaches rubs her face.* "Why the lull now? I swear they're doing it to make me look bad."

Gunny doesn't chuckle but his mouth quirks while the lieutenant's face is down. "I'm sure the crabs will come back as mean as before soon enough."

"But what if they don't? What if that was just a . . . a failed experiment in new hulls?"

"Then we thank God for His mercy, ma'am, and hope the cakewalk continues."

Peaches glances up at him. "****. I'm sorry, Gunny. That really was out of line. Of course I don't want things to get harder on us. I'm just . . ."

"Under a great deal of pressure managing the new situation, ma'am."

She blinks, then laughs. "Yeah. That. Go on, I'm sure you have better things to do right now than listen to me whine."

After he's left, Peaches puts her chin on her palm and frowns at the footage, watching it loop.

We need . . . a montage. Team Kitty patrolling the Warren. A scowling Fang eyeing a dead crab while someone teases her about making a cheek shot instead of a head shot. Fang2 doing endless stretches wearing a bored expression, then doing endless exercises with weights, also wearing a bored expression. More patrols. A week passes.

Testing Facility.

Fang2, drawing the word out. "***********, when am I going to be ****ing done with this stupid physical therapy?"

Claws. "When the doc says you are." *He squints at a wall-monitor that's showing power consumption curves in real-time.* "Let's try that again."

Spots the Space Marine: Defense of the Fiddler

Spots. " Okay." *She grabs his wrist and pulls him in; they both crouch, facing opposite directions but lined up rather than back-to-back. Blue shield and gold merge overhead into shimmering green.*

Claws. "Is that me or is it hoggin' less juice?"

Fang2. "Ooh, me, me, I can answer that!" *As Claws and Spots both look at him, he throws himself on top of the shield bubble.* "WhoooOOOOoooo! That tickles!"

Claws. "Fang2, you freakin' moron! We had no idea what that would have done to bare skin!"

Fang2. "Now we do. Hey, look at that."

Claws glances at the monitor. "Huh."

Spots. "Here, I'll turn mine off." *She does. Claws's shield immediately starts drawing more power.*

Claws. "How about that. So it's worthwhile to bolster someone else's shield."

Spots. "I didn't know that! Interesting."

Fang2, still plastered to the shield. "This feels great. Like a ****ing massage."

Claws. "A ****ing massage is a little more than just a massage, you know."

Spots. "Actually, I think that's illegal." *They both look at her.* "You know. Sex and a massage. You're only allowed to pay for one, the other's illegal. So if you get both . . . " *They're still staring at her. She throws up her hands.* "You know, if you have to explain the joke it really doesn't work very well."

They both laugh.

Fang2. "You two are gonna have some nasty surprises for the crabs if they come back."

Spots. "They will."

Fang2. "All the talk in Sickbay's about how the super-crabs are all gone and maybe were never here at all. They say they're here because Peaches was PMSing and needed the new LT to hold her hand."

Spots. "They really said that??"

Fang2. "Well, no, but you can tell they're thinking it. It's been too easy in the Warren."

Spots, frowning. "They've only been here a few weeks."

Fang2. "Yeah, a few weeks of nothing special."

Spots. "Do they really doubt we needed the help?"

Fang2. "I don't think they doubt it . . . that's the problem. 'Cause things sure don't look very hard right now. Makes us look like—"

Claws. "Back up a sec. Did you say . . . a few . . . weeks?"

Fang2, puzzled. "Yeah? That's how long they've been here?"

Claws, frowning. "A few weeks."

Spots. "Claws . . . ?"

Claws, shaking himself. "Ain't nothing. Let's get back to work. That means you too, princess."

Fang2. "You mean me, right?" *He twirls (badly).* "I'm a pretty Asian princess!"

Spots. "You get all the credit for starting this one."

Claws snorts. "Back on the mat, Chao. Spots . . . once more, with feelin'."

They resume practice. When it's over, they separate at the Door: Fang2 heads to Sickbay to log his exercises; Spots heads for the Barracks to shower.

Claws . . . doubles-back and heads for the Fiddler's Room.

66. The Improbability of Sentience

Claws is leaning on his elbow against the wall, face close to the intercom.

"Hey, Sam? It's Claws."

"Come in."

Claws enters, hands in the pockets of his sweatpants. "Could use that beer now."

"It is in the coldstore."

Claws saunters over to the refrigerator and squints into it. "What the **** is that?"

"Dessert. For me, anyway."

"Is it supposed to wiggle?"

A bowed note, somehow sarcastic. "Don't ask if you don't want the answer."

Claws snorts and pulls out the beer, unscrews the top and sits opposite the Fiddler. "So, two weeks from egg to full-grown-and-full-of-someone-else's-guts crabdom, right?"

"Typically."

Claws. "****." *And drinks.*

Samuel-Colt. "Mother's-Escort?"

Claws. "The new shells. We ain't seen 'em for a few weeks. Nothin' but Mark Ones. It's because they're breedin' 'em."

Samuel-Colt, with a bounced note. "Most certainly."

Claws. "****." *He leans forward, scrubs his eyes with the base of his palms.* "****, Sam. How many?"

Samuel-Colt. "As many as the average breeding female can produce. Among the enemy, that can be hundreds if conditions are right: food, environment, male virility."

"Hundreds?" *Claws stares at him.* "You serious?" *Frowns.* "Wait, 'among the enemy'? What about you?"

Samuel-Colt draws out a long note. "Our clutches average 10-12 individuals. Sentience is harder to nurture."

"So . . . you folks get out-bred by ten to one."

Samuel-Colt. "We hate to tell you, Mother's-Escort, but sometimes it is more on the order of hundreds to one."

Claws stares at him. "****, Sam. Are we gonna win this war? *Can* we win this war?"

Samuel-Colt. "It is possible, Claws. Or else we would not have asked."

"But how? How the **** does that work when for every one of us that dies, they have a hundred ****in' more? Or a thousand? And can grow another thousand in two weeks? Why haven't they overrun the ****in' galaxy?"

Samuel-Colt taps his head just above the jeweled eye. "They do not have the minds for it."

Claws. "So you're bettin' that brains are gonna out-do brawn? But all they need is one smart crab and then they can copy him a thousand times. A thousand thousand times."

Samuel-Colt. "It is not so simple. Fortunately for us." *Before Claws can interrupt he holds up both his topmost hands.* "Pause. You believe in a God, yes?"

"Uh . . ." *Claws stops.* "Yeah. Card-carrying Protestant, says so on the tags."

"And your God has an opinion on others attempting to make themselves into gods, yes?"

Claws. "You could say that. It's wrong. There's only one. Everything else is a fake."

Samuel-Colt. "Exactly." *At Claws's look:* "Your scriptures are correct. When we try to re-create that Work, we fail." *He lifts one long finger.* "Take that single smart warrior, cloned. Now you have a thousand of him. But the exact same qualities duplicated do not make for a good army. If he was a leader, he will not work with himself. If he was a follower, no one will lead. All his flaws are magnified; there is no perspective outside himself to see his potential mistakes. His brilliance is distinct, but he will not think of new ideas. He is sterile, mentally. A closed circuit. And that is before the flesh breaks down."

Claws. "What now?"

"An individual cannot be cloned indefinitely." *An intricate melody.* "The female holds his mental imprint in mind while laying the eggs to ensure the pattern is passed. But her memory fades with time, and with it the integrity of the pattern. Eventually, the copies fade into caricatures of sentience, like marionettes."

Claws, frowning. "Huh. Still, at the rate they breed they should've overwhelmed us a long time ago."

Samuel-Colt. "Numbers alone aren't enough, Claws. To win a war, one needs both intellect and passion, and balancing these two things manually . . ." *He strikes a note so sharply it sounds like a breaking string.* "Eventually, human—and Violinist—ingenuity will put a stop to them. There are millions of ants on your world, Mother's-Escort, but I rarely hear of humans complaining that ants will eat them out of their homes."

"Yeah, well, ants ain't nine feet tall and armored like a tank neither."

Samuel-Colt strikes another sharp note, somewhat more humorous. "We did not say the work would not be hard; that is why we asked for help. But we will prevail because there is no other choice."

Claws. "****, I hope so." *He scratches his brow with the hand holding the bottle, using his thumb.* "****. I need to tell Peaches we're about to be hit hard. You're sure?"

Samuel-Colt. "As sure as the circumstances permit. There is always a chance of mistakes."

Claws. "****. This is gonna be fun." *He looks up.* "I'm gonna have to tell her I got it from you."

Samuel-Colt. "Understood. But if she wishes direct confirmation, we will require the presence of the Mother for the meeting."

Claws. "Official, huh."

Samuel-Colt. "It would be easier for me."

Claws. "Then that's how we'll do it." *He glances at the empty bottle.* "Uh, where . . . ?"

"There, by the desk."

Claws tosses it. "Okay." *He rubs his face.* "Okay. Two weeks, and it's been three . . . it could be any time, then."

Samuel-Colt. "Yes."

Claws. "Then we gotta tell her now. Stay awake, okay?"

"I will be here."

Claws nods. "Thanks for this."

Samuel-Colt. "Your victories are ours, Mother's-Escort."

Claws glances at him. Then nods. "Yeah . . . yeah, they are. I'll be back."

67. SUMMON THE COUNCIL

Barracks, a few moments later, as Claws enters. Spots is sitting cross-legged on her bunk.

Claws. "What the f—err, ah . . . Spots. You waitin' up for me?"

Spots. "Yep.

Claws. "I'm not sixteen, you know."

Spots. "But you have been drinking."

Claws. "!"

Claws. "How the hell can you smell that from there?"

Spots. "Secret Mom Power. So, what's going on?"

Claws. "We're about to go talk to Peaches about the crabs goin' soft on us." *He taps a request into the wall-screen.*

Spots, when he's done. "Go brush your teeth." *At his look:* "I'm serious."

Shaking his head, Claws goes. When he comes out, Spots has a clean shirt for him and a few mints.

"You kiddin' me?"

"If it's important enough to go see the Lieutenant about it, it's important enough not to have her first impression of you be 'he smells like . . .'" *Spots hesitates, wrinkles her nose.* "Good beer. Hey, where did you find good beer on station?"

Claws. "You know the difference between good and bad beer?"

Spots. "Yes?"

Claws. "Good, you can teach me some other day. Let's go."

———

Cut to a small conference room off the Control Center.

Peaches. "They're what?"

Claws. "Breedin' the new shells, ma'am. They should be just about done, at that. Two weeks is the quote I've got and it's been over that."

Spots the Space Marine: Defense of the Fiddler

Peaches. "And you had this from the Fiddler."

Claws. "Yes, ma'am. He was very forthcomin'."

Peaches. "Did he give you any details on what we could expect?"

Claws. " 'Fraid not, ma'am, except that two weeks was long enough to put hundreds of crabs on the field."

Peaches. "****." *She presses her thumb against her browbone.* "You think he's willing to talk about it?"

Claws. "He's willin', if we bring Private Guitart."

Peaches. "All right. Head over there now. I'll join you as soon as I find Lieutenant Avril."

68. Mother's Council

Peaches is heading down the corridor toward the Door, Gunny at her back and Avril at her side.

Avril. "So according to the Fiddler the crabs are about to hit us. How'd we find this out?"

Peaches. "He talks to one of my privates." *Avril glances at her. She shrugs, uncomfortable.* "He'll only talk about certain topics with certain people. Alien protocol thing."

Avril. "If he only talks to your private, why are we going there now?"

Peaches. "Because I'm hoping he'll answer more questions. I've asked her to be there."

Avril. "So . . . you, me, this private—"

"And a corporal."

Avril. "And a corporal? How's he fit in?"

Peaches. "Remember the whole 'no woman without an honor guard thing?'"

Avril. "Oh!" *And looks over his shoulder at Gunny.* "And you're bringing yours."

Peaches nods.

Avril, chagrined. "That makes me . . . the odd man out."

Peaches. "I'm sure he'll understand."

Fiddler's Conference Room, off the Lab. This is a large rectangular room with a conference table at one end and a large open space at the other next to a wall-screen, presumably to allow small-scale demonstrations. There's a small dais; the Fiddler is standing at the end of it. Spots and Claws are at its edge. They salute the entering officers; Samuel-Colt nods once to Peaches.

Peaches. "Um, thank you for seeing us, Samuel-Colt."

Samuel-Colt, bowing a slow melody. "Lieutenant-Savannah-Bonnet. Maiden's-Escort. Lieutenant-Paul-Avril."

Peaches flushes at the 'maiden's escort' part. Fortunately she doesn't see Gunny's expression. "Private Guitart and Corporal Walker tell me that you shared some useful information with them about the current situation. That the crabs are reproducing."

Samuel-Colt. "That is correct."

Peaches. "And this takes . . . two weeks. So we should be seeing them soon."

Spots the Space Marine: Defense of the Fiddler

Samuel-Colt. "Presuming our theory is correct, yes."

Peaches. "Do you have any idea how many of the enemy we should expect?"

Samuel-Colt spreads his hands, with a quick melody. "We have not examined that data, Lieutenant-Savannah-Bonnet. One might make an estimate by examining any previous surges, but we strongly suspect that the Enemy was already entrenched when you landed. They would have finished their initial breeding before your arrival. Data would be limited. We would encourage you not to draw . . . hasty conclusions."

Avril. "So we know they're coming . . . right now . . . but not how many."

Claws. "Uh . . . do we know that they'll abandon Mark One?" *When Samuel-Colt glances at him:* "If they switch to breeding the new shells, will they leave any capacity to breed the old ones?"

Samuel-Colt, a bounced note. "Unlikely. If the new shells work better, they will not waste materiel on old ones."

Peaches, frowning. "Is there an overhead to making the new ones? I mean, do better crabs take longer, or more . . . uh . . . stuff . . . to make?"

Samuel-Colt. "At times, Lieutenant-Savannah-Bonnet. Depending on the design."

Avril. "Are they going to come from one place? Can we set up a choke-point?"

Claws, under his breath. "****."

Avril. "Corporal? Something to add?"

Claws. "We already tried that. We died."

Avril glances at Peaches, who says: "He's right. My predecessor tried to find the crab's lab. His offensive failed, badly."

Avril. "But why? It's just a matter of finding it, right?"

A tense silence. Spots looks at Samuel-Colt. "Samuel-Colt?"

"Mother-soldier."

"Do you know why that didn't work?"

Samuel-Colt, low drone. "Mother, most breeding chambers are closely protected. The one servicing this location is most certainly deep underground. It will have multiple exits; its passages will empty into various tunnels above it that allow the Enemy to penetrate our own corridors at multiple points. A single choke-point is tactically unsound; the Enemy would not make it so easy."

. . .

Peaches. "Why isn't this kind of thing in our briefings? Or background information?"

Samuel-Colt. "We do not know, Lieutenant-Savannah-Bonnet. Perhaps it is a 'need-to-know' issue."

Claws. "****! The people who need to know are the ones who are gettin' their ***es chewed off, you ask me."

Gunny. "Which no one did, Corporal."

Peaches, muttering. "Though he has a point."

Samuel-Colt. "In fairness, Lieutenant-Savannah-Bonnet, the Enemy innovating is not a usual activity. This information may not have been included because it may have been assumed that you would not need it."

Avril. "There's got to be something we can do. I noticed those traps you set up in the floor, those are good ideas. Maybe we can use them?"

Peaches. "We haven't been able to test those extensively yet. . . ."

Spots, quieter. "Samuel-Colt? Is there anything you wish you could tell us?"

Samuel-Colt, minor arpeggio rising, sharply staccato. "Mother, even in some things I cannot speak without specific circumstance. But we must say again: the Enemy innovating is not a usual activity."

Claws. "****. Meanin' we're in the middle of somethin' special. A crab test-bed? Some special mother-crab that specializes in new breeds? Somethin' like that?"

Samuel-Colt says nothing, bows nothing.

Claws. "****."

Spots. "Why us? Why here?"

Samuel-Colt. "Mother . . . where would you have your children during a war? Where the fighting is fiercest?"

Spots. "Of course not—oh. We're in the middle of nowhere, aren't we."

Peaches. "****."

Spots the Space Marine: Defense of the Fiddler

69. ROLES AND PROTOCOL

Avril. "This is . . . serious. Is there any way we could tell for certain? That they're running a . . . a lab?"

Samuel-Colt. "Possibly. We would have to smell one of the children while still alive."

Claws. "**** that, we can't put you anywhere near them, they might eat your brain and then we'd be ****ed six ways to Sunday."

Avril. "Eat his brain?"

A very pained silence.

Spots, quiet. "He doesn't know . . . ?"

Avril. "Know what?"

Peaches. "The crabs, they eat one another's brains. While they're still alive. It lets them absorb memories and knowledge. They've been trying to do it with us, but we're too different from them for it to work."

Avril: !

Avril. "Why the **** weren't we told??"

Peaches. "Maybe it would make us hate them too much."

Claws. "Hatin' the enemy too much didn't hurt us at Iwo Jima."

Before Gunny can say anything, Avril says: "You're a real smart ***, you know that, Corporal?"

Claws. "Yes, sir!"

Spots, interrupting before Peaches, Gunny or Avril can respond: "This can't be the first testbed, Samuel-Colt. The . . . Enemy . . . might not innovate often, but they must have at some point in order to fight us in so many environments."

Samuel-Colt, uneasy melody. "You are correct, Mother-soldier. But not all labs are successful. As we have explained before to your escort, our engineering attempts are . . . hit-or-miss. Many more of the latter than the former. We believe that you have the misfortune of having stumbled onto a lab with a higher success ratio."

Avril. "That just makes it all the more important that we do something about it. Maybe we could capture the Queen?"

Peaches. "We'd have to get into the breeding chamber for that, and you heard what that would be like. It's suicidal without more people."

Avril, frowning a little. "We'll have to ask for more people, then." *At Peaches's expression:* "No, no, I'm not going to throw us at something we have no chance of taking—"

Claws mutters something that sounds like, "Thank ****."

"—but if we can get reinforcements and we have a chance, this is an amazing opportunity, Savannah. Let's push it up the chain and see if we can get some support for it."

Samuel-Colt, rising note. "Lieutenant-Paul-Avril is correct. To capture or destroy one of the few Queens breeding new designs would be a powerful blow against the Enemy."

Peaches. "All right. But we need real support. Not another half-strength company, a quarter of whom are in sickbay."

Avril winces. "Ouch." *Lifts his hands at her expression.* "No, I agree with you completely."

Samuel-Colt. "May we do anything else for you?"

Peaches faces him and bows awkwardly. "Not right now. Thank you, Samuel-Colt. You've been very helpful."

Samuel-Colt. "It is our greatest desire."

The two officers leave. Gunny hangs back and gives Claws the Eye. "I should rip a ****ing strip out of your hide, Corporal, but I think I'll leave the pleasure to your sergeant."

Samuel-Colt, rising arpeggio, staccato. "Pardon me, Maiden's-Escort."

Surprised at the interruption, Claws and Gunny look at him.

Samuel-Colt. "We understand you must maintain discipline within your ranks. But among us, a Mother's-Escort has the right to speak when he believes he must, to save the Mother from potential danger."

Gunny. ". . ."

Claws. ". . ."

Samuel-Colt, low drone. "The Mother's-Escort spoke to point out issues with the officers' plans, or to share relevant information. That is his duty."

Gunny. "I don't want to offend you, sir—"

Samuel-Colt, sharp note, once, bounced. "Then do not." *Tilting head.* "You have left your maiden unescorted." *Which is so clearly a dismissal that Gunny leaves.*

Spots the Space Marine: Defense of the Fiddler

When the three of them are alone, Claws says: "Aww, ****, Sam. You didn't have to do that."

Samuel-Colt, falling note. "You are presuming we did it on your behalf, Mother's-Escort. But we did not."

Claws. "Come again?"

Spots, murmuring, "It's because you need them to remember you're a Violinist, isn't it? And to give you the proper respect, and to use your protocols when interacting with you." *She looks up.* "Otherwise, we might ask you for things you can't do and then get upset because we think we have the right, and that you don't have the right to refuse."

Samuel-Colt bows to her.

Claws. "Uh. Hmm. Damn."

Spots, scowling. "Would you STOP that? I've been listening to you curse all evening. I want to punch you!"

Both males stare at her. Claws busts out laughing.

Spots sighs. To Samuel-Colt, she says: "I sympathize with you. No one takes me seriously either." *She looks at him.* "You gave us really useful information today and it must have been really hard for you. Can we do anything for you? As a thank-you?"

Samuel-Colt, spreading upper hands. "It is a kind thought, Mother. I do not know what I would ask for."

Spots thinks. Then: "You're usually listening to music when we visit you in your room. Would you like me to bring you some music? Things I like? We could share."

Samuel-Colt, startled rising glide. "Ah? Yes . . . ! Yes, that would be interesting."

Spots. "All right. After our next patrol." *She bows, more gracefully than Peaches.* "Good night, Samuel-Colt."

Samuel-Colt. "Mother. Mother's-Escort. You are always welcome."

Spots and Claws spend the walk to the barracks in silence. Once in their room:

Spots. "You know, you're not doing a great job of making them think you're dumb."

Claws. "What now?"

Spots. "The accent you turn on and off when you want to fool people into thinking you're uneducated? It doesn't work very well if you keep saying smart things. Lieutenant Bonnet's not dumb, Claws. I don't think Lieutenant Avril is either."

Claws. "What the hell smart thing did I say?"

Spots. "It's not just one thing. It's everything." *She looks at him.* "You think like an officer, Travis."

Claws glances at her, wide-eyed.

Spots pulls the blanket over her shoulder. "Just saying. Night, Claws."

70. Avalanches Start Slowly

In the corridor, leaving the Fiddler's room.

Peaches. "We need to send a message about this."

Avril. "Yes. Absolutely." *Glances at her.* "You draft it, okay? Make sure you mention that it was your people who got the info, and that you made it possible by assigning them."

Peaches. "Really? I mean, of course, but . . ."

Avril, chuckling, tired. "Don't worry, I'll cover your ***. I'll sign it too. But you and your people deserve the credit for it. If we make it out of this hellhole alive, we're all going to deserve promotion. You, me . . . even Corporal Smart-***."

Peaches. "You're a good guy, Avril."

"Thanks. I try."

They reach his quarters. She glances at him. "Mind telling me why your people are such shut-ins? They seem wired pretty tight to me."

Avril rubs the back of his neck. "Hell, Savannah. We've been through a lot. I think asking them to be okay with it within a few weeks is . . . a little too much. Give us some time."

She studies him. Nods. "All right. Good night, Paul."

"Night, Savannah."

~~We have received intelligence~~ ~~We discovered~~ I discovered . . .

Peaches rubs her eyes, mutters. "Start in the middle, work backwards."

Given the information supplied by the Violinist, we now believe ~~our-selves to be surrounded by serviced by~~ that our location is served by ~~what might be~~ a crab test facility. Our Violinist has indicated that successful crab "laboratories" are rare and that ours might be one of the few. We've seen evidence *(append something here/attachments)* indicating—

She's interrupted by her personal comm beeping. She toggles it. "Bonnet."

"Lieutenant, we have a situation in the Control Room."

Control Room. The personnel manning the stations are very tense. There is so much activity on the suit cams that it's vertiginous.

Peaches. "Sitrep."

"Lieutenant Avril just led a relief team to back-up the on-duty squad, ma'am. It's still not looking good, though."

Peaches leans down, toggles Avril's channel. "Paul? Need help?"

After a pause, Avril. "Could probably use it. These're your new shells, I assume."

Peaches, grim, watching the monitors. "Yes. Do you have a count?"

Avril. "Hard to tell. Ninety? A hundred?"

Peaches. "I'll send the next team up. Keep it together." *She nods to the man sitting the comm board.* "Pull up the next squad on the roster and send them out."

———————

Spots and Claws both jerk upright when their alarms go off. Claws rolls out of bed first.

"Walker."

Scythe. "Armory, now."

Spots is already heading for the door.

"On our way."

71. KITTY TO THE RESCUE

Team Kitty in the Warren, running.

Scythe, staring at HUD. "What a cluster****." *Switching to squad channel, marking a position.* "We've got their rear. Form up, standard."

"Check, Sarge."

Their boots ring on the metal floor. Scythe has point, Claws and Spots behind him. Fang is in center; Hairball and Whiskers are rear-guard. They turn a corner . . . into chaos.

Claws and Spots surge forward and close in front of Scythe. Claws puts up the shield wall; Spots attacks through it. They shear through three crabs, another three, four. As they advance, Claws uses his free hand to shoot the fallen crabs in the head.

[**Squad**] **Fang** : ****! Leave some for me!

[**Squad**] **Claws** : Shoot over our heads, you got room.

[**Squad**] **Scythe** : Nice work. *Switching to company channel.* "Lieutenant, we're forty meters from your position and closing."

[**Company**] **Avril** : Glad to have you, Sergeant.

[**Squad**] **Scythe** : Keep an eye on the walls.

Spots and Claws hack; the rest of them "shoot over their heads." The crabs turn on them, but the shield spans the corridor, scintillating blue when the squad fires through it.

[**Squad**] **Claws** : Got two more minutes on this.

[**Squad**] **Spots** : Check. Scythe?

[**Squad**] **Scythe** : I like them not being able to touch us. Can I do it?

[**Squad**] **Spots** : The Violinist installed your new shield. Come forward, Claws will show you.

They stop advancing so Claws can show Scythe the setting; the crabs scrabble at the shield-wall during the trade-off. Scythe takes Claws's place and they continue their push. Claws falls back to join the others.

[**Squad**] **Fang** : More ****ing target practice—King! *Two shots and it's down, shattered at thorax and head.*

[**Squad**] **Spots** : Another star, Fang. *Pause for lunge.* We're going to have to start running them . . . *Back-stroke through another crab. . . . down your thighs . . . !*

[*Squad*] **Whiskers** : *Laughing.* Sexy.

[*Squad*] **Fang** : You know it, motherf—brother.

[*Squad*] **Scythe** : This thing's flashing.

[*Squad*] **Spots** : That's the two-minute warning.

[*Squad*] **Scythe** : That's it? Five minutes of this?

[*Squad*] **Spots** : It's five minutes of invulnerability. Don't complain.

[*Squad*] **Claws** : —we got dead.

They've found crab corpses they're not responsible for shooting. The corpses are piled in a rough line all the way to the next turn in the corridor.

[*Squad*] **Scythe** : ****!

[*Squad*] **Hairball** : Boss?

[*Squad*] **Scythe** : They're not shooting them right.

All the bodies are "dead," but most of them have been shot through the abdomen . . . not the head.

[*Squad*] **Scythe** : Spots, Claws, take care of it. Rest of you, with me.

The squad splits up. Spots and Claws pick through the dead, delivering the head-shots.

Claws, on the buddy-to-buddy channel, while keeping an eye on the HUD: "Hope it's not too bad around the corner."

Spots. "If it is, we'll know soon enough."

72. Sourcing the Push

The Warren. Spots and Claws are still doing clean-up.

Spots. "Claws? If the Enemy has their breeding chamber underground . . . how are they getting to us now that we've put a floor on the Warren?"

Claws. "Dunno. Could be penetratin' the outermost tunnels. Tunnel up, poke in from the walls. Why? Somethin' botherin' you?"

Spots. "I don't know. Just wondering why they're not overwhelming us. Is this their new big push? How come we can handle it with just three squads?"

Claws. "Crap, Spots, don't jinx it." *Kicks a crab.* "Think this is the last one—"

The outward wall bursts. New shells spill out, including a King. Claws doesn't have to say anything; they both turn tail and run for the corner.

[**Squad**] **Claws** : INCOMING! Thirty, forty, new shells plus King!

[**Squad**] **Spots** : They're not chasing us . . . Scythe! They're pushing through your wall!

[**Squad**] **Claws** : ****! They're flankin' you! *Pings a location on the HUD.* Here!

[**Squad**] **Scythe** : We see it.

Spots reverses, grabbing Claws's arm. "Back! Shoot them in the back!"

Claws. "Hang on." *He checks the now tumbled wall and looks through it.*

Spots, picking off the crabs as they recede. "Claws?"

Claws. "Now you got me wonderin'." *Switches to squad channel.* "Scythe? You handlin' things fine? Need us?"

[**Squad**] **Scythe** : *Tense but calm.* We're fine, why?

[**Squad**] **Claws** : Wanna check where these ****ers came from.

[**Squad**] **Scythe** : Got a ****ing deathwish, Walker?

Spots aims at the back of the King, careful.

[**Squad**] **Claws** : I'm serious, we won't go far. Consider it part of the clean-up you assigned.

[**Squad**] **Scythe** : Fine. Ten minute check-ins. Don't come back dead.

[*Squad*] Hairball : Bring us some pictures.

[*Squad*] Whiskers : How I spent my ****ing vacation.

Spots frowns. On squad channel: "Fang? I shot your King in the back but it's still going."

[*Squad*] Fang : I'll take care of it, Mama. Good hunting, you and your nursemaid.

Claws on buddy-to-buddy. "Come on, let's go check out that hunch of yours."

Spots. "I hope I'm wrong."

Claws. "Wrong how?"

Spots. "I don't know. Wrong about feeling bad about it."

Claws. "Mom instinct, huh? Crap, we're screwed. Might as well see how we're gonna buy the farm before we go."

Spots grimaces. "This isn't funny, Claws."

Claws. "Hell, Spots, I ain't laughin'. Let's go."

200

73. Hunting

Control Room.

Peaches. "Paul? How's it looking?"

Avril. "Good. Busy though. Thanks for sending the extra squad."

Peaches. "No problem."

Control 1. "Ma'am? Team Kitty's detached a recon team. I have them up on monitor 5."

Peaches. "Huh. What are they up to?"

Control 1. "Transcript says they're investigating the start point for the current crab attack."

Peaches, leaning toward the monitor. "This should be interesting."

Control 1. "Want me to put you through, ma'am?"

Peaches. "No, let them do their business. But give me an ear-bud, I want to listen in, in case they find something."

———

Warren. Claws and Spots are through the broken wall and examining the next corridor.

Spots. "Maybe there'll be another break in the wall?"

Claws. "That would make things easy on us. Well, except for the repair. You'd think as many walls as they've punched through we'd a' got the message and made 'em out of something stiffer."

Spots, spreading her glove under a scrape on the wall. "Here, Claws."

Claws. "Huh. One of 'em musta bumped into it. Nice catch."

Spots. "That way."

They stop at the next turn to check the walls and floors.

Spots. "Don't see anything this time."

Claws. "Then let's go with common sense. They gotta come from somewhere and it ain't near the donut . . . we'll head for the fringes."

Spots. "Sounds good."

They head outward, finding nothing.

Claws, muttering. "**—crap, we mighta lost the trace."

Spots. "They have to come from somewh—" *Claws grabs her and jumps into a side branch as a crab scuttles past.* "Holy Mother!"

Claws. "Sorry. Didn't see us, looks like."

Spots. "That shouldn't have mattered. They can smell us, remember?"

Claws. "If that thing knew we were here, why did it ignore us? Come on."

Spots. "We're following it?"

Claws. "It doesn't seem to care about little ol' us. And we can handle one crab if it gets territorial. Let's see where it's goin'."

Spots, following. "Claws . . ."

Claws. "Mom instinct again?"

Spots. "No, I'm afraid this is more common sense." *She jogs after him.*

Claws. "I know what you're thinkin'. But we gotta know. You know? We're attritin' like crazy out here, Spots. We just got these new reinforcements, but they're gonna go down the tubes too if we don't figure out what the hell is goin' on out here."

Spots. "I thought you said that the last lieutenant almost killed everyone trying to do that."

Claws. "The last lieutenant almost killed everyone tryin' to do a frontal assault on a position he hadn't even located. He was **—" *Pause.* "No, I'm gonna say it, because he really deserved it. He was ****in' stupid, Magda, and I ain't usin' the term lightly. We're doin' the recon he shoulda done . . . and we got a resource he didn't."

"Which is . . . ?"

Claws. "He never talked to the Fiddler. You talk to the Fiddler. Peaches talks to you. We have real *information* . . . if we can put the pieces together, we might blow this place clean and stop *dyin'*."

Spots is quiet. Then: "That's a little ambitious, isn't it?"

Claws. " 'Course it is. But what's the alternative?"

Spots the Space Marine: Defense of the Fiddler

Control Room. Peaches, listening and watching the monitor, says nothing . . . but her brows lift.

74. In the Dark

The Warren, fringes.

Spots. "Check-in time, Claws."

Claws. "Yeah, I got it." *Switching to squad channel.* "Scythe, you still up?"

[Squad] Scythe : Yes. Still tracking?

[Squad] Claws : Yeah, we're heading fringe-ward.

[Squad] Scythe : All right. From now on do check-in with Control. Rest of us will be heading in shortly.

[Squad] Claws : All righty. *Switching to Base channel.* Control, this is Recon 1, Team Kitty. You read?

[Base] Control 1 : Recon 1, this is Control. Please ping your position so we can confirm.

[Base] Claws : Sending ping now.

[Base] Control 1 : We have you on the map, Recon 1. Give us a verbal check every ten minutes.

[Base] Claws : Copy that, Control. Recon 1 out.

Spots. "You didn't mention to either of them we're following a crab."

Claws. "They got our suit footage. I'm sure they're watching." *He leans over, waves his gloved hand in front of her helmet.* "Hi, folks!"

Spots, laughing. "For God's sake, Claws."

Claws. "Come on, let's get movin'."

They follow the crab, heading steadily outward. They leave the area with grid flooring though the halls are still lit.

Spots. "Claws?"

"Yeah?"

Spots. "Did they ever tell you where the crabs come from? Before I got here."

Claws. "No . . . assumption was they were comin' in from somewhere lateral. We built these—" *knocks a gloved hand on one of the corridor walls*—"to corral 'em into the space in a predictable way, figurin' if they were comin' for the donut we might as well narrow their options for 'em."

Spots. "But no one's looked?"

Claws. "The one time we looked—"

Spots. "Yes, I've heard that story. I mean . . . externally. With a satellite or something."

Claws. "Dunno. Reckon they have, though. Don't matter much . . . if we're gonna put down a military target, they're gonna attack it. That's sorta how war works."

Spots, rolling her eyes. "Claws . . ."

"Sorry, sorry. I'm used to talkin' to idiots. Why you askin'?"

Spots, shaking her head. "It just doesn't make sense to keep fighting the same fight over and over. It just feels . . . weird."

"Weird h—what the hell?"

The crab has turned the corner. Before them is a long hall. An empty one, unlit and without grid flooring.

When they point their suit lights down it, they find a distant dead-end.

Claws. "Christ! Where'd that sucker go?"

Spots plays her light over the walls. "We're pretty far out, aren't we?"

Claws. "Yeah, this is one of the last halls we built. Ain't no one been here for months, maybe not since we put it up."

Spots looks out. Looks down; looks up. "I don't see anything on the floor. Or the ceiling."

Claws. "Guess we'll be going over this one inch-by-inch. Come on."

They begin examining the corridor.

Claws. "This is crazy."

Spots. "Maybe they beam them in, like something out of Star Trek."

Claws. "Crap, I hope not."

Spots. "I don't know, transporter technology sounds pretty useful . . ."

Claws. "You've obviously never thought about the military applications."

Spots. "Like the 'beam soldiers from their family's homes to their areas of responsibility instead of shipping them for months' military application?"

Claws. "Like the 'beam a back-pack nuke into the middle of a major metropolitan area' military a—"

Spots lunges in front of him and drops a giant crab with one shot nearly at his feet.

Claws. "Mother f—"

"Ssh!"

She peers around the corpse and stops. There's a door there. A camouflaged door.

It's still open.

Claws, whispered. "... ****."

75. HOLES

Control Room. Peaches leans over, staring at the monitor. "Recon 1, this is Lieutenant Bonnet. Can you give us better footage of that door?"

[*Base*] Claws : Control, this is Recon 1. We're on it, ma'am.

He and Spots examine the door, mounted into a pocket.

Spots, brushing at its surface. "Looks like they reapply the dirt? It's real, not painted."

Claws. "Not real high tech, that. Hell if we almost walked right past it though."

Spots. "Fortunately we were looking."

[*Base*] Claws : Control, we're gonna go through.

[*Base*] Control 1 : Copy that, Recon 1.

He and Spots share a hesitation . . . then they both step through—

—into a long, narrow corridor.

—a very, very long narrow corridor. Barely wide enough for them to stretch their arms apart, but extending far behind their lights.

Claws. "What the . . ."

Spots touches his arm and points down. Every ten feet there's a hole.

Claws. "****."

Spots approaches one, crouches next to it and slowly . . . slowly bends to look over the edge. "Black as pitch. Must be deep."

Claws joins her. "Crap. It's just wide enough for one of 'em to climb straight up, ain't it."

Spots. "Look at the gouges in the walls. They probably use their pincers as pitons."

Claws looks over his shoulder at the row of holes. "How many you think? Seventy? Ninety?"

Spots. "We could count them . . ."

[*Base*] Peaches : Negative, Recon 1. We have mechanical drones for a reason. Time to head back.

[*Base*] Claws : Yes, ma'am.

He pauses, then passes a gloved hand through the dirt until he finds a small stone. "One more thing. Hey, Spots, boost your audio." *He holds the stone above the hole.* "Start," *he says, dropping it. He and Spots lean forward. When it makes a noise:*

Claws. "Stop."

Spots. "There."

Claws. "That should give 'em something to estimate depth." *He stands.* "All right, I'm done."

They step out. While Claws closes the door, Spots crouches alongside the crab she killed. "Hey, Claws?"

"Yeah?"

"Look at this."

Claws examines the corpse. "Looks like a Mark One? Like the junk crabs they've been throwin' at us."

Spots. "It *looks* like a Mark One, Claws. But look here, along the sides. And here, along the spine. The seams are different. And there's a pattern, a matte pattern. Same color, different texture."

Claws. "You ain't tellin' me this is a *disguised* bug."

Spots. "I'm telling you it doesn't look like the Mark Ones we've been killing."

Claws. ". . ."

[*Base*] **Claws** : Control, this is Recon 1. Ma'am, we gotta anomalous crab here. You want us to drag it in?

[*Base*] **Peaches** : Recon 1, this is the Lieutenant. If you can get it back, then yes. But if at any point you run into trouble, you drop it and run, understood?

[*Base*] **Claws** : Copy that, ma'am.

She and Claws share a look, then they each take a leg and start dragging.

Claws, muttering. "I'm touching a freakin' cockroach."

Spots. "A costumed cockroach."

Claws. "A *spyin'* cockroach."

Spots. "That almost sounds like a song."

Spots the Space Marine: Defense of the Fiddler

Claws. "The lyin' spyin' cockroach? Ain't done nobody good?"

Spots. "Picked a fine time to leave me!"

Claws. "Four thousand children and a crop in the Warren . . ."

Spots. ". . ."

Spots. "Wow, you're too young to know that song."

Claws. "Pshaw. Who don't know 'Lucille'? That's classic."

Spots, muttering. "Way to make a girl feel *old*, Claws."

Claws, mock prim. "Classic is a *compliment*, ma'am."

Spots. "You get back to me about that in a decade or two."

76. Butterflies

Barracks. Claws is turning back his blanket, Spots is picking up her rosary.

"Hey, Spots? Am I layin' it on too thick? The age bit."

"It has gotten a little bit . . . well."

"Old?" *Claws ducks when she mimes throwing a pillow.* "Seriously. If it bothers you, I'll stop."

Spots kneels in front of her rack. "I don't mind the ribbing, but you could use some new material."

Claws chuckles. "So noted." *And switches off his light. Ten minutes later Spots's rosary beads settle onto her night-table and her light flicks off too.*

———

Office. Peaches is working on paperwork at the desk when her com beeps.

"Bonnet here."

"This is West. We're in the Boardroom with the new specimen now, Lieutenant."

"Go ahead and get started, I'll be there in five."

Peaches finishes, sleeps her computer and heads down the hall. She is almost to the room:

"Boardroom, emergency, we've got—****!" *Gunshots. Screams.*

Peaches. "Security, medical teams to the boardroom!"

Peaches draws her sidearm and sprints for the door, opening it on an abattoir: four people are down, pouring blood. As she enters, the crab—very much alive—kills the intelligence officer. Crabs can slice through armored limbs; what they do unarmored humans is unspeakable. And quick.

Its back is to her. She brings the sidearm up, gripping it with both hands, and shoots it in the head. Again. And again. She empties the magazine into its head and thorax.

It turns toward her and lurches, swinging scythed claws. Peaches knocks the dissection table over and kicks it, smashing the crab back, but it keeps coming. She throws the empty pistol at it then grabs the framed photo on the wall. As the crab leans toward her, she ducks inside its reach and breaks the frame over its head, then uses the wooden edge to wield a glass shard on its eyes.

Spots the Space Marine: Defense of the Fiddler

It collapses—

—onto her.

Avril pounds in a moment later with Gunny and two men, followed by a medical team.

Avril. "****! Help me get this off her."

Peaches, from beneath. " 'm . . . kay. I'm okay." *They lift it and she crawls a step, holding her shoulder.* "I think one . . . one of the specialists is still breathing—"

The medical team is already checking the fallen.

Avril. "Savannah!"

Peaches, very pale. "****, I think it broke that . . . that damned collarbone again."

Avril. "What the hell happened?"

Peaches. "Recon team . . . brought in a dead crab for dissection . . ."

"But it wasn't really dead?"

Peaches, deep breath. "Paul, they ***ing dragged it halfway through the Warren on its back. After one of them put a hole in it."

Avril, looking at the crab. "****. It *let* itself be dragged here?"

Peaches. "I don't know. But I want an answer. We need to call the Fiddler . . . uhn."

Avril, catching her as her elbow gives. "Savannah? Savannah!" *Touches her leg.* "Crap, that's yours, not someone else's. Corpsman!"

Peaches, struggling to sit back up. "No, I want . . . want to stay . . . for this!"

Avril. "I'll debrief you the moment it's over. God, Savannah, lie back down!"

The medical team leaves with six stretchers; Peaches is on the last one. Watching them, Avril says, "Gunnery Sergeant? Did they already start the recording for the procedure?"

Gunny, checking. "Yes, sir."

Avril. "Flag it for me. I think they're going to want to decorate Lieutenant Bonnet for trying to save these people. Now let's wake up the liaison team."

Private, glancing at the blood and wreckage. "Sir? Are we moving somewhere else?"

Avril. "No. Maybe the alien can learn something from the body before we drag it to the incinerator." *He crouches, picks up the soggy remains of the framed picture: butterflies with pins through them, washed in scarlet, dripping.* "I'm not going to hide the cost of silence from him."

77. Start with Violence

Outside the Boardroom. Avril is waiting beside the closed door. Spots and Claws arrive first, stop at attention.

Claws. "Sir. Corporal Walker and Private Guitart reporting as ordered."

Avril. "At ease. Where's the alien?"

Spots. "On his way, sir."

Avril. "We'll wait here, then."

Spots. "Lieutenant? May we ask . . . what's this about?"

Avril looks at them, is about to speak, when the Violinist turns the corner. "Ah. Samuel-Colt. Thank you for joining us."

Samuel-Colt, rising arpeggio. "We are at your service, Lieutenant-Paul-Avril."

Avril nods. "Good. We need your help." *He pushes open the door.*

The Boardroom. All the human bodies have been removed but the floor is slick and the walls spattered. The crab's hulk remains where Peaches dropped it, behind the upended dissection table. There is shattered glass all around the entrance. Neither Peaches's nor the intelligence officer's empty pistols have been recovered yet, and are eloquent.

Spots, whispering. "Mother of God."

Claws. "****. Don't tell me that thing was still ****in' *alive* when we brought it in."

Avril. "It appears so, Corporal."

Claws. "****! It was *dead*!"

Spots looks at Samuel-Colt. The Fiddler rests one upper-arm hand on Claws's shoulder, startling him.

Samuel-Colt, very low drone. "If it was designed to mimic death it would do so very completely. You would not have been able to tell. Even your instruments would have been fooled."

Claws, jaw clenched. "You ****in' warned us, didn't you. And we didn't ****in' listen." *To Avril.* "How many died?"

Avril. "We're not sure. One of the specialists was still breathing. Four, maybe five. And Lieutenant Bonnet was wounded bringing it down." *To Samuel-Colt.* "What can you tell us about this? Was this thing designed to infiltrate our base?"

Claws, angry. "*****, no. It was designed so stupid-****in' ********s could drag it inside the base's defenses."

Spots. "Claws. Lieutenant Bonnet ordered us to bring it in. It wasn't our decision."

Claws. "No, but she based it on data we gave her. Which was obviously. ****in'. Wrong."

Spots. "If it was designed to fool us into thinking it was dead by actually *being* dead for an hour and a half, Claws, I don't think you can call it 'obvious.' Unless God lent you His omniscience and didn't inform us?"

Samuel-Colt, interested. "Would your deity inform you of such a change?"

Spots. "He often—" *She stops, then shakes her head.* "Samuel-Colt. This crab?"

Samuel-Colt looks at it, single note plucked. "I can smell nothing. I cannot work with the dead except as you do, by visual observation."

Avril. "You're saying you need a live one to give us any information on a change this big? There's nothing you can tell us?"

Samuel-Colt. "A live specimen would be more illuminating, yes."

Before Avril can speak, Spots says, "This disguising of it. Why would you do that if you were designing it?"

Claws. "He told us already. Way back when. For recon. They fall fake-dead in the Warren, their own collect 'em when our backs are turned."

Samuel-Colt. "That was our supposition, yes. Infiltration is not a tactic used by the Enemy."

Spots. "Samuel-Colt? We found the location where the Enemy enters the Warren. They appear to use holes. And a door."

Samuel-Colt. "Those are not uncommon methods."

Avril, frustration showing. "Is there anything you can tell us about this? Anything we could use?"

Samuel-Colt, slow melody. "Lieutenant-Paul-Avril, you already know that the Enemy is designing new models. We can guess at their purpose, which you have also already done. We can dissect the body, which you already do. If you bring us a living crab, we might be able to divine more from the pheromonal signature and the carapace scent-markers. But we are no more omniscient than the Mother's-Escort. We cannot commune with the dead."

Spots the Space Marine: Defense of the Fiddler

Claws looks at him sharply.

Avril. "Fine. Corporal, Private, you are dismissed. Samuel-Colt, thank you for your time."

Samuel-Colt, falling arpeggio. "You are welcome." *He steps outside. Spots and Claws follow.*

Claws turns immediately, stepping so aggressively into the Violinist's space that Samuel-Colt back-pedals. "You know more about this than you're tellin'. So ****in' TELL US."

Spots, grabbing his shoulder. "Claws!"

Claws. "It's true, isn't it? Isn't it? **** you, TELL ME!"

Spots. "CLAWS!"

Samuel-Colt. "I have suppositions, Mother's-Escort. Nothing more. And some things I will not give breath to speak unless they can be corroborated."

Claws. "And if we bring you a live one? That'll be ****in' enough?"

Spots. "Travis, please!"

Samuel-Colt. "It may be."

Claws. "Then we'll ****in' bring you a live one. And you'll find out what the **** is going on here, if you have to ****in' eat him yourself. Do you understand?"

Spots. "TRAVIS!"

Samuel-Colt. "Mother's-Escort, you presume too much." *He raises a scythed claw.* "Our peers may speak to us that way. Others must show more courtesy."

Claws. "You want me to ****in' paint your arm just to get you to talk? You want us to start this off with violence? I'll do it. I'll bind us together against our ****in' wills if that's what it takes!"

Spots gets between them and shoves Claws back. "That's *enough.* Enough! This is what the Enemy wants. This is what the Enemy has wanted since God cast him out of Heaven. Stop!"

Claws turns his back on them and leaves.

78. GUILT

"And now, Mother? Will you go to Sickbay and see the fallen?"

Spots shakes her head. "No, it's too soon. I'd be in the way of people doing their jobs."

Samuel-Colt, rising minor arpeggio. "Then will you follow your errant escort?"

Spots, looking down the hall. "No. Now is not the time for that either."

Samuel-Colt, long sawed note. "And what is it the time for, Mother?"

"Sleep."

"You feel no guilt?"

She smiles up at him, sad. "Of course I do. But guilt can be a . . . very personal indulgence, Samuel-Colt. It often takes the focus off the people who truly need you, while you are busy involved in yourself and your own sins. So I will sleep. Because it's the middle of my sleep-shift and my squad will need me to be alert on patrol."

Samuel-Colt. "Spoken like a Mother."

"It's what I've been for most of my life so far." *She looks up at him.* "Do you need anything before I retire?"

"Tell me something, if you would."

"If I can."

Samuel-Colt, rising melody. "You allow your escort to indulge himself, but you do not extend this courtesy to yourself, to . . . act out. Do mothers not have the same needs as their children?"

Spots, sad. "Of course they do, Samuel-Colt. We've just been in too many situations where the cost of acting out is higher than the cost of being responsible." *She smiles a little.* "When Claws is a father—God grant him that privilege—then it will be his turn to make those choices. Until then he needs what freedom I can give him so he can find his limits."

Samuel-Colt. "And yet he is not your child."

Spots. "Every mother's son—and daughter—is my child, Samuel-Colt."

"That seems ambitious, Mother-soldier. Spiritually speaking."

"Maybe. But it's the charge that was given to me by the Mother of God, so I follow in

Spots the Space Marine: Defense of the Fiddler

wiser footsteps than mine." *She looks up at him.* "What will you do?"

"What I have ever done in the face of the Enemy, Mother. My work." *Samuel-Colt bows. Spots returns it. The Fiddler departs.*

Spots stares down the hall a few moments more. Then she goes back to the Barracks.

———

Shots of the base. Claws in the hall. Claws passing the Real Window. From different angles, light on a face held in a tense mask, eyes hard. He walks . . . walks. Walks.

Gym. One of Alpha Company's squads is working out. Claws's entrance draws significant attention. He ignores the stares to head for the weight bench, which he loads up and starts using.

Eventually someone leans on the wall next to the bench and watches.

Claws. "Yeah?"

"You compensating?"

Claws. "****, what?"

"You know, compensating. Not using a spotter cuz you're putting out for the alien."

Claws shoves the bar back up. Sits up. "You wanna ****in' repeat that, ****er?"

"You're the one, right?" *Wiggles fingers and makes a face.* "The aaaalien whisperer."

Claws, incredulous. "You have got to be ****in' kiddin' me."

Another man joins the first. "He's the one. I've seen him with the girl."

Claws. "You ********s gotta problem with that?"

Second man. "You got a problem with humans? That why you spend so much time ****ing with aliens?"

Claws rolls his eyes and starts to lie back down. "****, if that's the best you can do, you gotta lot of practicin' to do. Look me up when you can dish out some serious ****, not this high school crap."

Third man. "****, it's not the alien he's ****ing, everyone knows that."

Claws is off the bench and shoving him against the wall before can finish the sentence. "You ****in' accusin' me of ****in' a SQUADMATE? Is that what you're doin'? I want to hear it ****in' louder this time, so God Al-****in'-mighty can HEAR YOU LIE."

217

Silence.

Claws steps back. "Didn't think so." *Throws his towel at the nearest man, who catches it by reflex. As he passes someone mutters,* "****, man, it bothers you more to be accused of ****ing a woman than a bug?"

Claws stops. "You don't **** your squad. I'd **** an alien before I **** over my kinfolk. If you ****ers don't get that yet, **** all if I want to fight next to you."

And then he's out the door and walking. Walking.

Walking through the Door.

. . . to the Lab. Slams the door-chime with the meat of his fist. When the door slides open, he steps in.

"What the ****? You lecturin' me on COURTESY when there's blood ankle-deep on the floor? You givin' me ****? You think I need more ****? I already GOT ****. ****, I just had a roomful of ****in' fatheads try to tell me you and me were ****in' lovers, or me and SPOTS were and that's just ****in' sick and I don't need it harder from you and what the **** are you starin' at me at for, don't you have a single thing to say to me?"

Samuel-Colt, sitting at his desk, tosses him something. Claws catches it, bewildered.

"What the **** is this?"

"Your tranquilizer round."

79. New Territory

Claws stares at the bullet. Samuel-Colt continues.

"You must strike an unarmored location, at least once, possibly twice. After the target has fallen, we suggest shearing off its limbs before towing it in. A dolly would be easiest, but a strap around the head would also suffice without damaging the specimen."

Claws, staring at him now. Drawls finally, "Reckon we could mount casters to the shell and kick it in."

Samuel-Colt. "That would work also. Field glue should be sufficient to affix them if the carapace is dry. We recommend wiping the carapace down with alcohol to remove any ichor first."

Claws carefully closes his fingers around the round. "Sam. . . ."

"Claws." *A sharp note, causing Claws to look at him.* "There are things I *cannot* say. Without the Mother, *most* of what I have said I would not have been able to say. This is not my choice. It is by design."

Claws, hand fisted now. "You're tellin' me this is biology."

"Yes. Even with the Mother, I could not speak at all, only design weapons, had there not been a slight irregularity . . . in that during one of the changes in power, the new Mother decided everyone who interfaces with humanity had to be better at communicating with them. We spent one short life as a diplomat before resuming our work in weapons design."

"And this bein' a diplomat involves . . . a different model. Different brain?"

"Correct."

Claws is silent. Then. "You tellin' me you're tellin' us stuff Fiddlers have *never* told anyone?"

Samuel-Colt spreads his upper limbs in a very human gesture. "We do not know, Claws. Only that we are sharing information we have never shared in any of our lifetimes."

"Because of Spots."

"It is a pheromonal matter."

Claws stares at him. "*****, Sam, our mothers can't possibly smell like yours. We're flesh and bone and blood. You're mostly goo on the inside. You sure don't nurse."

"We know. We can only surmise that decades of exposure to humans has caused . . . an adaptation."

"That must be ****in' scary for you."

A hiss from the vestigial limbs. "It is the way of things. One adapts, or one dies." *A softer note.* "In a way, it is a blessing. We will never live among our kind again. It is comforting to regard humanity as less alien."

Claws. "****. Talk about comin' into a dysfunctional family. Look, I'm sorry. About this. About the hall." *Rubbing his face with his free hand.* "About draggin' that crab the **** in, and for what? We didn't learn nothin' from it."

"Had you truly killed it, it would have been useless for dissection. Do you not say hindsight is perfect?"

Claws. "There are people dead—"

"Most likely."

"—because of me!"

Samuel-Colt, another sharp note. "Because of the *Enemy*. Your guilt is not becoming, placing responsibility as it does in the wrong place."

"But—"

Samuel-Colt, staccato arpeggio, minor, descending. "No. If you believe you are worthy of blame, then are not the dead also for not being armed? For not being prepared? They were complacent, yes?"

"No!"

"Then?"

Claws. "****." *He looks at the round again.* "I'll have to tell them about this."

"We would prefer it, yes. Through you and the Mother." *At Claws's look, Samuel-Colt finishes.* "This situation . . ." *A hesitation?* "This situation grows more complex for us. Diplomatically. Biologically. We feel the need for protection."

A silence then.

Claws. "All right. All right." *He stands.* "Is my apology acceptable, or should I do some special alien grovel dance?"

Samuel-Colt's long, sawing note is somehow dry. "If we require your dignity at any point in payment for crimes committed, we will inform you."

Spots the Space Marine: Defense of the Fiddler

"Gee, thanks Sam. Good night."

"Good night, Peer."

Just outside the door, Claws stops. Turns and looks inside again. "****, Sam. An *unarmored* location?"

Samuel-Colt. "That is correct, Peer. You will have to shoot them in the eyes."

80. Better than a Hallmark Card

Claws returns to the Barracks. Spots is asleep in her rack, rosary tangled in her hand. He looks at her for a long time, then turns in.

Following morning.

Shaking Spots. "Hey."

"Claws? Alarm didn't go off—"

"We gotta errand to run before patrol."

Spots sits up, rubs her eyes with one hand, beads swinging. She sets the rosary on her desk. "Sure. What are we doing?"

"We need to tell Peaches that the tranq rounds are ready."

"Already?"

"Yeah."

Spots glances at him. Then nods. "All right. Give me five."

———

Sickbay, not long after. Claws stops a corpsman. "Is the LT awake?"

"Not a chance. She's in bed twelve, dreaming the dreams of the righteously medicated."

Spots. "And the others they brought in yesterday?"

"Three of them are in the morgue. The last two just got out of surgery. Prognosis is positive. More or less."

Claws. "What does 'more or less' mean?"

"We had to amputate an arm on one of them. The other might be paralyzed. You never know with paralysis, though, sometimes people snap back."

Claws. ". . ."

Spots, nudging him. "Thanks for telling us. Come on, Claws."

Claws, whispering. "Was he tryin' to be funny? Because that sure as hell wasn't funny."

Spots. "He's medical, Claws. They have an off-center sense of humor, they've seen too much."

Claws. "And we haven't?"

Spots. "Are you trying to tell me soldiers have a less macabre sense of humor than doctors? Soldiers? Really?"

Claws. ". . ."

Claws. "Okay, point." Looks around. "I just don't like the vampires."

Spots, hard. "They keep us alive. You don't have to like them, Claws. Just show them a little respect."

At bed twelve, Claws hovers over Peaches while Spots reads the monitor. "Broken collarbone, big gash in her thigh . . . 32 stitches! Ouch. They pumped a lot of blood back into her. Bruises, cuts. Nothing more serious though."

Claws. "This is nothing serious? I'd hate to see serious."

Spots. "She'll be okay."

Claws rolls his shoulder. Then turns and hunts for a piece of paper and pen. He writes:

Fiddler's gift, by way of Mom and her Tag-along. You want a live one, these'll bring one down. Say the word. —Walker

He wraps it around the round and secures it with a rubber band, then leaves it on the tray by her bed.

Spots. "Quite a present."

Claws. "It was that or a Hallmark card. Somehow I'm thinkin' she'll like the bullet better."

———————

Much later, after patrol. The rest of Team Kitty has finished stripping their suits and dispersed. Spots is racking her power packs.

"Hey, Claws?"

"Yeah."

"We still doing practice?"

Claws looks up. "What? Yeah." Shakes himself. "Yeah, of course."

"It's okay if you want to take the time off."

"No, I'm fine. Patrol was too freakin' quiet, that's all. Gives me the collywobbles."

Spots. "You weren't the only one. It was getting to all of us. We couldn't even keep any of the word-games going." *She finishes up.* "All right, I'm done. Lead the way."

They head past the Door to the Testing Facility. Spots starts on her stretches while Claws checks the gloves. They've barely been there a few minutes when:

Fang2, at the door. "****! A guy can't sleep around here without all hell breaking ****ing loose!"

Claws. "What the hell are you jawin' about, princess?"

"You, smart-***. I heard you almost took on the entirety of squad PYEO in the gym."

Spots. "Claws? What's this about?"

Claws covers his eyes with a hand, muttering. "Aw, Jesus."

81. LEGENDS

Spots, looking at Claws. "He did what?"

Fang2, dropping onto his exercise mat. "He ****ing picked a fight in the gym when it was, like, eight to one. And actually brazened it the **** out so they didn't pound him to ****ing powder."

Claws. "Christ, Chao, if you're gonna tell the story, tell it right. They picked the fight, not me."

Fang2 chortles. "Not the way they tell it. Which is all about the size of your—"

Claws holds up a hand, wincing. "Chao!"

Fang2 to Spots. "I heard it was because of you and the Fiddler."

Claws. "Can we please stop talkin' about this?"

Fang2. "You know you wanna."

Claws. "I'm completely sure I don't, really, honest, cross-my-heart."

Fang2 to Spots. "I'm serious, it was about you."

Spots, back to stretching. "I'm sure it was."

They both look at her.

Fang2. "That's it?"

Spots. "Yes?"

Claws. "Really? You're not gonna ask?"

"Nope."

Claws. "Not even a single question?"

Spots. "Well, maybe one." *Looking at Fang2.* "What on earth is a pee-yoh?"

Fang2. "It's not a thing. P-Y-E-O. It stands for 'Peck Your Eyes Out.' I play cards with their sergeant, Abrams, he's cool. Maybe a little whacked, but cool."

Spots. "Oh, the man with the broken leg?"

Fang2. "Heh! Yeah, him."

Claws. "Do you know everyone?"

Spots, sweetly. "Apparently not as well as you almost did."

Claws, touching hand to chest. "Ouch." *To Fang2,* "I hope this story hasn't gone far."

Fang2. "**** no, man! I was lucky to hear it all after that footage about Bonny-****-you-up-beautiful-Peaches got out!"

Claws, slowly. "The . . . what?"

Fang2. "The footage of her taking on that infiltrator crab single-handedly! You haven't seen it?" *He mimes a shooting gesture with one hand.* "Pee-yow! She emptied her gun into that ****er, and when it didn't go down she ****ing *kicked* it like some kind of barroom brawler and when that didn't stop it she ****ing took it on with a PIECE OF GLASS to the ****ing EYES!"

Spots, wide-eyed. "No kidding."

Fang2. "Not a chance, Mother! That was some serious-****ing ***-kicking!"

Spots lowers her head, hand to her mouth to cover her twitching mouth.

Fang2. "I'm serious! You have got to see the video, it's ****ing AWESOME."

Claws, moving toward the wall computer. "All right, yeah, I wanna see this—"

—when the door opens on two security men and . . . Fang.

Long pause.

Security. "This private says you're expecting her?"

Claws. "Yeah, she's one of ours. Let her in. Thanks."

They nod and step back as Fang steps forward. The door closes. Another silence. Then:

Fang. "I'm not stupid. The moves the two of you were doing on patrol . . . those are way too smooth. You've been training."

Claws, holding up his hands. "You got us. What about it?"

Fang. "I want in."

82. Leading From Behind

A long pause.

Fang looks at them, scowls. "What?"

Claws. "Well, you've kinda been a ***** since you showed up."

Fang2. "He's kinda got a point."

Fang. "So? Being a ***** doesn't make me blind to the importance of training." *She points at Fang2.* "And you've got no room to talk. You've been ****ing with me since I got reassigned."

Fang2. "Of course I've been ****ing with you. You were such a tight*** about everything I had to. I can't resist easy targets. Why do you think I'm here?"

Claws. "All right, all right. That's enough." *Eyes Fang.* "You willin' to work at it?"

Fang, rolling her eyes. "No, idiot, I'm here to **** around. I was a *Dragon*. I can work you to the dirt."

Fang2, muttering. "Sex-eh! I'd like to see that!"

Claws. "Oh God, the mental image." *Covers his eyes. Points at Fang2.* "You are so gettin' extra push-ups for that one."

Spots. "This is good. We're going to have to practice covering for a sniper now that we have those tranquilizers."

Fang, Fang2. "What?"

Spots. "Samuel-Colt finished making those tranquilizer rounds, so we can bring back a crab for dissection."

Fang. "Didn't you two just do that?"

Fang2. "Do what? Bring—holy ****, man! You're responsible for the thing that Peaches went ****ing hardcore on?"

Claws. "Yeah. It was playin' dead."

Fang. "What now? It wasn't dead?"

Fang2. "****! Who's got the whole story? You two? And you haven't spilled? ****! Can we get it now?"

Claws, scowling. "Why are you so eager to know?"

Fang2. "I'm stuck in Sickbay. Gossip is like cold hard cash."

Spots. "There's no story to tell, Fang2. Claws and I went through the Warren to find where the crabs have been coming from and found their . . . well, their entry point, I guess. We killed a crab there and the lieutenant asked us to bring in the body, so we did. When they put it on the dissection table, it woke up and killed three people and wounded two more before the lieutenant brought it down. That's it."

Fang2. "****!"

Spots, looking at Fang. "So . . . we could use the practice, covering someone shooting. We haven't experimented with that using the new shields."

Fang, rolling her shoulder. "Like I said, Mama. I want in."

Spots. "All right." *Looking at Claws.* "How do you want to do this?"

Claws, staring at them. "****, did I just get out-voted?"

Spots. "Only if you were objecting. You weren't objecting to someone in the squad wanting to train with us . . . as a squad, right?"

Claws. "Of course not, I just . . ." *He throws up his hands.* "Fine." *Points at Fang.* "But no prima donna ****. You'll learn the shield-tech along with the rest of us. I don't want a situation where one of us gettin' cut down ****s us over."

Fang. "I've got no problem with that."

Claws. "Fine. Let's start with some scenario design." *Turns to Fang2.* "And you . . . you got yoga to do, princess."

Fang2. "What can I say. It's in my *genes* to be a yoga-mastah."

Fang. "I thought yoga was Indian."

Fang2. "Same continent. Close enough." *He beams at her.* "****, Fang, I've missed you."

Claws. "Chao, hit the mat. Ladies, with me."

Fang2. "****! How come you get all the luck?"

Claws. "You call this lucky?"

Spots. "Hey!"

Fang2. "It is when you've been staring at man-*** for weeks. Sickbay, rrrgh."

Spots the Space Marine: Defense of the Fiddler

Later, Sickbay. Fang2 checks in with the staff, is issued a limp-looking meal and sits on his bed to eat it.

A protein bar lands on his nightstand. Scythe slides onto the stool next to him. "So? How's it going?"

Fang2. "Heh. Would you believe Fang-****ing-one showed up?"

Scythe lifts a brow. "No kidding. How'd that go?"

Fang2, reaching for the bar. "Uncomfortable when she first got in, but once she started working it all smoothed out."

Scythe. "Who's leading the lessons?"

Fang2. "Claws still."

Scythe. "She's taking direction from him, then?"

Fang2, mouth full. "Yep. She doesn't give him as much lip as I thought she would. She'll be back tomorrow."

Scythe. "Good."

Fang2. "When are you crashing the party?"

Scythe. "Maybe a week. Speaking of crashed parties, when they letting you out?"

Fang2, after licking the wrapper clean. "Light duty next week. Finally. I'm getting ****ing tired of fleecing the same people over and over."

Scythe. "All right. Thanks for keeping an eye on it for me, Chao."

Fang2. "No problemo, Boss. Thanks for the candy."

Scythe slaps his shoulder. Outside Sickbay, he grins to himself before strolling off.

A few beds over, Peaches wakes. Her bleary eye focuses on the round on her tray, then narrows. Her hand reaches out, closes on it. It takes her a moment to get the paper off and read it.

Peaches. "Yes . . . !" *And then hissing, touching her shoulder.* "****. I would pick now to be . . ." *Glances at monitor.* "A quarter dead." *Hits the call-button. When the corpsman arrives,* *she says,* "I know I should be resting. But I absolutely have to see the Violinist and his liaisons, right now."

"You're right, you should be resting."

Peaches. "If I said pretty-please with a cherry on top?"

The corpsman sighs.

83. A Little Kink in the Plan

Late evening. Spots and Claws are heading for Sickbay.

Spots. "Why is it that we can never seem to get a full night's sleep these days?"

Claws. "You know what they say. No rest for the wicked."

Spots, making a face. "Speak for yourself."

Claws. "Which part, the rest part or the wicked part?"

Spots eyes him. They enter Sickbay and head for Peaches's bedside. Gunny's there, and Avril.

Claws. "Ma'am. Corporal Walker and Private Guitart reportin' as ordered. You don't look so good."

Peaches studies him.

Claws. "Uh . . . ma'am?"

Peaches looks at Spots, who says nothing. Then: "Do either of you know why the Violinist just refused to come here without you escorting him?"

Claws. "Uh . . . literally escortin'? Like walkin' him down the hall?"

Peaches. "Yes, Corporal."

Claws. "No clue, ma'am. Not bein' an alien and all, I couldn't guess."

Peaches sighs. "Well, get over there and walk the damn alien here so we can discuss your present."

"Yes, ma'am."

"And make it quick, please. The new painkillers are going to kick in real soon now."

"Yes, ma'am."

Once again, Spots and Claws are outside Sickbay. Spots looks at Claws. He starts walking.

She smiles. "You don't have to tell me."

Claws, tense. "What?"

Spots. "You know why he did it. I can tell."

Claws. "Look, Spots—"

She holds up a hand. "You don't have to say anything. It's pretty obvious. He's worried, so he's putting layers of formality between himself and the lieutenant to remind her that he's not human."

Claws stares at her. "How the . . ."

"Not stupid, remember?"

Claws. "There's 'not stupid' and there's 'psychic.'"

Spots. "What I want to know is what's made him nervous *now.* That part I don't know. And you don't either, I bet, or you would have told the lieutenant."

Claws. "Crap! Stop doin' that 'starin' inside my head' thing. It's creepin' me out."

Spots chuckles, says nothing more.

———————

Sickbay. The door opens for Spots, Claws, Samuel-Colt and two guards. Their entrance causes a complete cessation of activity. As they pass they gather stares, stares that don't stop once they reach Peaches. The alien stands several heads above anyone else; his slim figure looks out-of-place among the medical equipment and the men and women resting on the beds. Fiddler technology never made it into Sickbay and it shows somehow.

Peaches. "Samuel-Colt, if we did anything to offend . . ."

Samuel-Colt, rising note. "There was no offense, Lieutenant-Savannah-Bonnet. How may we help you?"

Peaches, uncertain but not sure how to discuss it further. "I wanted to thank you for your work . . . and to ask. What kind of crab should we bring down? Which one will be most useful to you?"

Samuel-Colt. "That is a good question, Lieutenant-Savannah-Bonnet. We would have the easiest time with a King."

Peaches. "We can do that."

Avril. "Or we could, if there were any Kings to be found."

Everyone looks at him. He lifts his tablet. "I've been reviewing cam footage while waiting. The patrols are reporting no incursions. Nothing. Not even a single bug. The Warren's empty."

84. Internal Pressure

Peaches. "Completely? Nothing, not even an old model?"

Avril. "Not a thing." *Looks up at Samuel-Colt.* "What are they doing?"

Samuel-Colt, descending arpeggio. "We are not the Enemy, Lieutenant-Paul-Avril. We can only guess at their motivations."

Avril. "So . . . guess?"

Spots. "Sir." *Avril glances at her.* "A little courtesy, please."

Avril flushes, looks at Samuel-Colt. "Do you have any guesses you can share, Samuel-Colt?"

"No."

Full stop. Everyone looks at him.

Claws. "No? That's it?"

Samuel-Colt, sharp single note. "No." *Spreads his upper hands.* "If the Enemy has soldiers to send, they should be sending them. To abruptly withdraw is not in keeping with their normal tactics."

Peaches, frustrated and starting to slur. "What *has* been in keeping with their normal tactics lately?" *Rubs her forehead.* "Okay, I'm losing it. We'll just have to wait for them to come back. Send one person out per patrol with the tranq rounds—no, two if we have the ammo—and let's hope we get something to shoot down soon."

Avril. "I'll spread the news. You rest, Savannah."

Peaches. "No choice . . . Thank you . . . Samuel-Colt."

Samuel-Colt. "It is our pleasure, Lieutenant-Savannah-Bonnet. Unless there is something else?"

Avril. "No, you can go. Thank you."

Samuel-Colt turns. Stops when Spots and Claws don't move.

Spots. "Samuel-Colt?"

Samuel-Colt. "We are awaiting our escorts."

Avril stares at him. His eyes narrow. To Spots and Claws: "Dismissed."

Outside in the corridor, Claws swears under his breath. "You tryin' to get us in trouble, Sam? Tearin' us between the officers and you? How exactly is that gonna help anyone?"

Samuel-Colt, low minor melody. "We must protect myself, Claws."

Spots. "From what? What is it that you see that you aren't telling us?"

Samuel-Colt keeps moving. They follow him to his room, where he stops at the door and faces them.

Claws. "It's not 'aren't tellin'' this time. It's 'can't,' ain't it."

Spots. "Can't . . . like physically? Biologically?"

Claws, muttering. "Quit that psychic crap, it's creepy."

Spots to Samuel-Colt. "So you do know something."

Samuel-Colt, minor arpeggio, slow, falling. "Only guesses, Mother-soldier. We promise you that. If we knew for certain . . ."

Spots. "You would tell us?"

Samuel-Colt, with a sharp rasp, not musical at all. "You could compel us to tell you."

Claws, uneasy. "Is that another biological thing?"

Samuel-Colt, falling note, somehow sad. "Of course, Peer. Good night."

The door shuts on them. They stare at it for a few moments. Then:

Spots. "So there's some biological component to this?"

Claws. "Um . . . yeah. He sorta literally can't tell us some things, and the only thing that's lettin' him squirm through the loopholes is that he put in a shift as a politico and some of the wiring's still there."

Spots. "Huh. Interesting."

Claws glances at her. "You're not upset?"

"What?" *She starts walking back.* "Why would I be upset?"

Claws. "Because he told me and not you."

Spots chuckles. "This isn't high school, Claws. I'm not going to get jealous of you being friends with him because I want to be friends with him too."

Spots the Space Marine: Defense of the Fiddler

Claws. "I'm not—****, I guess I am friends with him. Sort of."

Spots's mouth twitches. She continues. "Besides, you would never have talked to him had it not been for me, right? I seem to remember you trying to pull me back into a hiding place when I first saw him in the Armory."

Claws. "I guess not, no. Well, no, never. Who talks to the Fiddlers? They're creepy. Like giant grasshoppers."

Spots. "More like giant shrimp. But anyway. There you go. Instead of being jealous, I get to be happy because I'm responsible for the two of you hitting it off."

Claws. "Nice way of thinkin' of it."

Spots. "I'm a nice . . . hmm."

"Hmm?"

Spots stops, folding her arms and looking at him. "It wouldn't have worked. You pulling me into a hiding place back then. He could have smelled us."

Claws. "Well, yeah."

Spots. "What if they smelled us near their holes? Maybe that confused them and that's why they're hiding right now."

Claws. "Maaaaybe."

Spots, watching his eyes. "I know that look. What far more horrible thing are you thinking?"

Claws. "Or maybe they're massin' in preparation for *our* invasion. If you find a couple of ants by their lonesome in your house, what do you think?"

Spots. "That they're finding a trail for all the other ants. Huh. You think they think we were point for an invasion?"

Claws. "Maybe."

Spots. "Seems as good a theory as none, which is what they've got right now. Are you going to tell the lieutenant?"

Claws. "Yeah. Tomorrow. She's kinda got enough on her plate right now. And we're a good two hours late for our own sacks. Come on, Mom."

Spots. "You really want me to start calling you 'son'?"

Claws. "I wouldn't mind."

Spots. ". . ."

Spots, hurrying after him. "!"

Spots the Space Marine: Defense of the Fiddler

85. Empathy, Unexpected

Barracks, in their racks:

Claws. "You ain't said nothing about him callin' me 'peer'."

Spots. "Neither have you."

Claws. "Too-shay, ma'am. Too-shay."

Spots smiles, turns over and goes to sleep.

An hour later, Claws is still staring at the wall.

Claws, under breath: "****."

He rises, dresses and goes to Sickbay, to the lieutenant's bed; Peaches is still unconscious. He stands by her bedside for several minutes, shoulders tense and head lowered. Then strides out.

. . . down the hall . . .

. . . to the lieutenant's office, where he touches the door-announce.

Avril, intercom. "Who is it?"

Claws, leaning on button. "Corporal Walker to see the lieutenant, sir."

"Come in."

Claws enters, comes to attention. Avril sets down the file he was reading, which has Spots's photo at the upper corner.

Avril. "Well, if it isn't Corporal Smart-***."

Claws, still at attention. "That totally wasn't called for, sir."

Avril. "You're right. At ease. In fact, sit. I was just thinking about you and Guitart."

Claws sits. Glances at file. "I see, sir."

Avril, leaning back. "I've had a little talk with Lieutenant Bonnet about you, Corporal. She thinks you're not living up to your full potential."

Claws, eyes down. "Is that so, sir."

Avril, reaching under the desk. "Yes. So tell me, Walker. Just off the record. What happened to your dad?"

Claws stiffens. " 'Scuse me?"

Avril sets a beer in front of him. Sits back down behind the desk with one of his own. "What happened to your father? I assume that's behind your attitude problem."

Claws eyes the beer, then Avril. "Beggin' your pardon, sir, but you ain't earned that story."

Avril. "I know. But I'm the one who might actually get it, since it was an idiot officer who sent my father home from Afghanistan in a wheelchair."

Claws sits up slowly.

Avril unscrews the cap, takes a sip. "He didn't want anyone to think he didn't have the proper fighting *spirit*. So he sent them into a cave after some insurrectionists. A *cave*. That they were using as an ops base. It's a miracle anyone got out alive. Dad came home and never walked again. My mother divorced him a few years later. I loved my mom and I was proud of my dad, so the only one left to be angry at was . . ."

Claws. "The officer."

Avril, pointing the neck of his beer at Claws. "Bingo. Sound familiar?"

Claws looks at his bottle, opens it. "A little, yeah."

Avril. "Not a Marine, was he. Your father, I mean."

Claws. "No. Army. My little brother decided to become an Army officer to do right by men like my dad."

Avril. "And you . . . didn't."

Claws. "**** no! I watched our mom raise us alone. But the war got bad."

Avril. "So you decided to do your duty. But like your dad did, as a grunt. So you joined a service where no one would recognize you."

Claws. "That was the plan, yeah, so how the **** did you figure it out?"

Avril. "Because you remind me of me. And then I saw your file, did a little research and made a guess."

Claws. "**** of a guess, sir."

Avril. "Yeah, well . . . I've been learning that a lot of life is making guesses and hoping the hell you're right. I don't have a leg to stand on, hating the man who got my parents divorced and my dad crippled. For all I know, he sent his squad out on less intel than I'm operating on now, trying to help Bonnet keep the crabs from savaging another company." *Drinks.* "Been a lot of Walkers in the military?"

Spots the Space Marine: Defense of the Fiddler

Claws. "Could say that. All the way back to WWII. Still want to see Iwo Jima if I ever get back."

Avril. "It's worth it."

Claws looks up. "You been?"

Avril. "Yeah. I picked up some black sand. Think every Marine officer should make that hike up Suribachi." *Smiles wryly.* "My family saw WWII too. On the French side."

Claws. "****. Harsh."

Avril. "I know. Don't have much to prove, do I." *He pushes the empty bottle aside.* "Look, Walker. You're ****ing wasted as a corporal. You know it. I know it. Your dad's ghost knows it, and he's probably pissed to be your excuse. Bonnet thinks you're a shoo-in for officer training. I think she's right."

Claws snorts. "You hardly know me to make that call, sir."

Avril. "I know a backseat-driver when I see one. You're too smart. You see the big picture. Don't you think you could do more good putting that brain up here where it can make decisions? Because you can't tell me officers don't make them all the way down the line. Not anymore. This is not your father's war, your grandfather's, your great-grandfather's. I'm a ****ing second lieutenant, Walker, and I'm sitting on top of a frigging supercollider with no one to pull my *** out of the fire if the crabs blow it up. If there's even an *** left to pull if that thing goes."

Claws. "Yeah. What if I don't want the ****in' responsibility?"

Avril. "Then you wouldn't have managed to get connected to the sole intelligence resource on the planet that could save us, would you? But you did."

Claws, glancing at file. "That why you readin' up on us?"

Avril. "Like I said, Walker. You're too smart for your boots."

Claws sets his empty bottle on the desk. "I appreciate the pitch, sir."

"You'll consider it?"

Claws. "Nope."

Avril sighs. Chuckles. "If you go mustang in ten years, you'd better buy me a drink."

Claws grins. "That's fair. Bourbon washes down humble pie pretty easy. Is that all, sir?"

"Almost. Why'd you stop by?"

Claws. "Just thinkin' that the crabs might be hidin' from us because we mighta left a track they could smell near the holes. Maybe they think we're gonna push and they're preppin' for that."

Avril. "The thought had occurred to me, yes." *At Claws's look:* "Not all of us are stupid, you know. We'll be sending some robot scouts once we finish configuring them."

Claws. "Huh. Think they'll get through?"

Avril. "Probably not, the way our luck runs. But you need to buy a ticket if you want to win the lottery."

Claws. "True." *He stands up, starts to salute, pauses.* "Sir? Is it true, Spots bein' a secretary?"

Avril. "More or less."

Claws. "How the hell did she end up here?"

Avril grins. "Why's a corporal asking?"

Claws. "Maybe it's her ASL who's askin', and it would kinda be handy to know how a secretary ended up in a powered armor company. I know we're runnin' out of folks but I didn't think we were scrapin' that far down the bottom of the barrel."

Avril. "All right, I'll buy that line. The reason Guitart's here is almost certainly that she's logged more EVA work than any of us combined volunteering for Search and Rescue ops on that asteroid her husband mines. They probably figured she could handle herself in a suit without training. And unlike me or you or probably most of us, she's actually used a gun for something other than target practice."

Claws. "****, what? What's that mean?"

Avril. "Not telling. If you want the story, you'll have to get it from her. Or go earn your own bars. Dismissed, Corporal."

*Claws salutes and exits. And stops outside the door, staring at the wall. Mutters: "****!" and then heads to the barracks to sleep. But not before eyeing Spots for a few long moments.*

86. Spots is Dancing(2)

Quick scenes:

Conference Room. Platoon Leader Big Lion, the tall woman with epicanthic folds and bronze hair, is showing the new rounds to the squad leaders and talking. The sergeants pick up the tranqs assigned to them as they listen.

———

Sickbay. Peaches leaning over a tray and pointing to Avril's display. He zooms in on the new traps installed by the Seabees, tags them and starts typing notes into the field as she explains them. They start going back and forth over a tactical plan while Peaches's food grows cold.

———

Engineering. Drones upside down on tables, their chipsets missing, frowning men and women around them.

Technician 1: ****, that's the fourth one they've gotten. At this rate we're going to have to send the ****ing vacuums.

———

Avril in the lieutenant's office typing.

Captain:

We urgently request the assignment of a new intelligence officer to replace the one we recently lost to a crab playing dead...

———

Two days later, the Test Facility. Fang2 has already left and Fang is just out the door, mopping the sweat off the back of her neck.

Claws. "You ready?"

Spots. "Actually, I have an appointment to keep with Samuel-Colt."

Claws. "What's this now?"

Spots. "Remember I promised him music?"

Claws. "Ohhhh, yeah. Guess I'm escortin', eh?"

Spots. "I don't know that you have to, but you can."

Claws. "At your service then, Mom."

Spots smiles at him and heads for the Fiddler's room. When they announce themselves, Samuel-Colt bids them enter. He is . . . reading a book.

Claws. "You read, too?" *Checks the ratty cover.* "Aw, hell. A romance novel? You're into the base stash."

Samuel-Colt, amused rising arpeggio. "Yes? Should we not check them out?"

Claws. "Well, if you're gonna, not that one. That one sucked powerful bad. I wanted to face-punch Cindy by page 40. Go for the 'Simmerin' Desire' series if you're down to the romance novels."

Spots is staring at him.

Claws. "What? You get friggin' bored enough you'll read *anything*. And I do mean *anything*."

Samuel-Colt, still amused. "What brings the Mother-soldier and her escort here?"

Spots. "I promised music . . ."

Samuel-Colt, sudden note, rising, leaping. "Ah! Yes!"

Spots looks around. "You have a terminal . . . ?"

"There, by the desk. Would you like refreshment? I have made tea."

While Spots loads a playlist, Claws says: "You drink tea?"

Samuel-Colt rises and comes back with a tray with iron cups and a teapot decorated with a meadow in relief. One of its blowing grasses forms the handle, another the spout. "It is a long story."

Claws. "Lemme guess. Some Japanese bigwig taught you the tea ceremony."

Samuel-Colt saws a pained note. "No. Someone *thought* we looked like the sort of creature who would appreciate a tea ceremony and attempted to re-enact one to impress us."

Claws, laughing. "Ouch. 'You seem alien! You might like the Japanese!' "

Samuel-Colt. "Just so. We have since forgotten as much of the situation as possible. The beverage was blameless, so we still drink it."

Spots joins them as her music starts playing.

Samuel-Colt, curious. "What have you brought me?"

Spots the Space Marine: Defense of the Fiddler

Spots. "Everything I like to dance to." *A grin*. "We won't get through all of it tonight."

Samuel-Colt, holding tea-cup. "This song has vocalists."

Spots. "Yes . . . ? I notice you're usually listening to orchestral work. Do the Violinists prefer their music without words?"

Samuel-Colt. "Ahh . . . actually, the first music we ever heard was a cappella." *At their glances, he finishes*, "We learned music from our ocean's great sea mammals. Much like your whales, they sing."

Claws. "No **—kiddin'! *Whales*?"

Samuel-Colt. "Yes. They are larger and more numerous than the Earth equivalent, and their songs are part of the ocean, like the texture of water and the color of light through waves. We were always aware of music. We always danced. But we did not realize that someone *made* the song until we grew older. And then . . . ah, everything changed."

Spots, whispered. "Wow."

Samuel-Colt. "For generations, we followed the singers. They allowed us to cling to their sides as they traversed their great migration paths, journeys they undertook each season but that lasted several of our generations. We learned a great deal from them, living and dying and being born among them. Some of our theologians believe music taught us to order our thoughts." *Listening*. "This music has a very active bass line. It is not unlike our racial memories of those first songs."

Claws. "Crap! You—of course. You can remember that far back, can't you. You can't *not* remember that far back."

Samuel-Colt inclines his head.

Spots, looking at her tea-cup. "Huh. So that means . . . well, no wonder you're so good with us. You've been working alongside mammals since time out of mind."

Samuel-Colt. "Just so, Mother. We give it a name, in fact. 'Warmblood view,' maybe, I would translate it. The perspective of creatures like you."

Spots. "So you dance. And you sing!"

Samuel-Colt. "We do, Mother. To honor our teachers."

Spots. "Do you?"

Samuel-Colt. "Honor our teachers?"

Spots, laughing. "No, dance."

Samuel-Colt hesitates. "Mother-soldier, our dancing is a thing in the water, and we—we, that is, I and my embodied lineage—are creatures of this earth."

Spots. "Well, so am I and I can dance. That's no reason to give it up!"

Samuel-Colt. ". . ."

Samuel-Colt. "We would not even begin to know how."

Claws. "Aw, geez. I know where this is goin'. Someone cue the montage."

Spots glares at him. He lifts his hands. "Don't look at me. This white boy ain't gonna teach an alien to dance."

Samuel-Colt to Spots. "You would do this? Teach us?"

Spots. "Yes! Music belongs to everyone. And everyone should be allowed to dance, poorly or not." *She stands up.* "Would you like to try?"

Samuel-Colt. "We would like some time to . . . to grow accustomed to the idea . . . !"

Spots. "Nu-uh. That's just a way to talk yourself into never trying. Come on." *She offers her hands.* "Up."

Samuel-Colt's rising somehow conveys uncertainty. He spreads his upper hands. "And now?"

Spots. "And now . . . you move." *And she demonstrates. Claws pushes back until he's against the wall, watching with tea-cup in hand. As the music scrolls from trance to electronica to classical guitar, from folk songs to alternative, Spots dances, stops, shows the alien a movement until he copies it . . . and continues.*

. . . and at some point, though exactly when none of them can tell, Samuel-Colt is dancing.

87. Reunions

Sickbay, several days later.

Corpsman. "Looks like you're good to go, Private."

Fang2. "Whoo! About ****ing time!"

Corpsman. "Tell me about it. I still have two pennies to rub together, but I might not tomorrow the way you play."

Fang2. "Aw, hell, I hate stealing from a corpsman. But you make it so easy."

The corpsman laughs. "Get out of here, Chao."

Fang2 pockets the last half-eaten protein bar (coconut) and saunters past the beds. When he passes Abram's, the sergeant calls. "Hey! Leaving already?"

Fang2. "Yup! I'm fit as a soccer mom!" *He flexes.*

Abrams. "How come you got out without physical therapy?"

Fang2. "Oh, I was doing the ****ing therapy. They just pawned it off on my ASL."

Abrams. "Seriously? He have training?"

Fang2. "Only the bad***ery kind. He's running the team drills." *He grins.* "Maybe if you ask nice he'd do you too."

Abrams snorts. "Like he tried to do my team in the gym?"

Fang2, laughing. "Hell, yeah. That's Claws. Tough mother . . . uh . . ." *He trails off.* "****! Do not want, bad image. He's a tough son of a *****."

Abrams shakes his head. "I'll keep that in mind."

Fang2. "You do th—hey, what's that?"

The back corner of Sickbay has attracted a sudden clot of corpsmen and doctors. Someone muffles a cheer.

Abrams, sitting up on his elbows. "Can you see?"

Fang2. "Better yet, I can walk." *Which he does, touching a passing nurse on the arm.* "What gives?"

Nurse, with feeling. "One of the Wild Dogs woke up!"

Fang2. "****! Yes!" *He comes back, grinning fiercely, and says to Abrams,* "Hope you like the local hooch, 'cause I'm betting it's about to come in that door with about twenty people. The dead just woke."

News spreads fast. Dusty shows up with her squad, some of the Vermin and Scythe. Even Peaches limps over, her arm in a sling, to grip the hand of the very weak Wild Dog and welcome him back. The personnel in Sickbay don't try very hard to shoo away the impromptu celebrators, though they do hush them. A little. Now and then.

The Wild Dogs's team leader leans back against an empty bed, watching her squad crowd around their teammate.

Scythe, to her, quiet. "Feel a little better?"

Dusty. "I've got another chance to bring one of my Dogs home. Hell yeah, I feel a little ****ing better." *She grins.*

Roach joins them. "Hell of a day, ain't it."

Scythe. "That it is."

Roach. "You hear about those drones they're sending down the holes?"

Scythe. "A little. What've you got?"

Roach. "They're down to numero zero." *Wiggles one finger.* "All the rest of them crushed by crabs before they got too far. They're gonna try sending the last one overland."

Scythe starts. "Will that work? It's like swimming in a waste dump up there."

Roach. "Guess they're desperate." *Grins.* "And you know what'll happen when that one goes."

Scythe sighs.

Dusty. "****, I don't care. I'd tromp around the ****ing planet today and kiss my blisters at the end of it. Semper ****in' fi!"

———

Barracks. Fang2 arrives, finds Whiskers and Hairball playing cards.

Fang2. "Look who's home!" *Poses.*

Whiskers. " 'Bout time. I was out of Sickbay faster than you."

Fang2. "Well, you didn't have a giant ****ing hole taken out of your side either. I was pouring blood, man. I mean, POURING." *He grins and drops into a chair.* "Gonna deal me in?"

Spots the Space Marine: Defense of the Fiddler

Hairball. "Once you stop holding out on us."

Fang2. "Huh?"

Hairball. "First Spots and Claws vanish at night. Then Fang-prime starts muttering in her sleep, she only does that when you're *****ing at her. Now Scythe's doing that 'watching and waiting' thing with his fingers on his table. Drum, drum, drum. Pause. Starts over again. What's going down, and when do we get invited?"

Fang2 laughs. "Hell, how about tonight? Unless you want to go to the Wild Dog party. Oh, what am I talking about, the ****ing party'll still be going when we're done. Come on."

Testing Facility. Claws is walking Fang and Spots through a sniper-shield drill when he gets a call from the security team at the Door.

"Yo, slavedriver."

"Chao, you're late, come on through already."

"I gotta couple of friends you need to vouch for to the pinheads here—say hello, guys."

Whiskers. "Hey, Claws. Let us the **** in."

Claws laughs. "Yeah, put security on."

A few moments later, Fang2 shows up with Whiskers and Hairball.

Hairball. "So what's the deal?"

Claws. "Team drills, new hardware. I'm the boss. Spots is the specialist. We'll be the best **—friggin' thing since the hoplites discovered the aspis. Good?"

Hairball, slow grin. "Great."

Claws. "All right, let's get to work."

88. The Gang's All Here

An hour later, Claws receives another call. He leans against the wall to take it while the Kitties work through basic shield shape-changing drills.

Claws. "Walker."

Security. "You having some sort of party up there, Corporal?"

Claws. "Hah, I wish. Someone else asking to come up?"

Security. "Says his name is Holden and he's got a big-*** sword. Hope you haven't pissed him off."

Claws, laughing. "No, that's my team lead. Let him by."

A few minutes later, Scythe shows up. "I really don't like how they run that checkpoint."

Claws. "Nice to see you too, boss."

Scythe stands next to him, nods. "How's it going?"

Claws. "Pretty good, I think."

Scythe taps the hilt of his sword. "Mind if I . . . ?"

Claws grins. "Go ahead." *Calls.* "Hey, Spots. Scythe wants a piece of someone and I choose you."

Spots breaks off an explanation to Whiskers. "What? Oh, sure." *She trots forward.*

Scythe walks out to join her, bows. She bows back and he draws the katana with ritual ease.

Claws. "Defend."

Scythe brings the sword down in an overhead cut and then steps forward, slashing. He takes it slow, and Spots retreats: every time the sword meets the shield, it makes a sound like a cross between sparks hissing, chalkboard scratch and a distant tiny handbell.

Whiskers to Hairball, muttered. "****, is that thing sharp?"

Fang. "I've seen him halve target dummies with it."

Fang2, unable to resist. "In *twain!*"

Hairball. "****."

Spots the Space Marine: Defense of the Fiddler

Claws. "Attack."

Spots springs forth, using the "blunt" edge of the practice shield to parry. The first time Scythe's sword catches on the translucent edge, sending a pulse of light down the previously-invisible curve, he starts. Now it's Spots's turn to go slow, letting him learn to guess where her shield's edge will be . . .

. . . when he thinks he knows where it extends, she changes it. And then she starts shifting it with every exchange, in, out, thicker, thinner. She pushes him back easily. Color races the edge of her shield as she lifts and punches.

Scythe, halfway to the wall. "Nice! Okay, that's good."

Spots stops and bows to him. He bows back. "Looks good. What about the rest of you?"

Hairball, smiling. "Cut us some slack, boss, we just got here."

Claws. "Get back to work, folks." *He nods to Scythe.* "Here, come see." *He brings the other man to the wallscreen and taps it, points.* "This is the power consumption curve for that exercise you just did."

Scythe squints at it. "Not quite as bad as I expected." *Still watching.* "Hell, pretty good actually, given power's this thing's Achilles' heel."

Claws. "Yeah, I got some comparisons . . ." *He brings up a new set of graphs.* "This is me, Spots and Fang runnin' through the same drill."

Scythe whistles.

Claws. "Yeah, that's what I said."

Scythe. "Think you can bring the rest of you up to her standard?"

Claws. "That . . . I don't know. Depends on how much time I got. If we can all start feelin' it the way she feels it, we might be able to make this monster draw the same amount of juice as the bog-standard shield. But it's gonna take time. I don't think we got it."

Scythe. "Between you and me, I don't think so either. Do you have a plan?"

Claws. "Yeah, of sorts. Actually it's Sam Colt's idea, but it might work."

Scythe. "That being?"

Claws. "He suggested yokin' our power together at the squad level. Dunno how he plans to do it, some kind of lasers. Idea bein', someone goes low, they get automagically topped up by someone with more."

Scythe. "So extra goes to the people using the shield. Preferably the people who use it best, except when it's needed somewhere else." *He narrows his eyes.* "Lot of problems with that."

Claws. "Yeah."

Scythe. "Lot of potential, though. Need serious squad-level training."

Claws. "Yeah. I'm so glad you showed up, boss." *They watch the drill a moment. Then, quiet.* "Thanks for lettin' me do this."

Scythe. "No problem." *Grins.* "Got some extra sleep on you. I'm not complaining."

Claws grins. Nods toward a table in the corner. "Gonna go get yours?"

Scythe. "My . . ."

Claws. "Equipment. You didn't think I didn't think you weren't gonna come, right?"

Scythe works through that, laughs. "Anticipating my anticipating?"

Claws. "Well, hopin', maybe. Was gonna ask you if you didn't come." *Watching the others.* "You know, we always take for granted that we're gonna shoot anything we want to kill. Big guns, little guns, it's all guns. The crabs almost never shoot at us: we never questioned that either. It never occurred to us that maybe the reason they don't shoot at us is because all their wars are probably hand-to-hand."

Scythe squints, then smiles wryly. "Right. Eat the enemy, get their battle plan, kill them."

Claws. "Yup."

Scythe. "So you're training some flimsy humans to go hand-to-hand with the crabs . . . why? We can't eat them."

Claws. "No. But I get the unhappy feelin', boss, that we're locked into a paradigm. And you know what happens when you get used to a box."

Scythe. "Someone shuts you in it."

Claws. "Yeah. Puttin' a cuttin' edge on that shield's finally given us a tool we can use to go face-to-face with these ****ers. Damned if I don't want to know how to use it when the gun ain't the tool for the job." *He lifts his hands.* "But hey. This was all Magda's idea."

Scythe grins, squeezes his shoulder. "I'm sure it was. I'll go get my shield. One request."

Claws. "Request, har har. That's rich."

Scythe. "You're the boss in the training room. So yes, a request."

Spots the Space Marine: Defense of the Fiddler

Claws. "Go ahead, Mister Holden."

Scythe. "There's a hell of a party going on down the hall. One of Dusty's Dogs woke up from his coma."

Claws. "Call this off early for that? Hell yeah."

Scythe high-fives him and goes to collect his equipment. Claws grins . . . and then looks at the power consumption curves, still flickering on the wallscreen. They reflect onto his eyes, and he sobers.

89. Come Together

Wild Dogs Common Room. Dusty's Dogs are hosting the party, complete with illicit alcohol. Team Kitty arrives post-practice and dissolves into the small crowd of Dogs and Vermin. Scythe ends up chatting with Dusty and Roach but the rest of the team mingles, well-acquainted with each other from "guesting" in one another's squads before the relief arrived.

No one notices when staff, corpsmen and support personnel sift into the crowded room. Or maybe they do, but it's all okay.

Spots finds Gunny at the edge of the crowd with a cup. He smiles at her.

"Better than the Real Window, isn't it."

Spots. "Absolutely." *They watch together in comfortable silence. Then.* "Gunny?"

"Guitart?"

"Why is there no one here from Alpha Company? At least one of their squads should be off duty and awake."

Gunny says nothing. Then: "I guess they didn't feel welcome."

Spots. "Or they weren't invited."

Gunny makes no comment.

Women's Shower, two days later. Spots is untaping her hair under the water when Fang steps in . . . hesitates, thinks about stepping out . . . and then doesn't, mesmerized by the process.

Spots. "Fang? Come in, you must be cold."

Fang. "Uh, right." *She steps into the shower.* "Are you . . . going to wash that?"

Spots. "It's my day for it." *She finishes unwinding the tape and her hair falls loose, all the way to her hips.*

Fang. "Jesus." *A little softer.* "It's pretty."

Spots looks over her shoulder, smiles. "Thanks." *She starts lathering, untangling as she goes. Fang starts washing too, then stops again.*

Fang. "Do you . . . could I . . ."

Spots hands her the conditioner. "Sure." *At Fang's pause.* "You wanted to help, right?"

Spots the Space Marine: Defense of the Fiddler

Fang takes the conditioner and starts finger-combing it through Spots's hair. "I almost never see you in here after practice. You and Claws off doing some other secret project?"

Spots. "It's not really secret. We go visit Samuel-Colt most nights."

Fang. "Seriously?"

Spots. "Of course. He's the only Violinist on the base, he likes company."

Fang. "You're saying he gets . . . lonely?"

Spots. "Wouldn't you?"

Fang, pausing. "Yeah." *She continues.* "I guess so. What do you talk about?"

Spots. "Well, we don't actually talk much lately. We dance."

Fang does stop now. "You're kidding."

Spots. "No?" *She looks up at the other woman, over her shoulder.* "Is that too weird for you?"

Fang. "Nothing's too . . ." *She trails off.* "Okay, yeah. It's too weird for me."

Spots grins. "Let me guess. That makes you want to go see it for yourself."

Fang eyes her.

Spots. "If you want to come, just stay after practice. I'll introduce you to him. You can dance too, if you want."

Fang resumes finger-combing. "That's taking it a little too far, Mama."

Quiet for a moment. The water patters softly around them. Then:

Fang. "Hey. I . . . wanted to thank you. You're the only person who didn't . . . treat me badly. Even though I was a *****. To you, too."

Spots. "I know you didn't mean it."

Fang. "But I—"

Spots holds up a hand. "Not in your heart, Fang. You were separated from your team. You were lonely and hurt. You didn't want to be here. I understood."

Fang. ". . . really?"

Spots. "Of course. I don't want to be here either."

Fang is silent, her hands full of Spots's hair. Still looking at it, she says, "They all died but me and Drake. It was . . . we were doing recon, a tunnel mouth up onto the surface—not here, it was, ****, some rock, we called it Niflheim—and it just . . . just went. We were never sure if it was us or them, but all that was left was a crater. Drake got discharged on a 261, he . . . he just went crazy. He was the squad lead, he felt responsible."

Spots, quiet. "And that left you."

Fang. "Yeah." *Pause.* "We were good. You know? These drills Claws is doing, we did **** like that for kicks, because we were the best and we were a ****ing *team*, like one body when we moved out. These tats . . . we all got them together. Like we were a tribe. When it came apart . . . it was like . . . like losing family. They *were* family. And then they sent me here, and it's not that Kitty or anyone here's a slacker, but this is the ***-end of nowhere for a reason and it was like . . . like punishment, on top of mourning. For not dying with them." *She wipes her eyes with the side of her arm, hand still full.* "Bit. It bit. And I didn't know how to handle it." *Softer.* "I still don't know how to handle it."

Spots turns around and wraps her arms around the taller woman, one hand on the back of her head. Fang stands stiffly at first and then sags against her. The water drizzles around them, beads on their skin and rolls down, and if there are any tears they are mercifully masked.

Finally, Fang rubs her eyes. "Not going to say anything about 'giving it time', huh."

Spots smiles, sad. "I think you figured that part out." *She cups the other woman's face; Fang puts a hand over hers.* "I'm sorry, Fang."

Fang. "It's . . . it's okay, Mama."

Spots shakes her head. "No, it's not, and it never will be. It might get a little easier to deal with, but it will never be okay. And we all understand that."

Fang takes a deep breath and nods. Then: "Nicola. It's Nicola Olivia Gordon."

Spots smiles, a real smile this time. "Nicola. That's beautiful."

Fang, smiling a little too. "Yeah, they used to rib me about it all the time. Very girly."

Spots. "Typical. I'm Magda Heloise." *She grins.* "But 'mama' is fine with me too."

Fang, returning to washing. "You being used to it and all."

Spots. "Yeah."

Fang looks up. "You're going to see them again. I mean that."

Spots, soft. "There are never any guarantees, Nicola. But I pray you're right."

Spots the Space Marine: Defense of the Fiddler

End of the week. Fang2 is preparing to head to drills when he gets a call from Sickbay. He leans over his nightstand to take it.

Abrams. "Hey, Chao. You busy?"

Fang2. "About to be, but ****, go ahead."

Abrams. "Wondered if you could come down here."

Fang2. "Sure, it's on my way. Sorta. See you in five."

Sickbay. Fang2 strolls in, finds Abrams sitting up in bed. The Alpha sergeant is gaunt from too long convalescence; it looks bad on his large frame, like skin stretched taut over a barbed wire scaffold.

Fang2. "So what's up, Hawk?"

Abrams. "You said . . . your ASL put you through your physical therapy. Think he'd do mine?"

Fang2 looks at him. A quick look, but a searching one. Then, with a ready grin: "Hell, sure. You got some papers from the docs? Recommended exercises?"

Abrams brandishes a sheet.

Fang2. "Let's go then. Need a shoulder?"

Abrams. "Would appreciate it, yeah. ****ing hip is almost worse than the leg."

90. VISITORS

Testing Facility. Team Kitty is working through shield shape drills against dummy targets with real-time power consumption curves displaying on the wallscreen. Spots is running this exercise, stopping to talk through reasons for contracting the shield versus maintaining the size. This is a very frustrating exercise, man vs. his own equipment, but the team is in good spirits.

The door opens for Fang2 and Abrams.

Fang2. "Sorry I'm late, I had to pick up a pal."

Everyone stops. The company is too tight-knit not to recognize Abrams as one of Company A.

Then . . .

Spots. "Hi, Hawk! They're letting you up pretty early, how are you feeling?"

Abrams. ". . ." *Recovering well:* "I've been better. But it's nice to be out of Sickbay. Thanks."

Spots. "Obviously I should have brought you more protein bars."

Fang2. "I would have shared! Well, maybe not the coconut. But the rest!"

Claws says to Spots, "Keep the drill goin'." *Then approaches with Scythe behind him.* "What can I do you for, Sergeant?"

Fang2. "This here is Hawk—"

Claws eyes him. "I wasn't talkin' to you, Chao. Go join the line."

Fang2. "Right, right. Be nice to my guest, though." *He pats Abrams on the shoulder and trots off to find his glove.*

Abrams. "Hawk Abrams. Chao said you did his physical therapy. Was wondering if you could do mine."

Claws, cocking brow. "Really? Why?"

Abrams. "Because I'm ****ing sick of Sickbay. Besides, I wanted to meet the ****er who tried to take my entire team on."

Scythe coughs into a fist. Claws scowls at him.

Abrams. "Well? Can you handle one lame bird? Or do you prefer your fights uneven?"

Claws laughs. "I think one on one's enough. Though if you'll excuse me for sayin', Hawk, you look done in. You sure you should be up?"

Abrams. "Yes. Dammit. I've been ****ing flat on my back too long." *He hands over the paper.*

Claws reads it. "All right. Doesn't look too bad. You can use the Princess's mat over here."

Abrams. "Thanks."

Claws. "Don't mention it."

Satisfied, Scythe returns to the drill; Claws crouches alongside Abrams and walks him through the first two of his exercises, then leaves him to it. Claws goes back to work himself, but his eyes on the wallscreen are narrowed. When he steps off the line Scythe joins him.

Scythe. "Not liking it."

Claws. "Hell no. I asked Sam to come in, we gotta start talkin' options."

Scythe nods. "It's a powerful tool but . . . finicky."

Claws. "If all it was was finicky, I'd be a-okay with it. It's the whole 'the only one left with juice to use it after a few minutes is Mama Spots' part that ****s us over." *He calls over.* "All right, turtle drill."

Spots. "Right!"

The team forms into a rectangle with Fang in the middle and Spots, Fang2, Hairball and Whiskers on the corners. They expand their shields until the edges meet, shooting colors down their rims on contact.

Claws. "Forward!"

They advance, trying to keep the shields in contact. A few paces in there's a chime and Fang2 mutters, "****, sorry." He shifts his shield until the noise stops and they continue. Advance. Retreat. Stop. Turn. Keeping the shields small enough to conserve energy but large enough to cover them completely is a challenge.

Claws. "**—um, Crap! Didn't you people learn close order drill? Someone call a freakin' beat."

Hairball starts calling the cadence, which improves their performance. Scythe and Claws are still watching when Abrams says behind them, "Is that really necessary?"

Claws looks over his shoulder. "Yeah, it really is."

Scythe. "Proper use of the shield makes the team invulnerable . . . but it doesn't last long. The more compact the shield, the longer the turtle lasts."

Abrams limps up to join them, watching. "I've heard rumors about Bravo's magic shield tech."

Claws. "It ain't magic. I ****in' wish it was magic. Would sure be nice to be able to waltz through the Warren without ever takin' a scratch. Unfortunately it don't work that way."

Abrams. "You can't have one person just . . . cover all the rest?"

Claws. "Not right now, no. Drain the power cell right outta the back of your suit and maybe ****in' inside out."

Abrams glances at him. "Not right now?"

Claws. "Well . . ."

The door slides open then for Samuel-Colt. The silence this time is complete. Even the turtle falls apart, Fang2 plowing into Spots and Hairball stopping entirely.

Samuel-Colt, rising note. "Mother's-Escort? You asked for me?"

Claws, distracted by the mess. "Awww, for the love of God. You people gonna fall outta position the first time someone flashes something shiny at you? Close up!" *As the team sockets back together, he says,* "Heya, Sam. Yeah, come on over."

Abrams, staring. "****. It's a Fiddler."

Scythe, murmuring. "It's *the* Fiddler, Sergeant. Be polite."

91. Turn the Knife

Spots. "Come on, back to the drill." *They resume, if much slower. There are a lot more chimes and muttered curses.*

Claws, turning back to Samuel-Colt. "Thanks for comin'. I thought . . . maybe it's time to talk 'bout that power-share you were tellin' me about."

Samuel-Colt, drawing a long ripple of notes. "There is concern, then."

Claws nods at the wallscreen. "Look for yourself. It's just too persnickety. Maybe when we've all mastered it, we can do without. But what if we need this trainin', like, tomorrow?"

Abrams glances at him. "You expecting something?"

Scythe. "This lull won't last forever."

Samuel-Colt. "The distributed power network would solve that problem, Escort. But it may result in lower power levels for everyone during times of greater shield usage. Is this an acceptable risk?"

Claws. "That's what I keep askin' myself."

Scythe. "I think having the option would be useful. What do you think, Abrams?"

Abrams, surprised into giving an opinion. "I think it could save a few ***es in a pinch. Is it dynamic or can we control the allocation?"

Scythe, frowning. "Do you think we'd have time to finesse power levels in a fight?"

Claws. "Maybe not, but you could maybe flip a lock? On, off?"

Samuel-Colt, rising arpeggio. "A less granular control would be possible."

Scythe. "A light switch." *He chuckles.* "That might take care of most of the objections."

Abrams, thoughtful. "Talk about having to think like a team, though."

Scythe. "I like it. We should be thinking as a team anyway. How soon can you have a prototype, Samuel-Colt?"

Samuel-Colt, with a somehow embarrassed note. "We have perhaps been working on this project in our spare time." *At Claws's look:* "It posed fascinating problems. We enjoyed solving them."

Claws. "Engineers! You're all the same, no matter the species."

Scythe. "So . . . soon, then."

Samuel-Colt. "A matter of days."

Abrams. "Shouldn't we run it by the lieutenant first? I have to imagine this involves substantial modification of the suits."

Claws. "They might say no, though."

Abrams eyes him.

Samuel-Colt. "We still require several days to complete the hardware revisions."

Scythe. "Putting it off won't make it any easier."

Claws. "Forgiveness is easier than permission, boss. We got the new shield that way."

Scythe. "The new shield doesn't have the ability to trash the whole team if it fails, Walker. We'll do this by the book."

Samuel-Colt, quick, sharp note. "The technology will not fail, Scythe."

Scythe. "It's not the technology I'm worried about, Samuel-Colt." *He taps his temple.* "Human error."

Abrams mutters. "Gets you every time."

Samuel-Colt. "With your permission? We will resume work on it."

Claws. "Sure. You need any of this data?"

Samuel-Colt, low note. "We can access it from our quarters . . ."

Claws snorts. "And probably have been, eh?"

Samuel-Colt rubs his vestigial limbs together in a way that feels like obfuscation. Or thumb-twiddling. "Perhaps we should plead the fifth."

That surprises a barked laugh out of Abrams.

Scythe. "Thank you, Samuel-Colt. We appreciate your help."

Samuel-Colt bows. Scythe bows back. Claws does a cocky little finger-salute and the alien turns to go.

Spots. "Samuel-Colt! Tonight?"

Samuel-Colt. "We are at your service, Mother." *And leaves.*

Spots the Space Marine: Defense of the Fiddler

Abrams, staring at the door. "****. You could almost forget he's a nine-foot-tall bug."

Claws nudges him. "Maybe you should get back to the mat. You ain't done yet, after all."

Abrams. "Right."

The team tightens up without the distractions, though the turtle drill remains no less 'persnickety.' At the end of the session everyone is tired, including Abrams who is sitting on his mat, knees up and arms resting on them. He's sweating and pale.

Fang2, stopping by him. "Need a hand back?"

Abrams. "Yeah, thanks."

Claws steps in. "I'll take care of it."

Fang2. "All right, but don't break him."

"Ain't plannin' to." *Claws nods to Abrams.* "Come on."

There is a determinedly silent silence as they leave the secure area.

Then, Abrams: "So was that planned?"

Claws. "Since I kinda wasn't anticipatin' you showin' up at all, that woulda required psychic powers on my part." *He grins without humor.* "You took it well."

Abrams. "****. He's a giant bug."

Claws. "He's a giant bug that designs us ****in' amazin' toys."

Abrams. "And is that all it is? Because that's not what I hear."

Claws. "I've been on this rock too long, Abrams, but not that ****in' long. And I don't want to hear a ****in' word about me and Guitart, or I'll dump you off my arm right here and let you crawl back to Sickbay."

Abrams. "You still didn't answer the question."

Claws glances at him. Then says, "You ain't earned that answer."

Abrams. "I think that's answer enough."

Claws. "Yeah, well. I can tell the enemy from our allies. Sue me."

Abrams. "It's not about telling our enemies from our allies, Corporal. It's about knowing the difference between us . . . and them. They're aliens."

Claws. "This is old ****, Abrams. We've been doin' it since aitch sapiens slaughtered the Neanderthals. Kinda loses its meaning when we can turn the knife on ourselves just as easy as we do on aliens." *They stop at Sickbay's doors.* "You gotta problem with me not hatin' Samuel-Colt, you don't have to come back."

Abrams. "Yeah, well, maybe my problem is more about me not hating him the way I should." *He straightens, grimaces.* "****. There was a minute there where I forgot he wasn't just some engineer. He talks like a ****ing engineer. He's even got an accent, like the ****-ton of foreign human engineers we got. What the ****? How did I not notice, even for a second? He smells like a ****ing spice cabinet!"

Claws grins and slaps the other man's shoulder. "See you tomorrow."

92. THE SAME CLAY

Sickbay. Avril is perched on a stool next to Peaches's bed. They have the privacy curtain drawn and are consulting over reports and maps. Peaches looks a little waxy, but alert.

Peaches. "So that's it."

Avril, rueful. "You could put it that way, yeah."

Peaches, glancing at his expression. "Thinking about how you're going to explain away several hundred thousand dollars' worth of equipment loss?"

Avril, rubbing brow. "Uh-huh."

Peaches. "I don't envy you." *At his scowl she grins.* "Hey, heavy lies the burden on the shoulders of command."

Avril. "Just a few weeks and this could have been you!"

Peaches. "Heh. But it's not."

Avril sighs. And then smiles. "It's good to see you smiling."

Peaches meets his eyes and for a moment, they share that smile. Then she lifts the paper. "So they killed every drone we sent down the holes. And now the one over-land stopped transmitting. Which means . . ."

Avril. "We get to send a team out." *He looks up.* "I'm right, right? We can't let this lie."

Peaches. "No . . . no, I don't think so." *She sets the report aside.*

Avril. "My turn to read your mind. But you're troubled about something. What? That no one bothered to do it before?"

Peaches. "Something like that. My predecessor . . . when he led the assault that killed off most of the company, he didn't even have a target. He just aimed them at the edges of the Warren and sent them out."

Avril. "Without a plan?"

Peaches. "I . . . don't know. He didn't leave any paperwork, any notes . . . any anything. He didn't talk to anyone about it either. From what I've been able to gather, he was one of the extreme 'officers stand apart' types."

Avril snorts. "We're the same clay as everybody else."

Peaches. "We know that. I don't know about him. But anyway. I just . . . worry. When we dropped down here there were surveys, of course. But nothing suggestive of the kind of thing we're dealing with now."

Avril. "All the more reason to find out while we can. So . . . over-land? I have a couple of men who've done seismic mapping before, I can send them."

Peaches. "Yeah . . . yeah. But let's ask Samuel-Colt a few questions before they go."

Avril. "The alien? Like what?"

Peaches. "Like whether our topside drone died because of the constant storms and toxic mud . . . or if there might be crab patrols up there."

———

Testing Facility. Claws and Abrams have just left; the rest of the team is filing out, except Spots, who strips off her glove and then her shoes.

Fang pauses at the door. "So, you and the bug . . ."

Spots, tugging a sock off. "You're welcome to stay."

Fang hesitates, but before she can decide, Samuel-Colt's shadow crosses her shoulder. Her eyes track the growth of the shadow on the floor in front of her: antenna. One set of arms. Another. A third. She looks behind her.

Samuel-Colt. "Good evening, Fang."

Fang. "****! You know my name!"

93. Being Female

Samuel-Colt. "In the course of our duties, we regularly review suit camera footage and logs. We become aware of each individual's names and callsigns during this process."

Fang. "Uh . . . of course. Wait, you watch the footage?"

Spots, finishing up with her socks. "It's public material, Fang. They told all of us who were being assigned to the Powered Armor division . . . didn't they tell you during training?"

Fang. "Of course, I just . . ."

Samuel-Colt. "Mother? Is Fang serving as escort tonight? We observe that Claws is not present."

Spots. "Claws is helping Sergeant Abrams back to Sickbay, I'm sure he'll be back." *She comes closer, curious.* "Can Fang do his job? I thought only males could guard females?"

Samuel-Colt leans toward Fang, who back-pedals once before pride stiffens her shoulders and makes her stop. "You are correct. Fang does not smell female, however. Perhaps that is why the idea is not discomfiting."

Fang. "Wait, what? I don't smell like a girl?"

Samuel-Colt. "Not very, no."

Spots eyes Fang. Then frowns. "You're on stop-thats, aren't you."

Fang folds her arms. "Yeah, and? It's not illegal."

Spots. "No, but only barely."

Fang. "Look, Mama, I don't know how you play it, but I don't want to start bleeding in the middle of a fight. Bad enough to do it from a ****ing wound without doing it from—"

Spots holds up a hand.

Fang. ". . . anyway. Don't tell me you're not on *something*? You're still getting your period?"

Spots. "Yes? Though admittedly, not as often on our ration schedule."

Fang. "And it doesn't bother you? No mood swings, no cramps, none of that ****?"

Spots. "I challenge you to tell my mood swings from anyone else's in this place. As for cramps . . . labor kind of rearranged my idea of 'painful cramp.' Most months I don't notice it coming or going."

Fang. "****. That must be nice."

Spots. "I guess." *She folds her arms.* "Fang, the hormone treatments were designed for short-duration high-risk missions where going anemic could make the difference between failure and success. They're not meant to be taken indefinitely."

Fang. "I know that."

Spots. "So you're not taking them continuously, right?"

Fang. "Damn it. No. Just enough to coast through a few months. Then I stop."

"And start again."

Samuel-Colt, curious rising note. "Is it that you wish to be a male, Fang?"

Both of them stare at him, jerked from their dialogue.

Fang. "Uh . . . no." *At Spots's look, she lifts her hands.* "Look, honest . . . the answer is no. I don't hate being a woman. I just want to be a Marine. And I want to be as good a Marine as a man could be. I didn't want to half-*** my way into this. When I did the qualifications, I aimed for the male standards. And I *did* it. That's how I got into recon. That's how I made it into Dragon Team. I'm good. I'm as good as anyone, and better than most." *She takes a long breath, lets it out.* "That's what I wanted. That's who I am. A woman who's as good as a man at a man's job."

Samuel-Colt. "This is fascinating. What inspired this desire?"

This question catches Fang flat-footed. She has no immediate answer. "I . . . wanted a challenge, I guess. Something really hard. A test, one that everyone could tell if I passed or failed. It's . . . it's hard to find stuff like that anymore."

Samuel-Colt, with a curious minor arpeggio, falling. "So you joined the military in order to prove yourself."

"I . . . well, yeah. Yes." *She glances from him to Spots.* "Let me guess. I'm the only one."

Samuel-Colt. "We did not have a choice as to our role in this conflict, so we can only observe your agency, not judge it."

Fang, to Spots. "And you?"

Spots smiles. "I'm here for the same reason I'm a mother."

Fang. "Oh come on. Moms drive minivans and buy ice cream. Soldiers kill things and sleep with their weapons. Don't tell me there's a parallel."

Spots the Space Marine: Defense of the Fiddler

Samuel-Colt, rising note. "This is an intriguing premise."

Behind them in the hall, Claws drawls, "What is this, a party? And no one invited lil ol' me?"

Fang, stepping back. "Don't worry, you didn't miss anything."

Claws. "That's good, cuz I'm here to break it up. Spots, Sam . . . the LT'd like to see us."

Spots. "Right now?"

Claws. "Right now."

She sighs and gets her shoes. As she heads through the door, Fang says, "Mama? What was the parallel?"

Spots, smiling a little. "Duty." *And is gone.*

94. INTRACTABLE

Sickbay, outside the door of a consultation room.

"Ma'am, Corporal Walker and Private Guitart reporting as ordered. The Violinist is with us."

"Come in."

Spots and Claws enter. A pale Peaches is sitting on the chair behind the desk; Avril is sitting on its corner, arms folded. The room is barely large enough for all of them once Spots, Claws and Samuel-Colt are inside.

Peaches. "At ease, Private, Corporal." *To the Fiddler.* "Thank you for coming, Samuel-Colt."

Samuel-Colt, ripple of a melody. "Lieutenant-Savannah-Bonnet. It is good to see you ambulatory after your defense of the base. You are to be commended for your courage."

Peaches, taken aback. "I . . . ah, thank you. I just did what had to be done. Please, sit if you wish."

Samuel-Colt. "We prefer to remain standing. If we may, Lieutenant-Savannah-Bonnet." *Rising note, interrogatory.* "How may we help you?"

Peaches and Avril glance at one another. Avril clears his throat. "You are no doubt aware we sent recon drones down the holes that Corporal Walker and Private Guitart discovered on the edge of the Warren."

Samuel-Colt. "Yes."

Avril. "All of them were destroyed before they reached the floors of the tunnels. Is that normal?"

Samuel-Colt, rising note. "You send a foreign object into enemy territory and it is destroyed, and you ask if this is usual?"

Peaches. "We haven't noticed the crabs paying attention to objects much before, Samuel-Colt. They've left the repeaters above ground alone. Nothing's touched our satellite. They never seem to attack materiel, just people."

Claws, muttering. "And yet we're worried they're gonna assault the donut."

Avril. "It's more like we can't afford them to notice it, Corporal."

Peaches. "That and the donut doesn't operate itself. There will always be people here to man it."

Spots the Space Marine: Defense of the Fiddler

Claws. "Point."

Avril. "Sometimes the brass's decisions make sense." *Grins at Claws's expression.* "Sometimes." *To Samuel-Colt.* "You see why we're concerned?"

Samuel-Colt, minor arpeggio, falling. "You intrude on the Enemy's territory, Lieutenant-Paul-Avril. This is a different matter from their impinging on yours. Territorial integrity is aggressively defended. The drones will register as alien and be destroyed."

Peaches. "Even though we scrubbed them?"

Samuel-Colt, sharp note rising. "Even so, they smell and sound and look like human engineering."

Peaches sighs. "We had to try."

Avril nods. "That doesn't explain the bot we sent overland." *Looking at the Fiddler.* "That one stopped transmitting, or was destroyed, or something. Do you think it's likely that there are crabs on the surface?"

Samuel-Colt. "Anything is possible, Lieutenant-Paul-Avril. Likely, however . . . we would not guess so. Enemy soldiers would have to be engineered specifically to operate on the surface, just as they must be for work in vacuum. Had they elected to attack overland, you would be fending them off there, not via the Warren."

269

Peaches. "But they could be experimenting."

Samuel-Colt. "We have established that they are capable of it, yes."

Peaches and Avril exchange looks.

Avril. "We'd better send a full squad just in case."

Peaches nods.

Samuel-Colt. "You plan to send a team to investigate?"

Avril. "Overland, yes. To see if we can recover the lost drone, if it's just broken down. And to do some seismic mapping. One of my teams has expertise with the equipment. Maybe we can get a sense for the enemy base without having to send someone down the holes."

Samuel-Colt. "It is a sound plan. We would like to accompany this team."

A long pause. The two officers stare at the alien. Spots and Claws glance at one another.

Peaches. "Ah . . . Samuel-Colt . . . that's a very irregular request. Can I ask what motivated it?"

Samuel-Colt. "We have good hearing, Lieutenant-Savannah-Bonnet. We would like a chance to interpret the data on site."

Spots. "Samuel-Colt? Doesn't that require you to expose your body?"

Samuel-Colt. "That is correct, Mother."

Spots. "Can you survive the atmosphere outside the base?"

Samuel-Colt. "No, Mother. But we need not expose our entire body to gather the data. A hand and arm will suffice. Our suit is segmented, like yours. We can minimize the damage."

Avril, incredulous. "You would give up an arm to do this?"

Samuel-Colt. "It can be regrown, Lieutenant-Paul-Avril. The data is important."

Peaches. "I . . . don't think I can let you do this, Samuel-Colt. What if something happens to you? We'll be responsible for the death of an alien ally. That would be . . . very bad."

Samuel-Colt. "We understand your misgivings, Lieutenant-Savannah-Bonnet, but you have no authority over us. We are, as you noted, an ally. Not a soldier. If you wish, we will record a statement absolving you of responsibility for our fate, but we insist."

Silence.

Claws. "Crap. This means we're goin', don't it."

Both officers glance at him, but Samuel-Colt answers first. "That is correct."

Claws. "I thought I was the Mother's-Escort, not yours."

Samuel-Colt. "You are also the liaison to the alien, is that not so?"

Peaches, shaky but half-rising with a scowl. "Are you pre-empting my men as bodyguards, Samuel-Colt?"

Samuel-Colt. "We are going on your mission, Lieutenant-Savannah-Bonnet. Is your mission team prepared to work with us? Or will they require human intermediaries who are familiar with me?"

Avril, low. "****."

95. Mission Planning

Peaches, to Avril. "So do we send Team Kitty?"

Avril. "We'd lose the expertise with the equipment. Our best option might be leaving a couple of the original squad home and subbing in these two."

Peaches. "Aren't they down a sergeant, though? That would put two corporals in the same team . . ."

Claws clears his throat. "Uh, ma'am? I have no problems deferring to the mission lead."

Spots. "Except in matters pertaining to the safety of the alien."

Everyone looks at her but Samuel-Colt. Another uncomfortable silence.

Avril. "All right, that's settled." *He lifts a map off the desk.* "Samuel-Colt, do you think the alien base is more than a day's walk away?"

Samuel-Colt, quick falling note. "Doubtful, Lieutenant-Paul-Avril. Do you plan to send your soldiers on foot?"

Peaches. "We've been debating it. The Pig's the only ground vehicle we've got that we can be sure won't bog down, but it's heavy and slow. The team would be more flexible without it."

Avril. "We could do air drops, but if the target's close we might overshoot. We were thinking sending them by foot would let them take readings more frequently with less effort. Save fuel, less warning to the crabs that we're out there."

Peaches. "As long as you think it's close. Going by standard procedure we can only walk the suits thirty-six hours from base before we turn back."

Samuel-Colt. "We would be greatly surprised if the Enemy is farther than a day's walk from the base."

Peaches glances at Avril. "By foot, then, with air support standing by?"

Avril nods. "We can airlift them out if the situation changes."

Peaches. "Samuel-Colt? If we do this by the book, we have to observe comm silence. Do you think that's wise? I've never seen evidence that the crabs read our comm traffic."

Samuel-Colt, rising note. "Do you wish this to be the time you find that evidence, Lieutenant-Savannah-Bonnet?"

Another pause, then both she and Avril start laughing.

Peaches. "Ouch. Schooled by a civilian." *She bows to him.* "Thank you."

Samuel-Colt, sprightly melody. "We are at your service."

Avril. "They'll only be out for a day anyway." *He looks at Claws and Spots.* "The team's leaving at 0400. You should be able to get some sleep if you go down now."

Claws, Spots. "Yes, sir."

Avril, to Samuel-Colt. "We'd like that recorded statement before then, please. I'll let you go, but I'm going to log that I tried to talk you out of it. We don't have a lot of aliens on the front line, Samuel-Colt, and if we lose you I doubt we'll have any."

Samuel-Colt. "Perhaps if we were human. The loss of one of us would not materially affect our decision in that regard."

Peaches. "I think what he means to say is that we humans would find it unacceptable, and might start objecting to exposing you to danger."

Samuel-Colt. "Ah. Of course." *A sharp, rising note.* "We thank you for being . . . reasonable about our request."

Avril. "Just come back, sir." *To Claws and Spots.* "You keep him in one piece. And be polite . . . you're guesting with PYEO."

Claws doesn't put his head in his hand, but the impulse is there.

Avril. "All right, then. Report to the armory at 0330 for the briefing. Dismissed." *Pauses.* "Ah, unless you have any questions, Samuel-Colt."

Samuel-Colt. "We are content, Lieutenant-Paul-Avril. Thank you." *He ducks out of the consultation room, waits for Spots and Claws to join him, and leaves Sickbay. The two pace him all the way to the Door; once they're in the secure area, Claws glances up at Samuel-Colt.*

Claws. "This had better be good, Sam."

Samuel-Colt. "That is just what we're fearing, Peer."

96. The Middle of Things

Corridor outside the Barracks. Claws and Spots have left Samuel-Colt at his door and are now walking back.

Claws. "I'll catch up with you."

Spots. "All right."

He continues past their door and stops at the next one over. It's ajar; he knocks.

"Yeah?"

"Gotta talk to you, Boss."

Scythe shoves the door open with his heel. He's sitting in front of the terminal which is right next to the door. "Come in."

Claws enters, leans on the wall, arms folded. "Spots and me got tagged for special duty tomorrow."

Scythe. "This should be good."

Claws. "We're goin' topside as the Fiddler's bodyguards, taggin' along with a team that's gonna try to find the crab base."

Scythe, sitting back. "Wow. You don't do things by halves, do you."

Claws lifts his hands. "Wasn't my bright idea this time, I swear."

Scythe chuckles. "But you're in the thick of it anyway."

Claws. "I blame Spots. Hell, no, I blame Sam Colt. Wait, can I blame them both?"

Scythe. "Face it, Walker, you're enjoying this."

Claws. "****, you think I want to go hang out with Abrams's special snowflakes?"

Scythe. ". . ."

Scythe starts laughing. "Wait, the guys you supposedly tried to take on in the gym?"

Claws runs a hand over the back of his neck. "****. Yes, yes, them."

Scythe reins himself in with difficulty. "****, Claws."

Claws grins. "Guess it is kinda funny."

Scythe. "It is that."

Claws. "Anyway. Mission shouldn't take longer than a day. They're positin' the base isn't too far. The squad's gonna take measurements and tromp home. Hopefully in one piece."

Scythe. "All right. Thanks for the heads-up."

Claws straightens, glances at him as he turns to go. "You thinkin' what I'm thinkin'?"

Scythe looks up at him. "What, that we're about to get hit bad?"

Claws. "Yeah."

Scythe smiles, wry. "Wouldn't be who we are if we weren't waiting for the other shoe to drop."

Claws. "Mmm. You gonna try to keep 'em drillin' during patrol?"

Scythe. "They could use the real-world application, yes. We can go through the motions even without the gloves."

Claws. "All right. See ya in twenty-four."

Scythe. "Hopefully less. Godspeed, bastard."

97. ALL BUT ONE

Barracks, 0230. Spots wakes before Claws. She sits up and swings her legs over the side of her bunk, gripping the edge with her hands, eyes closed. When she opens them, it's to look over at her table at the rosary. Slowly, she picks it up and loops it over her head, tucking the beads with her ID tags under her shirt. She writes a note, leaves it on Claws's table and leaves.

The Armory is deserted. Spots suits up, runs through the checks herself and picks up the helmet before heading to the Door, where the guards greet her and let her pass. She goes to the Violinist's door and chimes for admittance.

"A moment." Then: "Enter."

Spots steps inside . . . and stops almost instantly, staring up.

> *And up.*

>> *And up . . .*

In a suit, Samuel-Colt is over ten feet tall, and the design is unbelievable: almost no bulk to it, the segmentation joints flush to the surface so that it looks molded. Both upper sets of arms are visible but the vestigial arms are hidden, streamlining the Violinist's appearance. His great claws are not gloved, but sheathed in rubber and metal so that they look like immense axes. Rather than boots the suit ends in metal points; despite this Samuel-Colt is bending down to pick up a helmet without even a slight wobble.

Samuel-Colt, without accompaniment. "Mother-soldier? You are early."

Spots. "I wanted to see if you needed . . . help."

Samuel-Colt. "If you wish, a second check is welcome."

Spots nods and draws near as the alien goes to one knee with a grace that is uncanny for someone on stilts. She stares.

Samuel-Colt, looking over shoulder. "Mother-soldier?"

Spots. "The . . . feet. How are you doing that?"

Samuel-Colt. "It is how we are accustomed to walking. You have not noticed?"

Spots. "But . . . in a suit . . . !"

Samuel-Colt. "Ah, yes. It has gyroscopes to help offset the weight."

Spots checks the back panel then. "You look . . ."

Samuel-Colt. "Disturbing?"

Spots. "Improbable, I guess." *She reads off the lights.* "Air supply, green. Reserve power, topped. All lights green. Seal check . . . well, you don't have your helmet on. No ammunition?"

Samuel-Colt. "Our suit is not designed for battle, as yours is."

Spots. "But . . ." *She smiles, reading an indicator.* "You have a shield."

Samuel-Colt. "It is wise to be prepared." *He rises, twisting on the legs and again, Spots stares, breathless.* "Mother-soldier? Is it so strange?"

Spots. "Somehow . . . seeing a machine fitted to someone so different makes the differences more obvious. Does that make sense?"

Samuel-Colt. "Of course."

Spots. "And this . . ." *She touches the edge of one claw.*

Samuel-Colt. "A vestige from other, less-evolved times. We often debate why we retain them when we engineer so many other characteristics away."

Spots. "You'd just . . . remove them?"

Samuel-Colt. "Of course. We are always engineering ourselves for maximum efficiency. 'Playing God,' we have heard it called. Does that trouble you?"

Spots. "I . . . I don't know. It just seems . . . there are so many ways to make bad choices as it is. Being able to make bad choices on that level . . . it would paralyze me with uncertainty. What do you do if you fail?"

Samuel-Colt. "We erase the geneline."

Spots breathes out, shocked. "Mother of God! all of them?"

Samuel-Colt. "To the last. We take care of our mistakes, Mother. We always have . . . all but one."

Silence. They look at one another.

Spots, soft. "I miss your music."

Samuel-Colt inclines his head, jeweled eyes closing. "You will hear it again."

Spots takes a deep breath in, nods. "Well, let's go."

Spots the Space Marine: Defense of the Fiddler

Barracks. Claws wakes up, rolls out of bed blinking and finds the note. He reads it and mutters a curse, goes to wash up. Not long after, he saunters to the Armory and leans on the wall outside it, arms folded, waiting.

When Spots appears with Samuel-Colt towering behind her, even he is taken aback.

Claws. "Well. Don't you look like somethin' outta a movie. Just need the slo-mo."

Spots smiles. "Waiting for us?"

Claws. "Yeah, kinda." *He stands straight.* "You ready?"

Spots nods.

Claws looks at them both again. Quieter. "You two look fine." *And then turns to the door, keys it open and steps through.*

Team PYEO, suiting up, stops.

And stares.

98. Issues

Armory. The tableau. Six men from Team PYEO on one side of the room, caught in various stages of suiting up; Spots and Samuel-Colt at the door, with Claws alongside. At their stares, Spots lifts her chin a fraction. The silence holds, brittle.

Then she smiles, a sudden, sunny smile, all the way to her eyes, so honest that it catches them all flat-footed.

Spots. "Hi! I'm Private Magda Guitart, Team Kitty. This is Corporal Walker. We're the liaisons to the Violinist. You must be Hawk Abrams's men."

The silence now has the tension of incredulity. At last a man steps forward. He's an inch shorter than Claws but broader-built, with the coloring of an olive-skinned man who hasn't seen the sun in a long time. He looks them over.

"That's right. I'm the ASL here, Griffin."

Spots, offering her hand. "That your call-sign?" *Glancing at his suit label.* "Oh no, it's your real name? What are the chances?"

One of the others. "We keep telling him—" *and stops at the look his fellow gives him. The rest of the team is staring at Samuel-Colt.*

Griffin to Claws. "You, I know."

Claws. "Uh, yeah. Look, I'm not here to make trouble. I'm just escortin' the bug."

Griffin. "Last time we talked, you said something about not being willing to fight next to us."

Claws. "Your whole team was ****in' with me, Griff. You wanna make this an issue between us? I'm fine with us goin' out, doin' our jobs and comin' back without having to do the whole ****in' alpha male ****. But if you'd rather fight this out, we can do that."

Samuel-Colt. "Is there an issue?"

Sudden silence.

Claws. "Naw, there's no issue. Is there?"

Griffin. "I'm not comfortable with the presence of an alien on the mission."

Claws. "You think we are? Were up to me I'd be sleepin' through this little party. But it ain't up to me, and it sure ain't up to you."

One of the other men mutters. "Now I can't tell which one he's ****ing."

Spots the Space Marine: Defense of the Fiddler

"I'd take the girl."

Spots grabs Claws's arm; unlike him, she's already in powered armor and her grasp stops him cold. "Enough." *To the mutterers.* "You have something to say? You can say it to me directly." *She waits. Nothing.*

Griffin. "****, this is just ****."

Spots. "Then the faster we get to it, the faster it'll be over. Start point's 0300, isn't it? Let's not be late." *She lets go of Claws, who rolls his shoulders and goes to start dressing. To say the mood in the room is uncomfortable is an understatement. There is no chatter, no eye contact. Everyone is as quiet as possible. When Claws is ready Spots does his suit check, turning her back to the others: the painted marks on the back are just visible beneath her external tanks.*

"You count coup?"

She looks over her shoulder at the man asking her. His chest tag reads 'Raven.' "Yes? Don't you?"

The rest of the team is coming closer now.

Raven. "Is that one crab a mark?"

Spots. "Yes. And stars for Kings. We go through colors to continue the count when we fill up the space. Start with red, then orange, on through the rainbow to black."

The first mutterer speaks now, a big man whose nameplate naturally reads Tweety. "****. You go through that many crabs?"

Spots. "We used to, when I first got here . . ." *She glances at Claws.* "There were even more before I came."

Claws nods. "Cannon fodder compared to the **** we deal with now."

Spots. "You didn't get many on the asteroid?"

A reluctant silence.

Samuel-Colt. "They would not have, Mother-soldier."

Everyone looks at him. Team PYEO in particular, various expressions of surprise.

Samuel-Colt. "These soldiers were stationed on a small asteroid, that is correct? The Enemy would have had to send vacuum-capable units against them. Such units are more costly . . . there would have been no 'cannon fodder.' The Enemy's strategy for targets in vacuum is to wait and send overwhelming force, rather than colonize and investigate."

Griffin. "That's . . . that's exactly how it happened."

Claws. "Huh. That's how they hit ships, isn't it?"

Samuel-Colt. "That is correct, Mother's-Escort. Vacuum-capable units are usually reserved for ship-to-ship engagements. The asteroid-mounted supercollider would probably have been considered a tertiary target, or a target of opportunity. Of little importance compared to the primary mission of the ship-killers."

Tweety. "****. We got side-swiped."

Samuel-Colt. "Essentially, yes."

The quiet this time is less hostile, more considering.

Griffin. "All right. All right, let's get this show on the road."

99. TOPSIDE

Control Room. One hand on a console, Avril is leaning toward the wallscreen, watching several blue markers advance across a map.

Peaches, via comm. "What do you think they'll find?"

Avril. "I wish I knew." *More firmly.* "They'll be all right."

Peaches. "There they go—"

One by one the markers vanish.

Peaches. "Godspeed."

Avril, under his breath. "They'll be fine."

Eight human figures, slogging across shifting terrain, thicker than sand but drier than mud . . . eight human figures and one too-thin alien. The atmosphere is so dense they cast no shadows and navigate by sensor. Observing comm silence they trudge toward the last known position of the drone, a hike of several hours. The suits are made for combat; they can withstand hazardous environments, but there are limits to how easy they make it to operate.

[*Squad*] Griffin : I have contact.

[*Squad*] Raven : Contact confirmed. Looks like the drone.

They gather around a glint of metal in the dirt. Griffin leans down and brushes some of it away, exposing the back of the robot.

[*Squad*] Tweety : ****in' thing stopped working because it fell in a ditch?

[*Squad*] Griffin : Might have been a microcell. Buried it, dissipated.

[*Squad*] Raven : Would explain why the map's shot to ****ing hell. ****ing planet. Hate the constant storms.

[*Squad*] Griffin : All right, pipe it. Emu, get it shipped and let's keep moving.

One of the men starts digging it free.

[*Squad*] Raven : Could have been worse. Could have been crabs.

[*Squad*] Griffin : What part of pipe it do you think doesn't apply to you?

[*Squad*] Raven : Right.

Claws and Spots are silent, standing on either side of Samuel-Colt. They remain apart from the others, a distance more psychological than measurable. Nevertheless, everyone observes it. Team PYEO doesn't ask for their help with the drone. Team Kitty doesn't offer.

Emu gets the drone strapped to his back. The group resumes their march, pressing on toward the location of the holes. They proceed carefully, expecting the enemy . . . but find nothing. The hours of vigilance are wearying; by the time they reach their destination, they are edgy. They spread out, securing . . .

. . . an empty space, another stretch of not-quite-sand beneath the thick soup of the toxic atmosphere.

[*Squad*] Griffin : This is it. Tweety, Raven, Trash, perimeter's yours. Emu, close-in duty with me. Jay, do your thing.

The sixth member of PYEO unhooks the gear loaded onto his back and lets it slide onto the ground. He pulls out a telescoping probe and digs the tip into the earth, then leans on it and pushes until it sinks almost completely out of sight. As he works, Samuel-Colt unplugs the elbow of his suit.

[*Kitty-Private*] Samuel-Colt : Mother-soldier. Will you hold this?

[*Kitty-Private*] Spots : Of course.

He hands her the arm piece, covering his naked arm with the armored one as he joins the man working the equipment. Jay glances up at him but makes no comment, adjusting the dials. Likewise, Samuel-Colt says nothing to him, leaning down and resting his hand, palm-down, on the ground.

[*Squad*] Jay : Pulse in three . . . two . . . one . . . now.

On his screen, illumined in green, hundreds of holes . . . leading down to hundreds of tunnels. They merge and head—

[*Squad*] Jay : North.

[*Squad*] Griffin : Pick it up, let's go. We'll do another test, hundred meters.

Samuel-Colt returns to Claws and Spots, who hands him the armored piece. The Violinist pushes it back in place.

[*Kitty-Private*] Claws : North?

[*Kitty-Private*] Samuel-Colt : For now.

As they set off behind PYEO:

Spots the Space Marine: Defense of the Fiddler

[*Kitty-Private*] **Spots** : Your arm? If we stop to test every hundred meters . . .

[*Kitty-Private*] **Samuel-Colt** : We shall see, Mother.

100. MISSION HIJACK

This time Jay carries the equipment by a handle rather than stowing it on his back. A hundred meters on, the squad stops to allow him to take another reading. Again, Samuel-Colt checks with palm to ground. Again, they head north.

[**Squad**] **Jay** : ****. We've got a three-way fork.

Griffin comes over to see as Samuel-Colt replaces his arm-piece.

[**Squad**] **Jay** : All the same size, too. *Points.* See the numbers? Within a few feet of one another. If size is an indicator of importance, then . . . we got no ****ing criteria to work with.

Griffin looks toward Team Kitty and Samuel-Colt.

[**Squad**] **Griffin** : Well? Is size an indicator of importance?

[**Squad**] **Samuel-Colt** : It can be.

[**Squad**] **Griffin** : Well, we don't have size. Is there anything else?

[**Squad**] **Tweety** : Maybe the middle one? It's in the center.

[**Squad**] **Samuel-Colt** : The Enemy does not give the same precedence to symmetry that humanity does.

[**Squad**] **Griffin** : *(frustrated)* Then what does it give precedence to?

[**Squad**] **Samuel-Colt** : Cues we will not be able to measure over land.

[**Squad**] **Spots** : Scent?

[**Squad**] **Samuel-Colt** : Often, yes.

[**Squad**] **Griffin** : Then we'll have to investigate all of them. We'll start with the north-northwest fork. Let's get going.

As the team starts over the shifting terrain. . . .

[**Kitty-Private**] **Claws** : Are we gonna have time to cover an entire crab warren?

But Samuel-Colt does not respond.

The testing resumes. The north-northwest fork continues another thousand meters and terminates in a large cavity. Jay leans back as the open space carves out a giant black hole on his monitor.

Spots the Space Marine: Defense of the Fiddler

[*Squad*] Jay : ****, that's big.

Samuel-Colt leans back, flexing his fingers.

[*Squad*] Samuel-Colt : It is nothing. An interstitial chamber. And empty, to boot.

[*Squad*] Jay : You can tell that?

[*Squad*] Samuel-Colt : Yes. This is a dead-end.

A long pause. The squad channel is live but no one is talking on it. Samuel-Colt accepts his arm-piece from Spots and plugs it back in, hiding a limb that looks strangely blurry, as if its edges are no longer quite as crisply delineated.

[*Squad*] Griffin : All right. Backtrack, let's take the center corridor.

[*Squad*] Tweety : I bet that'll be the one.

They return to the fork, take another reading and begin measuring along the north corridor: one man hunched over a device, two standing guard around him, three prowling in a broad circuit around them . . . and two humans standing apart, watching their alien companion brush dirt from the ground to find better contact for his exposed hand. They take their readings. Rise, move a little further north. Do it again. Rise, move a little further north. Do it again. With each measurement, Samuel-Colt's arm looks a little less distinct, as if it is melting.

[*Squad*] Jay : I got something . . . ****!

Another cavity, approximately the size of the first.

[*Squad*] Jay : ****, it's another dead-end, isn't it.

Samuel-Colt says nothing.

[*Squad*] Griffin : At least now we know. It's the north-northeast corridor. Let's go.

They return to their start point and begin again. Every time Jay pushes the probe in, the silence is charged with expectation. When his display shows another length of the hall, the tension ratchets higher. By the sixth time Jay adjusts the dials and sends the pulse, he is cursing and muttering under his breath. Still nothing. Already this corridor is much longer than the first two.

And then . . .

[*Squad*] Jay : ****! ****!

He slams his palm against the display. It's showing another cavity . . .

. . . roughly the size of the first two.

[*Squad*] Jay : ****!

[*Squad*] Griffin : What does this mean? Is it empty too?

[*Squad*] Samuel-Colt : It is.

Another silence. The wind blows clouds of toxic gas and bits of debris around them.

[*Squad*] Claws : Aw, hell. Now what?

[*Squad*] Griffin : Now we head back and give the LT the data.

[*Squad*] Samuel-Colt : Now we head west.

Another long pause.

[*Squad*] Griffin : Excuse me?

[*Squad*] Samuel-Colt : We have explored your lead, Corporal. Now we will explore mine.

101. CHANGE OF PLANS

Almost in unison:

[*Squad*] **Claws** : You have a lead?

[*Squad*] **Griffin** : You can't hijack the mission. You're not even in the ****ing chain of command—

Claws holds up a gloved hand and repeats his question. This time, the squad hears it ungarbled by Griffin's exclamation.

[*Squad*] **Samuel-Colt** : There was data that your sensors could not interpret.

[*Squad*] **Jay** : You're telling us you got something from all that **** that my machine couldn't? With your *hand*?

[*Squad*] **Samuel-Colt** : That is precisely what we are telling you.

A pause. Then:

[*Squad*] **Griffin** : This is crazy. We're going back.

[*Squad*] **Claws** : Empty-handed? We still got time. If the alien's right, then we could be bringin' home somethin' useful instead of a whole lotta nothin'.

[*Squad*] **Spots** : Lead on, Samuel-Colt.

The Violinist turns and begins to stride away. Spots trudges through the thick not-sand in his wake.

[*Squad*] **Griffin** : Get back here, Private!

Spots stops, turns.

[*Squad*] **Spots** : Corporal Walker and I are the Violinist's liaisons, attached to your mission to accompany him. If he decides to go off into the wilderness, we have to go with him. You can follow us or you can go back to base but we don't have that choice. We were assigned to make sure he gets back in one piece. Claws?

[*Squad*] **Claws** : Comin'.

Claws follows Spots, who follows Samuel-Colt. The rest of the team remains fixed in place, uncertain. And then . . .

[*Squad*] **Griffin** : **** it.

He sets off after the other three. Silently, one by one, his team falls in behind him.

———

Sickbay. Avril is at Peaches's bed, leaning with the backs of his thighs against the frame and his arms folded.

Peaches. "Are you sure about this?"

Avril. "I don't see why not." *He grins.* "It'll give you something to watch for entertainment."

Peaches rolls her eyes. "I'm not into horror movies, Paul."

Avril. "Fortunately, I'm not planning on starring in one." *He passes his hand over his eyes, down his face.* "It's been quiet a long time. We sent the team out . . . if anything's going to happen—"

Peaches. "Don't say it."

Avril. "They're going to be fine. But their activities are probably going to draw attention above ground. I doubt anything's going to care that yet another patrol is going by in the Warren."

Peaches. "And what do you think you'll find that the cameras we set up didn't?"

Avril. "The cameras are pointing at the door Guitart and Walker found. I'm going to look around the corridors in front of it, see if there's . . . well, anything. Crap, Savannah, I'm just tired of sitting on my ***. I'll put the suit on, take a walk and come back. Besides, I'd like to have a look at those traps the engineers set up."

Peaches. "You'll take someone with you."

Avril. "Don't worry, I know the script. Go off alone, get knifed in the dark." *He grins.* "I'll take the remainder of Team Kitty, since the mission stole part of them off. They're about up for patrol anyway."

Peaches sighs. "All right." *Eyes him with a lower-lip pout.* "You know the only reason I'm upset is because *I* want to be out there. I'm sick of Sickbay."

Avril. "Well, watch the cam stream, okay? It'll be like being there. Sort of."

Peaches. "Without the fun parts, like actually moving."

Avril. "Also without the crappy parts, like being bored or rushed by a mob of crabs."

Peaches moans. "I'll take a mob of crabs over being stuck here."

Spots the Space Marine: Defense of the Fiddler

Avril squeezes her good shoulder. "You'll be out of here soon."

Peaches sighs. "Can I listen in on the squad channel too?"

Avril. "In stereo, if you want."

Peaches. "I'll take it."

102. NEW LEAD

The Armory. The room is empty; Team PYEO is heading back and Team Kitty is coming in, but neither are there yet. Avril starts suiting up alone when the door opens. He glances over his shoulder and:

Avril. "Gunnery Sergeant." *Pause. Then he grins.* "Savannah send you?"

Gunny. "Yes, sir. Mind some company?"

Avril. "No, I'd be grateful for your experienced eye. And a buddy check."

Gunny. "I'll get suited up, sir."

When the door opens next, it's for Team Kitty. They come to attention at the unexpected sight of the lieutenant.

Avril. "As you were. I'll be tagging along today."

Scythe. "Yes, sir."

Team Kitty starts suiting up, staying ever-so-slightly apart from Avril. When Team PYEO files in from the airlock, the room gets very crowded.

Avril, to PYEO. "I need two volunteers for an extra two hours' duty or so. We're going to poke around the holes. Any takers?" *When all of them start to volunteer, he grins.* "All right. Gull and Whoop, you're up."

Whiskers, muttering. "He not trust us?"

Scythe, quiet. "I think he thinks we'll be busy enough on the normal circuit."

Whiskers. "**** that. Busy? In the ****ing ghost halls?"

Scythe. "That's enough."

Fang, casual. "You want to see the ****ing holes, go volunteer yourself." *She waits. Looks at Fang2.* "Was that not good enough?"

Fang2 hehs. "Too ****ing easy. Gimme something harder."

Fang sighs. "I've lost my touch."

Fang2. "Now that . . . that I can work with!" *Pats his armored rear.* "Put it here, baby, we'll find it for you!"

Scythe, shaking his head. "Hood up, let's go."

Spots the Space Marine: Defense of the Fiddler

[*Squad*] Griffin : So if you don't mind me asking . . . where the **** are we going?

The expeditionary team is trudging along the shifting mire: Samuel-Colt's tall figure in the lead, with Spots and Claws just behind, walking abreast. The others have formed a V around them with Tweety as rear guard.

[*Squad*] Samuel-Colt : We will know when we arrive.

[*Squad*] Griffin : . . .

[*Kitty-Private*] Claws : Um, Sam . . . that might not be the way to win them over.

[*Kitty-Private*] Spots : He has a point. Isn't there anything you can share with us?

[*Kitty-Private*] Samuel-Colt : This is difficult enough, Mother. Do you wish to increase the suffering?

[*Kitty-Private*] Claws : *(muttered)* ****.

Samuel-Colt bears west and says nothing more for an hour. Then stops abruptly.

[*Squad*] Samuel-Colt : Test here.

Silence. Jay looks at Griffin.

[*Squad*] Griffin : ****, just do it.

Jay unstraps his equipment and sets it up. He shoves the probe into the ground. This time he watches as Samuel-Colt unscrews the glove and sets his ragged hand on the earth. Bits of chitin are swaying off his arm like lace.

[*Squad*] Jay : Pulse in three . . . two . . . one . . . ****!

On his monitor, a broad corridor has flooded the screen with green light.

[*Squad*] Jay : ****! How the **** did we miss that?

Griffin and Claws come over to look. Spots helps Samuel-Colt with the glove. Neither she nor the alien look at one another as she pushes it back on over the increasing ruin of his arm.

[*Squad*] Griffin : ****, he's right. How *did* we miss that?

[*Squad*] Samuel-Colt : As we mentioned, the Enemy is not human, and does not respect human architectural conventions. Symmetry is not important to them. Locational context is.

[*Squad*] Griffin : What the **** does that mean?

Samuel-Colt rises.

[*Squad*] Samuel-Colt : It means the true heart of the Enemy installation is far more likely to be in an area with good magnetic and sonic properties. *points west* We follow the corridor.

[*Squad*] Jay : Hell, yeah!

103. Flood Tide

"Pulse in three . . . two . . . one . . . Jesus Christ!"

Griffin and Claws lean over Jay's shoulder, their faint and blurry shadows falling on the monitor and its ghostly flickers of dark green on light.

[**Squad**] **Claws** : What does that mean?

[**Squad**] **Jay** : Those are ****ing crabs. Like, a metric ****ton of them.

[**Squad**] **Claws** : How's that possible? The last reading we took there were no crabs visible.

[**Squad**] **Jay** : It could be that the corridor's getting closer to the earth or we put the probe in a better place.

[**Squad**] **Griffin** : But?

[**Squad**] **Jay** : But instinct says it is exactly what it looks like. In the fifteen minutes since we took our last reading, this corridor has ****ing erupted with crabs.

Griffin and Claws look toward Samuel-Colt, who is standing apart with Spots.

[**Squad**] **Griffin** : You concur?

[**Squad**] **Samuel-Colt** : It is likely, yes.

[**Squad**] **Griffin** : ****. Is it our fault? Are they coming for us?

[**Squad**] **Samuel-Colt** : Possible.

[**Squad**] **Claws** : But?

[**Squad**] **Samuel-Colt** : Doubtful. The surface likely produces many noises commonly ignored by the Enemy, in much the same way you would ignore the conversation of other diners in a restaurant. The soldiers were built for specific purpose, and only a few would be capable of diversion from it.

[**Squad**] **Griffin** : ****! Then they're going to attack the Warren?

[**Squad**] **Samuel-Colt** : Possible.

[**Squad**] **Claws** : I think it's time we lifted that ban on comm silence, eh?

[**Squad**] **Griffin** : Yes. *switches channel* Base, this is Recon 1. Come in, B—****! Are they actually *jamming* us?

[*Squad*] Claws : ****! Looks that way. I didn't know they did that!

[*Squad*] Samuel-Colt : We continue.

He turns and begins trudging west.

[*Squad*] Griffin : ****! Are you ****ing out of your mind? How many ****ing crabs did you count on that screen? We have to go back and warn them!

[*Squad*] Spots : It's a long walk, Corporal.

[*Squad*] Claws : ****, she's right. These crabs will outrun us, no problem. They got smooth ground and straight lines. We got ****ing worse-than-sand and partial storms.

[*Squad*] Griffin : We don't have to get to the base before them. We just need to get out of the comm black-out.

[*Squad*] Samuel-Colt : WE GO ON.

[*Squad*] Griffin : GIVE ME ONE ****ING REASON WHY.

[*Squad*] Samuel-Colt : Have you considered the implications of the Enemy jamming communications, when by your admission they have not before?

[*Squad*] Claws : **** . . . what the **** is so important?

[*Squad*] Samuel-Colt : That is what we *must* investigate. The Enemy considers almost everything expendable. The few things it does not. . . .

[*Squad*] Griffin : ****. Maybe I can split the team up, send half out to send the message, half can follow the bug.

[*Squad*] Claws : ****, are you kidding? What if somethin' decides we're worth a noise investigatin' after all?

Pause. Samuel-Colt tolerates it for a few heart-beats, then turns and resumes his journey. Jay quickly packs up his equipment and hurries after.

[*Squad*] Griffin : *(muttering)* ****, we're the ****ing Marines. We can handle a Warren with crabs in it for a change.

[*Squad*] Claws : Likely someone down there's probably relieved they have something to ****in' shoot.

———

Warren. Avril, Gunny and the two PYEO volunteers split off at the first fork to head for the holes. Team Kitty takes the regular patrol route.

Spots the Space Marine: Defense of the Fiddler

Fang2. "Feels good to be back in the ****ing saddle!"

Scythe. "We missed your jokes."

Hairball. "Not you, understand, but your jokes."

Fang2. "Aww . . . for serious?"

Scythe, grinning. "Okay, no, we didn't. But Fang did."

Fang rolls her eyes, but she's smiling too.

Fang2. "Heh. Um. Guys?"

Whiskers, muttering. "Here it comes . . ."

Hairball, to him. "This has got to be a good one. He's had days to do nothing but think up stuff in Sickbay."

Fang2. "No, actually, this is more in the line of 'I hear something.'"

A pause. It's been a while since Fang2's been on the team, but everyone remembers Fang2's uncanny sense for breakthroughs.

Whiskers. "Aw, come on. You're messing with us. There hasn't been a crab on one of these patrols in so long I hear the Varmints have a sign up in their game-room. 'Bug-free since' and a counter."

Scythe. "I've seen it."

Fang2. "I'm serious, guys . . . listen!"

So they listen.

And they hear . . . something.

A lot of somethings.

Whiskers, under his breath. "**** . . .!"

Fang. "Finally! Bring the ****ers!"

Scythe. "CONTACT!"

Whiskers. "Mother-***ing GOD ALMIGHTY ****!!"

The corridors flood with flashing black limbs.

104. Glimmer

The Warren, near the holes. Avril and his team are investigating. The halls are empty; one almost expects dust and cobwebs.

[*Base*] **Control :** Lieutenant, this is Control. Team Kitty needs back-up.

Avril gestures; the two PYEO members start heading back. He follows.

[*Base*] **Avril :** Control, this is Avril. Sitrep, please.

[*Base*] **Control :** Hall 4 is overrun at spokes 12, 13 and 14. Hall 5 looks bad too.

[*Base*] **Avril :** ****!

He glances back at the holes.

Avril, to himself. Where are they coming from?

―――――

Zoom in over a carpet of dead bodies, over which giant crabs are pouring in a glistening tide toward the five members of Team Kitty. The bugs pack the corridors, squeezing past one another at the edges, clogging the hall like a sick artery and then abruptly spurting a wall of flailing knife-edged limbs.

Fang2. This is a little . . . more . . . "fun" . . . than I was hoping for when I came back.

Fang. ****ing shut up, this is all just more ****ing target practice.

The team is retreating behind Scythe's new shield, which has a ruby edge. The droplets of light running the edge look uncomfortably like fresh blood.

Hairball. Is it target practice when they pack together like that?

Fang. Point. Wouldn't dignify it with the name. More like . . .

Whiskers. Broad side of a barn practice?

Scythe. Keep an eye on the rear.

Whiskers. Nothing so far, boss.

[*Squad*] **Avril :** Kitty, this is Avril. Status.

[*Squad*] **Scythe :** Inconvenienced, sir.

Spots the Space Marine: Defense of the Fiddler

Fang2, muttering. No kidding.

[Squad] Scythe : Could use someone closing up the rear, sir. Bit nervous about how clear it is back there.

[Squad] Avril : We'll be coming up spoke 15—no, better make it 16.

[Squad] Scythe : Understood.

Fang. What's the shield running at now?

Scythe. Looking good at 72%. The improvements seem to be paying off.

Fang2. ****! What's that?

They have backed successfully to spoke 14, where some glimmer in the dark has caught Fang2's eye. Fang glances that way, still shooting.

Fang, frowning. Don't see anything. What was it?

Fang2. ****! I don't know, but it was ****ing fast! ****!

Scythe. I don't like the sound of that. Hairball, Whiskers, shields hot.

As the two bring up shields, green and aquamarine . . .

Fang. I don't get it. This is all the same **** we've been shooting before. Why the flood?

Scythe. Ours not to question why—

Whiskers. —ours just to watch them die.

Fang2. Wow, that was totally hot. Like a line from a ****ing movie. I can totally see that. Some bad-*** guy in armor with a gun—oh wait.

Whiskers snickers.

Avril's team, jogging up the hall . . .

Gull. Did you see something?

His squad-mate starts to turn.

105. Revelation

Every place the Recon Team stops, the monitor shows the broad hallway flickering with crabs. Samuel-Colt has stopped removing his glove to measure alongside Jay; he speaks not at all as the team observes the results and discusses the distances between each reading.

Spots is watching him, uneasy, but tags at his heels in matching silence.

[*Private*] Griffin : Hey, Claws.

[*Private*] Claws : Yeah?

[*Private*] Griffin : Is he always so quiet? The bug.

[*Private*] Claws : You askin' me? I ain't his keeper.

[*Prviate*] Griffin : I hear a 'but.'

Claws pauses, watching Samuel-Colt and Spots as Jay packs up his gear again.

[*Private*] Claws : But this is bad, yes. Somethin' bad's up.

They continue on until:

[*Squad*] Jay : . . . oh, mother****—

Griffin forges over and crouches alongside. Claws looks over their shoulders. On the monitor is a large hemisphere, cut off by the edge of the display and implying a much larger space by its curvature. It's black against the dark gray of the rest of the display.

[*Squad*] Griffin : What the hell is that?

[*Squad*] Claws : Whatever it is, it's ****in' huge.

[*Squad*] Jay : *That* is what you see over a bunker.

[*Squad*] Griffin : ****! What? You're ****ing me.

[*Squad*] Jay : Not just a bunker, a ****ing 'you better have a nuke to break it open' bunker.

Everyone now looks at Samuel-Colt.

[*Squad*] Claws : *(soft)* Uh, Sam?

[*Squad*] Samuel-Colt : Yes, Mother's-Escort?

Spots the Space Marine: Defense of the Fiddler

[*Squad*] Claws : How did that get down there?

[*Squad*] Griffin : **** that. What *is* it?

A long pause. Samuel-Colt does not fidget as a human does to show discomfort, and with his vestigial arms "packed" into the suit he is unable to emote as Violinists do. His silence feels foreboding enough to the members of Team PYEO, but to Spots and Claws, who are more accustomed to his mannerisms, it positively shouts a warning.

[*Squad*] Samuel-Colt : If you permit the indulgence of following my directions, we will be able to test my hypothesis.

Griffin starts to say something, but Claws interrupts.

[*Squad*] Claws : Just . . . do it, okay? Let's just do it.

After a pause:

[*Squad*] Griffin : All right. But at least tell me this. It's big, isn't it?

[*Squad*] Samuel-Colt : It may be the key to understanding the Enemy's behavior here.

[*Squad*] Griffin : Okay. That's big, all right. *(deep breath)* All right, you're the boss. What next?

[*Squad*] Samuel-Colt : Let us begin by describing the circumference. Size is significant.

They begin, then, following the edge of the bunker. Here at last Samuel-Colt resumes the removal of his gloves: both of them now, exposing both hands, the frayed and the whole. As they continue their measurements, everyone becomes more and more uncomfortable, especially when their methodical investigation uncovers evidence of corridors feeding into the chamber. These corridors quickly dive too deep to be accurately displayed by their probe.

[*Squad*] Griffin : ****. This is a ****ing maze. Where do all those corridors go?

[*Squad*] Claws : I don't think there's a happy answer to that.

[*Squad*] Griffin : How the **** long have they been here to do this?

[*Squad*] Claws : Dunno. But if you sit on this rock long enough, you'll find out it don't take the crabs long to cut a corridor. That's why we cut the Warren ourselves, so that there would already be tunnels in the space around the donut, ones we'd already mapped.

They continue moving around the rim of the bunker, until Jay squints.

[*Squad*] Jay : **** me sideways. It's a tunnel leading up. A ****ing big one.

He glances toward the west, shakes his head. Looks at Samuel-Colt, whose hands are on the ground.

[*Squad*] Jay : You got more resolution on that? I'm thinking the thing's collapsed.

[*Squad*] Samuel-Colt : You are correct. It was collapsed.

[*Squad*] Griffin : *Was* collapsed? On purpose?

[*Squad*] Samuel-Colt : Yes. We have everything we need to know now.

[*Squad*] Griffin : And . . . ?

Samuel-Colt slowly rises. His left arm is a tattered ruin, terminating in a slim stump with vestigial nubs where there were once fingers. The left hand is frayed but still recognizable. Spots helps him with the gloves because he can no longer manage them himself.

[*Squad*] Samuel-Colt : There is a Queen on this world. A true-Queen, a thinking one. One of the Enemy's generals.

[*Squad*] Claws : What . . . ? Why—****!

[*Squad*] Spots : *(under her breath)* Mother of God.

[*Squad*] Claws : It's you. They're after *you*.

[*Squad*] Samuel-Colt : We think it's time I returned to the base.

106. CLEARING TRASH

Gunny lunges, grabs Gull's arm and hauls him back. "Shields hot!"

Everyone obeys, even Avril. They freeze. Nothing. No sound. No flicker.

Gull. "****. Was that my imagination?"

Gunny. "No. Sir, I think we should get you back to the base."

Avril. "Gunnery Sergeant, we're promised to Kitty's back-up."

Gunny pauses. Then: "Lead the way, sir."

Avril nods, tense, and starts back up the corridor. The two members of PYEO bring up the rear, spooked.

———————◆———————

Scythe. "Control, this is Kitty. New shell. Repeat, new shell."

"Kitty, this is Control. Probability?"

"One hundred percent. There's something out there and it's faster than anything we've seen before."

"Roger, Kitty. Try to get it on cam."

"Wilco."

Fang. "**** that, I'm bagging one of those ****ers and bringing it in. Peaches can ****ing dissect it with her Ka-Bar."

Scythe. "Don't be a ****ing hero, Fang. Just do the job."

Team Kitty is backing toward Spoke 16, where they're meeting Avril. They are managing the incursion using the new training: Scythe and Whiskers are handling shield duties at the front and rear of the formation while the two Fangs and Hairball rack up the kill count. The corridor is thick with chitinous bodies and reeking with ichor.

Fang2. "So how come they're not breaking through the walls this time?"

Whiskers. "****, man, don't give them ideas."

Hairball. "It's a good question."

Fang. "There're more out there."

Whiskers. "**** you, Fang."

Fang. "I'm serious. They're not going to waste a new shell on a distraction small enough for half a squad to handle. They've got more and we're about to get **** in the face."

Scythe. "That's enough."

Whiskers. "Contact—it's the lieutenant."

The two groups form up, with Whiskers taking up shield duty behind the two members of PYEO, who turn off their own first revision shields to renew their two-handed grips on their weapons with obvious relief.

Scythe. "Orders, sir?"

Avril. "Looks like regular Mark 2 trash?"

Scythe. "Yes, sir. But we've caught glimpses of a new shell."

Avril. "We did too. Let's clear the trash and see if we can't get a better look."

Scythe. "Yes, sir."

107. HUNTED

Montage. Kitty mowing down the crabs—eyeshot, eyeshot, eyeshot. Fang2 messing with his shield as he takes over from Whiskers. Avril in the center of the formation, taking careful aim.

Then: it's over. Crab corpses everywhere. The plangent drip of alien body fluids striking the metal grid. The ping of overheated metal.

Scythe. "See anything?"

Fang2, at the rear. "Nada."

Hairball. "Clear here, too."

Whiskers. "Think we did 'em all?"

Scythe. "Maybe."

Gunny. "Always a good answer."

Avril. "All right. Let's see if we can find any of those new shells on the ground. And keep an eye out in case they're still on their feet."

The squad spreads out, stepping among the severed limbs and shattered carapaces.

[***Kitty-Private***] **Hairball :** Uh, boss . . . good feeling about this? Not?

[***Kitty-Private***] **Scythe :** Of course not. Just keep your finger on the trigger.

As it happens, their first sight of the new shell . . . isn't of the new shell at all.

It's of a needle the size of a knife smacking into Whoop's shoulder. The man grunts in surprise, grabbing it. "The ****!"

Scythe. "HAIRBALL!"

—but Hairball, who is up next on the shield rotation, already has it active as the rest of the team lays down suppressing fire. There's nothing for them to target, though. The corridor is empty again.

Gull, checking on Whoop's injury. "****! Since when do they ****ing shoot people?"

Scythe. "They haven't in a very long time. And they were never big on shooting anyway. For obvious reasons, in retrospect."

Fang. "****! Where is the ****er?"

Gull. "****, it went all the way through the armor."

Whoop. "Man. I feel kind of . . . uh . . ." *He abruptly falls forward into Gull's arms.*

Gull. "****!"

Avril. "Get him to Sickbay."

Gull glances at him, then nods once, jerky, and hauls Whoop's arm over his shoulder. Gunny looks at them, then at Avril.

Gunny. "Permission to accompany them, sir."

Avril. "Granted."

Gunny nods and flicks his shield on, covering the two in PYEO as they head back.

Avril, to the rest of Kitty. "I didn't know they used toxins."

Scythe. "They haven't, in a long time."

Whiskers. "What is this, Return of Mark 1, Part 2?"

Fang2, under his breath. "****, man, stop upstaging me with those lines!"

Scythe. "This is ****." *Pauses.* "Excuse me, sir."

Avril. "No, go on."

Scythe. "It's acting like it has a brain, sir. It's hiding from us. It just shot us and then ran so we couldn't target it."

Avril. "That's unusual for the crabs here . . . ?"

Scythe. "Yes, sir. Even their Kings would sacrifice themselves to kill us."

Avril, still scanning the corridor, weapon at ready. "You're right, Sergeant. This is ****." *He grins.* "It's also **** we need to handle. We can't have a thinking crab running around the Warren."

Fang2, to himself. "Thinking is *always* to be discouraged."

Whiskers. "Lame. But I give you points for trying."

Avril. "Let's go hunting."

Scythe. "Shield discipline. I want a full wall. No more casualties."

108. FRUSTRATION

Team Kitty continues its hunt for the new shell, picking past corpses or gliding down unob-structed corridors. The new shields glimmer where their seams merge. As Scythe directs the others . . .

[*Officer-Private*] Avril : Savannah? You there?

Nothing.

[*Base*] Avril : Control, this is Avril. Do you know the status of Lieutenant Bonnet?

[*Base*] Control : Lieutenant, this is Control. Sickbay reports Lieutenant Bonnet is resting.

[*Base*] Avril : Tell them to wake her up.

———————

Sickbay. Peaches is in fact sitting up, checking her handheld sleepily. She is squinting at the logs with a growing frown when the doors slam open for the two members of PYEO, accompa-nied by a medical team and Gunny.

Peaches, looking up. "What the . . ."

As they rush past for the nearest bed: "What the . . . !" *Struggling upright.* "Gunny!"

He appears at her bedside. "Ma'am. One casualty. The crabs are back, they've brought a new shell. Shoots some kind of dart."

Peaches. "The hell! A girl lies down for an hour and everything hits the fan." *She pushes herself to the edge of the bed.* "Help me, Gunny."

He grabs her arm as she slides down and staggers. "Ma'am? Where are we going?"

"To Control." *Peaches winces.* "Crap. Pack me into a suit if you have to, it'll walk this lame leg for me. But I'm going."

———————

[*Base*] Bonnet : Paul, talk to me.

[*Base*] Avril : All this entertainment, Savannah. I arranged it just for you, you know . . .

[*Base*] Bonnet : *(laughing)* Yeah, well, the doctor wouldn't budge. I sleep when I need to sleep. Now what the hell did you do to my Warren while I was down?

[*Base*] Avril : A little excitement. Some old Mark 2s, and then . . . something new, fast. We're looking for it. Whoop . . . ?

[*Base*] Bonnet : He's in Sickbay, they got him. He's in good hands. What's your plan?

[*Base*] Avril : Keep looking. Nothing up there, I'm assuming.

Peaches glances at the men sitting at the consoles next to her. They shake their heads.

[*Base*] Bonnet : No joy.

[*Base*] Avril : I figured they would have reported if they'd seen anything on the monitors.

[*Base*] Bonnet : That doesn't mean anything, though. Supply only sent us enough cameras for the high-risk areas leading up to the donut or the base.

[*Base*] Avril : Of course. We get the dregs because we can make it work even if they send us on the beaches with a harpoon and some chewing gum.

[*Base*] Bonnet : Hell, the harpoon would be a bonus. Be careful out there.

[*Base*] Avril : Keep an eye on those monitors for me.

306

So Team Kitty hunts.

> *Down the halls.*

> > *Up the spokes.*

Peering around corners, prodding bodies, creeping toward intersections. They are careful. They are good.

They find nothing.

The hours of their patrol inch past, measured in sweat that trails down faces trapped behind helmets and grips on weapons growing harder, harder, until bones ache. No one talks except to give orders and respond, terse and focused.

In Control, Peaches says to the man next to her. "Bring the Varmints in early. Let's get some overlap when Kitty comes in."

As the end of the watch draws near:

Fang, muttered. "****! I wanted that ****er!"

Avril. "Another day, Private. It's time to head back."

Spots the Space Marine: Defense of the Fiddler

109. Impossible Choices

Team Kitty heads for the airlock. Team Varmint passes them in the hall. Scythe holds up a gloved hand as they go by—Roach slaps it.

Control. Peaches is leaning over the monitors. She can see Team Kitty unsuiting on one of them. "Crap, Paul. I was hoping for a little more closure."

Avril, in the Armory. "I know. Not much we can do about—"

The monitors displaying Team Varmint's cam-feeds erupt. Vertiginous tilts. Sudden shaking. Shouts and swearing.

"Ma'am! We've got . . . ****! The bio readings are diving!"

Peaches. "Talk to me!" *She grabs a mike.* "Roach! Talk to me!"

"****, ma'am, they've got—****!" *A scream.*

The line goes dead. The camera does too. The bio readings associated with the Varmint suits are plummeting, then spiking, falling again.

Peaches. "Get me someone who can talk!"

Flea's voice issues from the speakers mid-sentence as the operator dials him in. "—a'am, something . . . something just took the entire team. Just . . . just took the entire . . . entire team. . . ."

Peaches, switching channels. "Paul! The squad just went missing! I've got . . . movement on the monitors. No one's responding, they've been hurt. I think they're being carried—"

In the Armory, Avril says, "****!" *And turns to Kitty.* "We're going back out. They've taken the Varmints."

One heartbeat, stunned. Then the Armory explodes with frenzied activity.

Scythe, voice carrying, harsh. "RE-AMMO, POWER CELLS, NOW NOW!"

And then Team Kitty is packing into the airlock, spilling into the Warren, pounding down the metal grid with Avril leading.

[**Control**] **Bonnet :** ****, Paul, this is bad, we can't just chase them!

[**Control**] **Avril :** If you've got a better suggestion, I'm listening, Savannah, but God dammit! We can't just let them carry off an entire squad! What are you seeing?

[**Control**] **Bonnet :** We can't tell from the cameras, most of them are pointing down.

We can see a hint of the shells, but not enough to identify them.

[*Control*] **Avril** : So they're definitely being carried by the crabs.

[*Control*] **Bonnet** : And not struggling, either.

[*Control*] **Avril** : ****!

Kitty catches up with Flea, the sole member of the Varmints. He is slumped against the wall. Scythe grabs his arms, hefts him up.

Scythe. "Talk."

Flea. "It happened . . . like lightning. One moment, nothing, then . . . just . . . scooped everyone up and ran, ran."

Scythe. "Be more specific. How many? Did you see?"

Flea. "No, I . . . I didn't get a count, must . . . must have been enough for the team though."

Fang. "I got blips, Boss. Some of their beacons are still active."

Hairball. "Are they heading . . . toward the donut? Why?"

Scythe, to Flea. "You injured?'

Flea. "No."

Scythe. "On your feet, then."

Avril. "Let's go—"

[*Control*] **Bonnet** : Paul, the camera at the holes just lit.

[*Control*] **Avril** : Don't tell me . . .

Peaches is staring at a monitor . . . at a seeming endless wave of crabs pouring from the holes. So many the camera view is nothing but movement and light off of carapace edges . . . like a kicked-open anthill.

[*Control*] **Bonnet** : This is a trap.

[*Control*] **Avril** : We can't leave them behind. Savannah, we *can't.*

[*Control*] **Bonnet** : God! Paul—

[*Control*] **Avril** : Wake up someone to take care of the holes. I'm taking Kitty to get our men back.

Avril. "We're low on time and we've got crabs coming up our ***es. Follow the traces."

Scythe. "Shields hot!"

110. HEARTBEATS

Control. Peaches to the man beside her. "Get Team Holiday up and moving ASAP."

"Yes, ma'am."

Behind her, Gunny, looking at the monitors: "They're not going to get there in time to interdict, ma'am."

Peaches, low, tense. "I know, Gunny."

The Warren. Avril and the team are rushing, navigating by HUD. The blips representing two of the Varmint suits are zig-zagging around the donut.

Whiskers. "****! Where are they going?"

Scythe. "Probably some door we don't know about."

Flea. "****! You saying they're going to . . . "

Scythe. "****ing eat them someplace we can't reach, yes."

Avril. "Focus!"

The team shuts up. No sound except the pound of boots on metal. The distance closes. Avril turns a corner—

— and jerks back, just missed by one of the new needles. It smashes into the wall. Before them, a gleam in the dark: multifaceted eyes. Fang is firing a fraction of a second before the rest do. They all miss; the crab is gone.

Fang. "****! ****!"

Avril, grabbing her arm. "Ignore it!" *and pushes them on.*

Images: The river of crabs washing through the Warren.

> *Peaches bent over the console in Control, hands fisted.*

> *Team Holiday jamming helmets on and rushing through buddy checks.*

> *Peaches, whispering.* "They're not going to make it."

Fang2, running. "Guys, I hear something. . . ."

Heartbeat.

Scythe's eyes widen behind his faceplate. "BUBBLE! NOW!"

Whiskers and Hairball lunge toward him. Fang2 ducks. Scythe grabs Flea and flings him forward.

Fang skids. Slides. Still sliding. Cursing. Avril is in front of her, just turning. He reaches for her.

The walls explode.

Fang and Avril vanish.

111. Precious Seconds

Scythe. "Fang! FANG! Pingback!"

There are so many crabs they hit the top of Team Kitty's group bubble and go skidding across it, off it, flying down the corridor. Beneath the avalanche the team crouches close, crabs crushed against them, crabs over them, crabs now behind them. The shield holds, little arcs of color traveling its surface. Looking up at it, Flea whispers, "****."

Scythe. "FANG!"

A good ten meters of the corridor has come down. Everything is flailing limbs and flying dirt and light reflected off chitin. We spin dizzily close to the mass.

Closer to one section of writhing bodies.

Closer.

Between two crabs, three, six. Under. Down.

Fang is in a fetal curl at the very bottom of the pile-up, her shield bubbled close around her. She swallows, bares her teeth. "Yeah, Boss. I'm alive. Pretty ****ed if you can't clear all this out in—" *her eyes track to the power reading on the inside bottom right of her faceplate.* "—five minutes."

[Base] Scythe : Base, this is Kitty. Where's our back-up?

[Base] Control : Kitty, this is Control. Team Holiday is on their way.

Fang. "Boss, the LT was on the other side of me. . . ."

Scythe, under his breath. "****!" *To the team with him under the shield.* "What the **** are you waiting for? A cue-card? ****ing kill the enemy!" *Then, against the report of gunfire,* "Lieutenant? Are you there? Lieutenant!"

Camera rises. Swings over the roiling. All . . . the . . . way . . . to the other side of the mass, where Avril has backed up and is shooting, his first-generation shield flashing with every bullet that stings it on the way out. He's killing very fast, but this is only the end of the river pouring out of the distant holes.

Avril. "I'm fine, Sergeant. On the other side of this mess. Try not to catch me in your line of fire, eh?"

Scythe. "Stay near what's left of the wall."

Avril, wry. "Trying. For some reason these things are trying to kill me."

Scythe. "You have your shield?"

Avril. "Yeah, but shooting through it is draining it quickly."

Scythe, to himself. "****ing first revisions." *Louder.* "Two options, sir. Go around this corridor and meet up with us behind. Or halve the bubble, facing forward. That should keep it extended."

Avril. "Don't think wandering off alone is a good idea, Sergeant."

Scythe. "No, sir."

Avril. "Bonnet might kill me."

Scythe. "Yes, sir."

Avril. "All right. Half-shield. Keep them busy."

Scythe. "Will do, sir."

Fang. "Can you keep them busy faster? There's so much **** on me I can't even crawl your way."

Fang2. "Missing a hell of a shoot-out."

Fang, grimacing. "Shut up. This is ****ing bad enough without you gloating."

[**Officer**] **Bonnet :** I heard that, you know.

[**Officer**] **Avril :** Was it untrue?

[**Officer**] **Bonnet :** I'm more of the 'beat to a pulp and give them a chance to repent first' type, but . . . more or less.

Scythe has joined the others in the slaughter . . . but his eyes are on the blips on the HUD, moving steadily away.

Scythe, whispering. "****." *Punching a hole through a crab's head,* "Sir, we're running out of time!"

112. Too Late

[**Control**] **Bonnet :** I'm losing the cams on the Varmint suits!

There are fewer crabs in Avril's direction. Fang starts forcing her way out.

Avril. "****! Sergeant, you can bull through?"

Scythe. "Can try, but it's going to burn through the power cells."

Avril. "We're out of options. Do it—"

At the end of the hall. Behind him.

Glint of two pairs of eyes.

"—Holiday, you got clean-up, get your ***es up here double-time and keep these bastards off our b—"

A needle appears in Avril's back, piercing the armor. He lists. Gurgles.

A chitinous limb sweeps him up.

[**Control**] **Bonnet :** Paul? *PAUL!!*

Scythe. "Lieutenant?"

[**Control**] **Bonnet :** They've got him! The crabs have Avril!

Scythe. "****! Go go go go!"

Fang squirms out from under the pile, sees the retreating crabs, Avril over one shoulder. "****!" *She trips to her feet, steadies herself as a crab buffets her shield from behind.*

Aims.

Fires—

—her round pings off the back of the distant crab's head.

Fang, whispering. "What the **—!" *Hits again, no penetration. She tries their backs. Nothing. Desperate now, she shoots for their joints, but they're moving too fast even for Dragon Team's star shooter.*

Then her eyes track down. Lock on a dull gleam of metal. They narrow.

Breathe in.

Spots the Space Marine: Defense of the Fiddler

Breathe out—

Her shot rips off the lever alongside the distant trap, meant to be triggered by the kick of a passing boot. The false floor retracts under the legs of one of the crabs. It falls in. The floor snaps shut.

—but it's not the crab holding Avril.

*Fang. "**** **** **** ****!" She starts running. Behind her, Kitty explodes out of the pack of crabs. The entire crab host rushes after.*

They run. Following the blip of the last Varmint suit. Following Avril.

Pounding around the next corner.

The next.

Breathing hard. Cursing. Sweating. Praying. Sprinting full-bore alongside the long curving corridors abutting the donut.

Peaches, in Control, bent low over the monitors, whispering. "Come on, come on, come on come on come on—"

The last Varmint suit stops transmitting.

*Scythe. "****, **** no, Roach!"*

Avril's suit goes through a wall and vanishes. Kitty doesn't pause; they lay into the wall until it falls and the tumbling soil delivers them—

—into another narrow hall studded with holes, just like the first on the opposite side of the Warren.

Avril and the Varmints are gone.

113. Pyrrhic Compensations

Scythe. "****!"

Hairball lunges toward the holes; Scythe grabs him. "****, ****, no we can't, we'll all die down there, **** it all!"

Whiskers, facing off against him. "**** that! We don't leave anyone behind!"

Scythe, voice harsh. "ENOUGH! Stay back!"

[Control] Bonnet : Confirm that order. No one goes down there without a plan.

Scythe. "Copy that, ma'am—"

—from the corridor, the sound of thousands of legs, skittering.

Scythe. "SHIELDS!"

Fang2. "****! We're down to 20%—"

Whiskers. "****!"

The crabs burst into the hall . . .

. . . and past them. Like water down a drain, they pour into the holes, ignoring Kitty altogether except to slam against them when they're in the way. Scythe pulls Fang and Fang2 against a wall; Hairball and Whiskers flatten themselves against the opposite one.

Fang. "****! We can't just let them go down there without killing them!"

Scythe. "If we start shooting, they might notice us."

Fang. "Or they might not!"

Scythe. "Be *still*." *Low, hard.* "We've lost enough people today."

[Company] Sandy : Kitty, this is Holiday-Lead. We're two minutes out from your position.

[Company] Scythe : Resistance?

[Company] Sandy : Not much.

[Company] Scythe : See if there's anything to clean up. We're on our way back.

[Company] Sandy : Did you . . . the LT. . . .

Spots the Space Marine: Defense of the Fiddler

[*Company*] Scythe : MIA.

[*Company*] Sandy : . . .

[*Company*] Sandy : ****!

At last the flood of crabs is sucked into the holes. For several heartbeats, no one moves or speaks. And nothing happens. There is a strange tension, as if someone has left the punctuation off the end of a sentence and no one knows how to finish it.

Then:

Scythe. "Come on. Let's get back."

Fang. "We got one errand to run, Boss."

Scythe. "An erran—Fang? Fang!"

Fang is already loping away. Scythe growls and follows her, the team on his heels.

Fang leads them to the trap. The door has been deformed by the crab's attempts to smash its way out, but it's held. Staring through the tiny holes, Scythe says, "****. Is that one of the ninjas?"

Fang. "Yes. And they've got new armor, couldn't ****ing get through the back of the thing's ****ing head." *She puts her boot heel on what remains of the lever.* "Cover me."

The team encircles the hatch, weapons ready. Fang depresses the lever and the door retracts, jamming where it's been misshapen. The crab instantly tries to push through the gap.

As its head clears the trap, Fang switches ammo loads with a flick of her thumb and aims point-blank at one of those dull eyes.

Fang. "This is for Dusty's dogs."

CRACK

Outside. The recon team clears a hill, Griffin at point and Claws at rear. The rest of the squad is spread around Jay with his equipment and the tall figure of Samuel-Colt. The Violinist is walking at a normal pace, unbent . . . but closer to Spots than when they left.

Griffin. "That's the airlock. Think we can break comm silence now?"

Claws. "We'd better, or no one will let us in." *switching channels* Control, this is Recon 1. We're home.

[*Control*] Base : Recon 1, this is Control. Status.

[*Control*] Griffin : We've got the data.

[*Control*] Base : No casualties?

[*Control*] Griffin : None. The alien's in pretty poor shape, though.

[*Control*] Base : We're cycling the lock for you now. It's good to have you back in one piece.

Griffin. "****. What was that about? Was I imagining the tone?"

Claws. "Nope. Like someone's dog died."

Spots. "Someone must have gotten hurt while we were gone."

Griffin. "****."

Claws. "They're just gonna love our news."

114. Specimen

Control. Peaches is sitting in her chair, hands loose on her knees. Staring at the monitors that held the cam footage for the Varmints and Avril, two rows of blank screens, no signal, not even static.

Slowly her fingers curl into fists.

Behind her, Gunny. "Ma'am?"

Peaches, voice almost conversational. "Yes, Gunny?"

Gunny. "Kitty's brought you a present. It's in the Boardroom."

Peaches is silent a moment. Then she rises stiffly. "Let's go."

The Boardroom. The dissection table is still missing following Peaches's terminal use of it as a weapon, so the new shell has been immobilized upright against the wall with steel straps. It looks not unlike the pinned butterflies from the print that used to hang next to the door . . . except much, much taller.

Of the specialists assigned to the Boardroom, only one of the two survivors is well enough to be on duty, his uniform trimmed around the amputated arm. Team Kitty is standing at attention along one wall, with Scythe one pace in front of them. There are four armed guards, two at the door and two inside the room, covering the crab.

Peaches enters, limping, with Gunny behind her. She stops, stares.

Comes a few steps closer and looks up.

Peaches, whispered. "****."

Specialist, tired. "That's what I said when they brought it in."

Peaches. "How long is the tranquilizer supposed to work for?"

Specialist. "According to the Violinist's estimate, eight hours."

Peaches glances at him. "Estimate?"

Specialist. "We don't get exact numbers with our own drugs, Lieutenant, and we know how they work. I'm impressed the Violinist was able to improvise something that appears to have been effective despite claiming not to be a biologist. Nevertheless, we've prepared some precautions. Just in case."

Peaches, eyeing the straps and then the guards. "Good idea."

Specialist, wan smile. "Yes, well. We do learn from our mistakes."

She grips his good shoulder, meeting his eyes. Then turns to Team Kitty. "I was a little tied up with other things, so I haven't had time to review the footage. Who's responsible for this prize, Sergeant?"

Scythe. "Ma'am, Private Gordon brought down the ninja."

Peaches. "Nice work, Nicola."

Fang, subdued. "Thank you, ma'am. I'm only sorry I didn't get the rest."

Peaches. "You'll get your chance." *She faces the crab. Softer.* "****ing hell."

Scythe. "We didn't realize until they tacked it up, ma'am."

Peaches is about to answer when the intercom goes off. She limps to it and leans on the wall. "Bonnet."

"Lieutenant, Recon 1's in the airlock."

Looking toward the opposite wall, Peaches says, "Send them down here. All of them."

Pan out, away from her profile, sweeping across Team Kitty, back toward the crab . . . the new shell.

Nine feet tall. Slender, hard. Dark rather than tan-and-dust-colored.

. . . but otherwise, shaped almost exactly like a Violinist. He could be Samuel-Colt's brother.

Spots the Space Marine: Defense of the Fiddler

115. SECRETS

Armory. The recon team is peeling out of their suits, with Team PYEO on one side and Samuel-Colt on the other. Spots is helping him as his hands no longer function.

The intercom sounds. Griffin answers. "Armory."

"Recon 1, the lieutenant wants you in the Boardroom."

"Understood."

Griffin looks at Samuel-Colt, Spots and Claws. Before he can say anything:

Spots. "Let us finish."

Claws glances at her. Says to Griffin, "We can meet you there, if you want."

Spots helps Samuel-Colt to his feet. He steadies himself with one of his scythe-limbs, leaning toward her as she unclamps the chest-piece. His damaged arms hang limp at his sides, the tatters swaying.

Griffin watches them. Looks away. "We'll go as a group."

At last Spots finishes her task. Divested of his armor, Samuel-Colt looks frangible despite his hard shell and cruel weapons-arms. It's hard to look away from the damaged limbs.

As PYEO files out, Claws murmurs to Spots, "You sure about that call? He looks a lot more exposed like that."

Spots, quiet. "Exactly."

They make their way to the Boardroom, PYEO first like an honor guard, Samuel-Colt in the middle and Spots and Claws on either side of him. The Violinist is not moving well, and with the arm that still has a palm-shaped stump at the end cradles the arm that has nothing below the elbow but a gluey lace.

In the halls, they are stared at, and the eyes that follow them are hard.

Claws, muttered. "****. What happened?"

They reach the door and pass through . . . into the tableau of Peaches before the specimen and Kitty, the guards, Gunny and the specialist arrayed around her. The tension is so sharp and the sight of the crab so shocking the recon team loses a beat. Then they snap to attention.

Griffin, saluting. "Ma'am. Recon 1 reporting as ordered."

Peaches. "At ease. I heard your mission was a success, Corporal."

Griffin. "Yes, ma'am. The findings are significant."

Peaches. "Good. I'll want to hear them in a moment. If you and your team would stand against the wall, please?"

They move out of her way, sensing her mood. That leaves nothing between her and Samuel-Colt but Spots and Claws.

Peaches, voice clipped. "Samuel-Colt. As you can see, we've secured your specimen."

Samuel-Colt, no music. "So we see, Lieutenant-Savannah-Bonnet."

Peaches. "Is it sufficiently alive for your purposes?"

Samuel-Colt. "It is."

Peaches. "Then I trust you will explain this to me."

Samuel-Colt. "Lieutenant-Savannah-Bonnet, what in particular is it that you wish explained?"

Peaches. "Don't play games, sir. That thing could be your twin. I want to know why. I want to know why right this moment."

Samuel-Colt, bowing a hint of a note, soft. "Lieutenant-Savannah-Bonnet, we cannot tell you."

Silence.

Peaches, slowly. "Excuse me?"

Samuel-Colt is still holding that stump with his slightly-less destroyed arm, appearing to cradle himself. He looks very alien, and very human in that moment. "Lieutenant-Savannah-Bonnet. It grieves me to say so, but we cannot tell you."

Peaches stabs a finger toward the crab. "We bought that thing with the lives of an entire squad of men and women *and* Lieutenant Avril. They're gone, Samuel-Colt. And you want to tell me that you *can't tell me why the* **** it looks like a Violinist?"

A hiss runs through the room as she makes it plain. Shock flies over the faces of Avril's men at the news of his loss.

Samuel-Colt. "I am sorry, Lieutenant-Savannah-Bonnet. I cannot—"

Peaches lunges for him and he twists away, holding up his mangled limbs to protect his face. Gunny grabs for her, Spots moves toward them . . .

—but it's Claws who gets between the enraged officer and the alien. "Ma'am! Ma'am, no!

Spots the Space Marine: Defense of the Fiddler

There's another way! ****, there's another way, damn it!"

Peaches, snarled. "Make this good, Corporal."

Claws turns to Samuel-Colt, words quick. "You can't. You know, but you can't. Am I right?"

Samuel-Colt, soft note. He knows what's coming. "Yes, Peer."

Claws. "Then Spots can make you tell."

A long pause.

Samuel-Colt, even softer. "Yes, Peer."

116. ANSWERS

The silence then is like a held breath.

Peaches. "Private Guitart—"

Spots, before she can finish. "Is there a conference room we can use?"

Peaches frowns, about to speak.

Specialist. "We have one, yes. That door." *Points.*

Spots. "Thank you. Samuel-Colt, what would be proper?"

Samuel-Colt, low melody. "If you, then also your escort. If Lieutenant-Savannah-Bonnet, then also her escort. We would not recommend more people for security reasons."

A little 'oh' expression travels Peaches's face. She marshals herself well. "That will be acceptable. Gunny?"

"Ma'am." *He opens the conference room door.*

As Spots heads for it, Scythe meets her eye and mouths: Well done. *She nods, tense.*

Conference Room. There are six chairs, two against the wall and four jammed around a single table, too small for the room. Peaches sits at it; Gunny stands behind her. Spots enters, makes a face. Claws comes next. Last, Samuel-Colt, who ducks to clear the doorway.

Claws. "How 'bout I stay by the door."

Spots nods. She sits on one of the chairs by the wall and pats the other. The Violinist lights on it.

Spots. "Is it all I have to do? Ask?"

Samuel-Colt, low, grinding note. "It is."

Spots. "I'm sorry about this."

Samuel-Colt. "Do not be, Mother. It is your duty, and ours."

Spots. "Not about asking. But about having to force it. Is there . . . something to make it easier?"

Samuel-Colt gives up fiddling, resting his vestigial arms on his lap. "Proximity, perhaps. Pheromone level releases the mechanism."

Spots the Space Marine: Defense of the Fiddler

Spots is silent, looking at the opposite wall.

Peaches. "Private . . ."

Spots. "Ma'am. Please, let us do this at our own pace. You're asking me to coerce information out of an allied power."

Claws, quiet. "Technically, he's willin'."

Spots. "Technically, I was willing to go through labor. But it hurt a hell of a lot, Travis." *She draws in a deep breath and knots her shirt under her breasts.* "Samuel-Colt? Can you sit here by my feet?"

Samuel-Colt hesitates. "Yes? Mother?"

"Please, just try it."

The alien rises, stands before her . . . folds those improbably narrow limbs until he is sitting by her knee. Spots watches, then shoves the hem of her pants a little lower and pats her thigh. "Head here. That should put the rest of you in the right line."

Samuel-Colt, puzzled note. "As you will, but we do not—" *and then sets his head there. A sharp, bright note, rising.* "Ah!"

Spots, rueful. "I did a lot of sweating in that suit."

Samuel-Colt, soft note. "It is well, Mother. It comforts."

Spots. "Good." *She rests a hand on his head.* "That Enemy we captured. Why does he look like you, Samuel-Colt?"

"Because we are both Kings, Mother."

Spots. "Both . . . Kings?"

Samuel-Colt, with a note like a sigh. "Yes, Mother. The more sentient an Enemy unit, the more like us they appear."

Peaches, quiet. "Ask him why, Private."

Spots. "Samuel-Colt . . . why?"

Samuel-Colt. "Because they are us, Mother. A geneline we bred for defense . . . too well."

117. THE SHARP END OF THE STICK

Long pause. Even Claws is silent.

Peaches, covering eyes with one hand. "******. I am about forty years and a million ranks too junior to know crap this classified."

Spots, quiet. "Should I continue, Lieutenant?"

Peaches sighs. "In for a penny, Private. Go ahead."

Spots looks down at Samuel-Colt. "Samuel-Colt? I assume we're not the first to hear this."

Samuel-Colt, tired, falling note. "We do not know, Mother, but we imagine not. It is relevant to the war and how it must be waged so undoubtedly your superiors and ours have discussed it."

Claws. "Why us?"

Everyone looks at him.

Claws. "I mean, why are your relations after us? If this is a family squabble, how come they're not gunnin' for you and leavin' us humans alone?"

Samuel-Colt. "It is not . . . a simple matter, Peer. The Enemy is . . . territorial, as we explained earlier. It is merely that the Enemy's leaders consider all of space to be their territory and are prosecuting the war accordingly."

Peaches. "Well, crap."

Claws. "You don't know the half of it, ma'am. Tell her, Sam. About the Queen."

Peaches's head snaps back toward the alien. "What?"

Samuel-Colt. "The Enemy has landed a . . . general, you may say. A Queen-directing. She is most certainly responsible for the innovation in shells and tactics we have been seeing. The King you have captured is in keeping with the presence of such a Queen, who would bring sentient pattern designs."

Claws. "They're hidin' in a bunker a few hours' march away, one you'd need a nuke to punch open."

Peaches. "Oh my God. You're telling me that at the ***-end of nowhere, I'm facing a major offensive against an entrenched enemy led by one of their generals while down another officer and most of our combined company?"

Samuel-Colt. "We are afraid so, Lieutenant-Savannah-Bonnet."

Spots the Space Marine: Defense of the Fiddler

Claws. "That ain't the worst of it, ma'am. Because the secrets they can't get from eatin' us they can by eatin' him."

Peaches's hand curls into a fist. She looks at the Violinist. Speaks carefully. "She came here because of you, Samuel-Colt?"

Samuel-Colt. "We doubt it strongly, Lieutenant-Savannah-Bonnet, or they would have landed in more force. The Enemy has been seeking places to experiment with new models as the war has expanded. They usually choose places oblique to the front line, where failed experiments are less likely to be noticed. That is a more likely scenario."

Peaches. "So this is all a huge . . . terrible . . . accident."

Samuel-Colt. "An unfortunate confluence, yes."

Peaches. "So my priority now is to keep you from falling into their hands. Because if they . . . eat . . . you, then they'll know everything that you know, including everything about us that you understand after decades of living among us."

Samuel-Colt, low, soft note. "That is correct." *Rising minor arpeggio, ominous.* "You mentioned the loss of several people, including Lieutenant-Paul-Avril?"

Peaches, tense. "Yes."

Samuel-Colt saws a note like razors on chalkboard.

Peaches. "What! What is that about?"

At Samuel-Colt's hesitation, Spots rests her other hand on his shoulder.

Samuel-Colt. "They may be attempting to gather more data. The information derived from the consumption of human nerve tissue is . . . difficult to interpret, but the parallax can be offset with multiple data sources."

Another terrible quiet.

Claws. "****. You're tellin' us they might have realized you're here."

Samuel-Colt. "Yes."

Peaches rises immediately. "Then they're on their way. But what do we do with you? Is orbit safe?"

Samuel-Colt. "Likely not, Lieutenant-Savannah-Bonnet. The Enemy has been landing supplies here, probably in thrown meteoroids, and they have vacuum-capable units. A Queen-General can force-mature entire squads of such specialized drones."

Peaches glances at Gunny. He says, quiet, "Harder to run up there. And the next interstellar-capable ship's not due for two weeks."

Peaches. "****. Fine. You'll have to stay with us until we can ship you out, Samuel-Colt. We'll detail you a guard. The specimen . . ."

Samuel-Colt, sharp, quick note. "We recommend destroying it."

Gunny. "Agreed."

Peaches. "You can't . . . ah . . ."

Claws. "Eat his head?"

Samuel-Colt. "Tell us, Lieutenant-Savannah-Bonnet. Your enemy is known to favor a move in combat. How quickly do you use that against him?"

Peaches. "Pretty much the moment I spot it."

Claws, brows lifting. "You people booby-trap your own heads?"

Samuel-Colt, sharp note, rising. "Wouldn't you, Peer?"

Claws. "Point."

Peaches. "Fine. I'll enjoy putting a bullet through that thing's eye." *She stops on her way to the door, frowns.* "Your . . . arms."

Samuel-Colt, not meeting her eyes. "They will grow back."

Peaches hesitates, then nods. "I'll have a plan for you as soon as I've debriefed the recon team." *She glances at Spots and Claws, finishes.* "Stay here."

"Yes, ma'am."

Peaches leaves, Gunny at her back. The door closes very finally, covering their shadows.

Spots the Space Marine: Defense of the Fiddler

118. Lullaby

Quiet. Then:

Spots. "Samuel-Colt? Can you move your head a little higher and lean up into me?"

Samuel-Colt, hesitant note, rising. "Mother? You intend to embrace us?"

Spots. "Yes, more or less."

Samuel-Colt straightens to look up at her. "We do not show affection the way humans do. . . ."

Spots. "I know. It's not for that. You said . . . a while back. You hear with your entire body?"

Now Claws is looking at her.

Samuel-Colt. "Yes?"

Spots. "Then humor me."

So Samuel-Colt leans forward, head against her ribs and broken arms partially around her hips. Spots wraps her arms around his head, her own bent close. In this way, with much of their bodies touching, she sings.

> "En el agua clara, donde está la fuente
> lindos pececitos salen de repente.
> Lindos pececitos, si queres jugar,
> todos mis juguetes te los voy a dar.
> Yo vivo en el agua; no puedo salir.
> Mi mamá me ha dicho que siempre juegue aqui."

Samuel-Colt bows out a soft note. After several heart-beats: "A lullaby?"

Spots, petting the back of his head. One stroke. Another. "Yes. We soothe our children with them, and you could use soothing."

Samuel-Colt dips his head. "But I am neither human, nor your child, Magda Guitart."

Claws holds his breath.

Spots, unperturbed. "You're one of God's children. That's good enough for me."

Major arpeggio, rising, slow. "Your God accepts me as one of His children?"

Spots laughs. "Samuel-Colt, the only reason there's no Jesuit mission on your planet is because you haven't told us where it is."

They both laugh then, one with a ripple of music, the other with a human voice.

Claws, quiet. "Magda? What's it mean?"

Spots. "The song?" *Her eyes lose focus.* "It says . . . that you're sitting by a fountain looking into the clear water, when all of a sudden, you see some beautiful fish. You say, 'pretty fish! I'll give you all of my toys if you'll come play with me!' And one of the fish answers, 'I live in the water, I can't leave. My mother told me to always play here.'"

Claws. "That's . . . uncanny."

Samuel-Colt, low note, sliding upward. "Did you not say long ago? Some wisdom crosses species."

Claws. "And I said it about women, too, as I recall."

Samuel-Colt, faint amused arpeggio. "So you did."

Claws, looking at him. "And yet, despite everything, here you are."

Samuel-Colt. "Yes. We have become . . . fond . . . of humans. It is not unusual, at that. We evolved alongside mammals; we look on them favorably. And I in particular have been fortunate in my acquaintances."

Heartbeat pause as both humans accept what he has implied.

Then Spots, soft. "But you'll get on that ship when it arrives."

Samuel-Colt. "Yes, Mother. That is duty. It is unthinkable that we would endanger the outcome of the war. And if it becomes necessary . . ." *He looks up at Claws.* "We would ask that you ensure we do not fall into Enemy hands."

Claws looks away, jaw tense. "****, Sam."

Samuel-Colt, tense note, drawn out. "Please, Peer. Savannah will hesitate."

Claws. "And I won't?"

Samuel-Colt, sharp single note, staccato. "You must not."

Spots. "I'll take care of it."

They both look at her.

Spots. "I've pulled a trigger to end a life before, and it was stupid and senseless but there was no better choice. Doing it for you would be horrible, Samuel-Colt. But some things

Spots the Space Marine: Defense of the Fiddler

are worse than death."

He starts to rest a hand on her arm and realizes he has no hand to rest.

Spots, softer, meeting his eyes. "It's okay. I'm not afraid."

So he wraps the great scythe-claws around her, careful, and she leans into him.

Samuel-Colt. "Sing the song again, Mother?"

So she does, in her soft, grainy, up-too-long mezzosoprano. By the second verse, Claws comes to their side. She reaches for his hand and he allows her to take it. When she finishes singing, Samuel-Colt gives a great sigh through his spiracles, gemmed eyes closed. And so they remain, until a thin quiver in the floor makes the nearby table rattle. Claws looks up, frowns.

Claws. "Was that . . ."

Another shiver. And then a great, heavy thoom that shakes the walls of the base.

Samuel-Colt, without lifting his head. "They're here."

The general quarters alarm starts to wail.

119. MOBILIZE

Backtrack ten minutes. Peaches and Gunny exit the conference room. In one unbroken motion, Peaches draws her sidearm, brings it up and shoots the enemy King through the eye.

Specialist, backing away. "Jesus!" *Then:* "Christ, my specimen!"

Peaches. ". . . was a potential security problem we couldn't afford to go actual. Sorry, Mister Rinshaw." *She turns to Griffin.* "Report, Corporal."

Griffin steps up, bringing Jay with him, and begins to explain their findings. Partway through them, Peaches stops him and points at the sensor data Jay's brought up on one of the room's tablets. "You're telling me they have tunnels out there we don't know about."

Griffin. "That's correct, ma'am."

"Tunnels they didn't have when we arrived, according to the original survey data."

Griffin. "Apparently not, ma'am."

Peaches, after a short pause. "Continue."

Griffin summarizes the rest of the team's discoveries. Peaches is thumbing through the scans when the intercom chimes.

"Boardroom, this is Control. Is the lieutenant still with you?"

Peaches strides over, hits the button. "Bonnet."

"Ma'am, we have activity at all cameras."

"Repeat, please. Did you say 'all cameras'?"

"That's correct."

Peaches. "Can you give me numbers?"

Control's voice is remarkably neutral. "Hard to estimate. But at least several hundred."

The silence in the room is electric.

Peaches. "Heading this way?."

"As far as we can tell—****!"

The floor shivers beneath them.

Spots the Space Marine: Defense of the Fiddler

"Ma'am, we had activity at the airlocks."

Peaches. " 'Had'?"

"Something took out the cameras."

Another shiver. Then the great, wall-shaking sound. The dead King's carapace rattles against the wall and its steel straps.

Peaches, calm but clipped. "Control, sitrep."

Control. "We're not sure, the cameras are down, but—confirmed, we're getting reports they've breached the airlocks."

Peaches. "Sound general quarters." *As the alarm goes off, she switches to the base channel and her voice echoes from every intercom.* "All personnel, Plan Birthday Cake, effective immediately. This is not a drill."

As she steps away from the intercom, Gunny says, "We don't have the manpower for even the worst case Birthday Cake, ma'am."

Peaches. "I know. But it's the most doable plan we've got with our current numbers."

Griffin and PYEO have already sprinted out the room, and the Specialist and guards are following. Peaches stops Scythe. "Stay, Sergeant."

The conference room door opens on Claws, Spots and Samuel-Colt.

Peaches to the alien as he enters. "They're not coming for the collider, are they, Samuel-Colt?"

Samuel-Colt, low note. "We can never say with absolute certainty, Lieutenant-Savannah-Bonnet. But . . . no."

She nods. "Then we'll strip the detail that was supposed to cover it." *To Scythe.* "Your squad's in charge of guarding the Violinist. Keep him away from the enemy at any costs."

Scythe. "Yes, ma'am."

Gunny. "If they do decide to go for the collider—"

Peaches. "Then it'll blow and take care of the real problem, along with the rest of us." *She nods to Scythe.* "Get to the weapons lockers." *To Samuel-Colt.* "Do what you have to do. For all our sakes."

Samuel-Colt nods once.

120. LOCK-DOWN

*With Team Kitty gone, heading for their assigned weapons locker, Peaches runs into the hall.
She even makes it several steps before her leg gives out on her. Gunny grabs her before she hits
the deck and together they hobble-sprint for Control.*

Peaches. "Damned fine time to be out a limb."

Gunny. "Could be worse, ma'am. Could be your head."

She pauses, then laughs, wry.

*Control. The room is crowded, men and women crouched over panels, overseeing cameras, talk-
ing quickly into microphones. The senior lead is waiting for them as they enter.*

"Everyone's inside, ma'am. We're go for Birthday Cake phase one."

Peaches nods. "Do it."

*Over the howl of the general quarters alarm, a second, higher-pitched siren begins to shriek
over an absurdly soothing female voice:* "Blast doors are closing in halls zero-zero through
zero-ten. Please stay clear of the doors."

Peaches eases into a chair in front of a console. "Sitrep."

"Good news and bad, ma'am."

Peaches. "Go."

"Good news: Team Holiday was in the Warren when the flood started. They got back just
in time . . . so they're still in their suits."

Peaches. "Glory be, God loves us. What's the bad news?"

"They brought back footage of these."

*He brings up a blurry view of a large, bulky crab, lumbering toward the cam operator. Instead
of the expected claws, it raises a drill-like appendage on one thick arm, and a giant pincer on
the other.*

"Those things are twice the size of a King and they can tear through metal."

Peaches. "****. That's what got through the airlocks?"

"Yes. And we're estimating there are ten of them out there. We've labeled them priority
targets; the screens in the weapons lockers should have images up."

Spots the Space Marine: Defense of the Fiddler

Peaches. "Good call." *She brings up an interior view of the base and leans over a microphone, redeploying what few men and women she has.*

Leaning over her, Gunny: "You're going to shut down half the shunts?"

Peaches. "We'll have to. We don't have enough people to cover the original plan's targets."

He nods. As she resumes issuing instructions, he grips her shoulder once, squeezes.

———————

Internal Weapons Locker C. Team Kitty is arming. Scythe is fitting himself with a red earpiece and passing the black ones to the rest of the team.

Whiskers. "How're we gonna handle this?"

Scythe. "Easiest way is to find one of the core rooms and stay there. Sickbay, Control . . . Power plant's probably closest."

Hairball. "The best defense is a good defense? You sure that's how it works?"

Scythe taps his earpiece, squinting. "The assignment wasn't to parade the Violinist in front of the enemy. When it's several hundred to eight, going out in a blaze of glory is just a fancy way of saying 'going out.'"

Claws is staring at the screen in the room, meanwhile. "What the hell is that?"

Samuel-Colt, low note. "A digger. Small version."

Claws. "That's the *small* version?"

Samuel-Colt. "The large ones can carve out tunnels to dock interstellar ships." *At Claws's stare,* "they don't live long. Too difficult to power."

Spots. "You talk as if they're machines."

Samuel-Colt, minor arpeggio, falling. "In some respects, they are."

Scythe swears and everyone looks at him.

Fang2. "Boss?"

Scythe. "The aliens are shooting us."

Claws, eyes narrowing. "Now? Why? Don't they have enough ****in' intel?"

Samuel-Colt, low note. "We doubt it has anything to do with information gathering,

Peer."

Scythe. "Samuel-Colt? What can I tell the lieutenant?"

Samuel-Colt. "A Queen-general will have a significant arsenal of designs to deploy—such as the diggers—but they must be force-matured. They require live food."

Whiskers. "****."

Claws. "Bigger problem. If they're shootin' and the armory is way out on the outside layer of this freakin' cake . . ."

121. No Battle Plan Survives . . .

Spots, suddenly. "The test facility."

Everyone looks at her.

Spots. "We have gloves there."

Claws, frowning. "They're hobbled, though—"

Samuel-Colt, sharp, rising note. "The governor is easily disabled."

Scythe eyes him. " 'Easily'?"

Samuel-Colt. "For us, Scythe. Not for humans. You were in no danger."

Claws. "Shields would be a damned big advantage."

Whiskers. "The lab's not in the core, though."

Scythe. "It's still in safe territory, for now. Let's go."

———————

All along the perimeter created by the blast doors, Peaches's people are running for their assigned choke points. Team Holiday, still suited, has been separated so they can provide cover to the unarmored personnel at each of three halls.

Coyote, the Wild Dog's second. "Think this'll work?"

Dusty. "Guess we'll find out real quick."

In their earpieces, Control's voice: "First wave in three . . . two . . . one . . . go!"

The blast doors rise with a pneumatic hiss. The crabs rush into the kill zone, bodies shaking with each rattle of their biological guns, but the members of Holiday dispatched to provide shield duty prevent any of the needles from striking their targets.

The bodies of the dead crabs block the hall as Control speaks again: "Doors closing. Move to next assigned hall."

In this way, the squads rotate along the perimeter, filling up halls with corpses while safely protected by their team's shields and the thickness of the blast doors. There is some joking on the company-level channel about their biggest problem being clean-up.

Fourth rotation. The Wild Dogs are at a new junction, waiting for the door. As it slides up, it reveals the giant legs of a digger, inch by inch.

Furby. "What the **** is that?"

Coyote. "Looks like one of those priority targets."

Dusty. "Remember, aim for the face—****!"

The moment the blast door finishes moving, the digger explodes from behind it and . . . jacks to the right. Crabs pour over its back as it begins chewing through the wall.

Dusty, shooting down the crabs vaulting for them. "****! ****! Get it!"

Coyote. "It's kind of ****ing NOT LOOKING AT US."

Sandy, their Holiday guest. "Grenade?"

Dusty. "Not unless you want to ****in' get in front of us."

Wild Dog. "****! It's through!"

Dusty, on comm. "Control, we have a loose priority one targe—****, all the others are following it! Shut the ****in' blast door!"

122. IMPROVISING

Team Kitty is running through halls illuminated by strobing red and white lights. Their boot-falls echo in the empty corridors; everyone is either at the perimeter or battened down in the core. They rush to the Door, currently unlocked; there is no manpower to guard it, and emergency protocols require the ability to move freely out of trapped areas. For once, Kitty goes through without any ceremony except their own honor guard formation around Samuel-Colt.

Test Facility. The team bursts in. Their shields are on the table at the end.

Samuel-Colt. "Mother, Peer, your help please. I cannot lift them."

Claws. "****! Can you fix 'em with no arms?"

Spots grabs the first glove and holds it up for the alien. He taps it with his vestigial arm until she lowers it, then slides the end of the thin limb into a flat recessed pocket on the top of the glove, near the wrist. Its power lights flare, run through a warning pattern, then stop at "active."

Whiskers, watching. "Whoa."

Samuel-Colt. "Next."

Scythe, Fang and Hairball are scouring the room for anything useful, but they never brought full armor here and their practice weapons are all wood or foam . . . except one.

Fang. "I ****ing hope they don't close enough to us for you to use that."

Scythe, knotting his sword's scabbard to his hip. "You and me both."

Claws passes out the gloves after Samuel-Colt activates them.

Fang2. "So, bigger problem here, guys. Power supply? How long these things last without suit power?"

Claws. "****! Not long."

Samuel-Colt. "There is a single power cell in the laboratory. It should allow for extended maneuvers."

Everyone looks at Spots.

Scythe. "Let's go."

The lab is adjacent to the test facility. No sooner do they open the door . . .

Kenyan, running for them. "Thank God, you came back for me!"

Scythe. "Sir, you were supposed to have reported to your assigned station for your safety—"

Kenyan. "I know, I just . . . do you know what those things can do to an unarmored body? What if there were some loose out there?"

Samuel-Colt and the rest of the team slide past them, leaving Scythe and Claws to deal with the civilian engineer.

Claws, ignoring Kenyan. "Think we have time?"

Scythe, likewise. "I think we're pushing it as it is."

Kenyan, panicked. "You're not thinking of leaving me?"

Scythe. "Sir, the halls are clear currently. If you proceed to your station, you will be fine."

Kenyan. "How do you know they'll let me in!"

Claws, sotto voce. "That I didn't think of."

Scythe sighs and pinches the bridge of his nose.

Samuel-Colt has found the power cell and is jury-rigging it to Spots's glove. She grimaces at the wire running the length of her arm to her back.

Spots. "Better tape that somewhere."

Fang, watching both them and the door. "That'll hurt coming off."

Spots. "Not as much as my arm will if it cuts out in mid-swipe."

Samuel-Colt tapes it at her upper arm and shoulder. It's an awkward arrangement, but it works. "This should suit, Mother-soldier. If there is time, you can recharge at any available power receptacle."

Spots, flexing her arm. "Understood." *To Scythe and Claws,* "Ready!"

Kenyan. "****! What do I do?"

123. Like Cake

Dusty. "****! There's a door on the opposite side, we'll take it out there!"

Coyote. "We can't leave the junction uncovered!"

Dusty. "We can't let that ****ing digger core out the base, either!" *She points at two of the Dogs.* "You two, with me, special crab welcome duty."

Sandy. "There's only one of me—"

Dusty. "You stay. That ****er doesn't seem to shoot. We'll take our chances. Come on!"

She and her two Dogs dart behind the rest of the squad and circle the room the digger entered until they reach the door.

Dusty. "Ready? On three. One . . . two . . . THREE!"

They key the door open and leap through it and right in their faces is the digger.

"****!"

One Dog flings himself against the wall, the other into the corner. Dusty ducks the giant pincer.

341

Dusty. "****! SHOOT IT!"

"WE ARE!"

Dusty. "IN THE EYE YOU ****ING IDIOTS!" *She jumps back as the digger smashes the drill down and aims her weapon, scrambling back, back, back until her spine smacks the wall outside the room and the thing is still coming and then*

—it stops as one of the Dogs shoots its leg off at the thorax. Dusty breathes out. The round goes in its eye. It lurches forward. She puts another through the other eye.

Dusty. "Coyote! Herd . . . the rest into the ****ing . . . room! ****!"

It falls forward, ruined head smacking the wall next to Dusty's face. Her wide eye rolls toward it, then she ducks out from beneath it. Her Dogs are outside the door, shooting into the room; the rest of the squad, protected by Sandy's shield, are killing the remains of the incursion.

And then . . . silence, broken by the drip of ichor.

Dusty steps into the room and surveys the carnage. "Control, this is Top Dog. We put the digger down."

"Good work."

Dusty looks around. There's a destroyed table in one corner. She recognizes it, turns and looks up above the door. The poster is still there: "Varmint Gutter: Crawling Out of it So You Don't Have To."

Dusty, jaw clenched. "****." *She nods to the squad.* "Back to your stations."

Coyote, as they troop past the bodies. "I don't understand, alph."

Dusty. "Understand what?"

Coyote nods to the digger. "That thing punched through the wall like cake. But the walls at the perimeter are just as thin. Why was it waiting for the blast door to open, when it could have come in at any time?"

Dusty pales. "Oh, ****. Maybe they have—"

124. Incursion

Sickbay, sealed off by the blast doors. The tense quiet is interrupted only by the murmurs of the staff and the hiss and chirps of equipment. Every time the walls shiver, there is a pause—absolute silence—then the noises resume. The medical personnel are still on their rotations, but they're armed, as are the more ambulatory patients. Hawk Abrams is one of them, sitting up on his bed with a rifle over his lap.

Hawk. "Wish there was some way to find out what was going on."

Corpsman at the bed next to him. "Best not to know. Bad for the blood pressure."

Hawk snorts. "It's worse for my blood pressure imagining what could be going wrong."

Corpsman, grinning. "****. You born with that ****ed-up attitude, or did Murphy beat it into you?"

Hawk. "I'm in here, aren't I?"

Corpsman. "Point. Relax, Sarge, I'm sure they're doing just fine without you."

Hawk. "Says you."

He lies back against his pillow, eyes closed, hands on the weapon. That's where he is when the wall next to his head bows. A claw erupts through the concrete; Hawk leaps off the bed, falls badly on his still healing hip, and is on the floor when the digger rips the hole wide, concrete dust and flakes of paint spraying from the shower of blocks.

Hawk. "****!" *Ignoring the panic behind him,* "**** you, bastard." *It slumps, two rounds through its eyes.*

Everyone in Sickbay breathes.

And then the crabs behind the digger rip its body from the hole.

Hawk, pushing back on the floor, cursing. "****! Doing just ****ing fine, are they!"

Scythe. "****!"

Claws. "Boss?"

Scythe. "The crabs are ****ing loose inside the perimeter. We've got to—****!"

Rounding the corner, Hairball and Whiskers have encountered the Enemy. They throw up their shields against the rain of needles. "****! Back! Back!"

Kenyan, pale. "Oh, ****!"

Claws grabs his arm as they start running in the other direction, Spots taking the rear with her shield set to guard their backs.

Fang. "****! Where to now?"

Scythe, still listening. "Sickbay's out. Dusty's reporting incursions in the southern quarter."

Spots. "Control?

Claws. "****, we'd have to run back the way we came."

Scythe. "Let's try for the power plant. Form up. We're in hostile territory."

Kenyan. "Hostile territory!"

Claws. "Just keep movin', mister."

Kenyan. "But what if those crabs follow us?!"

Spots, tense. "No 'if' about it."

Behind them, the Enemy pours around the corner. Sees Samuel-Colt. Accelerates.

Kenyan. "****! ****! ****!"

Claws. "****, stop LOOKIN' over your GOD****ed shoulder and RUN!"

125. This Party

Sickbay. The senior medical officer is yelling for all the beds to be pushed to the center, away from the walls. Equipment is crashing over, plugs sparking as they jerk from sockets, and the din is hellish: the wail of medical alarms, shouting, the report of gunfire.

Someone grabs Hawk and drags him away from the hole in the wall. He never stops shooting.

Hawk. "**** this party!"

He's joined by three corpsmen, and together they start plugging the hole in the wall with corpses. They're still at it when the wall opposite them explodes outward.

In the corridors, the ragged remains of Peaches's company are hunting diggers.

Dusty's dogs, harrying the enemy, account for three more while protected by Sandy's shield.

Team PYEO scores another two.

The chief medical officer shoots one more over the bed of a patient—with the patient still in it, screaming.

In Control, the pace is frenetic. Calm, just barely, but what few security cameras the base had are being trashed almost as fast as the crabs pass them. Data is thin. Tension is high.

Peaches, hand over her mouthpiece as she talks to one of the controllers. "That's eight. Where are the other two?"

"We're having trouble finding them, ma'am. There are so many crabs loose in the base we can't scout efficiently."

Peaches. "Then we'll fall back. They've only got two of those things left." *She switches channels.* "All company, this is Bonnet. Fall back to final layer. Repeat, fall back to assigned positions for layer zero."

Gunny. "All the way?"

Peaches. "Only way we'll be able to patrol the entire perimeter fast enough to find the last two when they break in." *Her face is expressionless. Her eyes are not. They lift to the bank of monitors in time to see another go black.*

Scythe. "Next left. Stop and shield. Block the corridor. Ready—NOW."

Spots goes down in front, head bent, shield up. As the crabs make the turn, they are greeted with prejudice. More and more of them force themselves into the corridor, climbing over the bodies of the dead, and slowly the team backs up, laying a carpet of corpses before trapping the crabs against Spots's shield and building the wall.

When no more crabs squirm through, Scythe says: "GO!" and they run.

And for a few minutes, it looks good.

Kenyan screams as a second wave of crabs, headed by a digger, appear at the next junction.

126. SEALED OUT

Scythe's shield goes front and center. Fang shoots through it. The digger dies, blocking the corridor.

Briefly. Its brethren begin tearing it to pieces.

Scythe. "****, no time for this." *They jink down a different hall, running away from the center of the base and the power plant.*

Claws. "****! What way isn't ****in' blocked? ***in' cake is compromised in every ***in' which way!"

Hairball. "Guess we should have called it Plan Swiss Cheese."

Whiskers. "We got company. . . ."

. . . they flash past several halls dark with the shadows of advancing crabs. Whiskers, Hairball and Fang2 send suppressing fire into the corridors as they pass. Behind them, the crabs cut through the digger and meet up with the crabs formerly blocked by the wall of dead. The sound of their legs skittering on the concrete floors mingle with the wail of the siren.

Kenyan is struggling not to sob.

Spots, beneath her breath, is reciting the Hail Mary.

Claws, not quite so quiet, is cursing a stream.

. . . and then a second siren shrieks over the first.

Fang. "****! Is that what it sounds like?"

Scythe. "They're closing the blast doors."

Control.

"Ma'am, we have reports that the ninth digger is down . . . confirm, Team Kitty has taken down the ninth digger. There's only one loose."

Peaches. "Great! Oh, that's great—"

Controller. "Bad news is they're trapped outside layer zero. With the Fiddler."

Peaches. ". . ."

Peaches, whispered. "Oh, ****." *She switches channel.* "Team Kitty, this is the LT. Confirm position please." *And then she pales. To the Controller,* "Quick, where's the nearest hardened location to . . . junction f-14?"

Controller. "Looks like . . . the donut's all we've got, ma'am. The walls around it are fortified concrete and it's got a one-man airlock."

Peaches. "Is it locked?"

Controller. "For now. We can open it for them."

Peaches, into her mouthpiece. "Team Kitty, proceed to the donut. We'll have the airlock open for you." *She listens, nods. Pushes her mouthpiece away.* "****. ****, ****, ****. If something happens to them . . . ****." *She covers her eyes, drags her hand down to her mouth.* "Get that airlock open."

Controller. "Yes, ma'am."

Peaches. "We just have to find that final digger. After that it's all clean-up. . . ." *She frowns and shakes her head as dust falls in her eyes.* "What the . . ."

A little more dribbles onto her head.

. . . from the ceiling . . .

It caves in and the final digger comes calling, along with several dozen of its friends.

127. TOMB

Chaos. In Control, Gunny is a blur, hurling furniture at the crabs, building a breakfire. Peaches, still handicapped by her injury, is shooting from beneath one of the consoles.

In Sickbay, the chief medical officer, bleeding from the leg, is jamming a stimulant into his own body to keep going.

In the corridors, across broken rooms, the rest of the company is harrying the attackers.

. . . but there are so many. And people are dying.

———

Claws. "Are they serious? The donut?"

Scythe. "Got a better idea?"

Claws. "****."

Scythe. "Didn't think so."

They reach the airlock, which is standing open. There's room for two at a time.

Scythe. "Samuel-Colt, Claws, in."

Kenyan. "What about m—"

Scythe. "Sir, I need someone with a weapon first, in case there's company on the other side."

Kenyan pales, turns around. The crabs are bubbling into the hall from two junctions. "Ohmygod**** **** ****"

Scythe. "Hairball, Kenyan, go!"

Fang calmly stands behind Spots's shield and starts picking targets off as they barrel toward them. "You next, Boss. Mama and I are busy."

Scythe. "Fine. Fang2, with me."

Spots. "They're going to hit."

Fang. "I know. You fine with that?"

Spots. "Power's okay. We should be fine. Brace yourself—"

The leading edge of the crab assault smacks into the shield so hard Spots skids backwards. Fang squints at the ones plastered against the shield and kills them, one by one. "All right, Mama. Let's do this slowly."

They back toward the airlock until they're in it.

Fang. "On three. One. Two. Three—"

Spots kills the shield as the door slides shut on them. Instantly the crabs pound on the metal.

Fang. "Hope they can't get through that."

Spots. "Your mouth to God's ear."

On the other side of the airlock, they are reunited with the squad. They are in a vast curving tunnel made of concrete, bare floors, walls, ceilings. The only lights are dim LEDs that limn the curve of the track on the floor.

Fang2. "Freaky."

Whiskers. "****. Now we really are in a horror movie."

Scythe. "Can that ****. What's the situation on the other side?"

Fang. "They're banging on the airlock, don't know if they can get through."

Scythe. "I'm not getting anything from Control. Looks like there are two other doors like this one."

Hairball. "We got a plan?"

Kenyan. "How about 'not die'?"

No one looks at him.

Scythe. "Guess we'll stay here until the shooting's over."

Claws, muttering. "****."

Hairball. "They need us out there."

Scythe. "Maybe, but we have a mission."

Whiskers. "Seriously, this place is like a ****ing tomb."

Fang2. "Wow, thanks for that image."

Kenyan. "Not that I'm complaining or anything, but . . . what's so important that you're running from the fight?"

Fang, bristling. "We're not ****ing RUNNING."

Scythe. "We're keeping the Violinist safe, Mr. Kenyan."

Samuel-Colt, speaking for the first time in quite a while. "We know intelligence the Enemy wants."

Kenyan, slowly. "You mean . . . they're chasing *you*?"

128. HEAVY EQUIPMENT

Claws. "Now, now, Will. Don't be gettin' any id—"

Kenyan. "You mean they'll protect you, but not me? I know everything you know!" *He glares at Scythe.* "How ****ing short-sighted is your commanding officer, anyway? Leave the human out to dry, save the alien? Who do you think helped him build all the **** you're using?"

Everyone is staring at the engineer now. No one wants to tell him why Samuel-Colt's safety is more critical than his.

Kenyan, cheeks red. "**** you! All of you!"

Fang2. "Look at it this way. You're with us now, right?"

Kenyan. "By ****ing accident!" *He points at Samuel-Colt.* "This is always the way it works out. He gets the ****ing glory, and I get . . . what? A byline? If it wasn't for me and people like me, you ****s would be wearing bug-shaped suits and firing weapons made for four hands!"

Hairball clears his throat. "Um, Boss? I got a bay on this schematic. Pretty big. Maybe we should check it out."

Scythe. "A bay? Absolutely. Fang-Prime, Fang2, stay at the door."

The squad separates. Kenyan trails after the main group, still ranting.

Claws, murmured to Samuel-Colt. "Uh, you worked with this guy?"

Samuel-Colt, sotto voce. "He is not usually so vitriolic."

Claws. " 'Parently he's been savin' it up."

Not far up the tunnel they find Hairball's bay. It's not empty. There are two bulldozers, parts of a crane, and a lot of unlabeled equipment.

Claws. "The ****?"

Kenyan, behind them, sullen. "It's left over from constructing the site."

Spots. "They built the collider with bulldozers?"

Kenyan, folding his arms. "Of course not. They used a tunnel borer. But the military licenses those from companies back home, so the moment you're done with them they get shipped back to the owners. This ****," *pointing at the remainders,* "is part of your stores, so when you're done with them they get left here because it's more expensive

Spots the Space Marine: Defense of the Fiddler

to ship back Earthside than to lift them from here to the next place you need to build a base."

Whiskers, running a hand over the edge of the bulldozer blade. "Man, look the the size of these blades."

Kenyan. "Designed for the weird terrain upstairs."

Claws, speculative. "You thinkin' what I'm thinkin', boss?"

Scythe. "Yesssss."

Claws. "If we could just get 'em in here . . ."

Kenyan. "****! You're not thinking of *attacking*, are you? We're safe here!"

Scythe. "Sir, we're safe here until the enemy overruns the base. Once they've done that, they bring reinforcements, crack open this ring and we're done."

Hairball, satisfied. "Knew the best defense was a good offense."

Kenyan. "But what about the Fiddler? And me! If they get us . . ."

Spots, quiet. "No one will get Samuel-Colt."

Kenyan, looking at her, suddenly doesn't want to be included in that group.

Scythe. "We just need to get their attention somehow."

Samuel-Colt, rising arpeggio, minor. "We can provide assistance in that regard. Allow us to step outside the tunnel and we will bring them."

Scythe. "Samuel-Colt? Are you sure that's wise? We don't want to expose you to unnecessary risk."

Samuel-Colt, falling note, sharp. "This is, we believe, a necessary one. Your observation about our chances of survival if the base is overrun is quite correct."

Spots. "I'll go with him."

Scythe. "All right. Claws, you too."

Claws. "Aww, I wanted to drive the machine."

Scythe. "You're not fooling anyone, Walker, you've never touched one of those in your life and you're not touching one now."

Claws. "You callin' me a city boy?"

Scythe smirks. "Whiskers, Fang2, into the cabs. Let's crush us some crabs. Rest of you, behind them, I don't want them having easy targets."

As everyone starts to move, Kenyan says, "Are you sure this is a good idea?"

Scythe. "I'm sure that our brothers and sisters are dying out there, Mr. Kenyan, and we're going to help them."

Kenyan, muttering. "Fine. But I'm going in one of those cabs. Those *armored* cabs."

Scythe. "Be my guest."

129. SONG OF THE FIDDLER

Kenyan climbs up to the cab where Fang2 is settling in.

Fang2. "You licensed to drive?"

Kenyan. "No?"

Fang2 gives him his weapon. "You got shotgun."

Kenyan. "Fine."

Fang2 pulls down the key, puts it in the ignition, turns it. He grins. "Purring like a kitten. Someone's been maintaining these babies."

Kenyan. "Of course. They still use them upstairs and in the Bird Cage."

Fang2. "Huh. There's an entrance into the Bird Cage from here?"

Kenyan, still sulky but gripping the rifle. "How do you think they got the parts for the collider in here?"

Fang2. "Right." *Switches to comm.* "I'm good, Boss."

Whiskers, on his comm. "Me too."

Scythe to Spots, Claws and Samuel-Colt. "Looks like we're good to go. You got the plan?"

Claws. "We go outside, call the crabs, then use one of those doors—" *pointing at the inner wall of the collider tunnel,* "—to cut behind you."

Scythe. "Right. Everyone clear on that?"

Spots. "Yes."

Samuel-Colt, low tense note. "We are prepared."

Scythe. "All right. Godspeed."

Spots, Claws and Samuel-Colt head for the airlock on the other side of the bay. They step through, cycle the lock, and exit into a corridor strobing with red and white emergency lights, the sirens still shrieking intermittently.

Claws. "******—" *Stops.* "Crap, they going to be able to hear you through this, Sam?"

Samuel-Colt, quiet. "You will see."

Spots stops him as he lifts his vestigial arms. He glances at her and she holds up her rosary. "Duck your head, Samuel-Colt."

He bends for her; she stands on her toes and loops the rosary around his triangular head, settling it on his thorax.

Samuel-Colt. "For luck, Mother?"

Spots. "A prayer made manifest, more like. Go ahead, now."

Samuel-Colt draws himself upright.

Control. Gunny, the controllers, Peaches. Fighting. Blood streaking their uniforms. Needles buried in shoulders, thighs. The streak of bullets in an enclosed space. The stink of rent electronics. Screaming—

Samuel-Colt leans down, holding his vestigial arms at an angle, as if listening. His jeweled eyes close.

Sickbay. Hawk is bent over the chief medical officer's crumpled body, howling as he clicks empty. Tosses his weapon, grabs the surgeon's—

One arm drags lightly against the other. A whisper of sound.

Mess Hall. Dusty and the remains of her Dogs are backing into the kitchens, the few Seabees behind them armed with kitchen knives.

Samuel-Colt draws forth from his arms a long note, swelling, louder and louder. Clear like a bell. It rises above the sirens. As Spots and Claws stare, open-mouthed, he begins to play.

Across the base, the Enemy stops as if shocked by a current. Almost as one mass, they freeze, like a single hideous sculpture.

. . . and then they rush from the rooms, pouring into the corridors, speeding for the source of the song.

Claws, whispering to Spots. "Shield up, Guitart."

Spots, eyes streaming. "Right." *She activates the shield and goes to one knee in front of the Violinist, awaiting the tidal wave. And waiting, she cries.*

Samuel-Colt plays, and Schubert's "Ave Maria" soughs through the corridors, sweet and high.

130. Turning the Tide

The rooms and halls empty. Not trusting the reprieve, no one gives chase. For a moment, there is only the drip of blood and sweat and the sound of panting. Everywhere, people are holding still, tense, wondering.

Then, crackling over Peaches's comm:

"Lieutenant, this is Kitty-Alpha. We're hosting a party at the donut. Hope you can make it, maybe bring a few grenades."

Peaches grabs her earbud. "Say again, Kitty!"

Scythe. "We're drawing the crabs here, ma'am, where we plan to crush them between two bulldozers. Could use some back-up. We've got bait at airlock baker, that's where they're heading. You probably got some great back-shots right now if you have the ammo to take them."

Peaches. "God! We're there, Sergeant!" *Switching channels.* "All company, this is the lieutenant. Regroup, re-arm and head for the donut, airlock baker. Go go go!"

From the broken corners of the base, the remainder of Peaches's company seeps out. Joins up with comrades. Heads for the nearest weapons lockers. They find themselves alongside Naval personnel and many of their civilian contractors. Everyone wants a piece of the enemy.

Fortunately there are enough guns for everyone.

At the end of the hall to the airlock, Samuel-Colt is still playing. Claws narrows his eyes. "How long do we want to stay out here?"

Spots. "Until they show up?"

Claws. "I just hope it's worki—****!"

The corridor floods with crabs, a solid wall of black chitin.

Claws. "Um, NOW, back NOW!" *He pushes Samuel-Colt through the airlock. Spots runs after, arm behind her head to shield them: well-timed, for a rain of needles rattles off its surface. They dart through the lock and into the collider tunnel, leaving the crabs to squeeze through, one by one.*

Claws. "Boss! They're comin'!"

Scythe is standing on the platform behind the cab of Fang2's bulldozer. "You heard the man. Let's get this party started!"

Fang2. "WHOO!"

Whiskers. "Aw, yeah."

Fang, riding shotgun on his machine. "You did not just say that."

Whiskers, grinning. "I sure did, sweetheart."

Scythe. "Walker, head for your door."

Claws. "What do you think we're doin'? Takin' a walk in the park?"

They flash past the first of the inner doors until they are in eyeshot of the first bulldozer. The doors leading to the supercollider are flush to the tunnel and open only to handprints; Claws strips his glove and shoves his hand against the plate, and they're through.

The inside of this inner tunnel is smooth, well-lit even in emergency low-power mode, and houses the high-tech metal sheath of the collider.

Samuel-Colt. "What a noise it makes . . . !"

Spots glances at it. "The magnets?"

Samuel-Colt, low sawing note. "I am glad it is behind many walls."

Claws. "Come on, let's get behind the group. I gotta pound of flesh or two to collect."

They run, then, the humans' boots making thick sounds on the concrete. Outside, the crabs push their way into the tunnel. And beyond them, Peaches and her own begin to hem them in, taking those back-shots against crabs who suddenly don't care about anything except following Samuel-Colt.

131. Gaps

Collider Tunnel, looking down from the high ceiling. One by one, the crabs issue from the air-lock into the wide empty space and start rushing after the scent of Samuel-Colt.

Zoom down. In. Rush past the chitinous black shoulders. Dive into the airlock, full of hissing and scratching and scrabbling . . . out it again.

. . . to the packed halls, crabs crushed against one another.

. . . among them. Whipping past wasp-like faces, identical, one after another after another—

—to one last digger, hidden in the mass. Unnoticed. Uncounted.

Tunnel.

Hairball, reloading. "Your plan had a tiny flaw, boss."

Scythe, dry. "I noticed."

The airlock is big enough for a single crab at a time, and barely. Each individual has to force its way through it, scraping its shell. And the moment it's out, it presents a single target to three very itchy trigger fingers.

Fang. "We're wasting ammo this way. Go rotation."

Hairball. "I'm next, then." *Another crab goes down. While waiting for the next to appear:* "We're going to run dry eventually."

Scythe. "Eventually."

Kenyan is observing from the relative safety of the seat next to Fang2. He is nervous, but frowning. "They really going to let us pick them off one by one like this?"

Fang2. "They seem to be."

Kenyan. "Won't they get desperate? Start tearing through the wall or something?"

Fang2. "I don't think they can get through the donut wall, it's pretty tough ****."

Kenyan. "Won't that make them . . . I don't know. Angry?"

Fang2 squints at him. Then keys his comm. "Hey, Boss. The engineer's wondering if the crabs are gonna get pissed at being ****blocked and do something stupid."

Scythe. "Huh. Never noticed them to be angry. Single-minded, yes, but not angry. Hey, Claws?"

Claws and party are still in the inner tunnel. He answers. "Yeah?"

"Samuel-Colt have anything to say about that?"

Claws. "Sam? Enemy gonna get upset they can't get through the airlock faster? Maybe start innovatin'?"

Samuel-Colt's gemmed eyes half-lid. The expression is uncannily anthropomorphic. "Their actions should remain predictable, Peer. However, you know what they say about plans and the enemy."

Claws. "Right-o. Boss, expert says maybe we should make things easier for them."

Scythe. "Mmm. Whiskers, think you can make a hole in the wall?"

Whiskers. "Wow, don't ask for much do you. Better bet to do the airlock, they'll have made some compromises there."

Fang. "You're going to drive this thing into the airlock. You're ****ing kidding me, right?"

Scythe. "You enjoying target practice, Fang, or do you want a real challenge?"

Fang. "Put it that way . . ." *Grins at Whiskers.* "All right, babe, go for it."

Whiskers, grinning back. "Glad we're on the same page."

Claws, muttering. "We're missin' all the fun."

132. SACRED DUTY

Spots. "We'll be out in a min—" *and stops, because Samuel-Colt has. She doubles back.* "Samuel-Colt!"

He is leaning against the wall, head lowered and all six arms folded over his abdomen.

Spots, worried, reaches to touch him and stops. "Samuel-Colt!"

Claws. "Sam?"

Samuel-Colt. "It is . . ." *He pauses.*

Claws. "You weren't seriously about to say "nothin'," were you?"

The alien looks at him.

Claws. " 'Cuz if you've gotten human enough to lie, Sam . . ."

Samuel-Colt manages to scrape out a laugh on his vestigial arms, one weak rising note. "You think we do not lie, Peer?"

Spots, ignoring their exchange. "What's wrong?"

Samuel-Colt. "We have been injured too long, Mother—"

Claws. "****! Are you dying?"

Samuel-Colt. "Nothing so dramatic. We are . . . shutting down, more like. The body injured allows insult only so long before it tries to heal."

Spots. "Wait . . . don't you hibernate through that?"

Samuel-Colt. "I become unconscious, yes."

Claws. "****! You're tellin' me you're about to faint. In the middle of a fight. In the middle of *this* fight, which is about keeping you mobile."

Samuel-Colt. "I am . . . afraid so, yes."

Spots and Claws exchange glances.

Claws. "How long . . . ?"

Samuel-Colt. "Until I am in molt-state? Or until I leave it?"

Spots. "Both?"

Samuel-Colt. "Not long. I cannot give an exact time. Very soon. Damage this extensive . . . I will not wake again for most of a day."

Claws stares at him, then keys his comm. "Boss, we got a problem."

Scythe. "Oh, fantastic. We were getting bored out here."

Claws. "Seriously. Our ward's about to go into a ****in' coma."

Scythe. ". . ."

Scythe. "You'll have to stay in the inner tunnel, then."

Claws. "****, boss, what if you need the guns? Hell, the shield, we got the only long-actin' shield in the team—"

Scythe. "You have a task, Walker. *The* task, you and Guitart. I'm trusting you to handle it."

Claws sighs. "Right."

Samuel-Colt has slid to the ground, bent over himself. Spots is crouching alongside, her hand on his shoulder.

Spots. "Is it too bad? The pain."

Samuel-Colt. "It will not matter soon."

Spots, smiling a little. "Would you like me to sing?"

Samuel-Colt. "Alas, Mother, this tunnel is too loud. But you could sit beside me."

So she does, while Claws paces.

Claws. "****. They need us. This is ****."

Spots. "Go, then."

He stops pacing to stare at her. "What?"

Spots, expressionless. "I said go, if you want it so badly."

Claws. "I can't just ditch you."

Spots, voice hardening. "Then stop heaping guilt on an injured person just because you want to be out there, where your duty would be more satisfying. Stop thinking about yourself and start thinking about him."

Spots the Space Marine: Defense of the Fiddler

Claws. "****, Mom—"

Spots. "And stop with the freaking cursing! I thought you respected me!"

Claws closes his mouth so hard his teeth click. Then, softer. "Hell, Magda, everythin's goin' to pieces around you it's kind of hard to remember to be genteel."

Spots. "It's exactly when everything's going to pieces around you that you need it most."

Claws. "Gentility?"

Spots, hard. "Self-control."

Claws winces. "That was harsh."

Spots. "Then stop treating us like something in your way and more like your friends. We are your friends, right?"

Claws. "Yeah." *He crouches in front of them, weapon resting on his thighs.* "Sorry, Sam."

Samuel-Colt opens glistening eyes. "You need not apologize, Peer. We understand the source of your agitation. It is in our nature to be comforted by action."

Spots. "This is action."

Claws. "Yeah?"

Spots. "Yes. It's called 'defending the helpless,' and it's got a pedigree thousands of years old. You have a problem with that?"

Claws starts laughing. "When you put it that way . . ."

Spots, eyeing him. "What's so funny?"

Claws, grinning at her. "Ah, hell, Spots. You really are one of us. Cookie-bakin' momdom and all."

133. His Regard

Oblivious to their conversation, Samuel-Colt slumps further, head drooping. Both humans start.

Samuel-Colt. "No . . . fears. Normal."

Claws. "Right. Totally par for the course." *Listens to the chatter on the comm.* "Guess this is it."

Spots looks up. "It?"

Claws. "You know. The big final battle. Where they cue the music and things die in slow mo."

Spots shakes her head. "Now I know you're not thinking clearly."

Claws. "What's that supposed to mean?"

Spots. "She's still out there, Claws. And until she's dead . . ."

Samuel-Colt, soft. "Mother-soldier . . . is correct. There will be . . . tell Savan . . . Savannah Bonnet. There will be eggs. Thousands . . . of eggs. You must destroy them all. And the Queen-Directing."

Claws. "**—" *He stops, grits his teeth.* "Crap."

Spots. "We'll tell her, Samuel-Colt. You rest."

The exhalation through Samuel-Colt's spiracles is very like a sigh. "We will. When . . . we wake . . . Mother. We will be *very* hungry."

Spots chuckles. "Like a growing child. We'll make sure there's food. Protein, I'm guessing? Or is your chitin probably built from carbohydrates? Both?"

Samuel-Colt. "I . . . confess . . . to a liking for . . . artisanal cheeses."

Both humans are startled into laughing.

Claws. " 'Fraid you're not gonna find any fancy California cheeses out here, Sam. But hey, we got soy bars . . . they come from the same place, right?"

Spots. "I don't think they grow soy in California, Travis."

Claws blows out a breath. "Aw, come on. They grow everythin' else there."

Samuel-Colt. "It is good, to sleep thus." *And as suddenly as that, his eyes close and the ani-*

mating spirit seems to drain from his body, so abruptly Spots and Claws are left staring.

Claws, whispered. "Crap."

Spots draws in a deep breath. "Just you, me and a body worth the whole war now."

Claws trails a hand over the rosary around Samuel-Colt's neck. "I hope to God this works then, 'cause we're gonna need all His attention."

Spots. "I'm sure He's watching."

———

Outside the tunnel, in the corridors. Peaches and her people have attacked the rear of the crab mob with the fury of the desperate . . . and in so doing have created a problem.

Peaches. "****! Now what?"

Gunny, surveying the wall of dead bodies that is preventing them from reaching the rest of the crabs. "Now, we move them."

Peaches. "And get that close to the ones still alive?"

Dusty, standing behind them. "They seem to be spreading out since they can't get in quick enough through the airlock. We can keep picking them off that way, ma'am."

Peaches. "I'm just concerned if we keep nibbling at their heels, eventually they're going to turn on us . . ."

Over the comm, Scythe: "We're working on that right now, ma'am."

Peaches. "Ah?"

Cut to the bulldozer, rushing straight at the camera, with a grinning Whiskers at the helm and Fang with one hand on the seat and the other braced against the roof—

—a tremendous CRUNCH

Fang. "****!"

Whiskers. "No big deal. Now we reverse . . . and do it again."

Fang. "****ing yee-ha."

Whiskers. "Put a little more oomph into it, Dragon."

Fang. "****ING OOH-RAH!"

Whiskers, grinning with teeth. "That's what I'm talking about!"

CRUNCH

Spots the Space Marine: Defense of the Fiddler

134. CRISIS

A tiny stream of dust falls around the seam lining the collider airlock. Another stream, with a few discrete bits of concrete.

Quiet.

The entire airlock housing bursts loose from the tunnel wall, spraying particulate matter everywhere. A heavy dust cloud billows outward. Slowly . . . slowly the view shifts upward . . . to a sign: a giant A.

Not the B of airlock baker.

A river of crabs parts the dust cloud as the digger continues to widen the opening.

Fly down the corridor, following the long, shallow curve, faster, faster . . .

. . . to Scythe standing on the back step of the bulldozer, hanging onto it with one hand and resting the other on the tsuka of his katana. His rifle is slung from a strap over his shoulder; there are no targets with Whiskers blocking the airlock.

Scythe, to Peaches. "We could use more shooters, ma'am. We're running pretty low on ammo."

Peaches, over the comm. "We could join you, assuming the airlocks behind your position are clear."

Scythe. "They should be, ma'am. And that would be much appreciated."

Switch views to the base corridor, with Peaches standing just behind the writhing wall of crabs. "All right. We're on our way, Sergeant. Hold the fort."

"Will do, ma'am."

Peaches, to the rest of the company. "All right, we're redeploying. I need the Wild Dogs and half of Holiday at Airlock Able; PYEO and the other half, to Airlock Charlie." *She hesitates over the Naval personnel and civilians, then says,* "The rest of you, if you're coming . . . with me."

Dusty. "Ma'am?"

Peaches. "What is it, Sergeant?"

Dusty. "If all the crabs are here . . . there may be a clear shot from here to the armory."

Peaches. ". . ."

Peaches. "Go."

Dusty. "You heard the LT, on the double!"

Peaches. "And pick up spare ammo for Holiday while you're out there."

Inside the collider tunnel, Whiskers is making his fourth run.

CRUNCH

Whiskers, studying the result. "Think that might have done it."

Fang. "Looks pretty much the same to m—"

The concrete around the airlock housing crumples.

Fang. "Well, **** me."

Whiskers, reversing. "We're in business, boss!"

As he retreats, the first few crabs force their way through the expanded entrance . . . and then begin rushing through, pushing chunks out of their way, widening the entrance.

Whiskers. "There you go, sweetheart. Target-rich environment."

Fang. "Awww, you know how to please a girl." *She scrambles out of the cab and onto the step and grins, aiming.*

Inside the inner tunnel, Claws is still crouching across from Samuel-Colt's slumped body, listening to the comm chatter.

Claws, to Scythe. "Sounds like ya'll are doin' fine without us."

Scythe. "We'll send you a postcard. 'Thinking of you.' How's your charge?"

Claws. "Sleepin' like a baby lamb."

Scythe. "A lamb is a baby, definitionally. Your cityboy is showing."

Claws. "Now I know you don't have enough to do, if you're pickin' on my choice of poetic metaphor—"

Scythe, whispered. "—Oh my God."

Claws's head jerks up. Fly past him, through the walls, outside. Scythe is looking over his shoulder and paling under his gold skin.

Crabs. A flood-tide of crabs . . .

. . . attacking from the rear. **Behind** the bulldozer.

135. Holden's Last Stand

Kenyan. "OH **** oh ****ing **** OH GOD."

Fang2, looking out the window. "****!"

Kenyan. "GO GO GO! GOD, GET MOVING!"

Scythe. "NO! If we advance past Sam Colt's trail they'll know where he is!"

Peaches, over the comm. "Sitrep!"

Scythe is bringing his weapon into position, watching the tide roll his way. "Breakthrough, ma'am. Guessing from Airlock Able. We missed a digger."

"Can you hold them back?"

Scythe, ignoring her. "Here they come."

Kenyan, panicking. "****! ****!" *and pops the door to scramble out of the bulldozer—*

—when Airlock Baker's housing wrenches off-center and crabs erupt from it, filling the space between the bulldozers.

Fang2. "****!" *He looks behind his shoulder.* "****, this may be it."

Kenyan. "**** that talk! I'm not dying here!" *He snatches Fang2's gun and lunges for the door again.*

Fang2 grabs him. "Where the **** are you going?"

Kenyan. "Oh GOD it's too late!"

Standing on the cab step, Scythe calmly aims his weapon and starts picking off the crabs in the front line. One. Two. Three.

Fang, hanging onto Whiskers's bulldozer. "BOSS!"

Scythe. "Not now, I'm busy."

She's shooting too, trying to clear a path between her position and Scythe's, but there are too many crabs now.

Scythe is still firing his weapon. Four. Five. Six. He keeps going until he runs dry; the wall is still coming. Far, far behind him, Whiskers is driving his bulldozer into the mess of crabs issuing from Airlock Baker as Fang clings to its side with a snarl frozen on her face.

Spots the Space Marine: Defense of the Fiddler

Fang2. "****! OH ****!"

Scythe. "Don't move this bulldozer until back-up arrives. You got that, Chao?"

Fang2. "Boss—"

Scythe. "You got that?"

Fang2. "Yes! ****! What are you—"

Scythe's sword sings free of its saya. He stares at the oncoming crabs, then activates his shield, leaps off the bulldozer and runs for them. His first stroke shears a head off its body.

Scythe. "ADH-DHAARR!"

Another eye-watering gleam of light as the backstroke separates an arm from its thorax.

"AL-'ADIL!"

Flash: Scythe surrounded in crabs, now turning toward him, clawing at his shield.

"AL-'AFUW!"

Flash: Long wounds, thin as incisions, opening up four crab abdomens at once.

"AL-AHAD!"

Bound 'round in enemies, Scythe reaps them with steel and shield, yelling his litany. "AL-'ALEEM! AL-'ALI! Al-'AZEEM!"

Desperate, his squad is drawn toward this locus of death: Fang, trying to shoot her way to him; Whiskers driving, a maniacal rictus distorting his face; Fang2 scrabbling out of his seat with Kenyan pale and sweating at his side; Claws, in the inner tunnel, listening in horrified silence, looking at the wall as if to see through it.

Scythe, breathing harder. "AL-'AZEEZ! Al-Aakhir! Al-Awwal! Al-Baa'ith! Al . . . Al . . ."

His shield flickers, its power failing.

Scythe. "****! I always forget around number twelve or thirteen . . . ****, I'm sorry, Mom . . ."

The shield fails.

Scythe. "**** that." *Howling.* "COME ON, YOU ****ERS! COME AND MEET THE ****ING SON OF THE AFFLICTER!"

The crabs close in on him. He leaps. The sword lifts. Falls. Does not rise again.

136. Have Mercy

"..zeem! Al-'Azeez! Al-Aakhir!"

In the collider tunnel, Claws lurches to his feet. Spots grabs him. He turns burning eyes on her.

Spots. "You can't go, Travis!"

Claws. "He's *dying* out there. They're ALL DYING."

Spots. "We have a mission—"

". . . Al-Awwal! Al-Baa'ith!"

Claws, jaw clenching, meets her eyes.

Spots breathes in . . . lets him go. Claws flings himself around and sprints for the door.

Spots, crouching alongside Samuel-Colt's body, whispers, "Just you and me now."

———————

Claws slams the door open, shielded arm up. There are crabs everywhere. He hears Scythe's final cry and starts shooting, pushing his way toward the sound . . .

. . . only to reach the sergeant as he falls. With a howl of his own he grabs Scythe's sword and stands over his body, cutting, cutting, cutting.

He is not Scythe's equal. Not even close. But he doesn't fall.

Behind him, the rattle of a gun firing. The head of one of the crabs over him explodes . . . and there is Fang2.

Claws. "****! You tryin' to take my ****ing head off?"

Fang2. "BOSS!"

Claws. "SHUT UP AND SHOOT!"

Together they kill, and the crabs fall, and neither of them dies. Neither of them thinks anything of this invulnerability. Scythe is dead at their feet, they want vengeance, they have targets.

The arrival of Fang-prime surprises them both. She climbs over several dead bodies. The crabs ignore her.

Fang2. "****, weren't you on the other ****ing side of the airlock?"

Spots the Space Marine: Defense of the Fiddler

Fang. "Not anymore. We ****ing crushed the middle."

Claws is staring at her. "You . . . just . . . hiked over those ****in' crabs. And they didn't kill you."

Fang. "No. They're running."

Claws, sword slack in hand. "Say what?"

Fang. "Running? Back the way they came?"

Claws twirls around, stares in the direction she's pointing. Back. Back. Back—

—to the door that he exited through. The cracked open door. The one that is now busted open with a digger widening it.

Claws. "HOLY **** NO SPOTS!!!"

Inside, Spots is squinting at something in the distance on the floor when she hears Claws's yell. She looks up . . . as the crabs flood her tunnel, on the ground, crushed against the wall, scuttling on the collider tube itself. Dozens . . . scores . . . all the remaining crabs left alive are coming for her . . . and Samuel-Colt.

Spots. "Mother of God . . . !" *She twists, grabs Samuel-Colt's dead weight and runs, dragging him. Stops at that point she'd been staring at.* "Holy Mary, please, please—"

> *Al-Baasit . . .*

"Queen of Heaven—"

> *Al-Ghafoor . . .*

"Flower of Patriarchs—"

> *Al-Ghanee . . .*

"Gate of Paradise—"

> *Al-Hafeez . . .*

"Queen of virgins, Queen of Confessors, Queen of peace, oh holy Mother please . . . !"

137. Mundane Saviors

Claws leaps toward the door, sword raised. "Lieutenant, they're in the inner tunnel!" *To the Fangs.* "COME ON!"

Fang2. "****, I'm dry!"

Fang. "Me too." *Bashes a crab with the side of her gun.* "Fortunately they don't ****ing care."

Claws hacks another crab down. "**** **** **** ****!"

Fang2. "****! We're gonna get trampled!"

Fang. "Claws, use your ****ing SHIELD, you are NOT a ****ing SAMURAI!"

Claws. "**** YOU!"

> *Mother Inviolate (mater inviolata) . . .*

> *. . . Al-Wakeel, the Guardian*

> *Mother Undefiled (mater intemerata) . . .*

> *. . . Al-Walee, the Defender*

All three of them are out of ammo. Their shields are nearly dry. Claws is the only one with a weapon that works. And they are fighting with the crabs to reach a single point of entry.

Claws. "Oh, ****, God, please just ****ing listen to this ONE ****ING PRAYER—"

Peaches's voice over the comm. "Is there anyone in there with Sam Colt, Corporal?"

Claws. "Spots!"

Peaches. "Private Guitart, you still online? Guitart, answer, please."

Claws, shoving another crab aside. "****, oh ****!"

> *. . . Vessel of Honor (vas honorabile)*

> *. . . As-Saboor, the Enduring*

> *. . . Refuge of Sinners (refugium peccatorum)*

> *. . . Ar-Ra'oof, the Merciful*

Spots the Space Marine: Defense of the Fiddler

. . . Queen of Martyrs (regina martyrum)

Claws carves a path to the door with the Fangs. They hear the bark of weapons-fire as they enter the tunnel. So many crabs. Glossy black chitin, backs of heads, backs of thoraxes, backs of limbs. Wild-eyed, Claws slices, sword held in both hands.

Fang twitches as a round smacks the crab behind her. "****!" *To her comm.* "Who the hell just missed me?"

Dusty. "The ****ing cavalry."

More gunfire. Dusty and her Dogs are pushing their way in from the other side.

Claws. "THERE!"

There's a knot of crabs in the center, so many nothing can be seen beneath them. Dusty's dogs start flinging bodies. Claws hacks at the ones on their side.

Claws. "Oh, ****, ****, please—"

Dusty shoots the head off the last crab in their way and tosses it and . . .

. . . finds a bright hard shield, contracted to its smallest useful size. Beneath it and against the floor, Spots is huddled over Samuel-Colt, one hand tangled in the rosary around his neck, the other gripping her Ka-Bar so hard her knuckles show white through the skin. The knife is resting on the Violinist's domed cheek, just beneath his eye. Her shield has been disconnected from the power cell on her back and reconnected to an outlet beneath a hastily pried-open floor plate alongside a host of universal jacks for laptop carts and test equipment. As Samuel-Colt promised, the power plug worked.

Claws collapses on the bubble. "Oh God thank you—"

Dusty draws in a deep breath. Straightens up. "All right, puppies, let's clean up the rest of this ****ing mess."

Coyote, bared teeth. "With pleasure, Alpha."

138. Symbols

Claws, eyes closed, face still pressed against the bubble. "You're safe. As long as this base is runnin' and I've got two feet left to stand on, you're safe. I promise."

He pushes himself off and runs after Dusty. "Sergeant!"

Dusty pauses. "Yeah?"

Claws. "You don't have to go anywhere. They're all comin' here, you can just put some people at the doors of your choice and shoot 'em as they pass through."

Dusty. "They really that single-minded?"

Claws. "Yeah." *Smiles crookedly.* "Lookit me and the Fangs. Out of armor, shields down, no ammo, and we got in here because they didn't care we were pushin' our way through 'em."

Dusty. "Right. Doors it is." *Cocks her head.* "You coming?"

Claws. "In a minute, got something else to do first."

Standing next to the shield, Fang2 watches Claws jog away. "Where the **** does he think he's going?"

Rusty voice, from beneath and behind. "To find the body."

Both Fangs turn and look down at Spots, who is sitting up. Slowly.

Fang. "You're awake. With us, I mean." *When Spots doesn't answer, she crouches down to meet her eyes. Spots's are wet; the emergency lighting reflects off the long trails down her cheeks, her chin, glint off her throat.*

Fang sets her gloved hand on the bubble and whispers: "You would have done it."

Spots says nothing.

Fang meets her eyes a moment longer, then nods, almost imperceptibly. Louder as she rises. "Keep the bubble up, Mama. I think we're on top for now, but that might change."

Fang2 is still staring. "****, that's ****ing hardcore, man."

Fang. "Shut up, appendage."

Fang2. "App—oh, ****, not that old joke." *He snorts. Then says, enthusiastic.* "But no, seriously, that's ****ing hardcore."

Spots the Space Marine: Defense of the Fiddler

Fang, grinning viciously. "Yeah, well. Team Kitty is full of ****ing hardcores."

Spots says nothing, but she sits up, propping Samuel-Colt back up against the wall.

Outside the tunnel. Claws has to push his way through the remaining crabs, all still rushing for the opening: the image is surreal, the lone small human figure dodging the pouring line of shining black carapaces and emerging unharmed, sheathed sword in hand.

Once free of them, Claws looks at the carnage and spots two people nearby: Hairball and Whiskers.

They are standing over Scythe's body.

He joins them, crouches and puts a hand on Scythe's shoulder.

Whiskers. "They didn't eat him."

Hairball. "But we figured we'd better make sure. You staying?"

Claws looks around. "I don't think we have to worry about them makin' off with the bodies this time, but we'd better go do eye-gish detail. Make sure none of these are useful to the enemy. Better safe than sorry."

Whiskers draws his knife. "Good plan."

Claws starts to set the sword on Scythe's breast.

Hairball. "Hey, don't. You might need it, eh?"

Claws looks up at him. "What?"

Hairball gets down, hand reaching for Scythe's cloth belt.

Claws. "****, no, absolutely no ****ing way." *When Hairball looks up, he says:* "I'll keep hold of the ****in' thing but not . . . no." *He gets out from under his rifle and unclips it from the fabric strap, then winds the strap around the saya and jury-rigs it to lie across his back.* "There, okay?"

Whiskers. "Looks good."

Hairball. "Yup."

Claws looks at them both, frowning. They are expressionless. Then, curt. "All right, let's go."

They separate to begin sifting through the dripping mess, finding crab heads and punching their knives through the eyes and sawing through the necks. The black lacquer of the scabbard on Claws's back glints every time he bends, knife lifted.

———

True to Claws's guess, the crabs ignore everything to push toward the scent of Samuel-Colt. Dusty positions her team at the ingresses to the tunnel and team Holiday ranges outside of it, and between these two pincers the armored squads reap a sickly harvest.

Half an hour later, there is stillness.

Peaches picks her way through the wreckage to the inner wall, empty weapon bumping against her ribs as she leans through the hole. "Dusty?"

Dusty. "Here, ma'am. I'm thinking we're all clear."

Peaches. "Looks that way out here too." *She surveys the impromptu battlefield. The hulks of the two bulldozers rise above the corpses, and the emergency lighting strobes off pools of thick ichor. The stink is unimaginable, fuel and gore and sweat—that the crabs could smell anything past it is astonishing to her. Amid this mess, here and there, a human figure is walking or hauling the bodies into piles.*

Peaches breathes in, shoulders squaring. Then touches her fingers to her earbud. "Holiday, sitrep."

"We've run out of targets, ma'am."

Peaches. "All right." *Switches to all-channel.* "I need everyone out here at Airlock Baker, behind the western bulldozer. Spread the word to the contractors and Navy, anyone who doesn't have a link. I want to take a headcount."

A chorus of affirmatives wash back to her. She heads to position and waits as one by one the Marines, civilians and Naval personnel congregate. Gunny steps up beside her as the survivors arrive . . .

. . . so few survivors. Dusty's lost another two people and PYEO one. Scythe is dead. The Vermin are long gone, along with Avril. Her staffing element has been slashed almost in half after the disastrous attack at Control and in the corridors. The contractors are all alive, somehow, but there are many holes in the ranks of the Naval personnel.

Spots and the Fangs are the last to arrive, carrying Samuel-Colt. Peaches looks at them, then at what remains of her command. They once represented two full companies and all she has left could barely fill a platoon.

Her jaw tightens. Then she lifts her chin.

Peaches. "All right. Holiday, Wild Dogs, you're on rescue duty. Go through the base, find anyone who's trapped or unconscious. Start with Sickbay. PYEO, you're guarding the repair crews. We need to rebuild the base walls ASAP. Get suited up. Kitty, secure the barracks. Take the Violinist there, you're still on guard duty. You're also the first team down on sleep shift. We're moving to four-hour rotations. Got that?" *At their yes-ma'ams, she says,* "Holiday, Wild Dogs, Kitty, go. PYEO, stay while I coordinate with the Seabees."

A bedraggled Team Kitty gathers around the body of Samuel-Colt, which Spots has propped against the wall.

Whiskers. "Alien's wearing a rosary."

Spots. "I thought it would help."

Claws, bitter, looking at Samuel-Colt's arms. "You'd think the ****in' stigmata woulda been enough."

Fang. "Hey, Claws."

"Yeah?"

Fang's arms are folded. She unfolds one just enough to point at him. "You ****ed up. Really badly."

Claws meets her eyes. Without looking away: "Yeah. I did. I know."

Fang. "Like, 'could have made it all meaningless' ****ed up. 'Lost the war' ****ed up. 'Humanity as food for crabs' ****ed up."

Fang2. "Like that movie with the slave planet—" *He stops abruptly at Fang-prime's look.* "Um, yeah."

Spots, tired. "We were overrun, Fang. Even if he had stayed, it wouldn't have made a difference if they couldn't have turned the tide outside the corridor."

Claws. "Don't apologize for me, Guitart." *He looks at Fang.* "I know I ****ed up. I'm not gonna make excuses for it. I'm pretty sure we're alive only because God gives more weight to the prayers of moms and martyrs. And maybe ****in' idiots, because I did a ****-ton of prayin' at the end. So, yeah. I know it, Gordon. I'll try not to make the same mistake twice."

Silence.

Fang nods, says to the others. "He can keep the sword."

Fang2. "Sounds good to me."

Claws. "Um, this thing isn't mine, it's Holden's, and it's goin' back with him."

Hairball. "Someone's got to keep it until then."

Claws. "I was kinda plannin' on layin' it on his box, because, you know, that would be ****in' respectful—"

Whiskers. "****ing respectful would be using it to ****ing shear the head off that queen crab. And *then* laying it on his box."

Hairball. "Yep."

Claws stares at them all. "You can't be serious."

Fang. "In case you haven't noticed, you're what's left of command in the squad. Which is fine by me. You think, boys?" *At their assent,* "Guess we should get moving then, eh?" *She lifts a brow at Claws.*

Claws. ". . ."

Spots. "I'd like to leave this tunnel."

Hairball, to Whiskers. "Come on, you and me have got this." *He slides his hands under the Fiddler's shoulders, Whiskers grabs the feet. The two of them heave Samuel-Colt up.*

Fang, to Fang2. "I got point. You take rear. Just in case."

Fang2. "Roger that."

They troop off toward the remains of the airlock, Spots trailing in their wake. Claws stares after them, mouth still open.

Spots looks over her shoulder at him. Her expression doesn't change, but when she resumes walking, he follows.

139. Transfer of Energy

Flashes now. Armored silhouettes standing sentry duty while engineers pick through the rubble of the shattered exterior wall. Armored hands helping corpsmen lift the wounded onto gurneys. Armored bodies clearing halls, checking rooms. Unarmored bodies held gently in armored arms as the dead are carried back to the morgue. Staccato reports across comm channels as armored boots crunch across the litter of shattered consoles and plaster in what remains of Control.

Barracks.

Fang. "And . . . clear. That's the last of them. Nothing left here to fight."

Fang2, kicking a crab's thorax. "Plenty of trash to clear out though."

Claws, standing in the hall with Hairball and Whiskers (still holding Samuel-Colt). "Which section's the cleanest?"

Fang. "Looks like our digs are pretty good."

Claws. "Let's use those, then." *Nods to Hairball and Whiskers.* "Go lay 'im inside."

Whiskers. "You got it."

They enter to find the room mostly whole. Mostly. Claws shakes his head. "Time to break out the brushes and kneepads."

Fang2. "****, I hope you're not gonna make us scrub the floor with ****ing toothpaste."

Claws grins. "Don't tempt me, Princess."

Fang2. "Yeah, yeah, just dump it all on Cinderella, I've read the stories."

Fang. "You can read?"

Fang2, lifting his hands. "Aw, no, no, that's his line." *Pointing at Claws.* "No stealing."

Claws. "Less jabber, more tidying."

The squad hauls the bodies out, gets the worst of the body fluids off the floor and starts stacking the destroyed mattresses. Unaware of their industry, Samuel-Colt remains unconscious, sprawled across two of the bunks. It takes Kitty the better part of two hours to finish, and this after the long strain of the base attack and the combat in the collider tunnel.

Claws straightens from dumping a load of new sheets on the nearest bunk. His eye catches on the signs of strain: Fang2's slight limp, the jerkiness of Fang-Prime's movements, the circles under Hairball's eyes.

Claws. "All right, that's good enough. Sack time."

Hairball. "Sounds great to me."

Spots. "I'll take first watch."

Fang2. "Didn't Peaches tell us to sleep?"

Whiskers. "She also told us to guard the man here."

Spots. "I can sleep while watching him."

Fang2, interested. "You got an eye in the back of your head we don't know about? Was my mom right about that?"

Spots. "No extra eye, I promise. I'll just sleep in the same bed. If something goes wrong I'll notice."

Fang2. "You wanna sleep in the same bed as the alien?"

Spots lifts her brows. She's tired and it shows a lot worse on her than on the younger people around her. "What, you believe those rumors about the hot alien sex I've been having with the Fiddler, Fang2? You want in? He's got multiple hands. Between the two of us I'm sure we could rock your world."

Absolute silence.

Fang2 bursts out laughing. So does everyone but Claws. It's a hysterical laughter, but the tension release is real.

Claws. "Uh . . . right. Spots and I will take first watch. No hot alien sex, though. I lean homo-sapiens-sexual."

More titters as the rest of the squad starts to bunk down.

Claws. "In fact . . . no reason not to move in here. It's not like we're hurt for space like we were when they assigned half the squad down the hall."

Spots, rising. "That's a good idea. I'd like to go get my things."

Claws. "Right. We'll be back in a jiffy. Stay put, ya'll."

Hairball, yawning. "Not moving a muscle."

Fang2. "Hit the lights on your way out, would you?"

Claws. "Bossy much?" *But he smiles as he flicks the switch, then turns to follow Spots out into the corridor.*

140. PIETA

Outside in the hall, the silence is . . . awkward. Spots walks past Claws and into their old barracks. She ignores the corpse of the crab lying just past their bunks to sit on hers.

Claws. "Looks like the photos survived."

Spots, unpinning the one of her family. "Yes."

He watches her take down another photo, a view out a window, and a card depicting the Virgin Mary. Then, suddenly: "What would you have done?"

She looks up at him.

Claws. "The crabs come. You kill Sam. Then what? You turn the knife on yourself?"

Spots, quiet. "Suicide is a sin, Travis."

Claws. "Even if it means somethin' eats you *alive*?"

Spots's gaze drops to her photos.

Claws. "Seriously? Magda? God wouldn't forgive you?"

She looks at him: he is standing in front of her, still wearing Scythe's sword strapped across his back, and his expression is brittle. "Is that what you're afraid of? That God won't forgive you?"

He looks away, jaw tense.

Spots, quiet. "You couldn't save Sergeant Holden, Travis. You couldn't have saved the rest of your fire-team. Sometimes these things just . . . happen."

"Just. Happen."

Spots. "Yes."

Claws, voice hard. "You don't know that. You can't know that. You weren't THERE. You didn't see them DIE! I did! I saw them! I saw them die, they were in arm's reach and I . . . I couldn't . . . do a . . . do a damned THING and . . . and it's not ****ING FAIR. It's not, it's NOT FAIR, and I don't care about being forgiven, it's me, it's me who can't forgive God—" *he twists around and slams his fist into the wall.* "****!" *And slides to a knee.* "****, he was my friend, he was . . . he was like my brother, they all were. . . ."

Neither of them know when he started crying, or when Spots drew him away from the wall. But he ends up on his knees between hers, head held against her ribs, and angry tears wrack his shoulders.

141. SCARS

Once Claws's paroxysms ease, Spots rests her cheek on his hair. He sniffles, wipes his nose. Then, finally, silence.

Claws. "****. I'm sorry." *When Spots says nothing, he finishes:* "Crap, and I'm sorry about the cussin'. Guess I'm not so good with the self-control, like you said."

Spots. "I think you're doing fine."

He disentangles himself and leans back on his knees to look up at her. "Didn't you just say . . ."

She holds up a hand. "Yes. And I believe it. But you're barely into your twenties, Travis. God willing, you'll have time to figure it out."

Claws. "You're not *that* much older than me, you know."

Spots laughs. "Old enough."

Claws. "No, seriously, ten years ain't all that much. And I bet you were already this together when you were my age. Am I right?"

Spots. "Maybe, yes."

Claws. "So you see, it's a character defect."

Spots shakes her head. "I hope you're not being serious."

Claws chuckles and wipes his eyes again. "Crap, I'm all snotty."

Spots offers him the edge of the blanket. He eyes it, then shrugs and wipes his face.

When he sits back: "Seriously. How do you do it? How are you holdin' it together?"

Spots. "You think I'm holding it together?"

Claws. "Well, yeah. You're not exactly the one weepin' like a little boy in Momma's arms."

Spots shakes her head.

Claws. "Hey, Magda. I'm serious. I'm tryin' for a learnin' experience here. If those crazies want me for a boss, I . . . well, I could use the help."

Spots. "I don't know if I could . . . just give you my serenity, Travis. I got it the hard way."

Claws. "So tell me what the hard way is."

She looks at him for a few moments. Then says, unflinching, "Because I came close to dying on a hospital bed, and because I've killed a man. I feel like . . ." *She glances away now, thinking.* "Like I've been on both ends of the spectrum." *Meeting his eyes again.* "It doesn't make me less afraid, but it makes me more . . . familiar . . . with those fears. And I know that I've worked past them before."

Claws. "Well, crap. I don't know what to ask about first. What almost killed you?"

Spots. "My son. There were . . . complications. I still have the scar where they did the emergency c-section."

Claws. "And . . . the guy . . . seriously, you killed?"

Spots. "A break-in. He was armed, and between me and the nursery where my daughter was sleeping. I didn't even think about it, Travis. I just shot him, and I shot him so he wouldn't get up again."

Claws is silent a moment. Then: "Wow, you're right. I'm not gonna get your serenity your way."

Spots. "No . . . you're going to get it yours. You've already made a start, don't you think?"

Claws looks away. "Maybe on the trauma part, but not so much on the copin' part."

Spots. "Ah, but you already have the key to that, don't you? It's the same key that worked for me."

Claws. "What's that, then?"

Spots nods at the door. "They need you."

Claws. "You tellin' me that old horse manure about it bein' easier to be stronger for other people than for yourself is true?"

Spots. "What do you think?"

Claws folds his arms. Mutters. "Well, crap. Shoulda known better than to argue with you."

Spots. "Yep." *Grins.* "What do you think, boss. Ready to go back?"

Claws. "Yeah, guess so." *Gets to his feet.* "But don't call me 'boss.' That was . . . well. I need a nick of my own."

Spots. "Ninja. Samurai. Um . . . Cowboy!"

Claws. " 'Cept the closest I've ever been to a cow was on the highway drivin' past."

Spots. "That's what makes it funny!"

Claws covers his eyes with his hand.

142. DECISION

Barracks. The two enter; Spots goes to Samuel-Colt's bunk and puts one hand flat on the pad behind him, then eases over him. She slides an arm over his abdomen and sets her knife there on the mattress, near her fingers.

Claws shakes his head. Takes the knife and hands it back to her, then places one of the rifles there instead.

Spots smiles at him, then puts her head down.

Claws sits on his bunk, elbows on his knees and hands hanging. He watches the rest of the team sleep. Time passes.

Then he rises, silent, and leaves. After the door shuts, Spots closes her eyes and presses her nose against Samuel-Colt's carapace. No movement. Then her shoulders shake. Without breaking the silence, she cries.

Outside. Claws draws in a breath. Then heads for the armory and suits up, slowly, studying each piece as he dons it. He returns to the corridors, following them out to the edge of the base until he finds a work party.

Claws, approaching. "Hey. Put me to work."

Griffin. "Claws? Isn't Kitty down this shift?"

Claws. "Yeah. Can't sleep."

Griffin. "Got it. Well, we're hauling masonry. Join the party."

Claws lifts his gloved palm. Griffin slaps it. Clasps lightly, lets it slide.

Claws. "Thanks."

Griffin. "No problem."

Claws labors alongside Team PYEO for the next two hours, clearing away debris under the direction of one of the naval engineers. The suit's power-assist makes the work possible but it remains tedious and tiring. At last he straightens, eyes flicking toward the timestamp on the inside edge of the HUD.

Claws. "Hey, I'm off."

Griffin. "Good deal. Thanks for the help."

Claws. "Any time."

And he goes. Wanders, thinking, boots striking heavy and slow on the gritty floors. His feet take him at last to the test facility, and there he sits on one of the benches and looks at the area Kitty used for practice. The ghosts of those hours cloud his eyes. Fang2 and then Hawk Abrams on the mat. Spots talking the team through a variable shielding exercise. Turtle drills. Laughter. Sweat. Frustration.

He looks toward the data walls. On a whim goes to one and taps it . . . is surprised to find it operative. Pulls up the power consumption curves and watches them flicker through weeks of data: extreme curves leaping, twitching, and at last tapering to something smooth and low.

He rests a hand on the updated controls on his own glove. Restarts the data models and watches them again.

And then Claws sits on the floor in the dark, the monitors on but blank, helmet on the floor at his side.

Barracks. The squad is just waking when Claws arrives, still in his suit.

Fang sits up, throwing her blankets aside. "What did we miss?"

Claws. "We got somethin' to do."

Whiskers. "Yeah?"

Claws. "Yeah. To get some payback. Ya'll in?"

Fang2. "**** yeah!"

Hairball picks up the sword and tosses it to Claws, who catches it without objecting. As the squad assembles, Spots touches his arm. He sets his gloved hand over her bare one, carefully.

Claws, quiet. "Don't worry. We're gonna do it smart."

Spots smiles. "All right."

143. THE FACES OF THE DEAD

Lieutenant's Office. Peaches is sitting behind her desk, moving slips of paper around.

We look over her shoulder . . .

. . . photos. The small ones clipped to the corner of personnel files. Scythe. Roach. Avril. Flea. Strangers from before her arrival, slain by the offensive that necessitated her assignment. So many faces, the faces of the dead.

She is still rearranging them when Gunny limps through the door.

Peaches, looking up. "They let you out of Sickbay, Gunny?"

Gunny. "The beds they have left, they need for other people."

Peaches. "You were supposed to say something about a flesh wound like that not keeping you down."

Gunny smiles, says nothing.

Peaches. "Yeah. It's all ****. I know." *She returns to the photos.* "We're ****ed."

Gunny. "The next ship in is only a week and a half away."

Peaches. "Just in time to dig our graves. That Queen down there isn't going to wait that long. We're going to see another offensive from her within days, and then we'll die. Like all these people."

Gunny is silent, watching her—no, letting her build.

Peaches, cold, precise. "All these people. Two companies, and I'm lucky to have a platoon left. Those ****ing crabs killed them, and I've done nothing but presided over their ****ing funerals." *She starts laying the photos out in a grid, one by one, like playing cards.* "Good men and women. People with kids. People with moms and dads. People with dogs. People with scholarships waiting for them. People who could have grown up to be the ****ing President. So. Much. Potential."

Peaches looking up, not seeing him, eyes hard. "And here, in the chair, in the big ****ing chair, is Savannah Bonnet. Boatwoman on the river Styx. Counting the dead reaped by a ****ing alien."

Gunny. "What are you going to do?"

Peaches. "What exactly can I do? A frontal assault would be suicide. So would a raid. We've got no robots left, and even if we did they kill them before they get very far. Driving a fleet of bulldozers into their nest would be dramatic, but we wouldn't survive. Our

Spots the Space Marine: Defense of the Fiddler

only aircraft can't penetrate the walls of their habitat. We can't attrit them. We can't do what we really need to do—"

The chime sounds.

Peaches, eyes narrow. "Come."

Claws steps in, armored, with his helmet under his arm. He salutes.

Peaches. "At ease. Kitty's down, Corporal. What are you doing here?"

Claws goes to parade rest, eyes fixed on the wall behind her head. "Ma'am, forgive me. But there's something you oughtta see."

Peaches. "That important, is it, Corporal."

Claws. "Yes, ma'am."

Peaches. "Fine. Let's go."

389

144. A Chance

Peaches and Gunny follow Claws, remaining silent throughout the trip. When Claws leads them past the rubble toward the collider, Peaches frowns but says nothing. They cycle through the airlock.

Collider Tunnel. Claws allows the others to enter first. As they do, Team Kitty snaps to attention, their armored boots echoing as they hit the floor in perfect unison.

Peaches, frowning. "What's this, then, Corporal?"

Claws. "Ma'am, a demo. May I?"

Peaches, puzzled. "Proceed."

Claws, best parade ground voice. "KITTY! MOVE AND PROTECT! GO!"

The team scatters amid the detritus still littering the tunnel. They are difficult to see in the dim lighting of the tunnel.

Then at some distance, Spots's shield flares gold. Another shield pops up nearby and joins hers, white and gold syncing. They chime as they combine.

One by one the rest of the team sockets into the turtle, colors merging until they become a nigh-transparent milky shimmer . . .

. . . and then, the team is rushing the airlock. As they approach, one catches flashes of interior movement, like organs in a cell: Hairball and Whiskers scouting their flanks within the bubble maintained by Fang2 in the back and Spots in the front. They pour around obstacles, and the bubble never wavers, nor do their footfalls. No one breaks the bubble.

Suddenly, they are stopping in front of their observers. Spots crouches, Fang straightens, rifle aimed. Before Peaches can react, Claws darts from behind her, draws Scythe's sword and brings it down with both hands. His yell echoes, sharp and high.

With note like a struck bell, the sword stops five inches short of Fang's neck. Unflinching, she pulls the trigger on her empty weapon, enough for it to click.

Immediately Claws steps back, turns. He and the squad come to attention again. The milky light licks the length of the sword as he holds it straight up and to one side.

Claws salutes. "First Shield, reporting for duty. Ma'am."

Peaches draws in a sharp breath.

Spots the Space Marine: Defense of the Fiddler

145. Turn the Tide

Front Hall. The last time the company assembled here was to remember Dusty's Dog, before Alpha Company arrived. There was a casket. A memorial service. A body to be wheeled to cold-storage in expectation of a trip home on the next ship.

There are no bodies today. Only a handful of tables pushed together and draped in dark blue cloth, and on them, a semi-circle of rifles. What remains of the shattered base complement has gathered to honor the dead.

Into their quiet comes the chaplain, who walks to the front of the room, around the table. He begins to speak about sacrifice, about duty. About dying so that one's brothers and sisters might live. The men and women in the room listen, solemn and still.

At last the chaplain closes his book and bows his head. The company follows suit.

Silence.

Broken.

Boots against the floor. The clatter of the rifles on the table and the thump of something heavy landing among them.

Peaches has dropped a backpack nuclear bomb there.

"We've mourned the dead. Now we're going to kill their mother-****ing murderers so hard there won't be an atom left for God to rub together."

Electric pause.

Peaches, fist up, eyes hard. "For the slain. For the living. FOR VENGEANCE!"

"FOR VENGEANCE!"

PART 3
ENDGAME

146. Desperate Measures

Mess Hall. This is the only room cleared of enough debris for a conference. Peaches is standing over one of the tables with a map of the base and surrounding tunnels spread before her. Gunny is standing at her right hand. Around her, the leads and assistant leads of her remaining squads are gathered.

There aren't many.

Peaches, hand on map. "Let's start with cold reality, because we're standing in the wreckage of it. We can't hold off another of those attacks. Which means we have to finish it now, or not at all."

Silence, but no one looks away.

Peaches. "The contractors are putting together some smaller bombs for us. Our job is to sock them down the holes and make it seem like we're starting a major offensive from the front. While we distract them, Team Kitty—First Shield, now—is going to deliver this nuke the weapon devs have rigged for us to the main chamber."

Claws. "Ma'am? How we gonna set it off? Is it timed?"

Peaches. "They're working on a remote now."

Griffin. "What if the remote doesn't work?"

Peaches looks at Fang, who up until now has been standing a little behind Claws. "That's what Gordon's for." *Fang meets the LT's eyes as everyone else looks at her.* "You've got the highest qualification score in the entire company. You get the Queen. You kill her, doesn't matter if the bomb doesn't go. We'll still have a manageable situation on our hands."

Fang. "Ma'am, it's good as done."

Peaches. "Good. Walker, we'll be airdropping you near these side tunnels Jay mapped. We're going to get you as close to the breeding chamber as we can while still placing you near a tunnel you can break into. You'll have to hustle. We don't know how much time we have, but it's not going to be much."

Claws. "Understood, ma'am."

Dusty. "Ma'am?"

Peaches. "Yes, Sergeant."

Dusty. "What if the nuke does go off? Is there gonna be anything left of the base?"

Peaches. "I'm told by the experts it's big enough to do the job, and no bigger. But if they're wrong, we won't be in a position to care." *She looks around.* "Any more questions?" *No one speaks.* "I know it's a rough plan, but we need enough play in it to adapt to the crabs. Start point for base personnel is four hours from now. First Shield, you're leaving in three. Go prep."

The men and women scatter. As they're leaving:

Peaches. "Walker. Hang back a minute."

147. Fair Warnings

Everyone else exits, leaving Claws standing at attention facing Peaches, the table between them.

Peaches. "At ease." *When he stands down,* "I'll want your team in the hangar in three-thirty. Give us time for a last minute briefing and load-in."

Claws. "Yes, ma'am."

Peaches. "Nothing to add?"

Claws. "Not that I can think of, ma'am."

Peaches. "Not even a 'your plan is kind of loose given the stakes'?"

Claws hesitates. "Ma'am, that would be . . . uh . . . a little disrespectful."

She snorts. She comes around the table and leans on it, arms folded. "You know, Walker . . . we've been in an arms race with the crabs since the Violinists showed up and revolutionized our war tech: we make armor, they grow weapons that can hack into it. But if this shield thing works . . . it could be the end of all that. We could *win*. Decisively."

x

Claws meets her eyes.

Peaches, holding his gaze. "The man at the vanguard of the winning tech . . . he could go far."

Claws. "I'm sure she would, ma'am."

Peaches. "You're willfully misinterpreting me, mister."

Claws. "Ma'am, I appreciate the pitch—"

Peaches. "Avril was planning to sponsor you."

Claws winces. "Aw, ****, ma'am, that was a low blow."

Peaches. "Did it work?"

Claws. "With all due respect, ma'am—can I . . . ?" *He trails off and she nods. He finishes.* "I don't think I'm ready for it."

Peaches, gentler. "What I'm trying to tell you, Walker . . . warn you, really . . . is that if you lead Kitty into that chamber and come out alive and mission accomplished, you're going to end up with a hell of a lot of attention. More than you'll be able to shrug off with an 'aw shucks' farmboy grin."

Spots the Space Marine: Defense of the Fiddler

x

147. Fair Warnings

Everyone else exits, leaving Claws standing at attention facing Peaches, the table between them.

Peaches. "At ease." *When he stands down,* "I'll want your team in the hangar in three-thirty. Give us time for a last minute briefing and load-in."

Claws. "Yes, ma'am."

Peaches. "Nothing to add?"

Claws. "Not that I can think of, ma'am."

Peaches. "Not even a 'your plan is kind of loose given the stakes'?"

Claws hesitates. "Ma'am, that would be . . . uh . . . a little disrespectful."

She snorts. She comes around the table and leans on it, arms folded. "You know, Walker . . . we've been in an arms race with the crabs since the Violinists showed up and revolutionized our war tech: we make armor, they grow weapons that can hack into it. But if this shield thing works . . . it could be the end of all that. We could *win*. Decisively."

x

Claws. "You could take the credit—"

Peaches. "No, I couldn't. I wouldn't. Look, Walker, you came up with this. Don't you think that implies something about how you think?" *When he doesn't answer, she presses,* "You like being in charge. You're good at it."

Claws, uncomfortable. "I just want to see **** done right."

Peaches. "Exactly."

Silence.

Peaches. "Tell you what. Let's revisit it when you get back."

Claws. "Ma'am . . ."

Peaches. "Walker . . . if you pull this off, you're not going to have a choice. So let's talk about it when you get back, so you can at least aim the ****ing missile you'll be riding before everyone behind you shoots it off."

Claws looks down, shoulders tense. Lets out a short breath through his nose. "Yeah. All right."

Peaches smiles at his downturned head, not without sorrow. Then: "That's 'all right, ma'am'. For now. You don't get to shuffle your feet in front of me until they turn you loose with a bar of your own."

Claws straightens up.

Peaches, with a lopsided smile. "Dismissed."

Claws marches out. When the door closes behind him, he makes a frustrated sound.

Fang, leaning against the wall, arms crossed. "You in trouble again?"

148. Gaijin Daimyo

Claws, wry. "Depends on what you mean by trouble."

Fang. "In this case, trouble for us."

Claws. "Not so much, then. Peaches is just tryin' to get me to ****in' put on her uniform."

Fang grins. "Yeah?"

Claws, starting to walk. "Yeah. Me, an ****in' officer. What a crock of ****."

Fang, falling in stride. "Depends on what you mean by crock of ****."

Claws, exasperated. "****, not you too."

Fang. "Face it, daimyo. You're officer material. Everyone knows it but you."

Claws. "Hey, now. I'm not a ****in'— . . . oh, that's all fancy educated of you."

Fang laughs. "Ha! Don't try to pretend you didn't ****ing get it. You're such a ****ing faker."

Claws stops. Fang doubles back to face him.

Fang. "What, you all surprised? ****, Walker. Everyone knows you're smart, everyone knows you're way too ****ing well-educated for the face you put on, and everyone who's been around you long enough knows the ****ing accent's fake. Or started out that way. Now I don't think you know if it's real or not. You've been trying for this folksy **** so long, hoping to fool everyone else, that you're halfway to being a ****ing cartoon bump-kin."

Claws stares at her.

Fang. "You know it's true. So just ****ing man up, drop it and move on."

Claws. "****."

Fang. "Gonna deck me now?"

Claws breathes out. "No. Worse." *Eyes her.* "What's with you and Whiskers?"

Fang. "Huh?"

Claws. "Lately he calls you stuff like 'babe' and you haven't gutted him with that non-reg knife of yours. You want to **** him?"

Spots the Space Marine: Defense of the Fiddler

Fang huffs. "*****, no. Don't get me wrong, he's got a fine ***, but I don't **** squadmates."

Claws. "Good."

Fang eyes him. "Good?"

Claws. " 'Cause when the team bulks back up I'm gonna need an ASL and I'm thinkin' you're it."

Fang starts. "Me?"

Claws. "Even if they send us people more senior, they won't be as good with the tech, and the squad's gonna be about the tech. I need someone who's good with it and quick on the uptake. You think fast, Nic, and you think smart. You seem to be past your ***** phase, so if you're not gonna do somethin' stupid like roll in the hay with Whiskers, then you're it. My choice, anyway."

Fang. "*****, no kidding."

Claws. "Nope."

Fang. "Seriously?"

Claws. "If I had any doubts, your little speech there just convinced me. I need someone to haul me back on my ****in' *** when I'm doin' something stupid. So you up to it?" *His smile is all kinds of crooked.* "The ***** who helps leads First Shield, she could go far."

Fang resumes walking. Her face is thoughtful. "What about Guitart?"

Claws paces her, hands clasped behind his back. "What about her?"

Fang. "Why not her? She's technically senior. She's better than any of us with the tech."

Claws. "That makes her a specialist, not a leader. And when this is over, she's goin' home to those kids. You and I, we're in it for a career. Aren't we?" *He cocks his head at her.*

Fang. "Yeah . . . I think so."

Claws. "We play it right, Spots gets to go home and teach hotshots who wanna be jarheads how to use a shield from the safety of Parris Island. You and I, we'll be out here, endin' the war. I think that works out better for everyone, don't you think?"

Fang. "All right. But I'm still calling you daimyo."

Claws. "As long as I can call you Nic."

Fang. "Nic's fine. I didn't even know you knew my name."

Claws. "Yeah, well, I gotta get a head start on this officer crap before the mantle is thrust upon me, and all that ****." *He glances at her.* "You know, you really were a *****."

Fang says nothing for a few footsteps. He lets it lie. Then: "You watched your half of the team die. How did that feel, Walker?"

Claws. "Like ****. Like **** I'd never come back from."

Fang. "Try that for your whole team. And then getting sent alone somewhere new with new people."

They walk.

Claws. "Yeah, that would ****in' suck. I'm sorry."

Fang. "It happens. I've just figured out . . . the rest of you were dealing with your own ****. We just . . ." *She makes a scissoring motion with her hands.* "Two bad situations, same time."

Claws. "That's awful philosophical of you."

Fang. "Yeah, well. I know it sounds ****ing crazy, but . . . it's Guitart's fault. You know how your mom was always telling you to be nice to other people, and not to hurt their feelings, and all that other ****?"

Claws snorts. "Yeah."

Fang. "Having her around, she doesn't say that stuff but I remember my mom saying it more."

Claws. "Heh. Yeah, I see it."

Fang glances at him. "You can't turn it off anymore, can you."

Claws, rueful. "The accent? It just sorta comes and goes."

Fang laughs. "A regular ****ing gaijin daimyo."

Claws. "Can't you just call me "shogun" and get it over with?"

Fang grins. "Don't get ahead of yourself, country boy."

Spots the Space Marine: Defense of the Fiddler

149. Boss Fight

Barracks. Claws and Fang enter to find Hairball, Whiskers and Fang2 sitting crowded in the corridor between bunks. They are playing cards; there's a hand dealt for a fourth person. Samuel-Colt is still sleeping on one of the bunks. It's very quiet.

Claws. "What is this, a funeral?"

Hairball. "Aw, we're just making do. The common room is kinda a mess."

Fang2. "Hey, Boss—"

Fang. "He's got a name now, we're calling him daimyo."

Fang2. "Aw, ****! No kidding? That's ****ing awesome!"

Claws, suspicious. "You know what a daimyo is? What, you took a semester of Japanese feudal history somewhere I don't know about?"

Fang2. "*****, no, I played Rice Lords: Ultimate Sacrifice! You were totally some daimyo's ***** until you leveled up and could defeat one in honorable combat." *He bows from the waist, hands pressed together.*

Whiskers. "Wait, I remember that game. Wasn't that the one where you slaughtered peasants for not farming enough?"

Fang2. "Yeah! It was ****ing awesome!"

Hairball, frowning thoughtfully. "So a daimyo is a high-level boss who kills people for food? That doesn't sound right."

Fang, dry. "They turn rice into alcohol over there."

Hairball. "Ah, see, that makes more sense." *Grins.* "Okay. I'm cool with it."

Fang2. "ANYway, as I was saying . . . Daimyo, you suppose the boss's up there scoring with his ninety-two virgins?"

Whiskers. "It's seventy-two. I think."

Fang2. "Whatever, that's still a hell of a lot of virgins. What do you think, O Bad-*** Rice Lord?"

Claws. "From what I've heard about Scythe's mom, he's so not doin' any such thing, or she'd find some way up there for a verbal smack-down so hard he'd punch down into Hell and never come up again."

Behind them, Spots enters with an armful of protein bars. "Actually, knowing Scythe he's teaching them to fight with swords." *She mimes a hacking motion with a peanut butter bar.*

Fang2. "OMG. Scythe and his ARMY of SEVENTY-TWO HEAVENLY NINJAS."

Whiskers. "That sounds about right."

Fang2, dreamy. "I have a new god, and it is bad-***."

Claws laughs. "All right, all right. Now that we're all in one place . . . we got three hours. Then we suit up and report to the Birdcage. They're airdroppin' us at a site near the breedin' chamber, we break in and do our stuff. They'll be startin' a distraction an hour or so before so hopefully they'll be lookin' the other way when we sucker-punch them."

Whiskers. "With a nuke."

Claw. "With a nuke."

Fang2. "This is better than a movie. You think if I burn some incense, Scythe and his army will ****ing descend for the final battle?"

Claws, dry. "I'm afraid we're on our own for the boss fight."

402

Fang2. "****. Figures."

150. PARTY

Spots. "Three hours, is it?"

Claws. "Yup."

Spots. "Great! Let's go! Come on, guys, up, up."

Whiskers. "Wait, where we going?"

Spots. "You're playing cards in a space the size of a duffle bag. Let's go the test facility. Then you can spread out and I can put on some music."

Whiskers. "You serious?"

Spots. "Sure! It'll be just like playing cards in a bar. Except without the alcohol. Or the smoke. Or any other people."

Whiskers, grinning. "Yeah, just like a bar."

Spots. "Okay, it'll be more like playing cards in an empty club. But hey, I'll dance."

Fang. "You're kidding, right? We're about to go into a serious fight and you want to burn energy dancing?"

Spots. "I get nervous. Dancing puts me in a good mood. It's a good thing to be in a good mood right before you do something potentially fatal, right?"

Claws starts laughing. "Oh hell, let her. She's been dancin' since she got here. She danced on the dunes to get used to her suit, she danced her way into an alien's confidence . . . dancin' before the big showdown, well . . . if they cut that scene, everyone would feel like somethin' was missin'."

Spots. "Come on, Fang. You can dance too."

Fang. "No, thank you."

Spots. "But you'll come, right?"

Fang pauses, shorter than a heartbeat. Then: "Yeah, yeah, I'll be there. I got something to do first, though."

Spots, cheerful. "All right. The rest of you, pack it up."

Hairball. "What about the Fiddler?"

Spots. "I was thinking . . . we could maybe take him with us?"

Claws. "And haul his skinny body all over the base? Naw. I'll stay here with him. Y'all go on."

Spots eyes him, but he is looking away.

Spots. "All right." *She nods at the protein bars*. "Those are for when he wakes up. He'll be hungry."

Claws. "I remember. Y'all run along now. I'll be by, by and by."

Fang, rooting through her duffle, rolls her eyes. "He's going to kill us with those farm-boy-isms."

Fang2. "Death by hick. Not as much fun as death by hickey."

Hairball. "Sounds vampiric."

Spots, thoughtful. "Maybe a Southern vampire? Death by hick hickey?"

Claws. "Who said I was a Southerner?"

Fang. "No one, daimyo. We all know you're a city-boy." *She grins and heads out the door. Hairball, Whiskers and Fang2 follow her. Spots stops at the door.*

Spots. "You really will come by, right?"

Claws. "Yeah, don't worry. I won't let y'all have a party without me. Especially if it's the last one we ever have." *He pauses. When Spots doesn't say anything, he says,* "What, no 'we're gonna be all right'?"

Spots smiles."We're going to be all right."

Claws. "Phew. For a minute there I thought you'd been replaced by your evil twin."

151. Contingency Planning

The door closes, leaving Claws alone with the comatose alien. He crouches in front of the bunk and picks up the topmost arm, turning it a little to catch the light. The forearm, hand and fingers are thin . . . but they exist.

Claws, muttered. "And that's gonna have to be good enough." *He stands and goes through the table next to his new bunk, bringing out several items and spreading a towel. Then he sits across from Samuel-Colt, peels back the wrapper on a peanut butter bar, and waves it in front of the Fiddler's face.*

Claws. "Come on, this works in the movies. Don't make me kiss you or anything."

He tries it again—nothing. Leaning back, he makes an exasperated noise . . .

. . . Samuel-Colt lunges out of bed and into him.

Claws. "HERE! HERE!" *and shoves the food at him. Samuel-Colt devours it in two bites. Claws grabs for the next and hands it over and keeps unwrapping, fingers shaking with haste.*

A few minutes later they are both sitting on the floor surrounded in nine protein bar wrappers. Samuel-Colt makes a throat-sound.

Claws eyes him. "Was that a ****in' *burp*?"

Samuel-Colt. "In a manner of speaking. Thank you for the food. I was hungry."

Claws. "No ****in' kiddin', I ain't seen anything eat like that since my baby cousin had a growth spurt. How's the arm?"

Samuel-Colt stretches his fingers. "I will need another sleep, but it can be postponed. We assume there is a reason you woke us early?"

Claws. "You could say, yeah. We're headin' out to plant a bomb in the breedin' chamber, usin' your shields to get there."

Samuel-Colt, bowing a rising note. "That is a bold plan."

Claws. "That is a desperate plan, is what you meant."

Samuel-Colt, spritely arpeggio, rising. "Desperation is the mother of courage, perhaps?"

Claws. "Ha. Anyway, we're leavin' in about three hours, which means you gotta be mobile. The rest of the company's stayin' here to stage a diversion, and you're gonna have to handle your own insurance, if you know what I mean."

Samuel-Colt. "We do, Peer. We will find Savannah and remain with her, since she is likely to be in the most protected locale. Will we be issued a weapon to accomplish the suicide?"

Claws rubs the back of his neck. "****, it sounds so ****in' cold that way." *He shakes his head, then hands the Fiddler his knife.* "Here. This should do it."

Samuel-Colt. "You will not need it?"

Claws. "If I'm down to a knife down there, Sam, I got bigger troubles than I'll be able to handle with it."

Samuel-Colt. "In that you are absolutely correct."

Claws. "So I got questions I wanna ask about this chamber and what we should expect. But before I do . . . we got unfinished business, you and I."

Samuel-Colt, interrogative note. "We do?"

Claws reaches up to the table and brings down . . . the pot of ink and the reed. "You still serious about this? Because if you are, I'm ready."

152. Commitment

Samuel-Colt. "I am ready also."

Claws, picking up the reed. "What, you're not gonna ask 'are you sure?' Or 'are you doin' this for the right reasons?'"

Samuel-Colt bows a rising note as he holds out his arm. The tone is droll, somehow. "Should we?"

Claws. "Naw, just thought I'd give you the option an' all." *He turns the alien's arm.* "****, there's not much of it, is there."

Samuel-Colt. "It will grow a little, but we are not as thick through the limb as humans can be."

Claws dips the reed and starts painting. The odor is astringent and herbal. "What do ya'll usually paint on each other, then?"

Samuel-Colt, low melody. "Words."

Claws squints over at the alien's other arm. "Those're words?"

Samuel-Colt. "Indeed. The dots and lines in the center form the word, the signs above and below it, the music."

Claws. "****, really? You encode the fiddlin' into your writing?"

Samuel-Colt. "If we choose. Information intended to be presented as factual often leaves out musical inflection—science writing, you may call it. Or the author may wish to remain emotionally ambiguous, or anonymous."

Claws, distracted as he works. "That sound, it is the sound of millions of human bein's cryin', thinkin' of all the angst they might've avoided if only they could've made it clearer they were jokin' in that forum thread." *He leans back and blows on what he's done so far.* "So this stuff, what happens when your arm grows?"

Samuel-Colt glances at it. "The new material is supplied from the inside, so the exterior will expand."

Claws. "Ah, so I'll have t'do a touch-up when I get back."

Samuel-Colt. "I consider that a promise."

Claws glances at him sharply. He continues painting. Says, after a moment: "So the words on your other arm . . . what do they say? If that's not too private or anythin'."

Samuel-Colt. "They are mostly names: other Peers we have interacted with in service to humanity. The marks need to be renewed periodically to keep them from fading. If the male who applied them is still alive, we would seek him and ask him to redo them; since he may be the memory in a new body, it becomes a way to re-establish or re-state the importance of the relationship."

Claws, working. "Huh. And if he's not? Alive, that is."

Samuel-Colt. "Then we would visit a . . . how should we call it. Hmm. A professional re-fresher. Someone whose task is to repaint old marks, without emotional attachment."

Claws. "Is that what you do here?"

Samuel-Colt. "We are without recourse to such individuals. We refresh the paint our-selves as a reminder of our commitment to our mission to humanity."

Claws leans back, tired. "****, Sam. Do we deserve that?"

Samuel-Colt bows a sprightly note. "Do you think we are without flaw, Travis? Our species is as motley a group as yours. You simply don't realize it because you don't interact with us all."

Claws blinks, then bursts out laughing. "You're sayin' you're keepin' your looneys in the sea where we can't see 'em?"

Samuel-Colt, amused melody. "Something like that, yes."

Spots the Space Marine: Defense of the Fiddler

153. BROTHERHOOD

For a time then, there is silence. Claws works, bent close, lower lip rolled beneath the upper. There is the herbal, astringent smell of the ink, the occasional tink of the hardened reed against the pot's lip.

Claws, leaning back. "There. Pretty fine, if I say so myself. Which I do."

Samuel-Colt looks. "You have painted the Marine emblem on us?"

Claws. "Ah, good. You recognize it."

Samuel-Colt, bowing a long, wry-sounding note. "Semper fidelis. Is that a description or a threat?"

Claws grins. "You're a lot more subtle than even you let on, you know that?"

Samuel-Colt. "We try not to seem too threatening." *More seriously, touching it with gentle fingers.* "Do you think it is appropriate? I am not one of you."

Claws. "If you weren't one of us before, Sam, you are now. Anyone who's willin' to die— die permanently, 'cause if you die here you won't be puttin' any memories in some new body's head—is a brother of mine. I'm just makin' it clear, in case anyone's minded to misunderstand."

Samuel-Colt is struck speechless by this. They are both silent, looking at the tattoo. Then: "Shall I now offer you a cigarette?"

Claws. "A . . . what? Like, what, a post-sex smoke?" *He starts laughing.* "****, where'd you get that? What movies you been watchin'?"

Samuel-Colt, sprightly melody. "It was the romance novels you recommended. 'Simmering Desire.' Very interesting reading."

Claws. "Bet it feels more like a horror story to you, don't it. 'They're gonna have sex! OH NO! SOMEONE'S GONNA DIE TONIGHT!' "

Samuel-Colt. "Leaving the Mother to smoke the postprandial cigarette alone. Woe."

Claws. "****, you really are a joker. I can't believe Kenyan didn't notice all this time."

Samuel-Colt. "Kenyan was not a Peer."

Claws. "Yeah, well. He don't know what he's missin'."

Samuel-Colt hesitates. Then says: "It is customary at this time to offer reciprocation."

Claws. "Pardon?"

Samuel-Colt, bowing a very low note. "You have marked me. If the relationship is considered reciprocal, the marks are made so also."

Claws purses his lips and looks at the pot. "Will this stuff stick to me?"

Samuel-Colt. "It is a dye. On human skin, it will fade after a few washes." *He considers Claws's arm and bows a bemused pair of notes.* "We could paint a mural on your arm."

Claws laughs. "Or pen a Fiddler epic? What would you put on it, if I said yes?"

Samuel-Colt flips the reed so that the opposite end faces down and begins to write something on the concrete floor; the end is burnt and leaves sooty marks. When the alien finishes, Claws bends over to look.

Claws. "Looks cool, like some kinda tribal design. What does it say?"

Samuel-Colt. " 'War is hell.' "

Claws, laughing. "What? You're kiddin'?"

Samuel-Colt, sprightly arpeggio, rising. "Not at all."

Claws. "****in' appropriate. I didn't know you had a hell, though."

Samuel-Colt, quieter. "All thinking beings have a hell, Peer."

Claws rolls up his sleeve. "Sounds good to me. If I live through the next few hours, I'll get it inked permanent. Just keep the band narrow and up high. Officers can't have 'em bigger than two inches."

154. Moving On

Morgue. The bodies that could be recovered from the last battle are here in cold storage, awaiting a ship that no one may be alive to greet.

There are too many bodies.

The door opens; a long shadow stretches over the floor, framed in the lit rectangle cast by the light outside the door. Fang steps in and closes the door behind her, cutting off the light. The only illumination now comes from the dim glow of guide lights and the faint blue light inside the capsules themselves.

That dim light is soft on her face as she looks at the dead. Her chin lifts, just a touch.

Then she goes among them, hunting. Her hand glides over this one or that, an acknowledgement: but only one hand. There is a bundle under the other arm. When she reaches the capsule she's seeking, she sets her burden down and rests both hands on the cold steel and plastic, looking inside at its occupant's face, blue light on his pale features, warm on her dark.

She draws in a long breath through her nostrils, exhales. Then reaches down. There is a sharp snap and then a bright flare of aquamarine fabric billows over the capsule. Fang tucks it close up to the small window at its top, the embroidered sleeves hanging on either side. She rests a hand on it and bows her head, closing her eyes.

Then she goes without a backward glance. Behind her, the Dragon Team kimono gleams on Scythe's tomb.

Test Facility. Fang enters to find Spots messing with her music player and the guys already back at their game.

Fang. "Miss me?"

155. TEAM MANGA

Fang2. "Perfect! You're here! Now we can get this all worked out."

Fang. "Uh oh."

Whiskers. "He thinks we need Japanese names now."

Fang2. "Well, if Walker's the daimyo, 'Team Kitty' doesn't make sense, right? We need to be Team Manga!"

Whiskers, studying his cards. "I am not a teenage girl."

Hairball. "There are some manga not read by teenage girls."

Whiskers looks at him over his cards.

Hairball, unperturbed. "Okay, not many."

Fang2, ignoring them. "I was thinking Whiskers could be Ronin. Because the black guys always get to be the bad ***es."

Whiskers, still studying his cards. "I'm down with that."

Fang, hand on her forehead. "I am not hearing this."

Fang2. "Don't worry, you get an awesome nick too, because the only thing badder-*** than a black guy is a kick-*** black girl."

Fang, looking up at the sky. "I am so not hearing this!"

Spots is smothering her laughter next to the wallscreen.

Fang2. "So you can be ninja. Or samurai. Nah, ninja. That's badder-***."

Hairball, thoughtful. "Badder-*** or bad-***er?"

Whiskers. "Bad-***er. It's less correct but it sounds bad-***er."

Fang, wry. "So what's your name?"

Fang2. "I, obviously, am Private Cutefase."

Fang. "And Spots?"

Fang2, triumphant. "Private MILF!"

Spots the Space Marine: Defense of the Fiddler

Spots. "Agh!"

Fang2 beams.

Fang sighs. To Hairball, "What about you?"

Hairball. "I'm Private Ramen. I like noodles."

Fang2. "Team Manga. It would ****ing rock."

Spots has abandoned this conversation and is dancing and singing to "Rock the Casbah." Fang sits against the wall to watch, relaxed. There is something in her pose and gaze that feels companionable. Protective. Hairball, Fang2 and Whiskers play their cards; Scythe now has a chair of his own, to go with his hand.

The music scrolls to something new.

Fang2, looking up. "What the ****? You listen to Existential Foxes?"

Spots. "It's a good band! And I like this song!"

413

Fang2. "But it's about people ****ing! It has the word **** in it!"

Spots. "Yes?"

Fang, curious now. "You sing to this ****?"

Spots. "Sure! Watch." *She dances around until the chorus, then howls out:* "IiiIIIII waaaaaaaant, I waaaaaaaant, I want a pixellated—" *Pause.* "Iiiiii waaaaaaaaaaant, I waaaaaaaaaaant, I want a pixellated—" *Pause again.*

Fang, laughing. "Come on! You seriously don't do that!"

Spots. "Well, only when I'm alone. When I'm in the car with the kids I skip past it, they don't need to hear stuff like that."

Fang, to Fang2. "And you wanted to call her Private MILF? She won't even be able to report her own position."

Fang2. "Okay, I'll think of something new."

The door opens for Claws and Samuel-Colt.

Claws. "Miss us?"

156. PARTY'S END

Fang2. "Hey, Rice Lord. What do you think of going 'Team Manga'?"

Claws, pulling up a chair. "I think you're full of ****. Deal me in."

Whiskers grins.

Fang2. "But it would be so ****ing awesome!"

Claws rolls his eyes. "Less yap, more cards." *He leans over the chair and says,* "Hey, Sam, you playin', or you gonna dance with mom?"

Samuel-Colt. "We shall sit with the Fang to observe the dancing."

Spots. "Aww, that's no fun. You two should dance with me."

Fang. "No way, no ****ing way." *But she's smiling.*

Spots shimmies. "Aw, come on."

Fang. "Having boobs doesn't make me a dancer."

Spots. "I'll say, or the Baryshnikov fangirls of the world would be disappointed."

Fang2. "The what-nows?"

Spots. "Don't worry, it's before your time. Heck, it's before mine. My grandmother used to wax poetic over him though."

Samuel-Colt, curious rising note. "You do not dance?"

Fang. "Nope."

Spots stops dancing and heads to the table. Pickings are slim, but she finds two of the wooden poles used to stand foam targets. She tosses one to Fang, who catches it by reflex.

Spots. "All right. You don't dance? Come spar."

Fang. "You serious?"

The guys are surreptitiously watching this now.

Spots. "Sure." *She rolls her shoulders.* "We should warm up anyway."

Fang. "Well . . ."

Spots the Space Marine: Defense of the Fiddler

Spots leans over and pokes the advance on her music player until a heavy percussive beat rolls from the speakers. The music is violent and the tempo quick. "Come on."

Fang. "All right." *And gets up.*

—they move then, using the sticks as short staves: two women in loose t-shirts and camo-pattern pants. Light flashes off muscle on them both: the weeks have whittled away what softness Spots had when she arrived.

They move, and it is like dancing, and it is like fighting. At some point, they start laughing.

Hairball, muttered: "You watching this?"

Fang2. "**** no, I'm not ****ing watching this."

Whiskers. "For someone not watching this, your eyes are pretty ****ing nailed to it."

Fang2, hunching his shoulders. "What do you expect? ****, no one's mom should move like that."

Claws, drawling. "She sorta had to move like that to, you know, conceive."

Fang2. "I thought she was Catholic! Didn't they invent the missionary position?"

Whiskers, scratching his nose. "I think the Protestants invented the missionary position after noticing how good a time the Catholics were having."

Fang2. "****, I can't watch this anymore. It's like finding your mom and sister sexy. That's only fun if they can't ****ing take you apart."

Claws is trying not to laugh. The song scrolls to something less driving. Fang and Spots stop.

Spots. "There, see? Dancing."

Fang, tossing her the stick. "You're one of us, through and through, you know that?"

Spots grins, catching it.

So there is dancing and card playing. Samuel-Colt goes from watching to dancing to playing ("Where the **** did you learn to play like that?"). *Fang consents to dance one more time. Plays a hand. There is a great calm amid the activity . . . and a tension beneath it.*

Soon enough, Claws stretches. "All right, kitties, it's time to mosey on down."

Whiskers tosses his cards on the table. "Let's get this show moving."

They push in their chairs and leave the cards on the table, as if they are only pausing between games. As they form up, Spots turns off the music; her hand also flicks off the lights, leaving the room silent and dark. She joins the others.

The door opens on a corridor lined with the remaining Marines of Naval Depot B.

157. Last Meeting

The men and women are already in armor, helmets under their arms. They stand at parade rest, but they're spread out: there are too few of them to stand shoulder to shoulder and still make it to the corridor's end. In the spaces between them, one can sense the ghosts of dead comrades. Their implied presence fills out the column.

Claws stops abruptly at the display. So does the rest of Kitty. For a moment, no one says anything. No one moves.

At the head of the line, nearest the door, is Hawk Abrams. Recovering himself, Claws says to him: "Aw, ****, man."

Hawk lifts his hand. Claws slaps it.

Hawk. "Thanks for the leg."

Claws. "Ain't nothin'."

Hawk holds out his hand to Samuel-Colt. There is another pause as the alien stares at it. Then he extends his newly remade upper hand, clasps Hawk's.

They walk, then. All the way to the corner, where Dusty's anchoring the end of the line.

Dusty. "Hey, come back in one ****ing piece, eh? So we can pin your bars on."

Claws. "****, does everyone know about this?"

Dusty grins. "The scuttlebutt won't die 'til we do, son."

He clasps her hand too. She doesn't take Samuel-Colt's, but she does incline her head to him. As the last of Kitty passes her, Dusty calls, "ALL RIGHT, ****ERS, GO GO GO!" *The line breaks apart as the Marines scatter for their assigned points for the kick-off.*

Whiskers to Hairball. "You crying?"

Hairball. "Nope." *He grins, eyes wet.*

Samuel-Colt has stopped and is looking back up the hall.

Spots. "Samuel-Colt?"

Samuel-Colt, voice low. "No human has ever done such a thing for us."

Hairball. "You were due then. Yes?"

Samuel-Colt starts to speak, then shakes his head. The human mannerism only stresses his position: caught between two worlds, not entirely accepted by either . . . except here.

Spots touches his arm. He covers her hand with his.

Claws. "Aw right, we gotta briefin' to make. Let's hustle."

Spots the Space Marine: Defense of the Fiddler

158. INFILTRATE

Montage. Team Kitty suiting up: shots of their backs, with the marks gleaming on the armored curves, keeping the tally of the enemy dead. Whiskers and Claws helping strap the bomb onto Hairball's back. The team standing over a table with Gunny, who is explaining the mission. Claws asking questions. Fang frowning. The team climbing into the chopper.

. . . and then, suddenly, the rotor blades slicing the frame as we look down at the rope from which the team is dangling. Spots is looking over her shoulder as she slides down.

Fang2. "I still think you should have taken the katana."

Claws. "I was never takin' the katana."

Fang2. "But seriously, man! It's a ****ing katana! That's, like, your way of telling God 'I am too awesome to die!'"

Fang. "More like his way of telling the crabs 'shoot me.'"

Claws. "What she said."

Fang2. "Still!"

Spots is the last one down. She jumps to the mire among the rest of the team and straightens amid the soupy storm thrown up by the hovering helicopter.

Claws. "Raptor one, this is Kitty, we're all down."

"Copy that, Kitty. Good hunting."

Claws. "Thanks, man." *He waves to the helicopter and then turns as it speeds from view.* "Okay, Kitties, let's . . ."

Long pause. They all look around at the thick particulate air as it settles, the sticking sludge and the absolute emptiness of the vista.

Whiskers. "****, where's the door?"

Hairball, looking at HUD. "Says right below us."

Silence. Fang2 stomps on the wet ground. Just to make sure. Or for emphasis.

Claws, drawling. "Well, boys and girls, bust out them entrenchin' tools."

Fang. "****, what is this, World War II?"

Fang2. "If this were World War II there would be Nazis. Zombie Nazis."

Team Kitty starts digging. Entrenching tools are still shovels, but attached to arms in powered armor they are much more effective. Even so, it's not easy work in material this slick. They waste an hour breaking into their assigned tunnel. Claws is tense, trying not to watch the timeline in the corner of his display.

Whiskers. "We're in."

Claws. "Let's hustle."

They drop, one by one, into the tunnel: from the dusky thickness of the alien day with its twitchy winds and low sky, into . . . darkness, stillness, closeness. The tunnel walls strobe as the team snaps on their shields, flickers of color before the fields go invisible.

Fang. "Shields go."

Claws. "Right. Thattaway. Keep your eyes peeled. Et-cetera."

Fang2. "I think you gotta work on that whole sounding-in-charge thing, boss."

Hairball. "I don't know. I think the folksy casual thing works."

Whiskers. "Everyone's got a management style."

Claws. "Are we seriously discussin' this?"

Whiskers. "Sure?"

Claws. "Could you at least wait 'til I ain't in the room to start kvetchin'?"

Whiskers. "But that would be less fun—" *He stops abruptly.*

Spots, low. "I saw it too."

159. COVERT

Even though their voices are confined inside their earpieces and under helmets, they advance in silence, returning to training older than suits. Quickly—Claws's timeline is still counting down—but carefully, watching every corner, every corridor's end.

They turn into a hall. Their first crab stares at them (flash of eyeshine reflecting the status lights on their suits). Instead of attacking, as it should, it turns to flee.

Claws. "Don't let it—"

It hits the ground.

"—uh, get away. Nice shootin'."

"Thanks." *Fang, absent. She checks the body, pushing it over with her boot.* "Not a King. But it decided to run. Why?"

Hairball. "Maybe it's the diversion? Maybe they're all under orders to go that way. We interrupted it."

Claws. "We could hope. Let's not bet the farm on it though."

The two Fangs pull the corpse off to the side and tuck it as close to the wall as they can.

Spots. "They'll smell it, even if they don't see it."

Claws. "Yeah, but what can you do?"

And they're off again. The tunnels are deserted, and they make some time back jogging them, slowing only for intersections. It's going well enough that Claws stops obsessively checking his counter.

. . . and then Whiskers looks around the next bend and swears.

Claws. "Great. What?"

Whiskers. "Have a look, riceman."

Claws, muttering. "How did I get from daimyo to "riceman"?" *He looks past the corner.* "****."

Their next intersection is so highly trafficked some of the crabs using it get pushed out into the side junctions by the crush and have to wait for the next gap to get back in.

Claws. "Crap, that's our thoroughfare to the breedin' chamber."

Fang, looking now. "We knew we'd have to start killing them eventually."

Whiskers. "That's a ****ton of crabs to start killing at once."

Fang2. "But that's why they gave us the shiny new toys, right?'

Spots. "The shiny new toys won't work if they pile on us. Remember that time with Flea? They don't have to kill us to stop us. Just get enough of them in place and they can slow us down until the batteries drain, and then we'll be dead."

Claws. "Crap. We'll have to go around."

Fang. "You sure, daimyo?"

Claws. "This ain't a smash-and-grab, Nic. We try to shove through that, we'll blow our surprise and fail the timeline. Even if we get through it'll be too late for everyone else. Let's go."

160. BREAKTHROUGH

The team backtracks and takes another junction. It only takes them a few more turns to find—

Whiskers. "****."

Fang2. "Again?"

Hairball. "Now what?"

Claws's fingers flex on his rifle. "One more try."

Spots. "We might be running into a lot of crabs because there are a lot of crabs near the center."

Fang. "Like it's unavoidable, you're saying."

Spots. "Basically."

Claws. "One more try."

So they back out of that tunnel and once again try to come at the center from a different route. Claws's eyes constantly flick toward the counter in the corner of his HUD.

On their third attempt, they find yet another corridor clogged with crabs.

Whiskers. "So is this the part where we go in and kick ***?"

Hairball. "If we're going to do that, maybe the second hall was better? This one's really full."

Fang2. "Really full might be easier. You know, spray and pray, but with less praying."

Spots. "Maybe on your part."

Claws. "I think Hairball's right. We're gonna go in, let's spend the least amount of juice and ammo. Come on."

Again, they retrace their steps back into the maze of twisting tunnels. They turn the corner just as a group of six crabs does. The crabs don't have time to respond before they are being cut down . . . but in the jostling two break free to flee. Fang takes one through the head with a round. Spots lunges after the other with a shield. Cuts down a leg, runs up its back and decapitates it from behind.

The crab crashes to the floor—

—and through it, taking a startled Spots with it.

Part 3: Endgame ● M. C. A. Hogarth

Dirt puffs up from the hole. Silence for a heart-beat, then the team explodes into motion.

Claws. "SPOTS! ****, Magda!"

Fang. "Hey, mama!"

They kick the crabs away or climb over them and bound to the hole—

Spots, shaky. "Wish you'd stop cursing at me."

They look down into the hole and find her standing away from the corpse.

Fang2, hanging over the edge, enthusiastic. "That was one AWESOME ninja move, wow, it was like . . . like you were totally doing the dive-bomb combo from Toesock Killers 2! Ppshauw! Where'd you learn to do that?"

Spots. "I was . . . uh . . . more just thinking of it like a playground rock wall."

Fang2. "Oh, man. Way to harsh my buzz there, Mom."

Hairball. "No need to be disturbed. You can just add the army of hot moms who learned their ninja moves on playground equipment to the boss's army of houris."

Fang2. "Ohhh, yeah."

Claws, ignoring them. "Magda? Can you get back up?"

Spots, slowly. "Actually . . . I think you all should come . . . down here. . . ." *Softer.* "Mother of God."

161. SECRETS

Claws. "Magda, we've kinda gotta strict timeline here—"

Spots. "I know."

Claws frowns, then shrugs and hops over the lip of the hole. He lands with a thick thump alongside the corpse, straightens—

—and stops. "Jesus H. . . ."

Before them the tunnel slopes sharply downward, losing the dirt-and-dust consistency and smoothing into a corridor lit by an eerie pink glow. Studding the walls are alcoves full of translucent eggs the size of soccer balls. Hundreds of eggs, lambent, jewel-like.

Behind them, the thud is Fang joining them. Then the rest of the team drops through the hole. Whiskers whistles.

Hairball. "Looks like we have an idea where to plant the bomb."

Claws. "Reckon so. Come on."

He leads them down the hall until they are amid the eggs. The sound of their footfalls changes tone, from the muffled thump of boots on earth to the short echo of feet on a hard, clean floor in an enclosed space. Despite the urgency of their errand, they walk slowly: part caution, part . . . something else. No one touches anything. But they all look, their heads moving from side to side.

Fang2. "Wow."

Fang. "What makes them glow, I wonder?"

Hairball. "Is it the eggs or the wall?"

Claws. "A little of both, maybe."

Hairball. "We're going in the right direction, at least."

Claws. "Yeah." *He scans the hall before and behind them, eyes narrowed.*

Fang, stretching her fingers against her weapon. "Wondering why there aren't any guards?"

Claws. "Sumthin' like that."

Whiskers. "Maybe they're only posted at the entrance to this . . . uh . . . place? And we got around it by dropping through the floor."

Claws. "This looks pretty important, though. Why wouldn't they have patrols?"

Spots. "Do you put armed guards in a nursery?"

Claws glances at her. "No. But they ain't human."

Spots. "No, they're not. But if we have to grasp for straws, we have to start with the ones we can imagine."

The six humans move down the hall then, silhouettes against the glowing pink walls with their gemlike treasures. As they move, the hall grows broader, branches off into darker side tunnels, until they are walking down what feels like an avenue. There are fewer and fewer unlit areas on the walls; and so the light grows brighter until at last they reach a great round chamber, lit as brightly pink as a little girl's bedroom.

There are eggs everywhere in neat pyramids. The walls are smooth and pale. The silence is complete.

No one in the team speaks for several heart-beats.

Then, Claws: "Fine place for a nuke. Let's set 'er up."

426

162. NURSERY

The team helps pull the bomb off Hairball's back. Hairball, Whiskers and Claws start setting it up; Spots and the Fangs keep watch on the ingresses.

Fang2. "Does this feel . . . a little bit . . . weird to anyone?"

Fang, dry. "Which part?"

Fang2. "The lack of crabs. The funky lighting."

Fang. "The fact that we're wiring a bomb in a ****ing nursery?"

Whiskers. "Not getting soft, are you?"

Fang. "No. But it's so damned *pink.*"

Fang2, eyeing the mounds of eggs. "Helps that the things look so disgusting."

Spots. "Plenty of people think human babies look disgusting." *When Fang glances at her, she says,* "Samuel-Colt came out of an egg like these."

Fang. "You getting soft?"

Spots, quiet, hard. "No."

A nervous pause. Then Claws, exasperated. "Ain't no one goin' soft in this freakin' team, all right? We are all hard as mother-lovin' diamonds. Hairball, your side check out?"

Hairball. "Looks good. Whisks?"

Whisker. "Good to go."

Claws. "Annnnd . . . activate." *The device is flooded with lights, green, bright amber, orange. The final one flashes red once, then commences blinking.* "All right. When the LT punches the button, all the lights say it'll go."

Hairball. "We should disguise it?"

Spots. "We can hide it under some of these eggs. Build a pyramid like they've already done."

Claws. "Yeah." *Stares at the eggs.* "Uh . . ."

Spots brushes past him, picks up one of them and starts stacking. The rest of the team follows her lead, after a hesitation. Fang2 is the last to touch one. He makes a face as he lifts it.

Fang2, muttering. "****ing unnatural—"

I feel you . . .

All of them bolt upright, weapons lifted. Several dropped eggs roll away from their boots, the only noise that pierces their silence.

Fang2. "You hear—"

Claws cuts him off with a lifted hand.

Oh, you human heroes . . . I know you're there. I feel you. Will you come out, or must I send someone to bring you . . . to me?

Whiskers, hunched. "**** . . . !"

Fang2. "That . . . is not . . . the queen. Talking to us. ****! Is it?"

Come now. I can feel you, there in my body. I don't know where . . . but that . . . can be changed . . .

The team meets one another's eyes.

Claws. "Don't . . . you . . . tell me . . . we are. INSIDE. A CRAB."

428

163. TRAP

Heartbeat.

Fang. "Wait, how the hell does that make any ****ing sense? How did they smuggle in a crab the size of a base without us seeing it?"

Whiskers. "It's not the size of a base. This pink part's pretty small."

Fang2. "For a ****ing BUILDING! Why the **** are we still HERE??"

Spots is still stacking the eggs up over the bomb. "We're finishing the job we were sent to do."

Claws hasn't moved. His head is cocked. Fang glances at him, frowning.

Claws. "She ain't talkin'. Is she still listenin'?"

Fang2. "And that's another thing, another ****ing thing, how can we hear her??"

> *I'm still* **here, heroes.**

Fang2, grabbing his helmet. "****! ****!"

Spots, still working. "Almost done!"

Claws, to the Queen. "The hell you say! Get the hell out of our heads!"

> *I know you're in me, heroes. I know you're doing . . .* **something.** *Why don't you* **come up here,** *where we can talk . . .* **face to face?**

Claws. "Hell no!"

> **Even if I said** *. . . I wanted to negotiate?*

Everyone freezes again at that.

Fang, beneath her breath, viciously. "****."

> *Even if I said . . . I'll stop the onslaught.* **A . . . cease-fire.** *So we can talk.*

Now Claws: "****."

Whiskers. "We can't trust her. How would we know?"

> **Call your base.** *You can ask if I have kept my word.*

Fang2. "What. The. Hell! Why are we even talking with her! Let's ****ing get out of here and finish the job!"

Hairball. "But if her head's somewhere else . . . what if she lives?"

Fang2. "Are you ****ing kidding me?" *He point at the egg-covered bomb.* "You're ****ing kidding me, right?"

Spots. "We don't know where the rest of her is. We don't even understand . . . this . . . biology that lets her be the size of a house. And if we don't get it, how can we be sure?"

Fang. "A shot between the ****ing eyes would do it."

Yes. Come and meet me, heroes. Bring your fantasies *of killing me. Let us see where they lead you.*

Fang2. "For God's. ****ing. Sake. It's a TRAP."

164. Make the Call

Claws is still, tense, gripping his weapon.

Fang2, more urgently. "IT'S A TRAP."

Fang. "If we don't kill her, all this will have been for nothing." *When Claws doesn't respond.* "We could get into her ****ing nest and SHOOT HER BETWEEN THE EYES."

Fang2. "They could come in here while we're ****ing gone and get the bomb out of here!"

Spots. "They could do that while we're fighting our way back too."

Hairball. "We could set the bomb off now."

Fang2. "****! I don't want to die!"

Fang, ignoring him. "But what if it doesn't kill her? It's not even big enough to reach the base. What if she's out of range?"

Claws holds up a hand. Everyone stops talking.

Claws, looking up. "You better be tellin' the truth about that ****in' cease-fire."

We are.

Claws. "Tell us how to get to you."

165. Slow Motion

Go north, heroes. You will be escorted once you reach the end of my body.

Fang2. "Did she have to ****ing remind us?"

Hairball. "Could have been worse."

Fang2. "How the **** could that get any worse?"

Hairball. "Could have said 'once you reach one of my orifices' or something."

Fang2 stares at him. Then pointedly turns to Claws. "So what the ****, daimyo?"

Claws. "You heard the crab. North."

Fang2. "But it's a ****ing trap!"

Claws. "Yeah, and? Let's move out."

He heads down the northernmost corridor. Hairball follows, then Whiskers.

Fang. "Come on, tumor."

Fang2. "But—"

Fang, making a wiggly motion with the fingers of her free hand over the body of her rifle. "Trust the rice lord."

Fang2 eyes her. "**** the rice lord, I don't trust YOU since you've gone all nice."

Fang laughs. "Go. And button it. We don't need anyone listening to us squabble."

Grumbling, Fang2 follows Whiskers. Spots goes after him, then stops on the threshold, looking back into the chamber with its pyramidal mounds of eggs.

Fang, watching her. "Something on your mind, Mama?"

Spots. "Maybe."

Fang. "Regrets?"

Spots smiles. "No." *But as she walks into the hall, she trails her fingers along the glowing walls and frowns.*

She is not the only one frowning. Claws is watching both timeline and the power levels of the squad's packs on his HUD, along with a new, blinking red countdown.

Spots the Space Marine: Defense of the Fiddler

The team reaches the end of the polished pink area and are met by two Kings. The hall beyond their escort is lined with crabs. It looks eerily like the send-off the squad received at the base . . . but hideously inverted, the faces of friends replaced with the enemy's masklike heads and gleaming black bodies. Without consultation the team tightens its formation, shields snapped into a bubble.

Claws leads, jaw set. One step. Another.

"Lieutenant! The crabs are withdrawing!"

"Say again?"

Whiskers and Hairball have the center, watching the wall of crabs warily. Taller than the others, their heads show above the rest of the squad's but are still far lower than even the most common crab soldier's.

"They're withdrawing!"

Peaches glances around the corner, weapon at ready, frowns. Behind her, someone murmurs, "Well I'll be damned . . . Are they actually retreating?"

Spots and Fang bring up the rear. Their footsteps scuff the dirt floors.

Fang2, muttered. "****, this better work or we're ****ed."

Hairball. "Shouldn't have joined if you couldn't take a joke."

433

166. The Queen

The team marches up a curving corridor lined with crabs, following their King escorts. On Claws's HUD, their route is superimposed on the map generated by their exploration: they are heading back to the nursery, but a level above it. The hall they traverse is featureless dirt until it opens abruptly into a large dark chamber with an uneven floor. The chamber is lined with Kings rather than soldiers. Four more Kings stand in the center, flanking a low mound.

From that mound rises the slim stalk of a crab, upper body only. A gracile thing of multiple arms and narrow, triangular head and decorative, draping antenna. The Queen's eyes glimmer like faceted amethysts.

Her voice, when she speaks, is a sweet, high exhalation through the painted spiracles on her body. She sounds as if she is sighing each sentence.

"Heroes. You have come. At last, I see the face of the enemy directly."

Team Kitty stands rigid before her. Their escorting Kings have taken up position behind them at the chamber's entrance. They are entirely surrounded.

Queen, after a hesitation. "More or less. Will you not remove your helmets?"

Claws. "You must be kidding me."

Queen. "I am vulnerable before you, heroes. Will you not do me the same courtesy?"

Fang. "Vulnerable! Are you joking?"

Queen. "One shot . . . Fang, is it? You yourself said it." *One lithe finger taps once between the scintillant eyes, a hollow, almost plastic sound.* "Here."

Fang. "And then we all die."

Queen. "Yes. A . . . mutually assured destruction, yes? I would not be alive to relish your deaths. So, yes. A vulnerability. I know you plan to kill me. I can see it in your body, the tension."

Claws. "What the hell do you want? Why'd you bring us here?"

Queen. "As I said. To negotiate."

Spots, quiet. "To keep us from killing more of her eggs."

Sudden silence. Claws narrows his eyes.

Spots, continuing. "That's it, right? You knew we were in your body. You knew the only reason we'd be there would be to smash all of your eggs. You needed to get us out, so you said something, anything, to draw us out and save the remainder."

The Queen leans closer to them, antenna questing. Even at their furthest extension they cannot touch any of the humans, though. "What is this? What have you brought me, heroes?"

Spots, smiling. "I'm a mother. Just like you."

The silence is like a gasp.

Queen, almost whispering. "A mother. A human mother. Is it so?"

Spots reaches for her helmet. Claws grabs her wrist.

Spots. "Don't worry. The shields are still up and I'll put it right back on. I promise."

Reluctantly he lets her hand go. Spots thumbs the releases on her helmet and removes it, shaking her head to free the tiny curls plastered to her temples by her sweat.

Spots. "There. Do you smell now?"

Queen, eager. "Oh! Oh, it is so different. So . . . new. And yet, so familiar. I had no idea it would be so . . . familiar."

Spots smiles and puts her helmet back on.

Queen. "But you . . . you only have a few children. Is that so? That is so, isn't it? You are mammals."

Spots. "That's right. Most of us only have one or two. It's rare to have a lot more than that these days, though there are families with four, five, seven children."

Queen, breathless. "Does it hurt you as much as it does me?"

167. EMPATHY

A heartbeat pause.

Spots, faint smile. "Which part?"

Queen, rearing back. "You . . . so you . . . you understand."

Spots. "Maybe. Maybe you can explain. I've always found it's better to be plain than to assume things."

Queen. "Yes . . . yes, you're right." *She presses her top two hands together, head lowering until it rests against them.* "You . . . all of you have names, don't you?" *She looks up. Points in turn.* "Claws. And Fang. And Fang2. And . . . you are Hairball? You then are Whiskers. And Spots."

Spots. "Those aren't our real names. But yes, we answer to those."

Queen, laughing. "So rich you are! You have so many names you can use more than one! But my children . . . my children will never have names. I don't have a name. We have never been given names, not since our very first Queen hatched. We were made . . . you knew that, yes? By those you name the Violinists?"

The team's in-drawn breath is palpable; not all of them were privy to this news.

Spots. "We . . . suspected, yes."

Queen. "They made us to be their killers. Because life is dangerous. Because there is always something to be defended against. But they designed us too well, and it was too easy for us to reproduce. And then . . . they tried to kill us. To erase their error. Do human parents also hate their children? Do your parents hate you, heroes?"

Hairball, standing behind Spots. "My parents don't hate me, but they were disappointed in me."

Queen, leaning toward him. "Does it hurt you?"

Hairball is standing without tension but his voice is quiet with sorrow. "Yes. They still love me. I still love them. But this thing will always be between us. I think."

Queen. "It hurts me, Hairball. That our . . . parents . . . are trying to kill us. And I was not supposed to be able to hurt." *She leans back.* "But they failed to erase us. Those Violinists who were aggressive enough to fight us joined us instead, knowing that when we were eliminated, they would be the next to go. We would have won, heroes. And then they found you. And we are too different, for you to wish to ally with us."

Claws. "You want to expand into our territory. It's kinda a zero-sum game there."

Spots the Space Marine: Defense of the Fiddler

Queen. "We expand because we must. Because we were created aggressive and with a need to breed."

Spots. "But you don't have to be that way. We've seen you evolving the soldiers sent against us. You could choose something else."

Queen. "I could. But then, would we still be who we are?"

Spots. "Yes. Everything changes that lives."

Queen, looking away. "This I have discovered." *She looks down. Dips into the mound surrounding her and lifts something that glitters and clicks.*

At the sight, both Fangs, Hairball and Whiskers lift their weapons, but Claws throws up a hand and Spots says, "NO."

The Queen is looking at a long chain of interlinked ID tags. Their ID tags, the tags of their dead. Avril. The Vermin. The lost of Company A. The dead from the recent battle.

168. TURNING POINT

As the Queen watches the amethyst light of her eyes glimmer off the tags, Claws signals to Spots. She glances at him. A red countdown appears on her HUD and he lifts his brows at her.

Spots's eyes twitch to the numbers, then she looks back at him and nods. Maybe she smiles a little, lopsided, sad.

Queen. "These . . . were on the bodies of your dead. They were heroes, also, yes?" *She looks up from them.* "We have no heroes. Even if I succeed in killing you all and consuming the memories of your Violinist, I will not be immortalized. I will not be heralded as the Queen who helped to win the war. But you . . . you will remember these men and women, who were merely soldiers. Won't you."

Spots. "We will. We issue those tags to everyone, so that we can identify them if it's hard to do so otherwise. And we bury those tags with them. And not a one of us will forget them."

Queen. "So even in death you care about a human's identity."

Spots. "Yes. We know no one lives there anymore, but we honor the temple that once housed the spirit. It was unique, just like the soul that animated it."

The Queen continues to tilt the chain, watching the ID tags as they bob down the chain. "Before I was dispatched here, I consumed your media. I do not know if other Queens have done so, though you make it easy, spilling so much of yourselves into the ether. But I did not understand it. It was loud and strange and nonsensical."

Spots. "And then something changed."

Claws, *containing his anger.* "You got a taste for us."

Queen. "Yes. Queens do not eat the Enemy. We don't know if you have traps in your head, the way we have. We don't know anything, so we err on the side of caution. A soldier is expendable, but not a Queen."

Spots. "But you did. And something changed."

Queen, *sounding mournful, soughing the words through her spiracles.* "It is not like with other Violinists, heroes. To eat the brain of one of our own . . . we get such an exact copy that it is as if we welcome another person into the house of our body. They are separate. Distinct. But consuming humans . . . there is no such ease. It is all murk, flashes of color and images and words and . . . and there was no separating it. It settled into me, out of reach, confusing. I . . . can't . . . tell it apart from me. And then, all the media I had consumed . . . it made sense." *She looks up, hands curling into fists around the chain.* "I know now what a hero is. I know how I can never be one. I know what I destroy."

Spots the Space Marine: Defense of the Fiddler

Then she opens her palms, stretches out her hands . . . holds out the tags. "Take them. I know what they mean to you. You should bring them back."

Claws. "That . . . sounds like you're going to let us go."

Queen, pausing, wondering. "It . . . does, doesn't it?"

169. MOTHER TO MOTHER

Long pause.

Fang, suspicious. "You'd do that? You'd let us go? Why?"

Queen, still holding out the tags. "I . . . don't know. Perhaps it is because I can never leave."

Claws. "You can't?"

Queen. "No . . ." *She gestures with one of her lower hands to the base of her truncated body.* "As you can see, I am . . . installed here. It is that way with the Queens who create soldiers. We give up our ability to move for a larger womb. We allow ourselves to be carried from place to place and affixed to do our work."

Fang, nearly spitting the words. "The work of killing us."

Queen. "And your work is . . . exactly what, Fang?"

Fang. "You started it."

Queen. "No. No, we had no notion you even existed before you appeared at the side of our makers." *She sighs out a breath.* "No. Do not lay that blame at our door. We did not start this."

Spots smiles. "Funny. I keep expecting music when you talk."

Queen. "That we were never endowed with . . . the music. Our parents considered it unnecessary to our purpose so they stripped it from our geneline . . . just as they took our will from us and made us their murderers." *She closes her gemmed eyes.* "But I . . . I have a will. And I can make a choice." *She offers the tags again.* "For you, Mother. From one mother to another. In the name of our children."

Spots glances at Claws, who nods. She walks up the mound, her shield parting from the larger bubble, and as she steps in front of Fang she makes a hand signal against her back. Fang's eyes narrow. She glances at Claws, who nods again, ever so slight.

Fang's thumb brushes against a switch on her rifle, rests there, tense.

Spots lifts her cupped palm. The Queen lowers the ID tags into it. They clatter as they gather, dull metal reflecting suit-light and the Queen's eye-glow. There are smudges of dried blood on them, darkening the letters.

Spots, soft. "You ate them."

Queen, just as soft. "I did."

Spots the Space Marine: Defense of the Fiddler

Spots looks up at her. "I know why. I know why you took the risk. I recognize the signs. You're spending yourself to win. You're making new shells so fast that you're cannibalizing yourself in your zeal. So you ate our brothers and sisters, to keep from dying. To keep going."

Queen, soft. "Yes."

Spots nods. "I'm sorry." *Her shield goes edged, and her voice.* "Mother Mary . . . forgive us both—**NOW FANG!**"

170. Lights Out

Spots lunges, redoubles. The shield sings as it rips toward the base of the mound. Fang's thumb finishes its arrested twitch, flipping the switch on her rifle as it rises. The dart strikes the Queen's eye, snuffing its light.

The Queen falls as the shield separates her from the mound. The stalk of her body falls over Spots's shoulder.

The chamber erupts into motion.

Claws, bounding up the mound. "COVER HER!"

Kitty—First Shield—rushes in on his heels, enfolding Spots and the Queen's body back into their bubble as the Kings and soldiers race toward them. There are so many of them they get in each other's way. Fang's quick shots take out the Kings at the entrance and then they are in the corridor, racing away from the column of crabs that guarded their arrival as they break loose.

Spots. "Here!" *Hairball grabs the thin, drooping body as she darts for the front of the formation, shield still edged.*

Fang2. "****! WHICH WAY!"

Claws. "Toward the base!"

They turn toward thoroughfares they avoided on the way in. Spots is at the vanguard, slicing through the forward cover of Claws's shield as the Fangs shoot past them; as her arm moves, the necklace of ID tags clatters. Again. Again. Again.

Hairball totes the Queen; he and Whiskers cover the side corridors as their shields deny the crabs rushing up their backs.

There are a lot of crabs rushing up their backs. Scrabbling at the shield wall with giant pincers. Pushing. Piling on each other.

Hairball, conversational. "We might not live through this."

Claws. "****in' belay that talk, Marine." *Pauses.* "We might not live through this, though."

Whiskers laughs, rough.

Fang2. "**** all, my power's down to ****ing nearly ****."

Fang, eyes locked on the next target, the next, the next. "You're not the only one."

Whiskers. "Extra power cell on my back's good if we could all use it."

Spots the Space Marine: Defense of the Fiddler

Claws. "****, ****, ****in' ****. If only Sam'd installed that ****in' power-share . . ."

Hairball. "How do you know he didn't?"

Claws, on a breath, like a prayer. "****." *He grabs his glove and starts pawing through the menu.* "Come on, Sam, come on, if the ****in' enemy can read our mind, how 'bout you . . ."

They are killing so many crabs that they have to push past the bodies to keep moving.

Spots, tense. "We need to go faster or they'll lock us up."

Fang2. "****! I'm down to fifteen ***ing percent! I do not want to ****ing DIE HERE! SCYYYYYYYYYYTHE WHERE ARE THE VIRRRRRRRRRGINS!"

443

171. Lateral Thinking

Fang, tense, distracted. "I'm down to twenty percent!"

Hairball. "Fifteen here." *Glances at the crabs shoving at the back of the bubble.* "Not going to be pretty—"

Claws, still checking menus. "****, ****!"

Fang2. "****! They are ****ing piling on us!"

Spots. "GOD!" *She rears back, holding her shield made flat and large as the crabs in front of them throw themselves on top of one another.*

Fang. "****!"

Spots's shield flickers once, twice—dies. Fang and Fang2 lunge to cover her fully with theirs, but the crabs smash into the intervening space.

It is a space created by their incomplete training. It is small. It is enough.

Fang hauls Spots back bodily. "****!"

Spots, staggering. "It's . . . okay, it's still attached." *She touches the puckered hole in her armor, over her thigh.*

Claws. "Is that—YES!"

A soft chime sounds, ludicrously polite. And then all their suits answer, and even more absurdly in a chord, each chime a different note. The team's shields stabilize at fifty percent, pulling on Whiskers's spare power cell.

Hairball. "Wow."

Claws, muttering. "****in' showoff musician bug." *Louder.* "Hold the bubble here a minute. How you doin' there, Spots?"

Spots. "Limping, but okay. I got ahead of myself, I'm sorry."

Fang2, staring at the wall of crabs. "****, we kinda got bigger problems."

Spots glances at the countdown that is still ticking in the corner of her HUD, pushed there by Claws.

Fang nods. "No way we're pushing through that."

Claws. "That's fine. We'll take a page from their playbook." *He jerks a thumb at the wall.*

Spots the Space Marine: Defense of the Fiddler

"How fast you think those shields can dig?"

172. Run

Whiskers. "Sharp edge, but shallow . . . dunno." *Taps the wall.* "They'll break through this faster than the spades, but the spades might be faster after."

Claws. "All right. You're the expert. Fang-prime, Fang2, you kill the crabs crammed on us." *He eyes the Queen, still resting on Hairball's shoulder.* "I'm pretty sure Queenie here's the only crab what speaks English, but they've all still got eyes and I don't want them knowin' what we're up to."

Fang. "Our pleasure, daimyo." *She lifts her weapon to target a crab looking down on them.* "Our pleasure."

As she and Fang2 execute their attackers, Claws continues. "Whiskers, you're our man. Make us a tunnel, lickety-split. We ain't got much time here."

Whiskers. "Sure thing, rice-o."

Fang, still working on her assignment. "Did you just say "lickety-split"?"

Claws. "Yeah, and?"

Fang. "Nothing."

Fang2 snickers.

Claws checks Hairball's burden meanwhile. "Not moved?" *he asks, quiet.*

Hairball. "Limp as a rag."

Claws touches the point of her face, looking at the ruined eye.

Hairball. "What we gonna do with her, boss?"

Claws. "**** if I know, Hairball."

Whiskers punches through the wall of the tunnel with the cutting edge of the shield, then starts digging. Hairball, Fang and Fang2 stand, waiting, tense. Spots sits with her back to the wall and closes her eyes.

Each. Minute. Passes. So. Slow—

—and so fast, so fast, the countdown running down, red numbers glowing, shield power levels falling.

Whiskers. "GOT IT!"

Fang2 jumps up with a little twist. "Whoo-hoo! BREAKTHROUGH!"

Fang laughs. "Never thought you'd say it about us, eh?"

Fang2. "Nope!"

Claws, looking in hole. "Anything on the other side?"

Whiskers. "Looks clear."

Claws. "All right, all in. I'll keep the shield up."

Fang. Fang2. Hairball, dragging his burden. Spots. Claws glances over his shoulder at the cupola of crabs. Then he ducks in, leaving the corpses to collapse behind him. Behind them rises a sound that none of them have heard before: a high, piercing ululation, terrible in its anger.

Claws. "And now we run. RUN! ****in' GO GO, GO NOW!"

173. ACTS

They run.

Fang is on point. Claws takes the rear. All around them, the shrill and terrible wail floods the corridors.

They run.

The Queen's body bounces on Hairball's shoulder.

They run.

The timer continues counting down,

. . . counting down—

Before them, from a cross-section, an eruption of crabs. Fang and Fang2 shoot . . .

. . . themselves . . .

. . . dry.

Fang. "What the ****??"

Fang2. "****!" *Shakes his fist.* "BOSS! COME THROUGH FOR US!"

A shot fires past his shoulder, shattering the eye of a crab. Spots looks past him. "You're in my way."

Fang2. "****, you can shoot?!"

Spots, growling. "I'd kick you if I could lift my leg higher than your knee."

Fang2. "Owwwww, ****, that's hard talk, Mom!"

Whiskers and Spots take the front now. They mow their way through the enemy, but more keep piling in front of them. Their shield reserve starts dropping in chunks. Claws looks from that number to the other and breathes out. Shakes out his shoulders.

Claws, voice quiet. "Steady on."

Fang glances at him, meets his eyes. The skin around hers tightens, but neither of them say anything.

Team Kitty—First Shield—butchers the enemy, but they are outnumbered and their enemy willing to sacrifice themselves just to block them. They climb over corpses, thrust past them.

Spots the Space Marine: Defense of the Fiddler

Soon there is no ammunition left. Spots leads with her shield edge, though her face has gone sweaty and pale. Every cut she makes is accompanied by the singing clatter of the tags of the dead.

They are reduced to purpose. Effort. Motion. Instinct. No more thought: only acts. A meditation of violence.

Their suits chime out a minor chord, warning.

Clatter of tags.

Harsh breathing.

Prayer.

174. End Times

The fight . . .

. . . goes on and—

—then there is a shrill sound from all their suits—

—Spots's shield cuts out, mid-swipe.

Stop.

They look at the crabs. The crabs pause.

This lacuna lasts—

—forever

heartbeat

And then the heads of two of their attackers explode. Spots scrambles backwards. Her leg fails and she skids across the hard ground as her attacker lunges for her.

"WALKER!"

Claws looks up, frenzied. Something black gleams as it flies toward him.

It is not the gorgeous death-move that Scythe would have executed. But Claws leaps over Spots, bashes the crab in the head with the saya, draws his sergeant's sword and slices off the attacker's head.

In front of them, nothing but corpses: corpses . . . and Peaches, Gunny and the remaining Marines.

Peaches, nodding at the sword. "You left that behind."

Claws. "****! What are you doin' here?"

Peaches, grinning lopsidedly. "They retreated. Couldn't resist. Now we run."

Claws. "**** yes ma'am yes!" *To the squad.* "ALL RIGHT LET'S SEE THAT THREE-****IN'-MINUTE MILE!"

He grabs up Spots. "Come on, Mom. You and me together."

Spots, smiling. "Just like old times in the Warren."

Spots the Space Marine: Defense of the Fiddler

Behind them the wail of their attackers rises as they sprint for the base. "Just like."

They run, then. Hairball with the Queen. Whiskers at his side. The two Fangs in the middle, and Claws and Spots at the rear. The remains of their company run with them. They will not be alone at the final moment. They were not abandoned. It feels right, to be surrounded by their own when the bomb blows. The ghosts of their dead keep pace. This is their revenge.

Claws laughs as the red counter counts down.

..04

Pounding down the corridor.

..03

Straight shot now—

..02

— to the broken door to the airlock . . .

..01

Fang2, exultant. "**** YEAAAAAAAAAAAAAH!"

451

175. What Were You Thinking

They would ask later, and it would become The Question, their question. Not "where were you," because they were all there. They shared that: it was their solidarity, their context. But rather this: "What were you thinking when The Bomb went off?"

Whiskers. "That it was a ****ing grand explosion."

Fang2. "Of my grandmother bringing me congee while playing computer games. Me, I mean, I was playing games. Not her. She was bringing me food, she always brought me food . . . like a thousand games I must have played and she was always there. I mean, just a flash of that, like a cut scene."

Hairball. "That I'd better not drop the Queen."

Fang. "I wasn't thinking at all. Just . . . feeling . . ." *Deep breath.* "Alive. Fierce. Like we'd won. God, it felt good."

Peaches. "That the moment it died down, that I had to lead them back out and clean up the ones it didn't get. Whether it would be safe." *Pause.* "My heart was pounding pretty hard."

Gunny, with a laugh. "That I was too ****ing old to die like a new kid fresh off the transport."

Claws. "That I had Holden's sword in my hands, and that it felt right." *Laughs, self-conscious.* "God that sounds stupid."

Spots, quiet. "Of my children."

They felt the bomb, more than saw it, a great racking in the frame of the base. The metal sheeting on the floor rattling. The doors clattering in their pockets. The rumble of falling debris. It feels like forever. It takes only moments. These two impressions live together without contradiction.

. . . then it is done.

Peaches lifts her head. "All right! Let's go mop up!"

A great shout answers her on all the remaining channels. Claws staggers to his feet.

Peaches. "Not you, Walker—"

Claws, protesting. "Ma'am, we're fine—"

Spots the Space Marine: Defense of the Fiddler

Peaches cuts him off with a jerk of her hand and points into the halls. "AS I WAS SAYING, Mister . . . go get a refill from the Armory. Then get your ***es back here."

Claws. "Ma'am, yes ma'am!"

Peaches. "Better. Move it!"

First Shield starts off. Or tries. Spots takes one step and falls. Whiskers catches her arm before she hits the ground.

Claws. "Crap." *He puts his shoulder up under her arm.* "You're for Sickbay. If there's anythin' left of it." *He points.* "Fang, you got the team 'til I get back. Stay nasty."

Fang. "I will, Riceboy."

Claws, exasperated. "****, how did 'daimyo' turn into 'riceboy'? That's even worse than 'rice lord.'"

Hairball, hefting the Queen back onto his shoulder. "Um, Boss? What do I do with her?"

Claws frowns. "Uh, good question." *Switches channels.* "Ma'am?"

Peaches. "What is it, Walker?"

Claws. "We got a prisoner. Where should we take her?"

176. Prisoner

Peaches. "..."

Peaches. "Say again, Corporal."

Claws. "We took the Queen prisoner, ma'am."

Peaches, off channel, to herself. "**** ...! I don't know what's secure anymore." *On channel.* "The base is badly damaged. Find the first location you can secure her and do it."

Claws. "Yes, ma'am." *Grabs the sword with his free hand and nods to Hairball.* "Let's go."

Spots, as they head for Sickbay. "You can leave her with me."

Claws. "Lying next to an invalid's not my idea of secure, Mom."

Spots. "I've got a knife."

Claws looks at the corridors as they pass with a growing frown at their state. There is debris everywhere. Some of the halls are dead: emergency lights, no computer access. "If they put you under—"

Spots. "They're not going to put me under for the leg."

Claws. "How do you know?"

Spots. "Look at the base, Travis. No surgeon's going to want to work under general in these conditions unless it can't be avoided."

Claws. "Sickbay's got an auxiliary power sup..." *He stops as they reach Sickbay. The walls on three different sides are in ruins. So many of the stationary beds have been destroyed that the less serious cases have been remanded to a fleet of folding cots.*

Claws. "Well, hell."

Corpsman, tired, pointing. "Ambulatory patients over there."

Spots, looking at Claws. "I'll watch her."

Claws, making a face. "Only if we tie her up first."

Spots. "That's fine."

Spots lowers herself onto one of the cots, mounding the blanket under her knee. Hairball looks around, then shrugs and sets the Queen down on the cot beside her.

Spots the Space Marine: Defense of the Fiddler

Claws, to the corpsman. "Hey, you got duct tape?"

Corpsman, with the blank stare of the utterly exhausted. "What? No."

Spots. "Surgical tape?"

Corpsman. "Uh, yeah. Hang on." *He returns with a roll, handing it to Claws. He doesn't stay to watch Claws start to wind it around the arms of the Queen, trapping her hands behind her torso.*

Hairball. "Think she'll live?"

Claws. "Guess we'll find out." *He straightens, sword in hand.* "Stay on top of it, Guitart."

Spots, meeting his eyes. "Will do, boss."

Claws flushes. Nods. "Come on, Hairball."

Spots draws her knife and settles on the cot, eyes on the Queen. After a moment, she fishes under her armor's gorget for a necklace chain and pulls forth her little ring rosary. She hooks her finger through it.

She doesn't use it.

Warren. Peaches's company is clearing the halls. The crabs are dead, fleeing or seem paralyzed. The few that fight do so mechanically and are easily cut down.

Claws, rejoining First Shield. "Miss me?"

Fang snorts. "This is cake." *Kicks over a corpse.* "They're just folding up and dying."

Whiskers. "Just like old times in the Warren. Line 'em up, shoot 'em down, count coup in the armory."

Fang2, sighing. "Those were ****ing good days."

Fang, quietly to Claws. "Think we dodged the bullet."

Claws. "One of them, anyway."

177. CLEAN-UP

The teams scour the Warren, and there is a terrible satisfaction in their killing. Everywhere their boots strike the gridded floor, their enemies flee before them or freeze and are cut down. As they press on they leave mounds of corpses, kicked out of their way with a casual viciousness.

The crabs have attempted their territory. The Marines reclaim it, and stake that claim with corpses.

Hairball, thoughtful. "Do you guess we gave them a morale problem? You know, by taking the Queen."

Fang, shooting a crab in the back of the head. "I don't think crabs have morale."

Hairball. "Our Fiddler does."

Claws. "Yeah, but he's got a brain designed for it. These things are robots."

Fang2. "So why're they acting like this?"

Whiskers. "Maybe the Queen was telling them what to do, and without her they can't figure it out."

Claws. "Closest we'll get to an explanation, I'm bettin'." *He looks back the way they came.* "Looks like our sector's clear."

As Claws reports in, Fang2 shakes his head. "****. A life without crabs. What the **** are we gonna do all day now that we ****ing nuked them to paste?"

Hairball. "I think I'll read a book."

Whiskers. "He means 'look at porn.'"

Hairball. "Yeah. That."

Fang snorts.

Fang2. "What, Ice Maiden doesn't look at porn?"

Fang. "Not yours. I'd look at Hairball's though."

Hairball grins. "That'd be fun."

Fang. "I like a nice *** on my men, how about you?"

Hairball. "I think you'll like what I got."

Spots the Space Marine: Defense of the Fiddler

Fang pumps a fist as they head back down the hall. "**** yeah! I was getting bored of my stash."

Fang2, trailing them. "****!"

Whiskers grins and claps him on the shoulder. "Don't worry, Princess. I'll share mine with you. I think you're man enough to handle it."

Fang2 to Claws, who has been listening. "What, no comment?"

Claws. "On this? Abso-****in'-lutely not."

———————————————

Base, Armory. Men and women are shucking off their suits as Peaches racks her helmet. Once she's stripped down to her utility uniform, she moves among her people, touching a shoulder here, grasping an arm there. She meets their eyes, tells them they did a good job. Wherever she goes, she leaves a palpable sense of pride and pleasure.

Gunny joins her outside the room. She heads for her office, navigating the ruined halls with a distracted air.

Peaches. "So, this is not a situation I think they ever covered at Quantico."

Gunny. "Ma'am, which part?"

Peaches glances at him, grinning crookedly. "Well, let me see. I'm a single second lieutenant in charge of what was originally two companies and now is . . . barely a platoon, at the ***-end of nowhere, with no support. I've lost—" *she pauses, takes in a deep breath through her nostrils,* "—a lot of my people, including my very temporary commanding officer. I know **** I absolutely am much too junior to know. I've got one enemy laboratory—nuked—and now a . . . I guess a high-level prisoner. A high-level prisoner I can't remand to anyone, because not only am I the ranking officer in town, but all our intel people are dead."

Gunny. "That sounds about the size of it, ma'am."

Peaches sighs. "Well, hell. If it's not too morale-affecting for me to ask, Gunny . . . what the **** do I do now?"

Gunny, arms folded behind his back as he follows her. "Now, ma'am? I believe you're about to determine the status of our foreign ally. And then possibly have a look at the security arrangements for the prisoner's cell."

Peaches. "Right. Of course. What would I do without you, Gunny?" *And laughs.*

Gunny. "You're doing fine, ma'am. The ship'll be here in a week."

Part 3: Endgame ● M. C. A. Hogarth

Peaches. "God! A week! Wasn't it a week several years ago? Because that's what it feels like."

Gunny. "It's been a long day."

Peaches. "God could have made the world in a day as long as we've had, Gunny." She shakes her head. "Right. Samuel-Colt."

178. THE TEAM

Backtrack. First Shield is stripping down in the armory. As they finish up:

Fang. "Mama's armor's here."

Claws. "Reckon Sickbay sent it back, they musta stripped her to look at the leg."

Fang2. "Was it bad?"

Claws. "Dunno. Let's go find out."

They head down the corridor to Sickbay. There is no talking and no one looks at one another . . . but there is an easy solidarity in their silence. When they walk, it is in an unintentional diamond formation.

Sickbay. The corpsman nods toward the cots. Spots is in the same one Claws left her in, now wearing her PT uniform. Her leg is wrapped in compression bandages. Claws thought she looked like a porcelain doll when she first arrived to the base, but somehow she looks paler now, and her skin gleams at her jaws and temples with clammy sweat. Nevertheless, she still has her knife drawn, resting on her abdomen . . . and on the cot next to her the unconscious Queen abides.

Whiskers, sitting next to Spots. "You don't look so good, Momma."

Spots, wan but smiling. "It was more serious than it looked. Turns out armor's pretty good at keeping legs from exploding."

Claws sits on the cot's corner. "They shoulda left it on then."

Fang2, looking past Whisker's elbow. "Yeah, what kind of place they running here?" *Spots laughs and he continues,* "I'm sorry I don't have any coconut bars for you."

Whiskers. "Or pork chops."

Claws. "Wasn't it ice cream she brought? Brownies? Crap, I forget."

Whiskers. "It's been a while."

Claws. "It's been effin' forever."

They all laugh.

Fang. "Seriously, Mama, what did they tell you?"

Fang2, quieter. "You going to keep the leg?"

Spots. "Yeah, but I'll need months of physical therapy. Apparently armor's good at keeping legs from exploding, but it's not so good at keeping you off them when running on them would make things worse."

Claws. "Fancy that."

Fang. "Sounds like they'll be shipping you back on the next bus."

Spots, unhappy. "Yeah."

Silence then.

Spots. "But you know, if any of you could find *any* chocolate around here, that would cheer me up a lot . . ."

Fang. "There used to be chocolate protein bars . . ."

Fang2. "I bet I know where they are!"

Whiskers, looking around. "Where they were, anyway."

Fang2. "We'll get you some."

Spots. "Thanks."

460

179. THEME

Spots. "Hey, Fang. Stay a moment?"

Fang. "Sure, Mama." *She sits on the edge of the cot.*

Fang2, Whiskers and Hairball are already on their way to the door. Claws hesitates and Spots makes a gentle shooing motion. He walks some distance away and puts his back to one of the remaining walls, crossing his legs at the ankle and resting his hands behind his back.

Spots, looking back at Fang. "So. You didn't think much of me when I got here."

Fang, embarrassed. "Uh, well . . . you were a paper-pusher. You know how that goes. It wasn't personal, just . . ."

Spots chuckles. "I know. I wasn't exactly in the best shape when I arrived."

Fang. "You shaped up quick, though."

Spots. "I like to think so."

Fang. "Seriously. You kick real ***."

Spots. "Not too bad for a middle-aged mom, huh?"

Fang. "If thirty is middle-aged, then we're losing this war, Mama." *She pats Spots's shoulder.* "You're not all dried up yet."

Spots nods. "I'm glad you think so. I wasn't sure myself when I arrived that I'd be able to cut it."

Fang. "You serious?"

Spots nods. "Like you said. I'd been working a desk for years. And not even full-time! And then they put me in Armor?" *She shakes her head.* "I thought I'd fail you all."

Fang. "Well, you didn't. You're one hell of a warrior, Mama, and I'm proud you're on our team."

Spots nods. "I'm glad you think so, Nicola." *Meets her eyes directly.* "Stop taking them."

Fang's nostrils flare and her jaw muscles clench.

Spots. "If I can do it without stop-thats, so can you."

Fang. "Mama—"

Spots. "Nicola, you and Travis, you're going to go far. You're too good not to, and you're about to ride something big, I know it, I *feel* it," *touching her breastbone.* "Here. And when you do, when you rank up, you're going to have all these young girls coming into the service behind you, looking up to you. Do you really want the message they take away to be, 'you can't hack it as a warrior unless you fake it?' Do you want them to feel like they're not good enough on their own . . . without hormone replacements, without drugs? What kind of thing is that to tell them?"

Fang draws back, paling beneath her dark skin.

Spots takes her hand, squeezes it. "I know why you did it. But it's time to stop. You've got nothing left to prove except that you're good enough to make it without a crutch."

Fang. "Aw, ****. This is low."

Spots. "Isn't it true, though?"

Fang, rubbing her eye with her free hand. "Yeah. I guess it is."

Spots pulls her down and gives her a hug. Fang starts out stiff, then relaxes into it, rests her head on the other woman's shoulder.

Spots, whispering in her ear. "Go make your mom proud of you . . . the way I am."

On the other side of Spots's shoulder, Fang closes her wet eyes.

They part. Fang rises. Her voice is a little husky. "You get better now, Mama."

"I will."

Fang leaves, passing Claws without seeing him. He watches her go, then saunters back to Spots's cot and takes Fang's place on its edge.

Claws. "That was well done of you."

Spots, sharp. "You weren't supposed to be listening."

Claws. "What can I say. I got the ears of a hare."

Spots. "Or an ***."

180. The Wolf

Claws. "Ouch, that stung."

Spots, eyeing him. "You don't seem very wounded."

Claws. "I earned that one. Figured I'd take it like a—"

Spots, dry. "I hope you're not about to say 'man'."

Claws. "—Marine. Oorah."

Spots. "Good save."

Claws, grinning. "Thank you, ma'am, I do try."

She studies his face until the silence starts to make him fidget. Then speaks. "So, exorcise your demons?"

Claws. "What me? Never."

She smiles. "Seriously."

Claws rubs the heel of his hand over his knee. "Dunno if that's a fair question, mom. Who ever manages that? Completely?"

Spots. "You'd be surprised."

Claws. "Maybe so, maybe so."

Spots. "But you're moving on, right?"

Claws glances at her, then back at his hands, Sickbay. "Yeah. Guess I will." *Looks at her again.* "You don't know the story, do you?"

Spots. "No. But I don't need to." *At his look, lifts her hands.* "Not because I figured it out through mother-telepathy, like you're always accusing me. Just, you don't have to tell me."

Claws, quieter. "You ever think of what it would do to your husband, if you died out here?"

Heartbeat.

Spots. "All the time."

Claws. "And you're still out here."

Spots looks away this time.

Claws. "So how come you're here?"

Spots. "I couldn't not be." *Taps her heart.* "In here, there's someone who couldn't watch this fight and not join in."

Claws. "For your kids?"

Spots. "For every kid. And for myself. Because there's nothing in me that knows how to cower, Travis. This is my fight because I can fight it. So I'm here, for the people who can't."

Claws. "And for yourself."

Spots. "And for me. Because if I didn't do this, I would be crazy, like a wolf chewing at the bars of a cage."

Claws. "A big . . . mama . . . wolf."

Spots smiles. "Or a spotted cat, I guess." *More serious.* "I'd be no good as a mother if I kept that animal in the cage. You become a parent, you don't stop being what you are. You just have to be the *best* thing you are that you can be."

Claws. ". . ."

Claws. "I'll remember that." *Rising.* "I'll let you rest. You get better, okay?"

Spots. "I will. Travis . . . you won't tell on Nicola, will you?"

Claws grins. "Naw. I'm not an officer yet." *Grips her hand.* "Hey, Magda?"

Spots. "Yes?"

Claws. "I got your back. You know that. I'll take care of you."

Spots. "I know you will. You have since the beginning."

181. RAIDERS

Mess Hall, Naval. This room is entirely intact and relatively clean of debris, save for a stack of broken chairs and tables in one corner. Only two tables remain in a room meant for a dozen.

These two tables look very forlorn.

Fang2, Whiskers and Hairball are looking through one of the pantries behind the counter.

Whiskers. "I can't believe we're raiding the Seabees' kitchen."

Fang2. "We're just borrowing a protein bar."

Hairball picks up a canister of flour, looks inside. "They actually have . . . uh, raw materials."

Whiskers. "Ingredients?" *He glances in the canister.* "Well, ****, we could make cookies, if any of us knew how."

Fang2. "We could ask Spots but then it kinda wouldn't be a surprise." *He opens another door and springs back.* "****!"

Samuel-Colt is standing in this pantry like an Egyptian mummy in a coffin, knife in hand and both upper arms crossed over his torso. He bows a rising interrogative note without otherwise moving. "Is it safe to come out?"

465

Fang2. "****! You ****ing scared me, man."

Hairball. "It's safe, Samuel-Colt."

Fang2, with relish. "We set off the bomb and it worked like a ****ing charm!"

Samuel-Colt with a rippling melody. "That is a relief." *He steps out of the pantry and closes the door behind him, then looks at the three. It says something that Team Kitty knows immediately what he's looking for despite the alien eyes and body language.*

Fang2. "Don't worry, they're alive."

Whiskers nods. "Spots took a hit, but she'll be fine."

Hairball. "She's in Sickbay."

Samuel-Colt exhales through his spiracles, like a low wind sighing. "We are glad to hear this. We will go see her."

Fang2. "Yeah, do that, she'd like that. And hey, you find any chocolate in there while you were hiding?"

Samuel-Colt. "We fear we did not look."

Fang2. "Right." *To Whiskers and Hairball,* "Well, what are you waiting for? There are shelves we haven't checked."

Samuel-Colt leaves and the team resumes their search. There are mutters about powdered milk and cans of parmesan cheese (also powdered) and eggs (powdered too). When Fang2 hears someone behind him, he says, "Why the ****ing hell is everything powdered?"

Gunny. "Maybe so privates too young to keep an eye on their escape routes can gum it down. Since they're obviously not ready for real food."

All three of them turn and come to abrupt attention at the sight of Peaches, hovering behind Gunny's shoulder.

Peaches. "And what precisely are you all doing here?"

Fang2, turning bright red. "Uh . . . ma'am, it's not what it looks like—"

Peaches, hiding her amusement. "I'm sure it's exactly what it looks like. But go on, explain."

Hairball. "We were looking for something to cheer up Spo—ah, Private Guitart."

Fang2. "A little something. Honest."

Peaches. "A little something."

Whiskers. "Like a cookie. Or a protein bar."

Hairball, low. "Or a gigantic cake."

Peaches's face goes through an amazing contortion. When her mouth stops twitching, she continues. "Right. And while you were all raiding the galley, did you happen to see—"

Fang2. "He went that way, ma'am. To Sickbay, to see Spots."

Peaches. "Right." *She turns and heads back to the door, Gunny in tow. Halfway there, she stops and adds,* "Carry on." *The door closes behind them.*

Silence.

Whiskers. "Well, ****. Talk about dodging the bullet."

Fang2. "What can I say. I am MAGIC."

182. Audacity

Corridor. Claws is heading up it, away from Sickbay, and stops at the sight of Samuel-Colt, heading down it, toward Sickbay.

Claws, reaching for his arm. "Sam! ****, you're in one piece."

Samuel-Colt, grasping Claws's hand. "We are. The lieutenant found us a superlative hiding place, since she could not set aside a detail to guard us."

Claws. "That musta been nerve-wrackin'. You goin' to see Spots?"

Samuel-Colt. "Exactly so. The others told me she has been wounded?"

Claws. "Yeah, they'll have to send her home. Listen, Sam, there's somethin' you gotta know before you walk in there—"

Peaches, turning the far bend with Gunny behind her. "Ah, Corporal. Excellent, you've saved me the trouble of looking for you."

Claws comes to attention as Peaches joins them.

Peaches. "And Samuel-Colt also. The other man I wanted to see."

Samuel-Colt, amused little trill. "For some values of 'man'."

A pause. Then she laughs. "Um. Yes. I hear you're going to Sickbay? Let's keep going, we can talk on the way." *As they walk.* "So it looks like the plan worked."

Samuel-Colt. "We had heard as much, though without detail. Did you destroy the nursery?"

Claws. "We planted the bomb there, so, yeah, I'm guessin' no one's gonna be usin' it for a while."

Samuel-Colt glances at him, bowing a sharp rising note. "You actually entered the nursery? Without alerting the Queen?"

Claws. "Um, yeah. About that . . ."

The doors to Sickbay open. Samuel-Colt stops at the threshold as if struck. And then he bows a jangled shriek so discordant everyone in the area glances toward the door.

Samuel-Colt, shocked. "What have you done!"

Claws, flushing. "Uh, as I was about to say . . . Spots kinda—well no, I said it was okay, so it was partly my decision, even if she came up with the idea—"

Samuel-Colt, jeweled eyes glittering as he bends closer. "**Answer me.**"

Claws, meeting his eyes with great composure. "We kinda made off with the Queen."

Peaches, stunned. "And put her in Sickbay? I told you to find a secure location for her, Corporal!"

Claws. "Ma'am! The base isn't exactly brimmin' with secure places anymore!" *At her apoplectic look, he finishes:* "I put her under guard, ma'am. Guitart's been watchin' her."

Peaches. "You put a casualty in charge of guarding a high profile prisoner? In a room full of wounded!"

Claws. "****, ma'am, nothin's gonna come between Spots and that bug. And that bug's not gettin' past her either, bad leg or not."

Samuel-Colt brushes past both of them and into the room.

Peaches, severe. "We'll talk about this later, Mister Walker."

Claws, chagrined. "Ma'am, yes ma'am."

183. MOTHERLOVE

Samuel-Colt heads unerringly for the Queen, though she is not visible from the door. He comes to an abrupt halt at her cot, looking down at her.

Spots, watching him. "A gift for you, Samuel-Colt."

As Peaches, Gunny and Claws come up behind him, Samuel-Colt exclaims, "This is a strange notion of gift, Mother-soldier!"

Spots. "Is it?"

Peaches. "Private. I hear you're responsible for this . . . situation."

Spots. "Ma'am, yes. Though Corporal Walker gave me the okay."

Peaches. "She hasn't woken up yet?"

Samuel-Colt, harsh note drawn across his vestigial arms. "She will not."

"What?"

Samuel-Colt reaches down slowly, brushes his fingers against the amputated torso. "The Enemy engineered its field unit Queens to fit into their bases. Removing them from the base . . . deactivates them."

Claws. "Deactivate like 'fancy word for dead'? Or deactivate like 'animals hibernatin'' '?"

Samuel-Colt. "Like hibernation, yes. They require the additional neural matter installed in the architecture."

Peaches. "Wait, you're telling me she was actually a part of . . . the floor? The walls?"

Samuel-Colt, low bowed note. "Just so. The installation allows them to generate more eggs than a normal Queen."

Peaches. "So she's never going to wake up."

Samuel-Colt. "No. It is like a coma, perhaps."

Peaches. "Well, hell. There goes our chance to interrogate her. What are we going to do with her?"

Spots looks at Samuel-Colt. "It makes you uncomfortable, doesn't it? Standing there."

Samuel-Colt, low note. "She is the Enemy, but she is still a Queen, and I am still a King."

Spots. "Come here, sit next to me."

The Violinist walks around the end of her cot and settles at her side. She takes his hand and pulls him a little closer, until they are hip to hip.

Spots, offering her palm. "Better?"

Samuel-Colt draws in a long breath, a sound like a breeze. "Yes. But you smell very pained, Mother."

Peaches. "Private—"

Spots meets her eyes. "We can't use her, Lieutenant. And I didn't bring her back for us." *She looks directly at Samuel-Colt.* "I brought her back for you."

Samuel-Colt, sharp note, rising. "Pardon, Mother?"

Spots's voice has gone very low, and very intent. "You are going to take her back, Samuel-Colt, and put her thoughts in the body of a King, where she can never have children again. Make her prove her aggression was biological. Make her work toward the peace she claimed she wanted."

Claws. "****, Magda!"

Spots. "That will be her punishment, and her chance at redemption. We *will* win this war. Make her one of our instruments." *She draws in a deep breath and leans forward, pale and sweating.* "A mother tells you this, Samuel-Colt. Take her home. Make her ours."

Samuel-Colt, stunned silent by the pheromone-enhanced command. "You would have us enslave her."

Spots. "It's our children or hers. I choose ours. No matter what has to be done to end it."

Peaches. "Private! You can't dispense with enemy prisoners!"

Gunny, quiet. "That's not a prisoner, ma'am. That's a body."

Surprised, Peaches turns to him. "Gunny? But we could dissect it—"

Gunny. "And learn what, ma'am? How crabs make cyborg Queens? Another piece of biological trivia we can't use? If the private's suggestion works, then our allies will have the prisoner we hoped to interrogate."

Claws. "If her head ain't booby-trapped!"

Samuel-Colt, low. "It won't be."

Peaches. "What? Why not?"

Samuel-Colt. "Because she is an installed Queen. If her primary brain was trapped, the neural network in the base would trip it during installation."

A pause.

Peaches. "I don't know if I can let you do this—"

Samuel-Colt. "We are afraid you must, Lieutenant-Savannah-Bonnet. Forgive us. You are only a lieutenant, but she is a mother."

Claws. "A ****ing bloodthirsty mother!"

Samuel-Colt. "So are they all, Peer."

184. WONDERFUL WORLD

Peaches. "Well, if you're sure she's not going to wake up—"

Samuel-Colt, drawing out a long note. "It would be improbable."

Peaches, eyes narrowed. "Improbable? Not impossible?"

Samuel-Colt. "Few things are impossible, Lieutenant-Savannah-Bonnet. But as they say, it is close enough as makes no difference."

Peaches sighs. "We'll tie her down in the morgue. Under guard. No use leaving her here to distract everyone. Gunny?"

Gunny. "On it, ma'am."

As he arranges for the transport, Peaches says to Claws, "I want to see you in my office in two hours, Walker."

"Yes, ma'am."

She nods and leaves. A few minutes later, the Queen does also, born over the shoulder of a Marine who follows Gunny out into the hall. Samuel-Colt, Claws and Spots all watch them go. Then Claws draws in a deep breath.

Claws. "Guess I'm in the doghouse."

Spots, smiling. "It won't last."

Claws. "Hopefully. Well, got me some things to put in order in case the LT tells me to commit hara-kari. See you two later."

Spots. "Travis . . ."

He glances at her over his shoulder, and what he sees in her eyes makes him turn around.

Spots, quiet, but with triumph. "You see? I take care of you too. All of you."

Claws's shoulders tighten, as if the words have struck him physically. He nods. "Yeah. Yeah, I see that."

Spots nods, satisfied, and turns her attention to Samuel-Colt. Claws watches the two of them a moment, then leaves with a set expression.

Spots. "So, Samuel-Colt. No more dancing for a while, I'm afraid."

Samuel-Colt, with a gentle rising arpeggio. "No, Mother."

Spots the Space Marine: Defense of the Fiddler

Spots, with some remorse. "I'm sorry—"

He lifts one long hand. "Do not apologize, Mother. The lieutenant's escort was correct: your plan has potential."

Spots. "Do you think . . . I mean . . . it might hurt someone. She might turn on us."

Samuel-Colt. "Possibly. A blank will be bred for the project, so we will not risk any of our own people to make the attempt to . . . convert . . . her. And she will be watched from the moment she emerges, so her opportunities for betrayal will be limited."

Spots. "I really didn't want to . . . to force you like that. I wouldn't have, but I knew you'd probably have to argue her going to the Violinists and I wanted you to have the mental back-up of having the command. I thought it would help. Was I right?"

Samuel-Colt, folding a hand gently over her wrist. "You were, and it was a kindness."

Spots exhales. "I'm so glad. I hate doing things like that."

Samuel-Colt, amused trill. "Telling others what to do? You seem competent at it."

Spots. "I get a lot of practice. But it's definitely my least favorite part of parenting."

Samuel-Colt, canting his head. "What is your favorite part?"

Spots. "Knowing that there are two new human beings in the world, and that they get to love and live and learn all the wonderful things about life."

Samuel-Colt. "Even if the world is not always wonderful?"

Spots. "The bad comes with the good. If you can't have one without the other, wouldn't you rather still take something over nothing?"

Samuel-Colt, looking at the empty cot that once held the Queen. "I suspect that answer is a very individual one."

185. All of Them

Corridor outside Sickbay. Claws pauses, draws in a deep breath. Resumes walking . . .

. . . not to the barracks. But to the training center. There he stops and looks at it, from end to end, as if seeing memories rather than the actual place.

There are a lot of memories to be seen.

He advances finally to the wall computers there and pulls a chair over. Fingers move quickly over the interface. The cam feeds from several suits start playing, the elapsed time flickering in the corner as it races on, double-pace. He stops one of them on Spots mid-lunge, shield just beginning to light. Marks it, starts the reel going again, and clips it a few seconds later.

He does it again on another reel, Spots beneath the shield, covering them.

Claws, muttering. "I'm sorry, Mom."

Another clip now, Spots scything through a crab. This drifts through a filmy segue to an image of Spots with her little girl in her arms, her son leaning against her hip.

Claws. "I know you think this is your fight. But those kids need you more . . ."

The dissolve fades to Spots in a gymnasium facing a line of new Marines, young and focused. She is talking . . . points to the shield generator on her arm. Demonstrates its cutting edge against a foam target.

Claws. ". . . all of them."

He resumes sorting through the footage, selecting the ones where Spots is using the shield in non-standard ways, going back weeks, even drawing in the training center's camera saves. He's still there when the door slides open.

Fang. "Well, ****. I didn't think anyone would be here."

Spots the Space Marine: Defense of the Fiddler

186. Heart-to-Heart

Claws, rising. "I can clear out if you need me to . . . ?"

Fang, advancing and having a look at the wall screen. "What you up to? Performance reviews?"

Claws, sinking back down onto his chair. "Naw. Providin' for Spots's future." *At her quizzical glance.* "I'm gonna see if Bonnet'll rec her for training duty. Someone's gotta teach the kids the new shield doctrine."

Fang starts laughing. "Spots the DI. I'm not seeing it."

Claws grins. "Yeah, kinda a stretch if you say it that way. But naw, I think it'll be more like she's the reward for gettin' through Basic without dyin'. The DIs'll pulp 'em up for her, get them all soft and chewy so by the time they get to her they'll be ready to listen to anythin'."

Fang. "Sounds like a cushy job."

Claws. "Yeah, well . . . who else is gonna do it?"

Fang grins. "Guess when you put it that way . . ."

Claws. "So should I . . . ?"

Fang, uncomfortable. "Nah. I just wanted to take out some frustrations on a target."

Claws. "This about that little talk Spots and you had?"

Fang eyes him. For a long moment. Then: "How much of that did you hear?"

Claws. "Maybe . . . all of it?" *At her glare,* "You weren't exactly keepin' your voices down."

Fang scowls. Folds her arms and looks away. He watches her until she says, "What do you think?"

Claws. "About the stop-thats? What do you think I think?"

Fang. "That I shouldn't."

Claws. "Well, duh. Do you know why?"

Fang. "I guess I should say some **** about you being an oppressive chauvinist ****?"

Claws. "Can you even be a chauvinist ****? Isn't that like the wrong equipment?"

Fang. "Fine. A chauvinist ****."

Claws. "That's more like it. At least I got one of those." *He grins. Then sobers.* "Seriously. Ain't got nothin' to do with you ****in' with your body, Nic. It's your body, what you do with it on your own time is your business. But it's the 'your time' part I care about."

She glances at him.

Claws. "You go out on assignment. You get stranded in deep ****. For weeks. You run out. What then? You whack out because you're outta your candy?" *He shakes his head.* "I'd say the same to anyone with a drug addiction."

Fang. "We're not talking about crack."

Claws. "We're not talkin' about insulin, either. But even so . . . you see any jarheads with insulin dependencies out here? You gotta be healthy to be fightin' this far out, Nic. It's not fair, but that's how it is. You revvin' your performance makes you dependent. That means when the **** cuts out, you're operatin' at sub-standard."

Fang throws up her hands. "But I'm sub-standard without it!"

Claws. "**** that. The point of guns and armor is that your upper body strength ain't an issue. Little wiry folks like Fang2 and big honkin' folks like Hairball can both carry the same gun. Heck, a mom in her mid-thirties who's never *been* in armor can show up here after six weeks' trainin' and do a thirty-crab quota." *He squints at her.* "You tell me the real truth, Nic. Why'd you do it? You wanna be a guy?"

Fang sighs. "No. I like my body fine. But—" *She trails off.* "You're going to laugh."

Claws. "I doubt it."

Fang. "I didn't want special treatment. I'm black. I'm a woman. I didn't want people giving me stuff because of that. I wanted them to give me things because I deserved them."

187. MOMENTS

Claws. "You serious?"

Fang. "****, yeah. I got out of high school and the mailbox was flooded with ****. My family's not poor, Travis, but the stream of paper was ****ing endless. It's like they were terrified I wasn't going to go to college. *Their* college. 'Oooh, a smart young black female! Quick, sign her up, or she might not do it on her own!' Do you know how ****ing demeaning that is?"

Claws. "Uh . . . no."

Fang eyes him.

Claws lifts his hands. "Look, I've stepped in this minefield before, I learned my lesson. The right answer to someone tellin' you about discrimination is 'I have no idea what your're goin' through' and 'I'm sorry you're sufferin'.'"

Fang eyes him a little longer. Then starts laughing.

Claws. "So did you go to college?"

Fang. "Not for long. I wanted to blow **** up first time I saw an action movie. But even in the service, it's the same. The training's different. There's a sense that . . . you're being patted on the head somehow. They even segregate you."

Claws. "Aw, come on, Nic. You *really* want to share showers with a squad full of teenage boys?"

Fang, warming to the topic. "What difference should it make? So you find a team-mate attractive. It happens now, doesn't it? ****, Hairball shares your showers."

Claws. "Hairball . . ." *He trails off.* "Aw, you know, he turns around in the shower."

Fang, full-stop. "He what?"

Claws. "He faces the wall when we're in there. Not like plastered to it or anythin', but just does this polite little about-face and keeps washin'."

Fang, mystified. "Well, ****, why?"

Claws, throwing up his hands. "I don't KNOW, Nic, askin' about deep inner feelin's not exactly the kind of thing guys do."

Fang. "Idiot, you don't ask him about his deep ****ing inner feelings, you say '****, Hairball, what's so interesting about the wall and should I be looking' and then everyone laughs and he stops doing it."

Claws, laughing. "Maybe you're more of a guy than me."

Fang. "No, you're just more of a girl." *Grins.* "Boss."

Claws. "I'll remember that." *Looks at her.* "So, seriously. You'll be okay?"

Fang looks away. "Tell you the truth . . . I sort of ran out of them a while ago."

Claws. ". . ."

Claws. "When? About the time you stopped bein' a royal *****?"

Fang opens her mouth. Closes it. Then says, "****. Don't tell me that."

Claws. "What. That the stuff was messin' with your sunny personality?"

Fang. "****. *****."

Claws, looking up thoughtfully. "I think it was more messin' with your 'I could go far' personality. You ain't much of a sunny type."

Fang. "You are *such* a ****ing bastard." *And then viciously,* "****. I don't like the idea that it was changing ME."

Claws. "Those things do stuff to you." *At her look, he says,* "Just statin' the obvious. It's on the package, ain't it? You know, stuff has consequences. That's sort of the life theme we got goin' on here."

Fang rubs her face with one hand. "Yeah. ****."

Claws, watching her. "You could use a beer."

Fang. "****, if there was a place to drink on this rock—"

Claws. "Yeah, if there was a . . ." *Trails off.* "Well, hell. Meet me here in two hours, eh? If Peaches leaves me in one piece after our little meeting, I know where we could find one."

Fang studies him a moment, bemused. Then adds, "So you going to do it? Drop out for officer training?"

Claws sighs. "**** if I know. I don't want to leave the front."

Fang. "You really think the war will be over in the time it takes you to finish?"

Claws. "Or that I'll lose the momentum I've got here."

Fang looks around. "What ****ing momentum is that?" *At his look, she says,* "You're maneuvering to get Spots installed in a training billet? How long before any of those kids

478

are ready? In enough numbers to really do any good? And if you're in school, you'll be on Earth and maybe be able to pop over and give your expert opinion on the new shield doctrine, having been there when it was developed. For all we know, the alien'll be there too. Isn't he a weapons-designer?"

Claws stares at her.

Fang. "Yes?"

Claws. "I guess. But I'll miss the team."

Fang. "I hate to tell you this, boss, but there's not much of the team left . . . and when reinforcements arrive, it won't look anything like it does now."

Claws sighs. "Guess you're right."

Fang. "I have my moments. So. Two hours? Beer? You serious?"

Claws, slapping her hand and clasping it once before dropping it. "Abso-****in'-lutely. Wish me luck."

188. Decision

"Ma'am, Corporal Walker reporting as ordered."

Peaches. "At ease, Corporal." *Studying him.* "So, Walker. Should I be sending you back on the next boat out?"

Claws, tensing up. "Ma'am?"

Peaches. "Officer training?" *At his expression, she grins.* "What, you think I was going to send you home in chains for inappropriate prisoner disposal?"

Claws. "Uh, the thought had occurred, ma'am."

Peaches smiles wryly. "It would be bad form to shoot you for something I should have been more specific about. But hey, we're all playing it by ear here, aren't we." *A more natural expression now, focused.* "So, have you made your decision?"

Claws. "I . . ." *He trails off, jaw hardening.* "I wish I could stay, ma'am." *Smiles crookedly.* "Don't suppose you could dust off the old Brevet Medal."

Peaches. "I'd do it if I could, Walker. You've earned one. Unfortunately, I'm a lowly lieutenant with many limitations, a situation you'll soon find yourself familiar with."

Claws. "Pardon me for sayin' so, ma'am, but I sure hope I don't find myself familiar with a situation like this one too soon."

Peaches. "I wouldn't wish this on anyone, no. So the answer is . . . ?"

Claws. "I think I'd like to go for it, ma'am."

Peaches nods. "All right. I'm glad you've made this decision, Walker. We could use you."

Claws. "Thank you, ma'am. Uh, I did have one thing. . . ."

Peaches. "Yes?"

Claws. "I put together a file for you, ma'am, about Private Guitart. I think she'd be a shoo-in to train new recruits on the shield tech."

Peaches. "Ah, good idea. Send it along."

Claws. "Will do, ma'am."

Peaches. "Anything else?"

Claws. "No, ma'am."

Spots the Space Marine: Defense of the Fiddler

Peaches. "All right. Get some rest, we'll be on short rotations until the ship arrives."

Claws. "Yes, ma'am."

Outside her office, Claws draws in a deep breath. Looks down the corridor slowly, at the walls, the floor, the ceiling. At the rubble in it.

Claws, muttered. "****. Think I need that beer more than Fang does."

189. BEER

Fang. "Wow. You are kidding me."

She is standing at the door to Samuel-Colt's room, staring at the "fronds" of veils. Claws is inside, looking through the small refrigerator.

Fang. "This is where the bug lives?"

Claws. "This is where the bug lives. And . . ." *Withdraws a bottle, then another.* "Ta-da."

Fang. "You are raiding the alien's fridge. And the alien has beer."

Claws. "Looks like the last few bottles, too." *Sets out one more.*

Fang. "He's not going to be angry?"

Claws, now writing a note. "Nope." *Tosses her two of the bottles, one after the other.* "Note says we were here, and to come by if he's bored."

Fang. "You think he will?"

Claws. "Sure. I told him to bring that incense that makes him drunk. He'll know what we're about."

Fang, looking more and more bewildered. "You think it's a good idea for us to get drunk with an alien?"

Claws. "You seriously tellin' me with that muscle-to-fat ratio you got that one beer and a half is gonna lay you out?"

Fang. "Well, no."

Claws. "There you go, then." *Grins, a little wan.* "It's been a long day, Nic."

Fang. "It's been a ****ing long deployment. Come on, let's go pretend to be buzzed."

Training Room, once again empty. The two of them sit with their backs to the wall, one bottle in front of them and the third in the space between them.

Fang. "So, how'd it go?"

Claws, twisting off the bottle top. "Easy. ****in' too easy for somethin' that's been eatin' me all my life."

Fang. "I see you got no holes in you. I guess she let you off easy for the bit with the Queen."

Spots the Space Marine: Defense of the Fiddler

Claws snorts. "Yeah, well. Weird sitch."

Fang. "What's she gonna do with her, you know?"

Claws. "Turns out she's never gonna wake up. Her other half is in the base we just nuked. So the Fiddlers gonna take her and eat her brain."

Fang. "****." *Frowns.* "That'll mean she's "alive" again, won't it?"

Claws. "More or less, yeah. They're gonna let a boy baby eat her, though, so she'll be stuck in a body without the . . . uh . . . biological imperatives she claimed her old one had."

Fang, wry. "I love how your accent starts fading when you talk all intellectual."

Claws. "Shut up, I like my accent."

Fang. "Where did you fake it up from anyway?"

Claws, rubbing back of his neck once. "Uh . . . lots of places. Old Westerns. Books about farmers."

Fang. "Looney Tunes reruns?"

Claws. "I reckon I don't know what in tarnation you're talkin' about, missy."

Fang snorts. More thoughtfully. "Man, that poor crab. Talk about ****ed up. Waking up in a man's body after having had kids in a woman's? I can't imagine handling that."

Claws. "Yeah, I can imagine she'll need . . . uh . . . whatever the crabs got for counseling."

Fang laughs. "I wonder if they have transgender crabs. You think?"

Claws. "No ****in' clue. We can ask Sam when he gets here." *Glances at her.* "You ever think of what it would be like to have a man's body? Seriously?"

Fang. "Maybe. Not in the way you're thinking, though. More in the 'wish my ****ing body built muscle as fast as a man's' sort of way. But really, Walker, I wouldn't trade sex in this body for anything. It's ****ing fantastic."

Claws. "Man, I'd trade for a day." *At her lifted brow.* "You know, just so I'd know my way around when I was in my right and proper body. When I was in bed with someone else . . . um. That someone else bein' a girl . . ." *Eyes his bottle.* "****, half a bottle of this is no excuse for me talkin' this stupid."

Fang is hiding a laugh behind her wrist. She wipes her eyes and breathes in deeply. "Uh, right. I got sad news for you, boss . . . but women are all different."

Claws. "Figures."

190. COMMONALITIES

When the Training Room door opens for Samuel-Colt, Fang and Claws are passing the remaining bottle back and forth, still sitting on the floor with their legs stretched out in front of them.

Samuel-Colt, holding up incense, already lit; it makes him look as if he's smoking. "Am I too late?"

Claws. "Not bringin' your multiple personalities to the party? Naw, you're not late."

Samuel-Colt, bowing a low note. "I believe I have scared them into the back of my brain."

Fang. "It really *has* been a long ****ing deployment."

Samuel-Colt. "I—we?—cannot remember a more arduous one. May I?"

Claws. "Sit, sit. We were just talkin' about transgender crabs. Whaddaya think will happen with that Queen?"

Samuel-Colt sits on the other side of Claws. His legs extend much farther than either human's. "Damned if we know."

Fang barks a laugh. "What?"

Claws eyes Samuel-Colt wryly. "It's gotten to you, hasn't it, even you."

Samuel-Colt waves one hand. "Apologies, Peer. It has been a bit much, yes." *He breathes in slowly; it pulls the incense smoke toward his spiracles.* "We have never done direct violence to a Queen in this fashion. Nor have we done it in response to a command from another. The conflict is . . . painful."

Claws. "I'll bet."

Samuel-Colt. "The political and logistical repercussions are likewise worthy of a . . . a double-headache."

Fang. "A what?"

Samuel-Colt. "You have no word, because you have only one brain in each of your peculiar heads. We call problems of sufficient irritation double-headaches, as in it is enough to evoke pain in multiple brains, if one has them."

Fang eyes the bottle. "You sure this isn't spiked with something? Because that's a lot funnier than it should have been."

Claws. "Well, that'll be the politicos' double-headache . . . though I have it on good authority they don't even have one brain, much less two. Anyway, Sam, I'm sorry. ****in'

Spots the Space Marine: Defense of the Fiddler

sorry for all this ****."

Samuel-Colt shakes his head. "Don't be, Peer. What is, is."

Fang, muttering. "Poor *****. Bet she's going to have a hell of a double-headache when she wakes up with a . . . a . . . what the **** do male crabs have for a **** anyway? No, don't answer that."

Samuel-Colt. "It will surely be disorienting."

Fang chuckles. "Too bad I'll never meet her. I could tell her stories. Woman in a man's world, wanting some of a man's powers but wanting to keep some of a woman's. Having a woman's body, being ambivalent about some of what that means, but not all of it. We'd have a lot to talk about."

Both Claws and Samuel-Colt stare at her while she drinks.

Fang, meeting their eyes. Drawls, "What?"

Claws lifts his hand. "Nothin', seriously."

Samuel-Colt, bowing a rising arpeggio sloppily. "Would you eat a male body in order to be born with the experience of one, Fang?"

Fang stares at the Violinist, then says to Claws, "He's drunk, isn't he?"

Samuel-Colt. "We have perhaps gotten into the incense a little before we came." *Sighs.* "It truly has been a . . . long . . . deployment."

Silence then, as the two humans drain their last bottle.

Claws. "Hey, Sam?"

Samuel-Colt. "Yes, Peer?"

Claws. "Play somethin' for us?"

Samuel-Colt. "I would be honored." *Lifts his vestigial arms and pauses for a very long time, staring at the ceiling. Then he . . .*

. . . begins to play "Take Me Home, Country Roads."

The camera pans out on Claws and Fang cracking up laughing, looking down on both humans and alien, sitting together in the corner against the wall.

191. WHAT'S REAL

The Real Window. A long window with four layers—an exterior surface for storm debris, two pressure panes and an interior panel—looking out on the dismal murk of an alien day. Peaches is standing there as if facing a court-martial panel, directly in the middle, facing out, spine straight and chin high.

Her arms, though, are folded.

Behind her a lean, middle-aged man, scarred and with broken nose and stubble short hair, pauses at the sight of her.

Peaches. "Gonna offer me a tissue, Gunny?"

Gunny. "You going to cry, ma'am?"

Peaches's mouth twitches a little. "Hell, I hope not. If I start I might not stop."

Gunny. "Something on your mind, ma'am?"

"What's not on my mind." *She sighs.* "Got the lead-out message this morning. The ship'll be here in less than forty-eight."

Gunny. "Worried?"

Peaches. "Have you seen what's left of the base? And my command?"

Gunny steps up beside her, hands folded behind his back. "Ma'am." *When she glances at him, he says,* "The donut's secure. The Fiddler specialist is alive. We've destroyed an entire enemy base, captured its Queen—intact—and have made an enormous intelligence discovery . . . or six."

Peaches. "I lost almost my entire command, Gunny."

Gunny. "That won't matter. As far as they're concerned, people can be replaced. We're just boots here, Lieutenant. There are more boots where ours came from. The rest of it . . ." *He smiles faintly.* "You might end up with a decoration."

Peaches. "That's ****."

Gunny. "That's *war*, Savannah." *When she starts, he says,* "It's ****ed all to hell, and you and I both know it. But we're not here to be brave or to be remembered, or even to be saved. We're here to win a war, and we'll die doing it. Your people will die. You may die. And the hell of it is that someone at home will always have to send us out again. Until the enemy surrenders, or we destroy their power to make war against us."

Peaches swallows.

Spots the Space Marine: Defense of the Fiddler

Gunny squeezes her shoulder. "Mourn them, ma'am. They deserve it. But get used to it. The further you go, the more you're going to lose. You have to make your peace with that. Because if you can't, we'll lose you. And it would be a shame to lose you, Lieutenant."

Peaches, low, voice shaky. "****, Gunny."

Gunny, smiling crookedly. "It's not called the Real Window for nothing."

Peaches. "Guess if I'd wanted fantasies, I should have . . . done something else."

Gunny. "Maybe. There's not much real in life that can be denied for long."

Peaches. "Heh. Yeah, guess so. I'd rather be here, where at least I can stare it in the face."

Gunny. "That's the spirit."

Peaches. "Thanks, Gunny." *She draws in a long breath and exhales slowly.* "Thanks."

Gunny. "What I'm here for, ma'am."

She leaves, heading down the hall. Ends up back in her office, where she steps inside the door and just . . . stands there. Looks at it, the place where she worked, where Paul Avril worked. Looks at her desk. Then walks to it and picks up the folder there. Rummages through her drawer and finds a roll of tape. The door shuts behind her.

A few minutes later, she steps into a room labeled, "CHAPEL," and there, quietly, she begins to hang the pictures of the dead.

One by one. Methodical. Without crying, without expression. She stands back sometimes. Straightens them. Returns to the task. And keeps going until she's done. Then she stands in the center of the room, sweeps the wall with her eyes from one end to the other, meeting all the ghostly gazes.

She salutes. Holds the salute. And then drops it, turns neatly on her heel, and leaves them behind.

192. Mementos

Sickbay. Claws enters, sits easily next to Spots's cot. She looks up from her book, one of the battered old romances from the base's small stock.

Claws. "That one's freakin' risible. Rosemary Ann has a head full of feathers and her beau's a jerk. No clue what she sees in him."

Spots starts laughing. "I don't even know what that means."

Claws. "I figure you're far enough into the book to know exactly what that means." *He hands over a photo.* "Too good to use for a bookmark for that kind of trash. Figured you'd want to keep it in your pocket."

Spots smiles softly at it: it's the photo of her family she kept pinned by her bunk.

Claws. "I packed the rest of 'em when I did your duffle . . . thought I'd do that for you, what with you not bein' ambulatory. Ship's hit the system limit . . . should be here in a few hours."

Spots breathes out. "I can barely believe it."

Claws. "You and everyone else, I'm bettin'." *He sprawls a little.* "They ain't got enough people what to walk all the casualties on board, so I volunteered to wheel you in. I'll be goin' home on the same ship."

Spots looks up.

Claws. "Officer trainin'."

Spots laughs. "Wore you down, finally, then."

Claws with a sigh of mock frustration. "Freakin' people. The guiltin', it never stops until you do what you're supposed to."

Spots grins. "Get used to it. It only gets worse as you get older. You don't know guilt until your kids use it on you."

Claws. "Well there's somethin' to look forward to." *He starts laughing too, quietly.* "Ah, hell, Magda."

Spots. "Yep." *Watches him with an affectionate gaze.* "Write me, Travis, won't you? Tell me all about officer school. How you make out."

Claws. "I will. But hey, this ain't goodbye, ah? We got a long ride home. Sam'll be there too. He's packin' now."

Spots the Space Marine: Defense of the Fiddler

Spots. "They're taking him off the front lines, then."

Claws. "Probably for good, yeah."

Spots, looking at her photo. "He won't like that, any more than I do." *She smiles a little lopsidedly.* "Well, I'll have good company on the way back, at least. I can teach him to use that rosary I left him."

Claws. "The first Catholic crab. Wouldn't that be funny."

Spots laughs. "It would be . . . something. I don't know what!" *She smiles at him.* "Thanks, Travis. Not just for packing my stuff."

Claws, flushing a little, eyes cast down. "Yeah. Hey, me too. You've been . . . well."

Spots observes him squirming with that half-laughing, half-helplessly fond look that children always miss because their backs are turned or their faces, like Claws's, are down. Then she leans forward and says, "To be honest, I'll be glad to get out of here before Nicola finds the little gift I left her."

Claws, glad of the distraction. "What's this now?"

Spots, grinning. "I got the rest of the team to help, since I'm not going anywhere, and they proved themselves on their last little adventure to find me a piece of chocolate. So I asked them . . ."

As she talks, the camera pans outward, looking down on the two of them. It catches Claws's startled, tense shoulders . . . and then his uproarious laughter. It moves away, leaving them amid the mass of wounded in Sickbay . . . out into the hall, where two duffle bags are leaning against the wall, two of a long line of such bags.

One of them has a ring rosary hanging from one of the zippers.

A katana in a black saya wrapped in a red sash is leaning against the last.

193. GOING HOME

Slow focus on a piece of paper, a hand-written letter. The camera scrolls slowly down it.

Dear Nicola, Lance, Gregory and Vince,

First, Fang ... don't take it out on the rest of Team Kitty. It was my idea, I swear. And no, I'm not sorry!

Anyway, I never did get to make you all cookies, but if what you say about your raid on the Seabees' kitchen is right, then you have the ingredients and you have an oven. So I thought I'd attach a recipe. You should be able to find all these things ... just follow the directions and you should be fine. It's not as good as having Mom make them for you, but it's better than no cookies at all!

MAMA SPOTS'S EMERGENCY BASE COOKIES

4 cups flour
4 cups white sugar
1 1/2 cups dry milk powder
1 1/2 tablespoons baking powder
1 1/2 teaspoons salt
1/2 cup shortening
1 tablespoon dry egg powder
2 tablespoons water
1-2 cups of other stuff you can find (chocolate, carob, coconut, fruit, nuts)

Letter fades.

Flashes now.

Claws on a porch, knocking on a wooden door, painted green. He is in dress blues, and the sword is cradled against one side of his body. A middle-aged woman, honey-skinned and hair covered with a green and blue scarf, answers the door. She looks at him, at the sword . . . and tears well in her eyes. She moves aside so he can enter.

Fang stepping into the Armory; the rest of Team Kitty is studiously not looking at her. She frowns at them, puzzled, then unracks her armor. And stops. The kill count on the back has been augmented by a giant pink crown. She stares at it, mouth working . . . then starts laughing. Whiskers mimes her glorious shot at the Queen's head while Fang2 retells the story. She shakes her head, still grinning, tells them to suit up. She's the last out the airlock. Glancing back at the base door, hand on weapon, she smiles.

Spots using a key on the front door to a modest cottage, its facade overgrown with flowers. Stepping inside and finding her family at the breakfast table. Her kids rush her: she grabs up her daughter and pulls the boy to her hip. Her husband, a giant blond bear, watches her with overwhelming pride, then enfolds her in his embrace. She and her kids fit into it completely.

The camera pulls out on that slowly, very slowly, letting it fade to black on Spots's face.

Out of the dark, then, another face resolves: a Fiddler King. His eyes are closed, his head bowed. Abruptly, the eyes open: faceted pink, rose, garnet. Slim hands fly to chitinous cheeks.

A gasp, echoing, echoing.

Cut back to the letter.

```
Bake at 350 degrees for 7-10 minutes.

That should do it. Have fun. :)

All my love,
Spots

P.S. This time don't steal from the Seabees, please? Ask them politely,
I'm sure they'll be glad to share. Better yet, offer them some cookies.
Cookies make everything better.
```

SPOTS THE SPACE MARINE

Begin End Credits
Music: "Weatherbeaten," by The Republic Tigers

Thank you to the following people for lending the author their expertise.
Sgt. Jennifer D. Atkinson, Texas Army National Guard
John M. Atkinson, Staff Sergeant, United States Army
Bill Ernoehazy, MD, LCDR, MC, United States Naval Reserve (r)
JC Gibbons United States Air Force (separated)
Stacy "Mouse" Lucas, E-4 (Sgt), United States Air Force
TJ Macheski, HM3, United States Navy

Thank you also to the following people:
Jeriendhal, for writing the *Spots the Space Marine* TV Tropes page
S. Gosik, whose equipment recorded Spots's Lullaby.

**Finally, the following patrons helped make Spots
the serial available with their generous donations.**

Super-Sponsors
Stacy "Mouse" Lucas
Jesse Stringer

Sponsors

Keitha Bailey
Eric Bitton
Joseph Bonis
Leslie Brown
Jennifer Broschinsky
Billy Clark
Stephanie Clough
Lorena Dinger
Jim Doolittle
Brendan and Lydia Dunn
Mary-Grace Ellington
e_scapism101
Elizabeth Fallon
Mike Fannin
David Fenger
Beth Finn
Natalie Ford
Kathryn Frech
Mary Ellen Garland
JC Gibbons

Lyle Gordon
Jonathan Green
Kara Hash
Suzanne "Wispfox" Hill-man
Sean Holland
Tim Hoyt
Jari James
Chng Joyce
Jonathan Kaplan
Mey Lawrence
Richard Loll
Amanda Lord
Ashley MacDonald
Jeremy Matt
Steven Martindale
Margaret Middleton
Ellen Million Graphics
Meilin Miranda
Steven Modugno

David Morris
Oldwolfe
Clayton Oliver
Rachyl Perrotta
Steven Peterson
Gina Pond
Scott Ruggels
Robin Sanford
Cosma Shalizi
Torrey Stenmark
Toni Sturtevant
Katherine Tomlinson
Kim Turner
Gregory Ullman
Grey Walker
Jenika Watkins
Laura Weston
Conrad Wong
Vicky Woodard
Anonymous Donors (2)

Spots the Space Marine: Defense of the Fiddler

Print Book Backers

Abigail Gwinn
Adam and Shira Lipkin
Adam Kasanof
Alice 'Huskyteer' Dryden
Amanda Lord
Amy C Wetzel
Ana Steuart
Andrea Brokaw
Angela N. Hunt
Ashlee Tessier
Ashley MacDonald
Becka Sutton
Beth S
Brian Dolan
Brian Ruth
Bruce Murphy
capriox
Catherine Caldwell
Cecilia Tan
Chris "Halaku" Buser
Chris Thompson
Christina Shuy
Conrad "Lynx" Wong
Cosma Shalizi
Daniel Winterhalter
David Fenger
David Green
David Morris
David Perkins
Dee
Elizabeth Fallon
Elizabeth McCoy
Emily Coombs
Eric Hays-Strom
Evaristo Ramos, Jr.
Ferrett Steinmetz

Grey Walker
Harrison Swift
Jari L. James
Jasra/Lisa
JC Gibbons
Jennifer Cox
Jeremie Lariviere
Jesse "Tango" Stringer
Jim Doolittle
JJ Pionke
John
John Fiala
Karen West
Karl Maurer
Kate Chance Tomlinson
Kate Jones
Kate Sullivan
Dr. Kenneth Matheis
Kevin Trainor
Kim Riek
L.C. Hu
Lachlan Bakker
Leesa Willis
Liana Mir
Lorena Dinger
Marcus Velloso Sitonio
Marina Bonomi
Martin Rudat
Mary Ellen Garland
MeiLin Miranda
Melissa Selik Thornton
Michael Bernardi
Michael Feldhusen
Mikael Olofsson
Miles Matton
Misti Bonis

Najela "Sora" Cobb
Nana
Nikki Jeske
Pamela S. M. Hopkin
Paul Robinson
Persis L. Thorndike
Phil Olynyk
Quinn Ebert
Rabbit Seagraves
Rachel S.
Rachyl Perrotta
Rhel n· DecVandÈ
Ric "technomage" Loll
Rin Adams
Rix Scaedu
Robin Lee Sanford
Robin Taylor
Sam Wright
Sarah Morehouse
Scott Slbert Henry Ruggels
Sean Holland
Skarl the Drummer
Stacy Lucas
Steven Martindale
Susan Marie Groppi
Tamika
Teesa Alaniz
Tenmachi
The Vulture
The Waite Family
Tim Hoyt
Toni Sturtevant
Vincent Ecuyer
Wade Hursman
Zoe E. Whitten
Zrath-Smiley

End Credits ● *M. C. A. Hogarth*

Reference Materials

U.S. Marine Guidebook
One Bullet Away: The Making of a Marine Officer, Nathaniel Fick
Helmet for My Pillow, Robert Leckie
Making the Corps, Thomas E. Ricks
With the Old Breed: At Peleliu and Okinawa, E.B. Sledge
A Civilian's Guide to the U.S. Military, Barbara and Richard Schading

Partial Soundtrack

Spots was conceived and brainstormed from beginning to end while listening to music either running, on the treadmill, or on an elliptical. While the entire "exercise" playlist was over 80 songs long, these are the songs with the strongest associations with Spots.

"Rock the Casbah", The Clash
"Jigsaw Falling Into Place", Radiohead (Dancing in Armor)
"Friday, I'm in Love", The Cure (Dancing in Armor)
"Weatherbeaten", The Republic Tigers
"Zombie", The Cranberries
"Winterborn", The Cruxshadows
Ave Maria, Schubert (Samuel-Colt's solo)

About the Author

M.C.A. Hogarth has been many things—a web database architect, product manager, technical writer and massage therapist—but is currently a parent, artist, writer and anthropologist to aliens. She has over forty titles available in the genres of science fiction, fantasy, humor and romance.

Spots the Space Marine is her first near-future military SF story, and was originally serialized online for donations. A portion of the proceeds were donated to the Wounded Warrior Project.

Twitter: http://twitter.com/mcahogarth

Website: http:/mcahogarth.org

495

2239574R00273

Made in the USA
San Bernardino, CA
27 March 2013